To Kell

CHARAS

The Illumination Chronicles
Book 2

Dominic McCafferey

one of the few, who know

D. McCafferey

Many thanks to Eddie Eden

Cover Design by Michelle Jukes
Formatting by Polgarus Studio

Website: Illuminationchronicles.wordpress.com

1

High up, in the deep and secluded valleys of the Hindu Kush grow fields upon fields of ganja. Some are tended and others are left wild.

The tended fields are known as bagicha. This best translates as 'garden'.

The wild bush grows abundantly on the hillsides. They are known as jungli, and yes, this literally means 'jungle'.

Generally speaking, the higher altitude the grass grows, the better the quality.

The bagicha fields tend to yield good value and predictable crops that get turned into a dark brown resin. The local name is Charas.

Charas is hand-made by quickly rubbing the flowering buds between your palms. This is done until the sticky resins gather together to form a coating on the skin. Then you have to press your thumb hard into it, peeling off layers of the dark tacky gum, bit by bit. After some time and effort you make it into a collection of little round balls or snake-like strings.

Eventually you will have enough to make a 'tola' or 10 grams. This is the standard amount sold in one deal. A good harvester can make 5, 6 or even 7 grams per day. It's a cash harvest and the only source of income for the locals. No other crops grow so high up in this mountainous terrain.

Jungli is a different story, as it's impossible to be sure of the quality. However, as long as you're at a decent height and remote enough to guarantee the fields aren't tended by the locals, it's capable of producing the top quality high on the planet.

As it's been left to its own devices, these fields often produce some strange yet completely natural hybrids, mutations and one offs. Amongst the dominant green you can find leaves and flowering heads of purple, black, brown and various shades of red.

It's amazing to witness the colours that adorn these special fields.

Some strains of these superior plants only exist until their lineage has failed to pass on their genes. This is complete chance, due to the chaos of the wind or the insects failing to pollinate it. Another possibility could be someone rubbing the head before it's had chance to pass on its unique DNA.

Random plants that may only survive one season are the dream smoke, as exceptional as it gets. This is true jungli.

'Jack Daniels and Pepsi, sir?' asked the Emirates air stewardess, smiling. She was dressed in her unflattering beige uniform. She was still a dazzling looking woman with perfect makeup and shiny hair.

Dean nodded and smiled back, an interaction that wasn't missed by Beki. She was his one-time probation officer, now partner in crime.

Beki jostled in her seat and accidently, with purpose, knocked Dean's elbow from the communal armrest and replaced it with her own.

This was enough for Dean to turn his head sharply towards her, stopping the love in at 35,000ft, only to see Beki's nonchalant eyes closing and a sarcastic smile flash across her lips.

The air stewardess placed the 'free' drink down onto the circular, slightly depressed area, leaving the small can of cola next to the clear plastic cup filled with large, yet hollow, ice cubes.

Dean focused on the intricacies of the ice, the cracks that seemed to be inside the cubes and the distorted colours of frozen white that surrounded those crystalline fissures.

He listened to the sound the ice made when the contents of a 20cl miniature of the charcoal filtered Tennessee Whisky was poured over it. He noticed the way it seemed to bump around as it made those popping sounds.

Most people think that Jack is bourbon but Dean knew better than that. He'd been given the low down on Jack one night when he and his number two, Spence, had shared a bottle.

Spence told him all about the history of Jack and where its distinctive taste came from. It's due to the filtering process, gently seeping through ten feet of charcoal to mellow the spirit and flavour the palate with smoky overtones.

Although he was six and a half miles high in a winged metal tube, repeatedly breathing the recycled cabin air, sitting next to a woman he'd fancied from the minute he'd first seen her on his way to a country he'd never thought to visit before three days ago, he was strangely calm. The lump of Moroccan Pollen he'd chewed before boarding was starting to bite.

He recalled the first time he'd laid eyes on Beki. It was from behind the misty shatterproof plastic screen, in the reception of a grimy probation office. He was waiting in reception to be seen by his new officer.

His dreams had come true as it was Rebecca Aston, who two minutes later popped her cheery head round the door and said, 'Dean. Dean Shelby, would you like to come through?'

They had flirted outrageously at times over that desk in the privacy of the soundproofed session room. They had gone their separate ways and fate had brought them crashing back together and flung them onward, into this trip to the unknown.

Beki couldn't settle. She felt a mix of excitement and anxiety. She picked up her glossy magazine called *Read*. It was left over from the summer and she browsed the '10 sunshine BESTSELLERS' section. She wondered how two types of Olma bags, the Felix leather handbag and the leather Coral Tote bag could be classed as best sellers. She'd certainly never heard of them before.

When she looked more closely it was the 'favourites' from *Read Direct* and the Clover Tote was available in 'putty', which she thought would go well with the uniforms of the air stewardesses on the Emirates flight. She could see them all running round various parts of the planet with putty coloured Tote bags from Olma at £255 a throw. They would all be going for lunch with each other along with the odd handsome pilot, or good-looking gay air steward. They would be spending a small fortune in some Brasserie on salad and fish. They'd be poking it around the plate while talking non-stop about the latest on board romance or the best place to bag a millionaire boyfriend.

She flicked through the pages and settled on a 'Veg Vs Meat' food swap article. She read about a veggie and a carnivore who'd swapped diets for a fortnight. She also thought about the food in Goa when she last went there with 'IT'. This was the new way she referred to her deceased boyfriend, Tom Fisher. He had turned into some kind of jealous psycho and attacked her back in Manchester. All this happened after Tom had somehow found out she'd started seeing his friend Aidy. She'd defended herself and in the process he'd … died.

She felt nothing but hatred for him at the time and she still hated him now. He'd gone off with another woman and god knows what had gone on. He'd not come back the same man. Her Tom would never have done anything like 'IT' had. Her Tom had been a gentle soul, always ready to please her as best he could.

She'd spent years dealing with the perpetrators of crimes and hearing the stories of how victims' lives were ruined by sexual assaults of all descriptions. She was not going to be a victim; she had no remorse about her actions and would do the same again.

The problem was, the police may not have seen it that way. One lesson you soon learn in the criminal justice game, is things are weighed heavily in the favour of men. If you think about it, the whole system was set up by men and is geared towards the protection of them and of their property. Rob a bank and you'll get a very heavy sentence. Kill a man and you'll get the same. Rape a woman and the chances are you'll either get off with it, as it's so hard to prove without doubt, or if you are found guilty you'll generally do a couple of years max. They'll get four years but serve two. Most sex offenders are very compliant and well behaved in custody, they keep their heads down.

The victims however will be serving a life sentence of guilt and shame associated with being violated. It will quite possibly ruin their lives forever.

Dean nudged her elbow. 'Sure you don't want a drink? It's free you know.'

She thought about how refreshing a G&T would be right now and balanced it out in her mind's imaginary scales by having a bottle of mineral water on the side. She knew the importance of keeping hydrated in the air. She'd taken an aspirin tablet just before boarding, as she'd heard it thinned the blood. Someone once told her it stopped long haul DVTs. She was a little worried about drinking alcohol with aspirin, as she was sure this combination would be bad for the liver, but hey, she was going on holiday. She was off on an adventure.

'Go on then, G&T. Get me a bottle of water, too.'

Beki had planned to be good but a nine hour flight with a two and a half hour stop in Dubai International Airport, without any kind of narcotic, was proving a challenge.

Dean hadn't mentioned the pollen he'd necked, as he thought she would go mad at him for taking drugs into the airport. Dean was confident that customs wouldn't be looking for anyone taking drugs into India. It would be the other way round. He'd have to be sensible coming home.

He pressed the cabin crew button above his seat. A 'ding-dong' sound alerted them to attend his every need.

When they had been waiting on the ground in Manchester an air stewardess had asked them if they wanted a free up-grade to Business Class, as the flight had been over booked. Of course they'd jumped at the chance. They had a pair of window seats rather than the usual three. There was more leg space and slightly bigger and better cushioning. There were more cabin crew per customer and drinks were available straight away after take-off.

Their air stewardess had come down the aisle and asked Dean if she could be of service. He'd thought she looked exotic. She had slightly brown skin, high cheekbones and full lips. She'd spoken English with an American twang. He'd ordered Beki's drinks and thought he may as well have a top up himself, so ordered another Jack and Pepsi.

The drinks were served and about ten minutes later another air stewardess took their order for either orange juice, champagne or a combination of the two, Buck's Fizz.

Both plumped for the champagne and within half an hour of take-off, Dean was feeling quite happy.

Beki was impressed with the service on board. After her initial reservations about the cabin crew she relaxed into being constantly fed little bowls of peanuts, along with several more G&Ts.

Food was served with proper knives and forks. They were made from metal, not plastic. The food was superior to the normal, just about edible, stuff you were served on most flights. Her minted Moroccan lamb and cous cous and Dean's chicken Chasseur were both really good. They got a selection of decent wines to accompany the meal. She had a Cotes de Castillion and Dean had a Chilean Cabernet by Erruzis.

It was now one in the morning UK time and Beki was just nodding off after the satisfying food when Dean started giggling to himself.

Steve Smart was sad about the demise of any of his operatives but he had to admit to himself that Charles Bates' death solved a problem he'd been reticent to deal with.

Charles had been around the game for a long time. Although his recent role, based solely in the UK was fine, sometimes more pressing engagements arrived at short notice.

Steve really did need an international team. His players needed to be capable of uprooting and digging down again within hours. This could possibly be on the other side of the planet.

The truth, Charles was getting to a stage in his life where he could not be relied upon. De-briefs from colleagues had thrown up tiny but glaring errors of judgement. Miscalculations may jeopardise not only the lives of his peers and colleagues but of the operation as a whole. There was a lot at stake here. Generations had come and gone, countries had changed their names and governments several times over.

At least three empires had ceased to exist since the operation's founders had first decreed that they become the world government. They operated their regime behind the governments portrayed by the media.

They had started in pre-history. Their identity closely guarded, even today. Now it was all smoke and mirrors. Everything changed with the onset in the last twenty years of the Internet and social media. They'd managed to remain out of the general broadcasting system and anyone who got close was either truly awake or branded a conspiracy loon.

Steve looked up key words in Google like Illuminati and NWO. He then typed in Poulis.

The first hit came up with site after site of conspiracy madness about programmed celebrities and 'secret' societies, getting you to look hard towards the smoke.

Really, how could something on the web be a secret?

The name Poulis was protected by the mirrors. Everything was reflected back at you. You could only see yourself in the Poulis clan, they were you and you never looked too closely at yourself. His employers were in the safest place they could be … occultly in plain view.

'What are you laughing about? Come on, what's so funny?' Beki asked as Dean's giggles became worse.

'Nothing.'

'Come on, share the joke.' Beki was getting mildly annoyed now.

'I've not had the giggles for years.' Dean's eyes were now watering and he was feeling very high. 'I think it's something I ate.' This set him off again as he realised that the pollen had now really kicked in. It was after eating the in-flight meal, kicking his digestive tract into action.

'What have you had? Are you stoned, Mr Shelby?' Beki said with an authoritative tone, the one she used with offenders at work.

'I'm wasted. Never knew resin could hammer you like this.'

'What've you had?' she asked, genuinely annoyed with him now.

'Some pollen. I ate it, just before we got on the plane. It's mad. I'm really flying now.'

Beki leaned over and pushed her 'ding dong', cabin crew

button. Within seconds the air stewardess was there. Beki ordered red wine and asked for a blanket as she was cold from the air con.

The stewardess eyed Dean cautiously. She was wary of his bloodshot eyes and the fact he was laughing and giggling far too much. Luckily she put it down to the alcohol. When she returned she brought him an extra blanket, too.

They both settled down and tried to get a couple of hours sleep. Dean was off like a shot, straight into the dreamless slumber cannabis creates.

Beki snuggled up to him as he slept. Her mind was racing from being so close to him. His scent made her head go fuzzy. What was it about him that she had always admired? What was it that turned her on so much? Would they be travelling as friends? Platonically keeping their distance in shared rooms, taking turns to have a shower and use the loo, possibly having to share a bed?

It hadn't dawned on her that it was all about rescuing him, changing him. Deep down she thought she was the only one who could straighten him out.

The thought of trying it on with him was making her feel sick. If anything was going to happen, he would have to make the first move. She always thought men should just take her. There was not a chance she was going to humiliate herself by being rejected by one of her ex-offenders. Maybe that was the reason for not sharing the dope with her. Maybe he didn't realise just how much she liked a smoke, or a chew. She certainly wasn't above a chew.

Her last joint had been in the car to the airport. It had

definitely worn off. She was resentful of his drug induced sleep because she wasn't going to get a wink before Dubai.

When Dean woke up she was leaning the other way, towards the window. For the last hour she had been staring at the tiny dots of light below. She figured they were boats on the ocean. Now she was looking for the first signs of light from the dawn sun.

The horizon was showing the initial signs of morning life. It was a faint glow of mauve in the distance that broke up the black as night sky.

There were signs of life on board, too. The cabin crew were up and about with snacks, extra blankets and drinks for the fussy business class passengers.

She sensed they were starting to descend. The engines seemed to reduce their forward thrust. Then there was a slight gliding effect, she felt it in her belly. The nose dipped imperceptibly.

Then it became official. The captain announced in his Australian accent that they were making their descent and approaching Dubai on schedule.

Dean opened his red eyes and spoke through his yawn. 'Are we in Arabia yet? I've always wanted to go to the desert.' He interlocked his fingers and stretched his arms upwards. Then he flopped them back down onto his thighs and shut his eyes again.

2

When the cell phone rang, he looked at the number. He opened the French windows of the hotel room and walked into the gardens alone.

The call from Steve Smart made Hue Brooks freeze in the forty-degree heat of the Kenyan afternoon. He worked hard to keep his composure and maintain his stiff upper lip. This became increasingly challenging when the words assimilated as fact in his brain.

Charles Bates was dead.

He considered smashing the cell phone to bits against the hotel's wall. He restrained himself. He'd only bought it the day before. He felt like the one person he had any feelings left for in the whole world was gone. They'd abandoned him. He was completely cold, even as lines of sweat ran down his neck. Inside he was empty and alone. He shivered as though someone had walked over his grave.

He took a deep breath before putting on the bravado again, as drops of sweat fashioned a pool on the top of his brow. He wiped them away with his icy hand. All the blood had rushed from his extremities. It was as if he was preparing to fight, to kill.

'Fell from a hotel balcony, eh, what a way to go. At least he had a touch of excitement before hitting the ground, Charles would have liked that,' Hue added.

Steve didn't know what else to say. Hue Brooks was someone he would have to get to know better, as it was usually Charles who handled the phone calls and faxes between them. He got back to business in their coded vernacular.

'Have you hit the ground running?' asked Steve. He meant: Have you made progress with the mission? He then winced internally as he caught what he'd just said. Luckily his inelegant terminology didn't register with Hue who was still in shock.

'All good here, our friends in the North have nothing to fear, it's all but done. We will be moving on in the next two days,' Hue replied, meaning the job in Lamu was going well and the operation in Somalia would be seen as a better option for investment in two days' time. 'I hope I can speak for Emile, too, when I say we will need some time to sort out the deceased business, when we return to Blighty.'

Steve knew this was code for sorting out Charles' assailants and before he ended the conversation he agreed to whatever was required on that front. He knew they were going to do it with or without his permission, so best to give Hue some space to work things out. Anyway, whoever did this was due what was coming. From all the feedback he'd been given on Hue Brooks, he was someone you did not want on your trail. If Emile Sarafian was up for it, too, then he almost felt sorry for whoever killed Charles Bates. Like us all, they were dead already. Only their demise was closer than most.

Hue found he was sat in the shade of a Mango tree in the grounds of his hotel. He wept into his hands. He cried and cried. Silently, the tears ran out in a steady stream. He emitted no sound. The odd time his head jerked up, his fingers parted and his eyes stared into the daylight. It was an involuntary action.

He eventually stopped the tears, gained control again. He had not cried since being a boy, aged nine. He'd been at boarding school in Germany. The International Alliance School was frequented by sons of high ranking military officers stationed abroad and wealthy business families.

It had an excellent reputation, first class results and a strict disciplinary code. If you strayed out of line you were hauled to the front of the class and 'slippered'. This meant bending over and touching your toes while a sadistic teacher used an old plimsoll to slap you on the bottom five to ten times. It was faux sexualised assault, a deliberate humiliation in front of your peers.

When you watched certain teachers beating the boys, the pleasure on their faces was palpable. They would go ruddy-cheeked and watery eyed at the power over the vulnerable child who was bent over and completely at their mercy.

Hue had ended up crying one lunch-time when one of his teachers had asked to see him in his classroom. The teacher, Mr Kinsey, was in charge of the Under Ten's Rugby Team. He sat opposite Hue at his desk made from polished hardwood. Hue recalled the sheen as the light from the midday sun beamed through the window, hitting the desktop, picking up the grain of the wood.

He was close to Mr Kinsey, but not touching. The teacher asked Hue why he had not done his best in training and at the recent trials for the team. Mr Kinsey said he knew he could do better and wondered why he was letting him down.

Hue had been bewildered, as he always did his best and would never have consciously underperformed. However Mr Kinsey was adamant he was capable of more than he was giving. Hue then started to doubt himself and started to back down from his standpoint that he'd always done his best. He started to 'feel' he had let Mr Kinsey down and started to make excuses for his lack of ability on the rugby field.

Hue didn't know why but his emotions got the better of him and he started to cry.

'Why are you crying?' Mr Kinsey asked, putting his hand on Hue's left knee, rubbing it now in a fictitious comforting motion.

'I don't know,' said the nine-year-old Hue.

'Yes, I think you do know.' Mr Kinsey insisted Hue did know and was just letting him down again because he couldn't admit he didn't want to do his best for Mr Kinsey.

It carried on like this for about another ten minutes. Hue in denial as Mr Kinsey slowly persuaded him that he was failing; working it and working it, so he could break the boy's spirit by re-writing history, rewiring the nine-year-old's brain and manipulating his emotions. Eventually the teacher wanted to get to the point where the boy was completely under his control. His next line was well practiced.

'Come and sit here, on my knee, while I comfort you.'

Hue felt like he had been in that classroom for hours on end and yet the whole episode lasted less than thirty minutes. He stood up, still in floods of tears.

The spell was broken by Mr Collins, who had been aware that Tobias Kinsey was abusing the boys, at least mentally, possibly physically. He'd burst into the classroom without knocking. He had his hand gripped on the brass coloured door handle.

Hue noticed his pink hands and white knuckles.

Smiling knowingly Collins asked, 'Is everything alright here, Mr Kinsey?' He was just letting Kinsey know that he knew he was up to something.

'Yes fine, Mr Collins,' Kinsey replied, 'Brooks was just going.'

And then it was over. The crying stopped. The memory was stored away.

Hue had sworn to himself that he was never going to cry again. He would not let anyone down again, either. From then on he buried his emotions in a world of discipline, sporting success and academic achievement. He'd sent out a signal so strong to Kinsey, that the teacher had backed right off. Kinsey then moved on to another boy who showed less resilience to his mind games.

A year later, mid-term, Mr Kinsey had just disappeared from the school.

Hue went through sixth form and left the school for the military at eighteen.

The fact that Hue was gay never entered into his personal life. He went out with girls for periods of time, usually about three months. That was when they moved on, disillusioned as he'd not tried anything sexually, nothing more than a kiss. When he did kiss them it made him feel vile. It was akin to kissing his mother.

He had no gay encounters until he was stationed back in Germany. By this time he was free most weekends as he delivered training to officers in the barracks midweek. They came from all over to hear about the theory of Psychological Intervention Assaults, of how to win hearts and minds in the field.

One weekend Hue had gone out for a stroll. He went into the heart of Berlin via train, as he had never been there alone. He'd wandered around the city; it was a humid summer night. He stopped, either by chance or design, at a bar called Rockies. Hue ordered a vodka tonic and sat at a table. He sipped the drink and before he'd finished it, another one arrived. The barman-come-waiter pointed out the gentleman who had bought it for him and Hue beckoned him over to say thanks.

The guy was German; his name was Gun, short for Gunter. They'd talked constantly, fluctuating between German and English until the early hours.

Hue never once told Gun anything truthful about himself or anything that would leave a trace back to the barracks. He'd told Gun he was a businessman who was just in town for the night. Gun took the signals and invited Hue back for a drink to his apartment. Hue declined and said he had an early start in the morning but it had been good talking and he gave Gun a false address and number in London. Hue left the bar and waited in the shadows across the road. How dare this fucker presume he was cruising for sex? He was repulsed by the very idea. He would get what was coming to him.

Hue had waited until the bar emptied, at about two in the morning.

Gun left alone and walked drunkenly along the pavement, swaying a little. He'd never thought about his personal safety in Berlin as it had never been a problem in his area. He walked to his canal side apartment block and paused at the side of the building as he struggled to recall which pocket he'd put his key in. He leant against the wall of the building. He produced his key triumphantly, very pleased with himself.

Hue had moved silently towards him after checking the area for cameras and working out where would be best to do the deed. The last part of his run was on grass and he was at Gunter's neck before the man had any idea he was there. One quick twist with the correct technique was all it took. The crack echoed down the side of the apartment building as his spine ceased to function and the central nervous system broke down due to the loss of connection.

Gun slumped into Hue's arms, a dead weight. He moved him into the shadow of the side of the building and thought about what he was about to do for less than a second before untying Gun's brown leather belt and Boss jeans. Hue took out his sexual frustration, as Gunter's body jerked impulsively. His bodily fluids began to evacuate and Hue had to be careful not to get contaminated. Hue had not banked on this surprise lubrication and inhaled the aroma like a Cuban cigar.

After he was done by a final death jerk from Gunter's poleaxed frame, he had to wipe the evacuated faeces from his penis. There wasn't much, as Hue had an unusually small member. This was another reason he'd shied away from sexual encounters. It didn't look too bad flaccid but it grew not an inch more when erect, it just went hard, not long or fat.

Hue dressed Gunter and picked up his body. He went round the back of the apartment building and came out at the canal. He dumped the body in the water and went on his way.

This was the start of his sexualised serial killing. It took place about four times a year, always in different parts of the globe. It was Hue's way of feeling some kind of emotion, although it had never resulted in him shedding a tear.

The Emirates pilot made an exceptionally smooth landing, they barely felt a bump. As Dean looked out of the cabin window he eyed the brand new, state of the art Dubai International Airport. Everything looked golden.

As they walked onto the runway and into the waiting shuttle bus, the dawn created the light of a new day.

The pink sky was quickly turning blue and hazy light adorned the runway. Women dressed in khaki uniforms ushered the passengers onto the bus. They reminded Beki of Muammar Gaddafi's female troop of bodyguards, the Green Nuns. They looked as serious, too.

Even at this early hour there was warmth in the dry air. Dean had the faintest of paranoid thoughts about the security but got a grip of his thinking and told himself there was no way anyone would know he was high. Even so he pulled down his Oakley straights from the top of his head to cover his eyes. The bus pulled away with a slight jolt, affecting a nervous laugh from some of the standing commuters, caught momentarily off balance.

The two travellers lined up in the airport along with most of the other passengers who were also in transit. The way Emirates work it, most flights go via Dubai and then people get to shop in the best duty free in the world. They all seem to make a purchase before heading off to their onward destination.

The transit desk was busy but efficient, the queue was

steadily decreasing and before long the travellers were walking down a corridor into the shopping malls.

The duty free has three almost identical areas selling everything from chewing gum to gold. The gold was not the 9-carat rubbish that mirrored the price of skunk back home. All the gold here was at least 18 but mostly 22 carat.

Dean noticed the stark difference in colour. This gold was deep yellow as if it was flowing. It was liquidity. The gold back home was brassy and shallow, as if it had no presence, no inward motion.

He looked at the watches and decided he liked the Tag's more than the Lex's even though they were way cheaper.

He looked at the rows of sunglasses. Nothing matched the Oakley's and he already owned a pair.

As he walked round the booze he became engrossed by the champagne. The prices were in dirhams and US dollars. He thought about getting some Verve but then thought about lugging it through customs in India. He felt worried about them wanting him to pay tax on it and drawing lots of attention to himself, which he didn't need. Then he imagined getting it in the ear from Beki.

Then he started thinking about Beki. Should he get her a little something? A bracelet of that yellow gold? Or even better, a necklace. He decided a necklace was a great idea but he'd have to lose her to buy it. She'd been walking round next to him staring at all the lovely things. He'd been aware of her wittering on about this and that. Although he'd heard the words and said 'yer' and 'suppose so' a few times, he'd not actually been listening to a word she'd said.

He turned to face her. 'I'm just going to the toilet. I'll meet you here, by the champagne. Ten minutes?'

'OK, ten minutes. I'm just going to look at the handbags, so if I'm not here I'll be there.' Beki pointed out where the accessories were and became giddy about all the Louis Vuitton, Burberry and Gucci bags on display.

Dean went off and wondered if she'd prefer a bag. Then thought about where they were going and how the last thing she needed was a posh handbag.

He went to the gents and quickly walked back to the gold counter.

On his way he noticed that there were people dressed like real Arabs, straight out of a film, wearing whiter than white gowns that reached the floor. They had proper headdresses with black rope around the tops.

It was like being in another world. There were families of Africans dressed in black gowns and headdresses, skinny Asian men in cheap shirts, sandals and slacks, fully veiled women who were dressed completely in black. There were some from head to foot in white. There were people who looked Chinese, people who looked a cross of Chinese and Asian. There were European businessmen with briefcases in suits. There were travellers with bags slung casually over their shoulders that milled about in stripy Nepalese cotton shirts and Thai fishermen's trousers.

There was all manner of humanity in this airport melting pot.

As Dean approached the gold counter he watched a fat man, dressed in light grey slacks and a pale blue shirt being served by one of the two Filipino women who worked there.

Dean watched closely as he bought a necklace. It was a strong chain with round coin designs that dangled down via smaller chains. There were four on the top layer, then three, two and one at the bottom to make a triangle shape. It was a nice piece and was a nice price, two thousand nine hundred and ninety nine dollars.

The fat man bought it with cash. He looked middle-eastern; he had a moustache and a hooked nose. He opened a briefcase that he'd been holding in his left hand and put the packaged necklace in amongst the papers and files. Dean noticed that the briefcase was attached to the man's wrist with a chain.

'Yes, sir, may I help?' asked the other woman from behind the counter.

'I'd like to buy a gold bracelet or necklace.' Dean waited but she said nothing so he carried on. 'It's for a friend.'

'How much you like to spend, sir?'

After seeing the fat man spend nearly three thousand dollars he thought he'd better up his game. Originally he thought about spending a couple of hundred but he brought it up to a grand. 'About a thousand.'

Before he'd finished she butted in. 'Dollar or pounds sterling, sir?' She was fierce all right.

'Pounds, please.'

'We don't have too much for that price, sir, maybe bracelet better OK?'

'OK?' Dean replied with a slight question in his voice.

She walked round to another part of the shop. She

beckoned him over with the slightest of smiles.

The counter was round and he moved over to see a tray of bracelets with dangly objects resembling charms attached to them.

Then there was the one. It stood out from all the rest. It was a gold rope bracelet and he knew she had to have it, he had to buy it. Nothing had a price on as they were all considered affordable. No one who knew they could afford to shop there bothered to ask the price of a bracelet, apart from Dean who didn't know the protocol.

'How much is that one?' he asked, pointing at the top bracelet.

She reached in and took it out without a reply. She handed it to him and he felt the weight. The design was fantastically intricate and he got lost in the twists and turns as the individual threads of gold moved through each other. That was the one, she would love it and without hearing the price he said he'd have it, after all, it was only a bracelet.

The assistant packaged the bracelet up and rang through the till the sum of two thousand three hundred and fifty three pounds, eighty-nine pence.

The chunky bracelet was not only well made but it was heavy. It was the most expensive piece on the tray, which to give the saleswoman some credit, was the least expensive of all her trays.

Most of her work was selling extravagant gold pieces to gulf businessmen, who'd been cheating on their wives. This was usually with various types of prostitutes, in various places in the world. They placated the wives with riches, to stave off any awkward questions on their return.

Some of them would joke about it with their friends as they each bought an expensive piece. They would talk in Arabic and presume she couldn't understand them but she'd got a decent grasp of their language. She could follow a conversation as she kept her head lowered and listened to the debased jokes.

'Do you know how much it cost me to get that blonde Russian to shit on the glass table? And look, I'm paying fifty times as much to my wife to stay home and cook a meal!' How they would laugh.

This one was different though, English for sure, she guessed looking at Dean, good looking, good body, no fat. They were all fat, her customers.

Now and again you would get the wives with their husbands and she honestly didn't know who were worse. The wives talked to her like she was a piece of trash. As if she was one of the prostitutes her husband went on 'business' trips to see.

The men were at least polite to her while the women seemed to be full of hate. They would almost spit as they ordered her around, getting her to fix a necklace on their piggy necks or a ring on their fatty fingers. All her rings were over-sized because all their fingers were so fat. She knew they just sat around all day and ate because she had friends who worked as domestics.

The Philippine community in the Emirates was huge and most were there to serve. It was a terrible life for the majority as they were treated like modern day slaves by most families. They were abused verbally, physically and often sexually. They had little chance for recourse because they were treated even worse by the police. If they went to the police for help they would often get worse from them than they suffered at work.

One time she'd met a housemaid who heard a story about a domestic who had been raped by the oldest son in the family. She went to the police and instead of helping her they'd called the house in question. They spoke to the father of the boy who'd said she had lied to cover up stealing from the family. As punishment the police gang raped her in the station cell.

She said she was lucky to be alive as they were talking about what to do with her body once she was dead. It was only by chance that they all got called out to an emergency so they let her live.

By comparison the job at the airport was easy. She had to deal with slimy men all day and sometimes bitchy women but she went back to her shared room after each shift and slept for at least five hours. She prayed every night and every morning for her family back home and sent money to her mother and aunty. Her aunty had no husband and she had two children. She didn't want the children to have to work. She wanted them to finish school. She had to get them a better life than the one in rural Philippines. There, it was stifling and humid. Work was in the back-breaking paddy fields. It was all day, every day, for your whole life. You earned practically no money. It was soul destroying. You became like a zombie, immune to existence itself. It was so hard.

When Dean heard the price he balked for a second and then remembered the card Beki had given him. It had belonged to her dead boyfriend and she'd told him the pin number, so he used it. What he didn't realise was the saleswoman was going to ask for the boarding card, too.

Dean was travelling as Beki's boyfriend and so far so good. He'd got through customs in England as Beki had 'tripped' over as the customs officer had got Dean's passport and he'd been distracted enough by Beki's show of bare legs not to pay too much attention to the photo. He was yet another short-haired male with the same features. It's hard to distinguish one from another when you see thousands of them a week. They're only looking for suspicious Irish or Asian males. The rest all blend into one on the way out of the country. At the transit lounge in Dubai the customs man had looked twice but as the passenger had been cleared in the UK for boarding, subconsciously he didn't want to admit there was anything amiss. It was just another tourist on their way to India, nothing to bother the UAE.

Boarding card, now where had Dean put it? He had the passport, that was now in his hand, but where was the torn off slip of card?

Dean was still high from the chunk of pollen he'd necked in Manchester. He started to develop the stoner disease called 'pocket fever'. This is where the same pockets, bags and eventually front of underpants are repeatedly searched until the patient becomes completely disorientated from searching the same crevasses, pouches and compartments. Eventually the missing article, which is usually your keys or phone, is found in the one place you haven't searched. This is generally a random place, as you think at the time it's a great place to carry an item. The disease is flaunted until the next pocket virus takes hold, usually the next time you're completely out of your tree.

Dean eventually found it, folded over in the buttoned down outside breast pocket of the denim shirt he wore. He handed it over to the now irritated saleswoman who thought there was something not quite right about him. However he pressed the correct pin, boarding card matched the name on the bank card and the gold was now his. She watched him go, watched his broad shoulders as he walked away. She thought how much he took the world for granted; she prayed he'd get a wake-up call from God, so he would realise how lucky he was. Then she moved onto the next fat businessman coming in from Mumbai who had just spent two days locked in a hotel room with a child, half the age of his daughter.

Beki was tempted but knew deep down she would be crazy to take a Burberry handbag to India. It was stunningly well made and she could admire the aesthetic intent of the design. How she loved the line of a Burberry bag. In comparison the others seemed rather gauche.

She felt Dean move towards her before the tap on her shoulder.

'Come on. Let's get a bottle of something before we go,' Dean said and they walked off together back towards the alcohol.

They decided on a bottle of Martel VSOP and Dean paid for it with the dead man's card.

Beki put the bottle in her bag and they went to their boarding gate to wait the half hour before they were due to fly the shorter leg of their journey to the East.

The plane took off on time but they were back in Economy. Beki had the window seat, Dean the middle and he'd already started chatting to the passenger in the aisle seat called Gaz. He was about thirty years old, had shoulder length curly black hair in a kind of bob. He seemed to talk non-stop, in a stream of consciousness that started and ended with him. It was amusing Dean no end. He was also a Mancunian, much to Dean and Beki's surprise.

'I don't stay at the Laxman. It's an overpriced brothel, mate. Come to the Narung, that's where it's at in Delhi, mate. I'll sort things when we get there, no worries,' Gaz said, as if that was the decision made.

Dean was happy to take up the offer and liked the way Gaz spoke. It was the way he just said it and that was that. He had heard the lad's life story in the last half hour and he was keen to keep him around. This guy knew the territory well.

Gaz told Dean he'd been going to India for the last six years. These days he rented a house in Goa for the season. Before settling on his current routine of six months in the sun he stayed in the mountains and advised Dean of the places he should go if he wanted to sample some local delicacies.

Soon they were down with a bump and a shudder, as the

plane vibrated over the runway.

Dean looked over Beki's shoulder at his first view of India. What a contrast to the Emirates runway. It was barren and dusty, even the actual runway looked uneven and if he was honest, unsafe. It was cracked and rutted. Tufts of faded wheat coloured grass sprang up from random crevices and there was a dust haze in the air.

Dean swore he could smell a faint stench of kaka but then realised he was still in the air conditioned plane.

They pulled down their bags from the overhead lockers and Beki looked round at the passengers. They were very different from the people who flew into Dubai. They were surrounded by pushy Indian families who all seemed to want to get out of the plane as quickly as possible. She reminded herself that she was India, not the more westernised state of Goa. This was real deal Delhi.

As they opened the doors of the jet, the heat ran through the aircraft as quickly as a cheetah chasing a deer. The smell that Dean had convinced himself had not been there, now really was. It smelt like a toilet at a festival.

They slowly edged their way down the aisle, said goodbye to the cabin crew and paused at the exit door.

Gaz stood at the top of the boarding stairs and inhaled deeply. 'Smell that,' he announced to humankind. 'That's really how the world should smell. None of the sterilised West here.'

Just then, he was shoved in the back by a marauding family, keen to get a seat on the awaiting bus to the terminal.

The bus was slow and packed. They alighted at the entrance of the arrivals hall and as the doors of the bus opened all hell broke loose. People pushed and elbowed each other; children were dragged by their arms, crying and wailing; single men were quickest and made a dash for the hall doors, foreigners were left standing in the rush.

As Beki, Dean and their new friend Gaz entered, it became apparent why the stampede had taken place. There was complete chaos as lines and lines of humanity queued in fan assisted hot air. Others waited around circular islands of baggage recovery tracks. They were already three men deep.

'Don't ya love it?' Gaz said and he waded into the baggage recovery mire as if he owned the place.

'Wait here, I'm goin' in,' said Dean and he handed Beki his small backpack, before following Gaz into the mass.

The baggage recovery was meticulously slow. The same bags seemed to go round and round with no rightful owners. Then all of a sudden, a heap load of new arrivals all came at once. This was followed by the crush of bodies, all peering over shoulders to see if theirs was amongst them. This put even greater stress on Dean's already strained mood. A mixture of the heat and dust, slight dehydration from the flight and a come down from the pollen, coupled with the beckoning culture shock that people knew nothing of personal space, was already getting to him. He had been on Indian soil for less than an hour and he was ready to swing it out with anyone who crossed his path.

Gaz looked round and said, 'Mine's here, mine's here.'

He then turned back towards the belt of black rubber and leaned in to retrieve his bag.

As Gaz vacated the crush, Dean squeezed into his space. It was like the most packed bar in the hottest club at the end of last orders. Then he spotted his bag. He looked hopefully for Beki's, as logic said as they went on together so they should come off together, but this was India.

Here Western logic must be turned on its head, jumped up and down on several different ways and then returned to its original position, misshapen and anointed with bhakti. The saving grace of Beki's bag having been one of the last to leave the plane's hold was that the queue at customs was slightly less than when they arrived.

Curiously, Gaz had waited with Beki and told her all about his life. She heard it all in the twenty minute wait for her bag.

As Dean triumphantly approached, with both their bags, each one slung loosely over a shoulder, Gaz smiled. 'Watch this,' then adding as he turned, 'every man for himself.'

He strode off commandingly into the booth at the end. It read: Diplomats, Military Officials and Freedom Fighters. The pair watched in awe as Gaz confidently checked through this empty counter and smiled as he got through unscathed.

'What do you think?' asked Dean. 'Shall we try it?'

'No flippin' way, not with your dodgy passport, remember,' Beki replied.

'I'm not using that one. I need a stamp on my visa or somefing.'

'No you don't, they just check it and let you in. Use Tom's.'

'Not a chance, Beki, I'm using mine.' Dean was struggling to keep his voice low. Their first domestic and they hadn't even had sex yet.

'Do what the flip you want then, I'm queuing up. It's not too bad now.'

Dean followed her into the main queue and they both watched Gaz on the other side. He was sipping a chilled bottle of Bisleri mineral water, waiting patiently.

They got through with no issues and joined him in the arrivals lounge. He handed them both a bottle each of the same type of water and they both gulped it down greedily.

'We'll get a pre-paid taxi, to Paharganj,' Gaz said. He broke out a wad of rupees from his hidden money belt and paid the fare at the pre-paid taxi booth outside the airport.

'We're going to have to change some money, Dean,' Beki said. Loud enough so Gaz could hear her.

'No worries,' said Gaz. 'Wait till you meet Abdul, he'll give you the best rate. This is left over from the last time. I always keep a few rupees for the next trip.'

The three travellers settled in for the ride through mid-day Delhi. With their cab windows down, horns were sounding all around, cows blocking the road, rickshaws weaving through impossible spaces at improbable angles, cyclists defying death every hundred yards, motorbikes darting with a continuous 'beep' of their thumb pressed horns, dogs with ribs like rakes at the side of the road, beggars spotting the white faces and dreaming of dollars, the continuous staring of the Delhi-ites as they spot the foreigners, momentarily entranced by their unconventionality, their difference, their eccentricity. Never once did the majority of the locals who laid eyes upon the foreigners have anything other than genuine interest in mind.

Though it was different for a fair-haired woman, the sight of her evoked some men to think baser thoughts. The Internet had given rise to images of western women that went mostly unchallenged in the minds of Indian men. They had no doubt that all western women were prostitutes. They all engaged in the kind of hardcore pornographic images they had etched into their brains. This was via the Internet café's screens, now common in small suburbs of the capital and in the more affluent homes.

As they reached the top of Paharganj, the taxi driver stopped and looked at Gaz. His eyes welled, as if to plead not to make him drive down there. Even the most experienced taxi drivers in Delhi could not face the throng of Paharganj.

Although he was tempted to insist, after thinking it through and realising it would be quicker to walk, Gaz gave him the nod. They all got out.

The relieved taxi driver didn't bother looking back and shot off to the airport to join the line for his next fare. He almost knocked down a beggar, who homed in on the whites, fresh in from foreign lands.

Gaz spotted the commotion and ushered the two down into the most famous traveller's street in India. There was

Khao San Road in Bangkok, Freak Street in Kathmandu and Paharganj in Delhi.

Dean looked up at the mass of cables centred on a wooden telephone pole. Beki stared at all the colourful saris and materials lined up in three open fronted sari shops. Gaz looked at nothing in particular and took in everything at once. He was always on the lookout for something out of place; someone too interested in him or someone making a sudden movement in his direction.

As they got deeper, there were constant taunts of, 'Hallo, England, come see my shop,' from the Kashmiris. They were all hoping to sell something and everything was available.

Whispers drifted in their ear as they went past of, 'You want boy?', 'Girl, young girl?', 'Brown?', 'Hash?' There was a new one for Gaz in Paharganj: 'Cocaine?'

He gave the cocaine wallah a second glance and then quickly broke eye contact, before the weedy little runt with glazed eyes and a runny nose could involve him in anything. Gaz quickened his pace and pushed past a man with a small stationary shop balanced on his head, telling himself not to do anything so stupid again as evoke eye contact with a street junkie.

Beki and Dean were now holding hands, dragging each other along at various times, both trying to keep up with Gaz.

He was slightly taller than Dean and had a pace on him, even in the crowded street. Dean was happy to let someone else take charge for once. The best thing about Gaz was he didn't ask any questions and so Dean didn't have to lie about anything. He could just be Dean Shelby. He wasn't leader of a Manchester gang, he wasn't a big cheese who demanded respect, he didn't have to keep a drug flow through the streets of his home town, he didn't have to defend himself and his position to every wannabe gangster in his hood, he didn't have to shag two women at a time, he didn't have to order the assassination of one of his oldest friends because they'd been stealing from him and he didn't have to tip old men out of hotel windows.

He just had to absorb everything around him. For the first time in years, in the midst of all this dust, dirt, chaos and madness, he felt free. Maybe for the first time in his life.

Eventually Gaz looked round and nodded his head to the side.

He left the Main Bazaar and took a right down a smaller, less packed side street. They followed a bend and there it was in all its faded glory, the Narung Hotel.

Outside, it was peeling walls of whitewash, with a bluish hue. There were two old plastic, once white now grey, chairs and a decrepit sign above them with HOTEL NARUNG in black capitals on yellow background.

Inside there was a reception desk and a fan that swirled the hot air around but kept the flies and mosquitos at bay.

'Hello,' said Gaz in a loud voice. He sounded hopeful. He then turned to the pair and said, 'Isn't it great, we're here, in one piece, thousands of miles, millions of possibilities for things to go wrong and none did. It's meant to be … Hello?' This time slightly louder he added, 'They'll be having a siesta. HELLO!' At last there was a noise from the inner depths of the manager's office.

A sleepy fat Indian man, dressed in brown shirt and trousers with buffalo leather sandals appeared at the office door behind reception. He looked wearily at the three guests and said in perfect Indian English, 'Room?' He paused and yawned, stretched his arms out. 'Double 450, single 290. Top floor extra, double 500, single 390.'

He looked on at the three without expression and Gaz asked the question the manager had heard a million times. 'Why is the top single 390?'

'Room bigger, with roof accesses.' Then the manager yawned again, stretching out his chubby hands shrugging up his shoulders.

'OK, one double, one single top floor. Is Abdul around?' Gaz asked as he produced his cash.

'Eh, Abdul. He just got out of jail. Back later.' The manager looked slightly cross with Gaz for asking, but the expression was fleeting.

They lugged their bags onto the chairs in the reception and filled out the forms for the hotel's registers. Dean used Tom's passport and visa numbers.

Beki was happy they had a double room together. They were all a bit tired and agreed to meet up in half an hour after getting a shower.

When Beki and Dean got into their room they realised there was no bathroom. The shared showers and toilets were in the opposite corner of the square block on their floor. There was a central courtyard and staircase that went up to each level in a stairwell. They were on floor 4, room 22 and 23.

Gaz's room opened out to the main square landing at the front. At the back he had a small staircase that led to the roof. This was the special 'roof access' he'd paid the extra money for. It was well worth the extra in stifling Delhi.

Not having a shower in the room made life easier for Beki, as she didn't have to worry about drying or dressing with Dean around. She went for the first shower, the water was tepid but in the heat that was fine.

She then went back to the room wrapped in a sarong.

Dean exited for his shower. When he returned she was dressed and was combing out her golden, shoulder length hair. He just had a towel wrapped round his waist. She tried not to look but couldn't help a glance at his body which was rather perfect. He had an athletic build that wasn't forced. This wasn't a bulgy muscled gym body, which would have turned her off. This was nature at its finest, a young man in good physical condition.

He went to the far side of the room and turned his back on her. He let the towel slip off his waist and quickly dried round his privates. He reached into his rucksack. As he looked into the bag she caught another sly peek at his bum. She got a bit more than she bargained for as he stood back up, giving her a flash of his front.

So he didn't think she'd been looking, she asked innocently, 'Are you ready, then?'

He slipped on his shorts and turned round. 'Yer, come on, then. Let's see what's going down.' Dean opened the door into the square balcony, walked out and leaned over, looking down to the reception on the ground floor.

Looking up, straight at him, was a raven-haired man with a mean look in his eye. The man looked away and said something in Hindi towards the reception area. The manager appeared and looked up at Dean. He said something to the other guy and walked off with a hand gesticulation.

Dean took this to mean 'whatever'.

Gaz opened his door and smiled excitedly. 'Come here, mate, got something to show you.'

Dean walked over to Gaz's room and there on the bed was a big plastic bag, the type you get at the supermarket. What was in it wasn't from Sainsbury's, though. Dean looked in at roughly two thousand dried magic mushrooms. He looked up at Gaz, wide eyed. 'They're for the season in Goa,' Gaz explained. 'Powder them down and sell them on. Eat a few myself of course, mate. Grab a handful for later, if you like.'

'Cheers,' said Dean. He did just that. He pocketed them and thought about when he'd last drunk mushroom brews.

'Last time I had these I was about twelve. Never looked back.'

'They're not your bog standard mushies from Derbyshire. These are handpicked from Wales, mate. The best of the best.' Gaz was obviously very proud. He spoke about the ill effects of inferior mushrooms and the almost mystical qualities of their fabled first growth Welsh cousins. 'No stomach problem with these bad boys. You can eat them fresh. If you tried that with the ones from the local school field in Manchester, you'd be tripping alright but you'd spend the first hour either puking or in agony, feeling like your guts was exploding from the inside. So because there's no stomach with them, you can eat as much as you want and all you get is blissed out.'

'I think Abdul's downstairs,' said Dean.

'Ace, come on, I'll introduce you. Just be warned he's probably a bit edgy if he's just come out of the cells again. They always give him a hard time. He's a good guy, no worries there, mate.'

Dean wondered if Gaz had spent time in Australia.

They walked down the stairs and Dean waited at the reception desk. Gaz walked over to an unmarked door. He gave a tap and waited. When the door opened it was the man Dean had seen at reception.

'Abdul,' said Gaz. Abdul looked at him indifferently. 'Gaz from Manchester, we meet again.'

Abdul responded with a surprised expression that turned into recognition. He sorted through his memory banks. He put the face, the tone of voice, accent and overall impression through his inbuilt computer. It spat out the faint recognition of someone he had done business with before. It would have been impossible for Abdul to keep everyone he'd met on record in his head. He was constantly meeting people staying at the Narung, where he lived. He knew them usually for no more than the half hour they needed with him. That was to sort them out with some charas, brown, opium, cocaine, speed, trips or pills. Occasionally it might be some fraud involving travellers' cheques or credit cards. If they wanted a prostitute he would give them a phone number of a Russian friend who worked for herself.

He stopped there and if anyone wanted anything else, then he showed them the door. Sometimes that was with the boot of his foot. He didn't want child rapists ruining his good name. He'd told Amir the manager a few times to get rid of certain guests because they were no good. He'd tell Amir they would bring children back to the hotel. Amir, along with his brother Ali, would immediately turf out the offending child molesters onto the street.

'What can I do for you? Come in, come in.' Abdul beckoned Gaz in. He turned to Dean waiting in the corridor and nodded his head up, indicating he came too.

'Abdul, this is my English friend, Dean. He's from Manchester, also.'

Abdul came over to Dean and shook his hand. 'Come in, welcome, welcome. Manchester United?' questioned Abdul.

'No, mate, they're from Salford. I'm with the real Manchester team, City.'

3

Hue and Emile were having dinner at the Paradise Restaurant. Hue took a sip of iced water just as the bomb they had planted that morning, hit its timer switch. It exploded with furious candour.

There was a boom and then silence. The birds had stopped singing their evening song, momentarily in shock at the sound. Then the vibration hit. It travelled up through the tree's roots, along their trunks and into the branches where the birds liked to perch and sing.

The two men exchanged a glance and Hue checked his watch. His Omega Seamaster gave the local time of 21:53. He knew the next explosion was at 23:53 and the last one was to be at 05:03 the next morning. They would be on the plane home by then, though. Their work was done here. They had unfinished business back home.

Hue had been thinking through the possibilities surrounding Charles Bates' demise. It could be the meeting went wrong with the new supplier, but why? All Charles was doing there was touting for business, making the hoodlum an offer he shouldn't refuse. Charles was diplomatic to the core and although Hue realised he had been drinking slightly more than usual, he was very capable of handling a shoddy back street drug dealer.

No, Hue thought, this was more professional than that. This was something to do with the policeman, Sol.

They'd applied a touch of pressure in the past but nothing too severe. He had no doubt that Sol was involved in this. When he returned to the UK he would do some searching about in the files they kept on the guy, get to know him and then go in hard. By the time they were through with him he'd be begging them to spill everything he knew and more about the events of Charles Bates' passing.

They rounded off a dinner of braised quail, asparagus tips and shark meat kebabs with a Cognac and smoke. They chose Hennessy XO and two Simon Bolivar cigars from Cuba.

They paid the bill, leaving an unremarkable tip. Then they headed off to their hotel to pick up their packed hand luggage. They would then take their booked taxi to the airport. It was a non-stop business class flight to Heathrow, BA of course.

Beki went out into the back street and walked over to the first booth she saw that sold a variety of items. She had on a vest top and shorts. The heat was building and she wanted some water.

The booth sold all sorts of day-to-day items and she presumed it must sell bottled water, too. She'd borrowed twenty rupees from Gaz.

The man in the booth smiled in a friendly way as she approached, he had a male friend who was standing outside the booth and they were chatting.

'Hello,' she said.

'Hello, madam,' said the shopkeeper, a young man in his early twenties.

His friend looked Beki up and down. It was as if he was undressing her, like he had X-ray eyes.

She pulled down her arms making sure nothing was showing from the side and smiled uncomfortably up at the shopkeeper, who kept his eyes fixed on hers.

'Do you have any water?' Beki asked in her Mancunian accent.

The shopkeeper looked at her baffled. What in the world was 'warter'? He thought and thought, looking about his shop's well stocked items. War-ter? War-ter? He turned for help to his friend, did he know what it was? But his friend was also bemused. A friend of his arrived and the shopkeeper asked him what the foreign lady wanted.

'Yes, madam, vat is it you are vanting?' The friend of the friend's English was considered better than the shopkeeper's because he worked as a rickshaw driver and dealt with tourists at the railway station.

'Water, just a bottle of water … war-ter.' Now Beki was

spelling it out the way they heard it. The confusion grew to palpable levels.

Then a couple of passing relatives of the shopkeeper's friend's friend, stopped by. They too tried to help Beki, who was now almost surrounded by willing but confused Indian men.

They were all trying to help her, as they ogled her breasts and legs.

The heat of the day peaked and they all just went round in circles until Beki could not say any more than what she had said already.

The shopkeeper sold many things but because his shop was down a back street off the Main Bazaar in Paharganj, he sold to locals, not tourists.

A few who stayed at the Narung used his shop for sundry items like toothpaste, soap, incense or candles but none had ever came to him asking for 'wartear'. That was how the translation was now being heard and passed around the group.

Beki made a glugging noise and mimicked drinking from a bottle.

Suddenly the friend's, friend's, cousin's uncle, who arrived late to the scene, twigged. 'VATA!' he announced loud and clear. This was to the dismay of all around but the shopkeeper and Beki.

'VATA,' he said again, triumphantly.

All the young men looked daggers at him as it was the highlight of their day crowding around the blonde English lady and trying to peek down her top. Now the genie was out of the bottle and the spell was broken.

'Vata. Bisleri?' the shopkeeper said.

'Yes, yes, yes. Bisleri. Wata!' she said. Then losing her guard flung her arms up, fist clenched giving a last gasp, eye opening view of her bouncing boobs to the small crowd. She caught herself as the collective eyes widened and pulled her arms in again.

'No, madam.'

'What?'

'No var-ter,' the shopkeeper said. He pointed down the street. 'Main Bazaar.'

Dean sat on the double bed next to Gaz in the small but functional bed-sit of the Algerian-Indian Abdul.

He'd lived there for the last four years, off and on. There had been some bouts in jail and a couple of trips to Japan.

The jail time had officially been for fraud, drugs and once for fighting. The fighting charge he deserved and the other times were because he'd not paid enough to the right policeman at the right time.

Abdul paid the local police chief and paid him well. He took about twenty per cent of his income. In return if some hippy got caught with a kilo or two of charas, the bounty came Abdul's way at a decent price.

It was some of the police charas that he was selling to Gaz. He went over the top about giving it a good cover story. The tale was of a friend coming down from the mountains with too much dope to take to Israel, so he'd off loaded half a kilo to Abdul. The friend was now happily dishing his smuggled charas out to the thriving Israeli psy-trance scene. He was doing the round of parties and making a fortune. He even told them the name of the village it was supposed to come from, Tishi.

He got a tola and opened it apart with his two thumbs. He placed it under Gaz's nose.

Gaz inhaled deeply from the pungent bagicha. It was like smelling the fruits of the earth.

Abdul knew that it was decent stuff. It was nowhere near the best, but for charas starved travellers straight off the plane, it was better than any deal they were going to find from some Kashmiri rip off artist on the street.

'Can I make a mix, mate?' asked Gaz, as he took hold of the dope from Abdul. He handed it over to Dean who was sat on the bed, taking it all in.

'Not here, mate, police problem. Take it upstairs. If there's an issue, bring it back. It's five hundred and fifty a tola. Good price, good smoke. You want to pay in dollar or pound, no problem.'

'I'll take seven tola. Dean, you want some?' asked Gaz.

'Erm, yeh, same as you, mate.' Dean went along with Gaz's deal and bought seventy grams of charas for him and Beki.

'One minute, wait here,' Abdul said and he was gone. He was off to his stash.

'He lives here?' Dean asked Gaz.

'Yes, mate. He's half Indian half Algerian, so has dual citizenship. His dad's Indian but lives in Algeria with his mum. But Abdul likes it here in Delhi.'

They stayed quiet whilst waiting for their man to return, always a slight nervousness in the air, sat in a dealer's room in a foreign country in a backstreet hotel known for its drug use. Especially with the outside temperature now pushing thirty-eight degrees. Clouds were forming above them as they sat motionless, pressure building in the air, a downpour inevitable.

Abdul returned after about ten minutes, beads of sweat had formed below his hairline.

'Getting hot now, rain's coming.' He reached into his combat trouser pockets, then spilled fourteen sticks of charas onto the bed.

They were all wrapped in cellophane; all roughly the same thickness and length. They all contained a good balance of active chemicals to give the user a real high. It was a proper Indian welcome.

They both paid in pounds as Dean hadn't changed any money yet.

Gaz wanted to keep his rupees from his last trip, as the exchange rate had gone down. He knew Abdul's rate was decent enough.

They popped upstairs and stashed the dope in Gaz's room, as Beki wasn't around with their room key.

'Come on, let's go buy a chillum,' Gaz said.

Dean followed him out of the hotel into the cloudy and oppressive afternoon heat.

The first thing Beki saw as she walked onto Paharganj, or the Main Bazaar, was a cold drinks stall.

She ordered fresh orange juice and watched the young man squeeze it into a glass from his juicer, straining it through a yellow plastic sieve that looked like it had never been cleaned.

'Sucra? Sugar?' asked the young man.

'No sugar, thanks.'

'Thirty five rupees,' he said. Then she realised she hadn't changed any money.

'Flip, I need to change money.'

'Money change? My uncle change money. You want?'

'Yes, please,' she replied, relieved.

With that he got on his mobile and spoke quickly in Hindi.

'How much?' he asked.

Beki had a money belt with about five hundred pounds. It was mostly a mixture of twenty and fifty pound notes. She thought fifty would bring the money changer to her, twenty might not be enough.

'Fifty pounds,' she said, confidently.

The young man spoke again for about another minute. He was bargaining his slice of commission on the deal. As he put the phone down he handed over the juice adding, 'Ice?'

Beki shook her head from side to side in the English manner meaning 'no' and took the drink. It was sweet and refreshing.

The young man was still waiting for a definitive yes or no as the head shake to an Indian could mean many things. In this context he took it to mean, 'I don't yet know as I've not tried it', but after tasting the juice she gave no more sign she wanted ice.

'You change hundred pound, better rate, OK?'

That would mean better commission for him.

'No, fifty's OK. Do you have any Bisleri?'

He reached into the fridge at the back of the booth. He produced a cold bottle of mineral water, condensation dripping off the side. It wasn't Bisleri but it was water and she was dehydrated. She took it and gulped down about half a litre, getting a slight brain freeze as it was truly ice cold.

'Hey, Beki, give us a go on that,' said Dean as he walked up to the booth with Gaz.

She felt better for bumping into the lads and passed him the bottle smiling. He had a good glug and then passed it to Gaz, who finished it off.

'I'm waiting to change money,' announced Beki. She nodded towards the vendor. 'His uncle's coming.'

'What's the rate?' Gaz asked.

'Oh, flip, I didn't ask,' Beki said.

'What rate?' Gaz spoke directly to the young man with a slight edge to his voice that said don't mess with me, son.

The young man suddenly went from really sharp businessman to halfwit. 'Uncle coming,' he said. He started shaking his head from side to side.

'Yer, and what's uncle's rate?' Gaz insisted.

'Good rate,' he replied.

'How many rupees to the pound?' Gaz was getting annoyed. 'Exactly.'

'Uncle coming, one minute,' said the young man. He

was now very aware that this black haired foreigner was not going to be duped like the lady.

He got back on his phone and told his uncle, the local moneylender, that the situation had changed and there were now three of them. He suggested a business opportunity had arisen that needed a change of tack. Instead of giving the lady a less than the fair rate they could give them all a fair rate and still make a decent profit. He was prepared to lower his commission if the deal went ahead. Samil, the moneylender thought it through and said to give them a rate of RS90 if they change £100 or more and RS85 for the £50. He anticipated they would go for the better rate. He would then sit on the £100 until the exchange rate was better for him to sell it and make an extra few rupees in the future.

By the time Samil arrived they were ready with a bonus note. So they all changed £50, Gaz included. He had to admit it was a good rate.

The young man got his commission, which went to paying off some of his debt to Samil, who had lent him the money to buy the juicer, so he could set up the business, albeit at an extortionate interest rate, that would most likely never be paid off. Or at least it wouldn't be settled for many years.

However the young man had an income, Samil the moneylender never squeezed him too hard and everyone was happy enough. This was the way India worked.

The three travellers walked down the busy Bazaar looking at all the sights and shops, taking everything in.

'I'm hungry,' announced Beki. 'Where's good to eat?'

She directed her question to Gaz, the font of all knowledge.

'Well, mate, there's only one place to eat on Paharganj, the Bright,' he replied and pointed up the street. 'It's down towards the end, though. Let's buy a chillum on the way.'

They walked as quickly as the crowds would allow. The sense overload was immense. The good smells like incense and spice shops were followed by bad ones like sewers and engine fumes. This was as the odd motorbike or rickshaw weaved its hesitant journey through the throng. They always seemed to have their horns blasting at any opportunity. The engines revving up blue smoke into the already polluted and dusty air.

As they passed an enormous white cow, Beki noticed it was eating a blue plastic bag. She was so entranced by this that she narrowly avoided stepping into a puddle, the sort that you really didn't want to step in.

As she looked down she could see all sorts of detritus on the dirt road. Small piles of rubble, bricks, piles of swept rubbish, discarded leaf plates with mangy dogs licking the last drops of food from the bowls.

She looked to her right as an overwhelming smell of rancid cooking oil hit her. She watched a seated man, expertly squeeze a sugary batter into the hot oil wok before him. He was making a round, then criss-cross motion for each bright orange jalabi to join the piles he'd already made.

They found the chillum shop Gaz had been looking for

and went inside. It was long and narrow and sold chillums in all shapes and sizes. From ones you could fit in your palm, to a huge triple cobra headed showpiece that cost five thousand rupees.

Dean was admiring it and Gaz told him there was a temple in Hampi where they smoked a five headed chillum. Gaz knew what he was after and bought a standard size piece in black clay. It was enough for the average mix. It had a clean polished shaft and a medium sized, decently grooved stone. The stone was big enough to retain some heat but not one of those stupidly long ones that always break and are too hot to handle after a round or ten of continual smoking.

He bought some safi. This was a square of white cotton with some kind of pattern printed on it in red. A small polished coconut mixing bowl and a woven woollen padded case in red, green and yellow with black cotton trim. Total cost RS 575, bargain.

They trooped on towards the Bright and they heard the first clap of thunder.

Dean caught a whiff of bidi smoke, herbal and aromatic; he wondered what the guy was at. It looked like a little handmade cigar. It looked good; he didn't know it was a poor man's cigarette.

Gaz quickened the pace and the other two followed. Main Bazaar is longer than you think on a busy afternoon, when everyone starts to rush around, trying to get things done before the downpour starts.

'Here it is,' said Gaz.

He shot left into a non-descript blue and white tiled restaurant with a huge tandoor oven at the front. It was perpetually being refilled with the handmade chapattis that were being rolled out next to it. The people rolling and roasting the bread were boys, both children and teenagers.

Inside there was an old man sat next to the till counter, reading the newspaper. There was another man taking the money and ordering everyone about. They were the owner and his son.

The place was about half full. There was a constant rush created by the waiters. They moved between the closely set tables with consummate skill, as if floating on air. Back and forth from the open kitchen area, through the low swinging doors they came, armed with small silver dishes of various spicy vegetarian delights. Then they'd collect tandoori chapatti from the front. The last thing to happen to the cooked bread was a flip onto an open gas flame, where the flat bread puffed up. It was then thrown onto the awaiting plate.

Ninety per cent of the clientele who sat round the small plastic topped, metal-framed tables were Indian men. There were four travellers that looked Italian to Gaz, a couple of Indian families and lots of single men and small groups of two or three who chatted intermittently as they held their bread in hand before scooping up some aloo gobi or sabji.

The waiter came with three stainless steel cups of water and a small stainless steel plate of salad that consisted of sliced onion, a sliced whole green chilli and a wedge of lemon. He didn't say a word, just looked and waited for the order. The menu was on the table and was a laminated card that was well used and very creased.

They all chose a dish and Gaz added a yellow dhal. He also ordered six chapatti, three Sprites and a mineral water. The waiter went off and minutes later was back with the order of rajma, aloo gobi, aloo mattar and the dhal, which had small crispy onions and mustard seeds visible in its turmeric infused neon yellow brightness.

The rajma was made of kidney beans in gravy, the aloo gobi was very, very spicy potato and cauliflower, done until it was nearly a dry mash, the aloo mattar was potato pyramids and green peas in a tomato gravy with the star of the show being the yellow dhal, tasty, spicy and perfectly cooked with just the right amount of salt and tamarind for the sour aftertaste.

The breads were crisp on the flat parts and soft on the fluffed up parts. Gaz braved a chilli from the salad and Dean following suit, soon regretted taking his bite of the green monster. The Sprite killed the burning heat in their mouths for thirty seconds, with their oversweet fizzy sensation and Beki asked Gaz if they did lassi. They finished the meal with three banana lassi and all chipped in to the bill of RS381, leaving RS400 with the tip.

Outside the thunder sounded again and they moved down the Bazaar towards their hotel, stomachs full and heads down because the first large drops of afternoon rain had started to fall.

They walked down the other side of the road and all of a sudden Beki thought she was going to puke because of the stench of stale urine. She looked up and saw several white urinals in plain view, down an alley off the street. Most had men either in mid- flow or shaking the drops off. Beki tried not to stare but it was impossible not to look.

Gaz explained the sight. 'Piss pot alley. If they didn't have it they'd just go in the street.'

As Beki had momentarily stopped she felt a slight tug on the hem of her top. She looked round to see a child, probably a girl but it was genuinely difficult to tell. The child had short hair stuck out at all angles like it had been backcombed with dust. It didn't look as if the child had eaten recently or at least this week. Dirt engrained her skin and her eyes seemed to be popping out of her face. The clothes worn were grey rags, ripped and nearly falling off.

With one hand still tugging at her top, the other hand went to her mouth with all fingers and thumbs touching each other, her fingertips touching her lips as the child repeated the word, 'Khana' over and over, moving her hand back and forth to her mouth as she spoke.

'Gaz?' Beki asked in a worried tone, which confirmed the fact she was well out of her comfort zone. 'What does khana mean?'

'Food, meal, something like that. Ignore it.'

Literally, it means 'I cannot survive without food', or in this case, without rupees.

Then, without time for Beki to protest, Gaz turned on the beggar, waving his hand and raising his voice to a command. 'Chalo. Chalo Pakistan,' and with this the girl was gone. She instantly disappeared into the moving mass of people.

Gaz didn't understand that if she returned to her gang master without the required amount of rupees for the day, she would face a beating, humiliation and starvation. She'd be forced to watch, as the other street beggars ate their tiny meal of leftovers from the gang master's dinner plates, her mouth salivating to no avail.

By the time they arrived at the Narung, the size of the drops had decreased but the frequency had increased. They weren't soaked to the skin but after another ten minutes they would have been drenched.

As they sat in Gaz's room on the top floor, they understood it had really started to come down. The noise as the rain hit the roof was crazy loud. Gaz dug deep to the bottom of his bag and produced his iPod dock and speakers. It was a Sony set up with a decent sound and it did drown out the rain, if not the thunder.

He put on some old psychedelic trance; morning music from 1992 called Digital Alchemy and started the ritual of making a chillum.

Dean and Beki had never smoked a chillum before and Beki's protestations of having a spliff, because it's quicker, were shunned by Gaz. He insisted the way to smoke dope in India was like this.

Why like this? Gaz heard the voice of Ariella, his Israeli girlfriend from last season, in his head.

Dean heard some voices from the floor below and left the room to have a look. Two girls and three lads, all with Southern English accents were talking and laughing from the floor below. He could make out they were talking about their travels and how they'd had enough of India, especially the girls, who said they were off to Thailand. The boys said they were going up to the mountains. Dharamsala then Manali, before heading back home to make some money.

Dean got bored and joined Gaz as he got out a cig from the golden and red box, emptied the contents into the mixing bowl by rotating it between his finger and thumb and watching, trance like, as the tobacco fell gradually out.

Dean noticed the cig paper was browned and slightly scorched. This was from Gaz 'roasting' the cig with a match placed under and around it, drying out the tobacco and giving it a slightly burnt flavour. He un-wrapped the clear plastic from the top of the charas stick and broke off tiny amounts with his thumbnail and let them fall into the tobacco. Then using his right hand thumb and first finger he gently worked the charas into the tobacco.

Dean had never seen resin like this, it reminded him most of some squishy black he had a few times as a kid, the stuff his dad's friends used to smoke.

When Gaz decided enough was enough, he carefully wrapped the plastic covering back over the charas stick and placed it next to the mixing bowl on the bed.

Gaz was still in England mode and was still treating charas with extreme reverence, this would probably last about a day and he'd slip back into his India mind and take all these luxuries for granted again. Stuff like never having to cook a meal, as he would always be eating at restaurants and cafés, never having to work, never having to get up for anything other than a bus or train, never having to want for company because when you travel everyone wants to know you, never having to answer to anyone about anything and never being straight headed for at least the next six months … starting now.

He poured the mix into the top of the chillum and gently tampered it down with his thumb. Once happy there were no erroneous bits of tobacco on the top edge he put the upright chillum into Dean's hand, as he was sitting on the bed to his left.

Dean held it for the first time. He felt the weight of the thing and gazed down on the boulders of charas in the mix. There were a lot.

Gaz ripped off a strip of the safi and dampened it down with the condensation on the outside of a water bottle. He wrapped it into a ball, squeezed out a couple of drops of excessive liquid from the damp cotton strip in a clenched fist, unwrapped it again, took back the chillum from Dean and wrapped the cloth around the smaller bottom hole.

He mimed to Dean the way to hold it and said, 'Puff on it until its going, get it red hot on the top, then take as big a lungful as you can, mate. Hold it in, before letting it out slowly.

'Important this, never let the end make contact with your lips, that's very bad chillum etiquette, always fingers and thumb to lips. OK, mate?' He returned the prepared tube to Dean who was taking it all in.

Dean held it as he'd been shown, which was in one hand with an open fist, always being careful to keep the mix end upright, as Gaz had mimed.

He put it to his lips, using his fingers and thumb of his right hand as the mouthpiece and Gaz lit up two Homelite safety matches, keeping the lit ends slightly apart to create a V.

Gaz placed the fire to the end of the chillum and raised his voice a notch louder, after each of the next words he preached, until he was almost shouting at the end. 'Shiva, Shakti, Kali, Laxmi,' he commanded as Dean chugged away. Gaz paused with the final verbal ablution, until the novice took a massive lungful. Then, 'ALAKH Niranjan, Bom Bholenath … BOOM!'

There are many different explanations for the chant. In Gaz's mind it meant: Invisible Light, Hail Kind Hearted Lord … The First Sound in the Universe.

Dean exhaled a huge amount of blue grey smoke and held onto the chillum for dear life. He looked wide eyed at Gaz who nodded towards Beki who was sat on the far end of the bed, slightly amused by Dean's red face, which seemed to say it all, as in 'What the hell was that?'

'Beki?' Gaz said in a questioning tone, 'you want some?'

'Too right.' She took the tube and chugged a couple of puffs before taking a lungful herself. She coughed a touch as it went down but held it like a trooper until she exhaled in a controlled manner that impressed Gaz.

She passed it on to him and as she did, she gently let Dean know there was nothing to worry about by leaning into him and letting her hand rest on the side of his thigh, a little too long.

Gaz held the tube between his two hands in a different

style than he'd shown them. The tube poked out from between the middle fingers of his clasped hands and the mouthpiece was a circle made with his thumbs, the left one over the top of his right. He took two chugs for show and then made a sharp 'SSWWW' sound as he sucked in some air with the smoke allowing him to reach the full capacity of his lungs, keeping it there for a few seconds and then letting out a slow, controlled exhale. Then they did it all again until the mix was ash. The last toke was by Gaz and then he showed them how to clean the chillum.

He popped out the remaining bits of ash with the hot stone that stopped the mix from falling through the tube, by tapping the top sharply into the palm of his hand. He let the contents spill gently into the hotel's ashtray.

'Never let the stone hit the floor as it'll break it. Then it's impossible to find another stone to fit right. Each tube is made with its own stone and that's that.' As Gaz spoke he tore off a long strip of the safi cloth and rolled it into a string. He coiled it up into the business end of the tube. It lay there like a waiting cobra, the end like its curved head sticking up from the top. He trapped the cobra head with his thumb against the edge of the tube and quickly, as it was still quite hot, blew a sharp blast of air down the empty shaft using his rounded finger and thumb as a mouthpiece. Expertly done, the very end of the cloth came out of the smaller bottom hole at the base of the tube. Perfect. If you get this wrong, even an experienced chillum head can appear amateurish.

He nodded to Dean to grab the cobra tail. 'Wrap it

around the end of your finger, mate, hold it tight.' He then did the same to his end. He rubbed the chillum vigorously up and down the string until he was satisfied it was clean. There was something vaguely sexualized about this and Beki got the giggles as the high came on from the rather good charas. It was from Pārvati valley, from higher up than Tishi, this was from Ranngi. If Abdul had known it was from a really high village it would have been 850 a tola, so the lads had got a decent deal. Abdul just paid the police a flat rate for whatever they had. Sometimes it was low quality but most often it was good. Abdul never overplayed it, even though once or twice he knew he had the best of the best, the fabled Malana cream or close to it. Like Manuka honey, there's far more Malana cream sold than is ever produced.

Gaz immediately started a new mix and that was it for the night, doors open on the top floor of the Narung, the three travellers smoked chillum after chillum, talked, giggled, laughed hysterically and got the severe munchies late in the evening.

Gaz went to buy crisps that the Indians called 'chips', peanuts you had to shell, 'chicki', which was sesame seed and toffee bars and a big bunch of fresh lychees, still on their sticks.

The rains had ceased and there was some freshness in the air. Any stray dust had settled, dampening down for the time being.

Dean went out a couple of times to buy cold drinks of Pepsi, Sprite, Fanta and Canada Dry ginger ale from the cold drinks stall on Main Bazaar.

Each time he went things looked a little stranger as the lights went on after dusk and the colours all seemed more vivid, the people milling around, causing a sinister effect.

There were more hippies about now, aimlessly wandering up and down, stopping to browse the shops without glass windows. The street was quieter and the beggars more obvious. There was a little lad with no legs sitting on a kind of homemade skate board. He was using his hands along the ground to propel himself forwards. As Dean stopped at the cold drinks stand he arrived with perfect timing at his feet.

'Baksheesh, Mista?' he said, holding out his hand. It was worn hard with callouses from moving himself around. He was filthy dirty, with the wide-eyed stare that cut you in two. 'Mista, only ten rupee,' he said with a flutter of his eyelashes. He flashed his cutest grin, exposing white teeth with red stains between them. 'Only ten rupee, Mista, ten rupee only.'

He would have gone on saying the same thing to Dean until he paid up or walked off. This hard Manchester gangster was almost reduced to tears as he ordered an extra Sprite, passed it down to the beggar, with a folded fifty rupee note in the palm of his hand, surreptitiously passed on to the boy in a move they both knew by heart, as smooth as melting ice cubes, practiced to perfection from countless street deals, thousands of miles away by one of them.

It may well have been from a past lifetime.

4

Sol was having his evening meal early as he was going out on a blind date later that night and didn't want to feel bloated or slow. He ate two poached eggs on top of steamed Sea Bass, salad and chips. Healthy fish and chips he called it. Sol took good care of himself.

He'd seen too many of his colleagues grow fat and lazy as the years went on and the job became more about sitting behind a desk than out there fighting crime. Not that Sol was particularly interested in that. The lines were blurred to the point of meeting and he knew from a philosophical point of view there was no right or wrong, good or bad, criminal or policeman. These were just aspects, labels and points of view.

This particular point of view was one he never shared with anyone and kept completely to himself. He wouldn't want to get into a discussion about morality with ninety nine per cent of his colleagues, as they weren't the type to think that deeply. Most people Sol worked with in GMP were decent enough but not too bright. The women were generally a lot quicker in the head than the men but were held back with institutionalised sexism. If you were black and female you had practically no chance of promotion through the ranks. He couldn't think of one female boss of any colour other than white. Life would be so tough, so laborious. There would be a daily, possible hourly, feeling of treading through treacle. It would be like trying to do your job stood under an apple tree with apples constantly falling all around you and you'd have to make sure you caught each one before it hit the ground, because if it did fall on the floor it would start to rot and if you picked it up and put it with the rest of the apples, pretty soon the whole applecart would be riddled with corruption and it would be your fault for missing the trick.

Sol was aware he had to catch all his apples, too. If they, meaning the institution, could pin something on a black, then it proved them right.

He'd seen white officers get away with a quiet word in the corridors from the bosses, whereas he'd have been hauled over hot coals.

This latest case had come close to him being hauled in. He'd been mixed up in it from the start, as he was being blackmailed and threatened by two posh spooks from London. One, the older man, had been thrown out of the balcony of a hotel during a meeting he'd set up. Dean Shelby, the gangster that did it was on the run, possibly now out of the area, possibly the country.

Sol had been waiting downstairs in the hotel lobby when

it happened. He'd got out of there sharpish and hoped whoever was scanning the hotel's camera footage and CCTV from the street hadn't recognised him as a cop.

As he finished his meal and put the dishes into the dishwasher he tried to think about what he would do if the remaining London spook had seen any CCTV footage and recognised him. They knew his family lived in the Islands, St. Kitts, and had made vague threats towards them. They had paid him well in the past and somehow seen to it that the bosses left him alone on this one but if he was caught on camera at the hotel, considering one of them was dead, he knew all hell could come down on him.

Sol went upstairs and showered, wore a nice white shirt by Without Prejudice, a pair of light grey trousers from The Kooples and his light brown Jeffrey West shoes.

His date was arranged by a work colleague, Dawn, who he'd been chatting to about the fact that people in the job tend to go for other people in the job. She'd said she had a housemate who had just moved to Manchester from London and was a freelance journalist. Dawn had said to Sol, 'She said there was too much competition in London and she was hoping to do some work for the relocated BBC or Granada in Media City. She said she was looking for a date and liked slightly arrogant, slightly obnoxious, workaholic black men, and I immediately thought, Sol!' Dawn had written down her name and number on a piece of paper and instructed he should ring her.

The date had been arranged the next morning for that night. They were meeting for a nine o'clock drink at the

Wah Wah Bar, nothing serious, just for laughs and good company. Her name was Isabel and she'd be wearing a black and white dress with a black handbag and coat.

Sol couldn't wait and he sprayed some Kenzo Peace onto his wrist and neck. He didn't shave as he liked the look of a short beard or long stubble, whichever way you looked at it. He knew most women preferred a clean skinned man but then he didn't want most women, he didn't mind if a woman shaved her legs, underarms or pubes, he was after connecting with the person beneath the superficial exterior. Beauty was only skin deep, it was their soul he needed.

5

In the taxi from Heathrow to Emile's workspace Hue
thought about his next move. He'd slept most of the flight
and was feeling fresh as a daisy. He thought about St. Kitts.
Solomon Cleaver had family there but it was a bit too
remote. Frankly he didn't have the time or resources to send
Emile so far away to apply the pressure he needed. It had to
be closer to home.

When they got through the doors, the security was tight.
They entered a workshop dedicated to the dark arts of the
assassin.

Emile switched on the computers, booted up the Tor
system and they entered the world of the deep net. This was
the place of dreams and nightmares where anything was
available at a price. The currency used was the Bitcoin and
Emile had been an early miner. He had enough to keep him
going eternally. He plied his wares as well as bought
services.

He typed the address of an agency he'd used before into

the search engine. It was one who specialised in being able to get to work immediately. It was called Speedseek. They were not cheap but like everything, you get what you pay for.

He got on 'chat' with one of their operatives, Jo90, and gave the details of the man they needed to shadow. It was a BM, Solomon Cleaver, DI at Excelsior GMP, 25a Linnets Lane, Didsbury, Manchester, M23 4MZ.

Jo90 said they would hear back from them by midnight.

'Cup of tea?' asked Emile.

'Earl Grey, slice of lemon?' Hue replied.

'Coming right up, I kept the lemons in the refrigerator, luckily. Must have known you were due a visit.'

Emile went into the back room where he had a kind of bedsit arrangement. He had a small stove, fridge, kettle, shower room and a hammock that was attached to the walls with metal hooks. He used two screwgate climbing carabiners for ease of attachment. This meant he could put the hammock up and down easily, creating space for a foldaway table and chair during the day.

Emile sniffed the steam from the boiling kettle to help clear his head from the air con induced nasal congestion he felt after the flight. He then made them both a cup of tea. He opened the biscuit jar shaped like a pig and put a few assorted Fox's biscuits on a small plate. He used a plastic tray to carry the drinks and platter of biscuits. The tray was decorated with pictures of rare cat breeds. His favourite cat on the tray was a pure white Khao Manee from Thailand. It had one blue and one green eye.

When Hue saw the tray he thought about his black and white cat, Arthur. He wondered if Arthur had missed him while he'd been away. Sometimes Arthur pretended not to recognise him on his return and other times Arthur fussed and meowed like he couldn't live without him. Hue thought it was probably more to do with the amount of food left in his tray than anything else but now Charles was dead, Arthur was all he had left in the world worth living for.

Speedseek used various ways to locate and shadow unsuspecting marks.

In the case of a Detective Inspector from Greater Manchester Police the job was best suited to a local private detective called Sheena Imaz. She was given the call and was operative within ten minutes. She lived in a South Manchester suburb called Heaton Moor and was parked round the corner from Linnets Lane Didsbury within half an hour of her instruction as the rush hour traffic had evaporated and the roads were clear. She left her silver BMW 1 series parked outside a row of shops and walked down to 25a to see if there was any sign of life. If the place was empty she would quickly check his bins to see if there was anything useful she could use to find him, check for open windows, ways to enter the property without suspicion and as a last resort, fake a burglary so she could sift through his personal space and find out more about him and where he might be. The difference in these cases was speed, the clients needed to know where the mark is right now. In this case the upstairs lights were on and so she thought about how he could exit the property if he went out at all. She looked up and down the street but there were no parking spaces left near to 25a. There was a space near the corner and she worked out she would be able to see anyone leave 25a from there, even if they walked off in the opposite direction. She turned round and was walking back to the car when she heard a door open.

Sheena immediately about heeled and slowly walked down Linnets Lane towards the sound of the door closing and the lock clicking shut.

She found herself walking towards the mark as he left the property and turned left towards her. No doubt it was him and they passed in the street walking in opposite directions.

Sheena slowed her walk even more and waited until he was around the corner. She was dressed in trainers, jeans, and a T-shirt beneath her black Berghaus Gore Tex jacket. She made the decision to sprint to the end of the lane and hoped to find him from there. She discerned he was going out somewhere nice, either a meal or a drink, possibly a meeting. He was well dressed and had a pace in his step that told her he was on time for something.

Sheena stopped and composed herself before turning out of the lane onto the main road. She looked both ways scanning the whole area in seconds. He was walking towards the tram stop on the other side of the road, heading into town. Sheena had no choice but to do the same. She kept a distance and was good at what she did but there was no escaping the fact they had crossed paths in the lane and if he was 'on guard' he may wonder why she was now on the tram into town. She paused before walking up the steps to the tram station platform, whipped off her jacket and reversed it to the dark grey and dark blue camouflaged interior. She opened the side pocket and put on her beanie hat. That would have to do; the reversible jacket might do the trick.

The tram ride to town was easy enough, no getting off at quiet, awkward stops, he was heading to the city as she had imagined he would. She followed him to a bar off Deansgate called the Wah Wah. Sheena wasn't really dressed for it but again, she had no choice, and without the coat, in T-shirt and jeans she was able to blend in. She ordered a drink and got chatting easily enough to two office workers who'd been out since five but had been doing a line or two to keep them sharp through the boozing. They were vaguely amusing and worked as letting agents in the city centre. All the while they talked and laughed she kept one eye on Sol and one on the door as he was obviously waiting for someone.

At ten past nine she arrived and he went straight over to meet her with a slightly clumsy kiss on the cheek. After an initial chat that Sheena tried her best to lip-read, he bought two cocktails and they sat in a booth. She had to re-position herself so Sol couldn't directly see her but she was able to gather they were at the 'getting to know you stage', possibly a first date. She had to feign interest in the two boy's increasingly vulgar banter as well as lip-read the woman's words, take in her body language and anticipate any sudden movement by Sol, so she could turn away if he stood up.

The boys got a bit cheesed off when they felt they were being ignored and she had to turn it on to keep them there for another drink. Men were so easy to manipulate, the word should be 'femipulate' instead. A few sex signals and they were both like slavering dogs waiting patiently for their dinner. She was strikingly good looking but she wasn't dressed to kill.

Sheena was half Iranian, a quarter English and the last part Irish, giving her an exotic middle-eastern look. She possessed a straight nose, black hair and green eyes. Her dad had been a refugee from Iran and settled in England, meeting her mum who'd escaped her Irish Catholic parents to be with him and she fell pregnant soon after.

Her dad had set up a business finding lost loved ones who had escaped persecution, torture, political violence and discrimination. These were things that back in the seventies went unseen and were ignored by government. She'd carried on the tradition but these days there were charities that did that work and so she'd branched out into more diverse areas of the missing person or the finding people game and Speedseek, whoever they were, paid very well.

At eleven thirty she watched Sol and the woman leave the bar and he hailed a black cab for her. They had a kiss on the lips but nothing too passionate before he waved her goodbye and he flagged another cab for himself. Sheena couldn't bring herself to flag a cab and say those immortal words; anyway she was going to have to get home and check in via her phone on the way, so she did hail a cab but avoided having to instruct him to follow another one.

As predicted, Sol headed home and Sheena reported back to her contact Jo at Speedseek the night's events and his current position. Jo said they would be in touch and she should remain on call for the next twenty four hours. Sheena agreed and drove home, back to her flat in Heaton Moor, straight to bed as she predicted an early start in the morning.

6

Back in the hotel Dean needed the loo. He walked across the landing and into the toilet cubicle. It was basically a hole in the ground with a footrest either side. As he squatted down he looked at a tap and a green plastic jug. His stomach was a bit rumbly, he felt like he needed the loo. His urine came out smelling beefy, as he was slightly dehydrated from constantly sweating in the heat and the plane journey before that, where he had drunk too much alcohol and not enough water. The plane food had lodged in his belly and clogged him up but the chillified aloo gobi and the change of continent had other ideas.

He squatted for about five minutes and started to see shapes and patterns in the peeling blue paint on the wooden toilet door. He started to sweat profusely. The rumble in his stomach was now turning into an ache, a rumbling achy pain swept over his middle. He was sweating so badly the drips were falling from the end of his nose. Luckily the chillums he'd been smoking were acting as a muscle relaxant and eventually he emptied his bowels. At first it was the solid stuff from the plane food. This was hard work to get out. It was a slow process, stretching his anal cavity to breaking point.

Just when he thought he'd finished, there was a severe pain in his lower abdomen, this was no longer a rumble or ache. An overwhelming feeling that he was going to faint took hold of his stoned mind. He had visions of fainting and being found slumped on a grubby toilet floor in a back street dive in Delhi, arse in the air by Beki. He hadn't found the moment to give her the bracelet yet or properly tell her how he felt. Felt? He'd never thought about a girl like that before.

All of a sudden his bowels exploded and he felt like he was urinating through his bottom. It was a major splurge of the chilli intensive variety, as the meal he'd had earlier just went right through him. If he thought he had been sweating before, now it was gushing off him, running freely down his face and neck. He composed himself and found the pain had ceased, more or less. There were a few minor rumbles but nothing like the agony he'd been in a couple of minutes before the watery poo. He knew the stinging he felt was just a curry afterburner and as he used his left hand, as per Gaz's instructions, to wash his bottom with a jug, he totally understood why they don't use toilet paper in India. It was cold, cooling water, non-abrasive to the tender spot. As he stood up there was another stinging feeling, but he was OK. The sweats had subsided and he exited the cubicle in relative peace.

He used the wash basin in the shower cubicle to clean his hands and returned to the other two who were now back in the room.

'Just in time to light this chillum,' Gaz said as he handed Dean the tube.

Beki had noticed a change in Dean since he'd arrived in India. He was more chilled out, which she thought was a good thing but he had lost a little of his edge, which if she was honest, she'd liked. Back home it was him against the world, but his lack of enemies, things to control, issues to solve had all gone along with the territory. Here he was anonymous, just another traveller in this huge subcontinent.

'You alright, Dean?' He looked a little peaky.

'Yer, fine,' he answered to Beki then turned to Gaz. 'Go on then, this is good weed we bought.'

'Shiva's best,' Gaz replied proudly. He went through his ritualistic mantra before lighting up yet another tube.

Dean was getting it now; he'd made a couple of mixes and watched Gaz start with the tubes. You really had to chug it a good few times to get the thing lit properly. So that's what he did, clouds of smoke filled the open room and he took a big toke before holding it in, ready to pass it along.

As he looked up with his lungful of smoke, there was a short fat Indian man stood in the doorway of the room watching what was going on. He waved his hand in front of his face and in an annoyed gruff tone said, 'Eh, you be careful, sometimes they bring the fucking dogs!' He walked off, leaving a slightly stunned Dean and a puzzled Beki.

'Who was that?' Beki asked.

'Ali, the night manager. Don't worry, they pay off the cops, they'd only bring the dogs here for a reason, for example if they had a tip off there were people with smack or someone had been grassed up with a load of dope they were taking home.'

Dean immediately thought of the conversation he'd heard before about the boys going home to make money. Could they be smugglers? His mind started to work overtime and now Beki was making another mix. It was getting late but he wasn't tired. The weed was like speed, it perked you up. The high was amazing but he couldn't seem to get rid of thoughts of a Delhi police raid on the hotel out of his mind. Rationally he knew the chances of being raided were slight, but the reoccurring nightmare of being arrested by the Delhi police on his first night in India wouldn't leave his thoughts. It didn't help whenever a dog howled or barked, and there were a lot of howls through the night. It sparked off a picture in his head of the police dogs sniffing out the seven tola of charas stashed in his room. He kept his mouth shut and carried on smoking but was content to listen to Gaz's stories of his travels interspersed with bits of advice about where to go, how to get there and where to stay once you'd arrived. Gaz was getting tired, though, and was making hints he wanted to get his head down.

Beki and Dean went back to their room and suddenly it hit Beki that she was really stoned and tired, too. She lay on the bed and was asleep in seconds after a few yawns, leaving

Dean wide eyed awake, staring at the ceiling, getting more and more paranoid with every dog who howled at the full moon.

At about four thirty in the morning Dean nodded off. He now knew that Beki snored. These weren't cute lady like snores; these were proper loud man snores. It was a snore down his ear that woke him at six and the Delhi day was already happening and although the sound of dogs howling had gone, it had been replaced with another rampant noise. People coughing to the point of retching filled the sound waves. At first he didn't know what it was and he went outside the room to the window below the roof. He looked out on the city rooftops and saw that lots of people spent the night outside on their own rooftops. They started the day with a good cough. Another reason Dean had to get out of the room was he needed the loo to get rid of his erection. He woke up in close proximity to Beki, neither of them had much on. They were both dressed in pants, she was in a vest top, and he was pushing against his boxers making a tent. After he'd used the loo, got dressed and settled back at the window, listening to the extremely un-erotic coughing cacophony, his member went back to normal.

After about twenty minutes of staring into space, Dean realised he had a ganjover, he was still stoned from last night's chillum session. The best way to get over a ganjover is hair of the dog. He went back in the room and Beki was still sleeping. She looked hot laying on her front, bare legs slightly folded to the side, bottom tight against her shorts.

Dean went to the stash and got a tola of charas. He

needed cigs and papers so he stashed the charas down his underpants and went down the hotel stairs, out the front door and onto the street.

The same booth Beki had tried to buy water from was open and they sold cigs but not papers. He went onto Main Bazaar and saw the morning work going on. There were no tourists and the shops were starting to open. What he saw were several old ladies in pale, pastel colour saris, using small brushes made of long hard bristles, tied together at the handle, half bent forward sweeping the streets. They were making little piles of dirt and waste. Then a young lad with a wood and metal cart came and swept the plies into a plastic hand shovel and into the cart. He wheeled it on, until the next pile needed shifting. He seemed to always be missing a few out along the way as if he couldn't keep up. Then suddenly an argument broke out between a shopkeeper and one of the lady road sweepers. He was shouting at one of the crouched women, it seemed she hadn't brushed all the litter up near his shop. He was having a right old go and only stopped when another shopkeeper intervened by standing in front of the angry man and cowering woman. The peacekeeper was gently moving him away, while using calming tones to placate him.

The clever street sweeper created piles of dirt and dust in the early morning, so it looks like the streets are clear of debris but they know as soon as the hordes descend this will all get kicked around and have to be cleaned up the next day, thus keeping them in work. The boy with the cart misses out sweeping the ones made purely of dirt and dust and just collects the ones with rubbish that the cows had missed.

Dean was glad it had calmed down because he was about to step up to the angry shopkeeper and tell him to 'shut up and shift it himself'.

Out on the street he felt more himself again. When he was with Gaz he felt a little out of his comfort zone. Gaz was confident and knew the score in India. He had no idea who Dean was or his full background, so gave Dean none of the credence that he was automatically afforded back home. Dean had no rep here, which was good and bad. He didn't have to keep his rep in place but he wasn't used to being a 'nobody' or anyone's subordinate.

He walked down the street until he found a shop selling skins and it also sold water so he bought a bottle. It wasn't too chilled, although it came from the fridge, no doubt due to the power cuts, or did the guy turn off the fridge at night? He stood there and downed the whole litre, leaving the empty bottle at the shop. This made him feel slightly bloated but good. He had cigs, skins and weed. Matches, he needed a light. The shop near the hotel definitely would sell matches and so he walked back down Main Bazaar, picking up a small box. As he went through the hotel entrance there was Abdul and Ali the night manager, sat smoking cigarettes and drinking coffee.

'Morning,' they all said to each other and he went up the stairs. The lads who were going to make some money were up and about, bags packed on their beds. They were just bumbling around, brushing their teeth and were definitely not smugglers, they looked more like students close up.

Dean went into his room and Beki was still asleep. He sat on the edge of the bed and started to build a joint. He took care not to put too much charas in it, as he didn't want to get too blasted, especially as it looked like he was smoking alone. As he sparked it up, he watched the curls of blue smoke rise up into the shafts of morning sunlight coming through the cracks in the door. The room was still dim inside but he watched Beki as he sat and smoked. It was as if she had some inbuilt radar for weed. He'd been careful not to make a sound but she woke up after he'd smoked about an inch of the spliff, stretched her arms wide, smiled at him and said, 'Is that for me?'

'Of course it is, good morning, beautiful,' he said and handed her the joint.

7

Arthur the cat liked sleeping during the day and prowling around at night but as Hue was back home Arthur took the opportunity of sleeping on Hue's bed, as the door was usually closed while he was away.

At five twenty Hue's alarm went off and Arthur was disturbed. They both got up and both did their morning stretches. Arthur stretched for half a minute, Hue for half an hour then put on his running gear and went out in the crisp air to jog a few miles before breakfast. He made time to do some kata, systematic moves in kung fu.

It was the day of Charles Bates' funeral, only heaven knew who would be there. He needed to be in a top class frame of mind to get through the day.

Hue didn't have any food in for a cooked breakfast so went to the Filling Station Café close by and had a full English, coffee and extra wholegrain toast with raspberry jam. He read the morning headlines and searched deeper into the FT for any news about Kenya. It made a speculative piece about the possibility of new trade links in the area without anything specific. *Planting seeds,* Hue thought and left the café for home.

Both Emile and he wore black to the brief service, which went as well as these things could go. There were some old military there and a few people Hue recognised as old school spooks, most retired or at least sleeping. Most of the spooks conversed with no one and left immediately after the cremation. Hue was looking for who could be Steve Smart, not that he would go and introduce himself, but just to know what he looked like would be an advantage. After all the possibilities had been eliminated by Emile, who seemed to know everyone's name, he gave up. If Smart was there he was under an alias and older than Hue imagined him to be. It was like guessing the appearance of a radio presenter, someone from Radio 4, who you had listened to for years and built up an image of how they looked in your head. Often they were completely different from the abstract construction.

The remaining mourners went for a buffet in the Maple Tree Inn, where Charles used to go with the older spooks back in the day. They all said what a great man he was and how they couldn't believe the news. Well, neither could Hue. He was going to prize the truth out of those northern scumbags and honour the memory of his only friend, or die in the process.

Sheena was dressed in a grey business suit with a black mac coat. She had a bag with a change of clothes and was patiently waiting outside the home of Sol Cleaver so she could break in and find out all she needed to about him and his life, before she filled a report to Jo.

He'd left for work at nine and she was walking round his kitchen at eleven and a half minutes past. His back door had a Yale lock, but he'd not bothered to use the deadlock as he had on the front door. She had already cut a plastic drinks bottle into the required S shape and flattened it, slipping it into the edge of the doorframe and up against the lock. She'd pressed her right knee firmly against the lower part of the door as she pulled the cut plastic bottle upwards pushing her weight into the door and used her free hand to jerk the lock backwards. There was a click as the plastic passed up and through the lock, the jerking motion freed the mechanism and she was in. It took about ninety seconds to get in the house, the other ten minutes had been her guarded wait to make sure he hadn't forgotten anything and returned home.

She found what she was after on a piece of paper in the front room. In rushed handwriting, there was a mobile number, Wah Wah Bar 9pm and the name Isabel Hart next to it. Sheena now had the name of the woman he was no doubt cheating on his girlfriend with and she had a quick snoop around before leaving via the back door. The lock clicked shut and the mark would be none the wiser, until his girlfriend confronted him about his cheating.

She called it in to Jo and was told she'd done a good job

and the payment would be in her account before closing on Friday. Sheena went on her way happy, as good feedback from Jo meant more work would come her way.

She was totally unaware of the future consequences of her actions.

Beautiful? thought Beki as she took the spliff from Dean. 'I don't feel beautiful, I feel like someone's been kicking me in the chest all night,' Beki said. She took a drag on the joint, held it in and slowly blew the smoke towards Dean but the fan above the bed circulated it into the room before it hit him. 'That's better. What we doing today, then?'

'Fancy breakfast? I'm starving. Anything but curry.'

'I know. That meal was spicy all right. I need a shower and then we'll go and explore, have a proper adventure.' Beki passed Dean the spliff and got out of bed. As she got up and bent towards him he couldn't help staring down her vest top as it gaped. He caught a glimpse of her perfect breasts. He remembered when he used to go and see her as his probation officer and he'd often walk out of the interview with a semi after imagining having her over the desk or against the wall.

She walked over to her rucksack and he watched her bend forward, searching in her bag. She was looking for clean knickers, T-shirt and bra. He watched her from behind and imagined just going over there and trying it on, making a move. Back home with one of the local girls, he would have had no problem with making a move and would have tried to get her to ring a friend to come and join in. That had been Dean's thing, two girls; it had become a habit. Dark skinned girls mostly, always two at a time whether he'd paid them directly or just with gram after gram of ching.

Here he was, scared of trying it on with one fair skinned, older woman for fear of …? What was it, fear of rejection? He thought she'd been giving him signals, sitting a bit too close. Thinking about it, she'd always been flirting with him, that wasn't in his imagination.

As he watched her walk out of the room and towards the shower it dawned on him that women unintentionally flirted with you as they walked away, or at least their bottoms did.

Dean smoked half the spliff and put it in the ashtray. He heard some voices down in the reception and walked to the balcony and looked and listened.

'Top floor full, no way, how long they stay?' A traveller was after their room. Dean struggled to hear what was being said as they had gone into one of the downstairs rooms. When they came out he heard the guy ask, 'You been paying baksheesh to the cops? I'm not staying on the first floor, mate. They'll be on ya before ya know what's hit ya.'

Dean couldn't place the guy's accent. He sounded Australian. He could have been from anywhere though.

He heard the guy coming up the stairs. As he got to the floor below he looked up at Dean. 'Hiya, mate, you staying on the top floor?'

'Yes, mate.'

'How long ya staying, matey?'

'Dunno. A day or two.'

Dean noticed Gaz's door opening and Gaz appeared on the landing. Wrapped round his waist was a green sarong. He was a fit lad, quite a hairy lad, too.

'OK, matey, I just arrived from London.'

Gaz leaned over the balcony and said, 'Yer, London's full of you Kiwis.'

'Gazza! Mate. How the devil are ya?'

'Not bad, Bob. Bring ya bags up. I've got a double you can share with me, mate.'

Gaz walked off to the toilet and nodded and said morning to Dean on his way past. Dean smiled and nodded back.

As he walked to the loo, Beki came out of the shower door.

Dean watched Gaz's transformation as he saw her. His head went up, chest out, standing straight and tall, almost blocking her way.

They started chatting and laughing. Dean walked back in the room fuming. Nobody in Manchester would have ever behaved like that with one of his women. The trouble was, Beki wasn't his woman. He was in a very different world and he didn't know if he liked it.

He sparked up the joint and had a couple of calming tokes. When she came in she was dressed in a T-shirt and shorts. He passed her the joint.

'Gaz's friend just arrived, he's from New Zealand.'

'Yer, I know,' Dean said in a sulky voice.

'Yer, I know.' Beki imitated him. He sounded like the guy in the wheelchair off the telly who had an overly caring carer. She used to watch it stoned with Tom.

Dean had never seen it as he didn't watch much telly and so didn't get the joke. It just put him in a bigger sulk that she was taking the piss. They were both tired and still jet lagged. Beki saw his face. 'What's up with you?'

'Nothin', I'm hungry, can we go and eat?'

'Yes, but I've got to get ready first.'

'Get ready? You are ready, how much readier can you get?'

'Just give me a minute, don't rush me please, Dean.' Beki handed him back the last bit of the joint. He took it and stubbed it hard into the ashtray.

Beki pottered about the room, doing this and that but nothing that allowed Dean to think she was actually doing anything. She was putting her clothes in separate plastic bags, moving them around in her rucksack. She put her toiletries into the side pocket of her rucksack. She towel dried her hair even though it would be dry in minutes outside. All the time Dean was getting more frustrated.

Eventually she was ready and they locked their door and Beki kept the key. They walked out of the hotel onto the quiet back street but by the time they got to Main Bazaar it was in full morning swing, absolute chaos. A small tide of humanity ebbed and flowed through the passage to Old Delhi. Backpackers in tight groups wrestled for space with Indian grannies out to buy veg from the market. There was, what looked to Beki like the children catcher's cycle cage, taking uniformed infant kids to school. There were skinny men carrying huge sacks balanced on their heads. Cycle rickshaws slowly edged for space and cows unhurriedly strolled towards the market, acting nonchalant and indifferent to being moved along by the mass. All of Delhi seemed to be out that morning and all of Delhi seemed to be bumping into and crowding Dean. With the already hot morning sun, with his grumbling stomach feeling like it might explode any second, all this combined was not helping his mood improve, at all.

They settled on a tourist eatery because they couldn't take much more local delicacies and it had a sign saying amongst other things: Toast, Honey, Jam, Coffee, Chai, Breakfast, Lunch, Dinner.

'That'll do,' said Dean. He took hold of her arm, just above the wrist and guided her through the crowd like she had special needs.

They sat at a dirty table with bits of jam left from the last diners' breakfast. It was attracting a small family of flies.

After looking at the menu, Dean went for coffee and buttered toast. Beki went for scrambled eggs on toast and chai, no sugar. The order was taken by a boy who should have been in school and they waited in silence, watching the hordes pass by the open front of the café.

The food arrived and it was truly dreadful.

Dean's coffee was weak and had about ten sugars in it. His toast was small squares of sweet sliced white bread, cold and charred round the edges but still soft in the middle. It's like it was 'toasted' on a flame, not a grill. The butter was in a small separate glass dish and tasted rancid.

Beki's toast had no butter, thankfully, and her eggs were not properly cooked. There were white bits as it had not been properly beaten and when she opened the eggs up they'd only been cooked on the outside, not through. To top it all, her chai had sugar in.

They both picked at their breakfast for a minute before Beki announced she wasn't eating it and Dean wanted to complain to the manager. Beki suggested they should just pay and go and Dean told her she could do that but he wasn't paying, so then she got her money out and asked for the bill. The boy waiter brought the bill and Beki paid and stood up and Dean was in a sulk again, still hungry, still grouchy and more frustrated. Then they had to fight through the hordes again and Dean felt he was in a zombie apocalypse movie and eventually, that made him laugh.

He stopped fighting his way back to the hotel, stood still and laughed.

Beki wondered where he was until she turned round and saw him giggling in the street. She went back a few paces. 'Are you alright?'

Dean shrugged his shoulders and replied, 'Yer, I feel like I'm in a film, a zombie movie. Come on let's go, let's get out of Delhi, today. Pack our bags and get on a bus somewhere.'

As Dean spoke, a Kashmiri hawker pounced on the tourist rush.

'Good mornang, how are yooou? Would you like to stay

on my house boat in Kashmir? Very beautiful boat, all meals included, I do you good price.' He sounded like he'd learnt English from an American pastor, a religion salesman on the Church of the Light channel.

'No thanks,' said Beki. She didn't like the look of this guy. He had a huge hooked nose and was very skinny. An archetypal bad guy.

'Why not, Kashmir very beautiful, no rain there, no monsoon, beautiful lake, beautiful houseboat, come look I have picture.'

He produced a photo album of his boat and really started the sales pitch about how wonderful it was and how everything was included in the price and he almost got Dean but Beki was having non-of it. She almost had to drag Dean away as he was really getting sucked in. God, those Kashmiri's are good, she thought as she told Dean that it wasn't safe there because of fighting between Indian and Pakistani troops, as well as local militants.

She stopped in a second hand bookstall and bought a *Heavenly Globe Guidebook*, a few years old but better than nothing.

She looked up Delhi and went to the 'Places to Eat' section. She found a place serving Continental Breakfast Buffet in Connaught Place and she told him they were going there to eat and that was that.

At the end of Main Bazaar they jumped in a tuk-tuk motor rickshaw painted yellow and black. It ran on gas cylinders and after about ten minutes dropped them at The Connaught deli's front door.

As they entered the air conditioned restaurant, they were seated at a clean booth by a well-dressed young man, aged about twenty. They were immediately asked in good English if they would like some mineral water and fresh orange juice. At that point they both started to relax. The buffet consisted of croissants, bagels, pain au chocolate, Danish plaits with maple and pecan. Cornflakes, Rice Krispies, Bran Flakes and creamy cold milk.

There was a lady who made fresh toast in a toaster on demand and little butter cubes in silver paper wrappers on the table. There was filter coffee and assorted teas, as much as you wanted.

The other customers were a mix of business people, foreigners like Beki and Dean but maybe slightly older. Indian families with unruly children ran around doing what they wanted, the parents not batting an eyelid at their irritating behaviour like climbing over the seats, crying, screaming and shouting.

'I don't think I'm up for this roughing it traveller thing, Beki, this is more how I roll.'

'Well, I'm sure we'll do a bit of both. You calmed down now, then?'

'Yer, this is one crazy country, ten minutes from this air con buffet there's people spending their whole life begging from a skateboard cos they got no legs. It's mad.'

They looked through the guidebook after they'd finished their food and both sipped coffee and water as they planned out their travels, getting along fine again, feeling like they'd known each other forever.

8

Hue and Sarafian caught the early morning flight to Manchester from London City Airport. Rather sadistic in his approach to life, Hue had booked them both in at The Bright Hotel, the same hotel his friend had died in. Hue broke rank from his favourite establishment, The Lowry, because he wanted to chase up any leads from the hotel staff about the events surrounding Charles Bates' death. He planned to do this with money or intimidation. Carrot or stick, Hue cared not which, but so as not to bring unwanted attention he would initially use charm and bribery to get what he desired.

Emile Sarafian was busy, slightly in his own world, preparing his potions and powders for the planned attack on the cop and his minx. Sarafian had thought long and hard about torture and came to the conclusion years ago that a bit of psychological threat was better than vast amounts of pain. The thoughts in the head were the key to success. If the right techniques were implemented then you didn't really need to use physical force.

When he had been with Martha, his now deceased wife, and they'd brought up their son Zak together, he was never able to use any psychological punishment successfully. He saw this as admitting defeat, meaning he could not outsmart a six-year-old boy and therefore had to use brute force to control him. After Martha had died Zak then went to live with her sister in Canada and Emile supported him financially but had no contact anymore. Torture was the same to him as disciplining a child; if he couldn't outsmart the victim, he had failed. Anyone could smash a man's balls or cut off their digits, but not everyone could leave the victim completely at a loss, with no hope left, no gods to turn to and so completely powerless and enthralled as to spill what was necessary to know and be left thankful for doing so.

This was Emile Sarafian's gift.

Hue received the call from Jo90 giving the required information about Sol and Isabel. He'd advised Jo90 that he may need further support in the coming hours and would appreciate the same standard of service as he'd just received.

They went to the front desk of The Bright Hotel and asked if they could rent a car, a saloon with a Sat Nav inbuilt. After a short phone call, the receptionist told him the car would be waiting outside within the hour, gave him the price and asked if he wished to be called when it arrived. He told her how good she was at her job and said he usually stayed at the Lowry but thought he'd give somewhere else a try. He gave her a story about the Hilton being full and found a room here no problem. She said something about there being plenty of capacity at present due to an incident they'd had.

'Really, what was that?' Hue asked.

'Well, we're not supposed to talk about it but there was a suicide here. A very nice gentleman got drunk and jumped out of the window, killed himself. Bookings are down, people cancelled,' Brooke, the pretty, nineteen-year-old receptionist confided.

Hue thought how she looked like all the other young people in Manchester. They conformed to the same fairly conservative apparel, girls with fake tans, long hair and too much make-up.

'Really,' said Hue, 'and you were working here that day?'

'Yes, I'd not been here that long and that happened.'

'How do they know it was suicide?'

'Well, between you and me there's a rumour going round the hotel, that it wasn't.'

'Really, tell me more. I like a good story.' Hue's eyes were unblinking, keeping Brooke in a trance like state.

She carried on as if glamoured by a vampire. 'Well, Maria, one of the cleaners was sure she heard voices coming out of the room before he jumped and the police kept asking the same questions about someone being in the room with him.'

'Did Maria, the cleaner, see anyone? Someone about the same time, leaving the room?'

'Yes, well she might have and not said anything.' Brooke embellished the story as if to tell him what she thought he wanted to hear.

'This is for you, Brooke,' he said noting her name badge, 'for sorting out the car.' Hue handed her fifty pounds in tens, turned round and walked outside, staring coldly at the passers-by, sensing who were the victims in the way they walked, the way they conversed with each other, the way they smelt.

Isabel Hart was excited about her meeting with Geoff Bowker, the new BBC manager for the team of reporters working on Breakfast. Since the relocation to Manchester, she'd heard through her contacts that Geoff had been using some freelancers to fill gaps during the transition. He'd been happy to take on those who showed promise with a temporary contract.

Of course she would love this but the first step was to be punctual, finding her way around in a new city wasn't that easy. Once she was there on time she knew she would make a good impression.

She thought about the tram but wasn't sure about the exact location of the stops, so decided on her car. She would park in the nearby shopping centre and have a look round the shops after the meeting. She listened again to Geoff's voicemail telling her she should come for an initial chat over coffee to his office after giving the time and place.

As Emile had her mobile number and had hacked into her voicemails, emails, Facebook and Twitter, he knew all about the meeting and a fair bit about her life. He followed her in the hire car to the parking space in the shopping centre. As they entered the car park he quickly found a space near to her and was out of his car and walking swiftly towards her, mentally weighing up her size and physical condition as he approached. He'd describe her as petite, medium height and preoccupied. He was confidant she was unaware of his presence and he spoke in a 'silly me' kind of tone as he waved a £20 in the air and said, 'Excuse me, do you have any change for the meter, it won't accept this note and I've not got enough coins on me.' This seemed a pleasant enough request from a well-dressed, well-spoken gentleman.

She didn't register any threat but her just-out-of-London habit replied, 'No, sorry …' and before she'd had time to finish the sentence he was on her.

Emile punched her once hard in the stomach and she dropped forward, winded and shocked. He opened her rear car door which had not been locked as she was faffing about, making sure she had everything for the meeting and had scanned the car to make sure nothing was visible to entice thieves, just as he'd approached her. He quickly overpowered her by a knee to the side of her jaw, as she was at the perfect height for this blow. He knew immediately that even if she wasn't out cold she would be unable to function properly as it was a sweet, if opportunistic strike.

Once he had her in the car, he gaffer-taped her legs and then her wrists behind her back. He taped her mouth, leaving her nose free to breathe. He'd acquired the car keys from her jacket pocket and was driving out of the car park with her slumped body down the footrest area of the back seat within minutes. He drove for about half an hour until he was out of the city centre, heading North on the M61.

He was doing a steady 70MPH on the inside lane, slowing down to 60 behind a line of three commercial HGVs. He called Hue as he drove.

'All good here in transit. The keys are on the top of the driver's wheel. I'll be at the location within the hour and will be good to go within two.'

Hue had booked a last minute cottage in the middle of nowhere for a three day break. There were no owners living next door and no immediate neighbours. It was in the forgotten land that encompasses the three Northern counties of Lancashire, Cumbria and Yorkshire. It was a two-bedroom holiday let by a river, just over the Yorkshire border. Apparently there were 'walks from the door' but the seclusion meant these walks were over desolate hills, worn flat from millennia of wind and rain. The keys were in a coded box in the porch and the blurb on the website advised bringing a torch.

Hue took a taxi to the car park, retrieved the hire car and went back to the hotel. He waited for the call from Emile before phoning Sol.

'Solomon Cleaver, this is Hue Brooks. I hope this is a convenient time to meet as I've some rather urgent matters to discuss.'

9

Beki took the lead regarding their future travel plans. It was dominated by the weather, the monsoon was coming to an end and they had a month before the cold spells took over the mountains. There were two ways of travel. It was either all bus or train then bus. As they had to get a bus anyway, they decided to do the whole trip that way. There were lots of travel agents in Delhi and so they went in the first one they saw that looked professional. Inside the offices of ACE Travel, Beki read the sign that told her it was Air Con Executive Travel and she quite liked that. Mrs Gulwati, the efficient lady who seemed in charge, advised them to go on the night bus, leaving the pick-up point across the road from ACE Travel at 4PM. She sold them two tickets for the 'semi-sleeper' bus, 2x2, Volvo and advised they lock all baggage and take a blanket. Mrs Gulwati was very nice, especially when they paid the RS1350 ticket price without haggling.

'You will be arriving in Manali at 6AM and I suggest

booking a hotel now for your stay, save any hassling from hawkers when you arrive,' Mrs Gulwati advised. 'The Manali Ashgrove is a good hotel, surrounded by peace and tranquillity on the road to old Manali.'

'How much is it?' Beki asked while thumbing her guidebook to see if it was listed.

'Let us see.' Mrs Gulwati looked on her computer screen. 'One room or two?' she asked no one in particular.

They both replied in tandem, a 'one' from Beki and a gallant 'two' from Dean, who presumed that that was the right thing to do.

Beki gave him a look that was a mixture of hurt and anger. She redeemed the situation by saying, 'One room will be cheaper, Dean,' emphasising his name, shoving the book at him and pointing at the price section. 'Look at the prices.'

'RS4500 for a standard room, twin beds and bathroom attached, colour television with cable, central heating, pure veg restaurant and bar, breakfast included. It's one of the premier hotels in the area and I've stayed there myself, super clean,' Mrs Gulwati almost sang. She always told foreigners places were super clean as she always told Indians it was super deluxe.

'It's gone up a bit since this book was written, says RS2750 for a double here.' Beki now passed the book to Mrs Gulwati.

She quickly scanned down and tried to find a common ground to continue the sale. 'This is indeed a very old book, madam, you are right. For you, best price RS4250, but no breakfast for this price, four stars, madam. Very good?'

'We'll have it,' Dean butted in, 'book it, I'll pay.'

'Very good, sir. Madam will be very pleased.' Mrs Gulwati went back to the self-satisfied state she'd been in minutes before and booked the room online, making a decent mark up and wondering if she would ever make it to Manali for a holiday herself. She would love to see and feel the snow and breathe the fabled Himalayan air.

As they walked out of the travel agents the atmosphere was hot and the sun was high. They took a rickshaw back to the end of Paharganj, Main Bazaar and walked through the midday heat and dust until they reached the turn off for the Narung.

On the roof, under a canopy, a chillum session was going full power. Psychedelic trance was blasting from the speakers of the iPod dock in the small sound system. Gaz, Bob, Abdul and another guy, who was never introduced and said nothing but constantly made mixes, were all sat smoking tubes, watching the kites fly around old Delhi.

The kite flyers all tried to take other kites down and there were bets flying around the circle of RS10 a time as to who would win the aerial battles.

'Come, sit,' said Abdul beckoning Dean and Beki to join them as they poked their heads up the stairs to see what all the fuss was about.

They joined the circle and Beki was immediately passed a chillum to light, very proudly, by Bob. He had to get up from his cross-legged spot and lean over to Beki to light the two match flame and use his own chillum mantra as he carefully kept a centimetre between the top of the tube and the fire.

'Bom, Bom, Boll-e-nath, BOOM!'

As she sucked, the mix caught and the smoke filled the canopy. Beki chugged on the chillum and then took a huge lungful. She kept it in and greatly impressed the other chillum heads with her capacity for weed. She passed it to Dean and he took a go, not as huge as Beki's but decent enough.

The chillum is best smoked on the third go as the mix is well lit and Abdul chugged clouds into the air until his theatrical pull into his lungs, followed by a swift exhale and a coughing 'Bom,' revealed his lung capacity to be damaged by years of drug abuse and Delhi pollution. There was a debate as to when the chillum was finished by Bob and Gaz as they didn't want to give Beki the dregs but didn't want to waste it either so after a short discussion and both of them having a good look into the top of the tube it was decided by Gaz that it was done, even though Bob reckoned there was a last toke in it.

Gaz tipped the stone out into the ashtray and there was more debate as to the amount of mix that was left as Abdul chipped in. 'Don't waste the mix man.' He directed his comments to Gaz. 'Seriously, that's good stuff. There was definitely another toke there.' Abdul used his finger to poke the remaining mix and proved his point. 'If that,' he said, now looking at Beki, 'was a fella, you'd have passed it on, you're sexist man.'

Bob carried on the mock assault. 'Yeh, mate, you sexist

pig, she took the best toke out of all of us.'

'Don't be a sexist waster, man, build another chillum,' added Abdul, then coughed some more.

The first chillum of the day for Beki and Dean put them back in the same state as they'd been last night. After another few rounds Dean went to his stash and tried making a mix with input and advice from Abdul, Bob and Gaz as to the amount of charas to use, how to toast the cigarette without burning it, how hard to tamper the mix down, how much water to put on the safi, the best way to hold the chillum and the reason they shouted the mantras as the fire hit the mix.

'BOOM was the first sound in creation,' said Bob, 'most of the other words are names of Shiva, the god of destruction, the cosmic dancer whose dance keeps the universe in a constant state of flux.'

Gaz added, 'Shiva, the smoker's god. He sits and meditates up in the mountains after toking chillums of wild ganja all day long. Check out those Sadhu Baba Ji's, those boys toke all day every day, then do crazy Yantras to Kailash or Armanath … barefoot.'

'You know, man, some of those Baba Ji's are beautiful. They give you anything man, seriously, bestow great gifts but some are dark, man, very tant-ta-ric, you have to be careful around those guys, man, for sure.' Abdul was serious faced and he bowed his head as he said a little Sufi prayer.

'We just booked a bus up to Manali,' Dean announced.

There were looks exchanged around the circle.

'Something wrong with that?' he asked.

Abdul replied, 'No, man, it's a good time to go, less tourist, less cops. It's going to be chilly at night. You have about a month before it's snowing, still some rain but mostly it's stopped.'

Bob carried on saying, 'Wow, good on ya, mate, are you on a mission?'

'Eh?' Dean didn't understand.

'Charas, are you on a charas mission?' Dean still looked blank so Bob carried on. 'I've a few contacts in Hampta and Thela. I'll give you their details before ya go, useful people ya can trust. Two seasons ago I went with one of them guys. Manu was from a village in Thela valley, out into the wild, mate, camped out a few nights in caves and spent the days rubbin' jungle. Best stuff I ever had.'

Bob got a pen and notebook from his shoulder bag lying on the floor by his side. He looked up the names of Manu and another guy, Hanuman from Hampta. 'These guys are good men, they know me so make sure you tell them Kiwi Bob sent you and give them my best if you see 'em.'

10

As Emile pulled Isabel, head first, arms under her shoulders, lifting as he hauled and dragged her from the car, she started to struggle. It made his job impossible as she writhed around. He dropped her half out of the car, her head and upper body lying on the wet gravel drive, her back arched with her legs propped up, still in the channel behind the driver's seat and the back seats. Emile crouched low, she'd stopped struggling now and lay still although she was breathing hard though her nose which was getting clogged up with watery phlegm. Her nose and eyes both running as she cried intensely.

He bent low, placing his hand onto her forehead, gently brushing her hair and skin. 'Listen carefully as I will not repeat this.' He paused, waiting until he knew she was calm enough to take in his words. 'If you continue to struggle and make my job harder than it has to be, I will rape you, anally.'

He paused again and watched the fear escape from her

brain into her eyes. 'Is that as clear as I can be?'

Isabel nodded her head. Emile would never carry out the threat but had found from experience that the threat of anal rape for both sexes was the best way of aiding compliance. Over the years he'd learnt that this was much more effective than physical pain as a deterrent.

He lifted and pulled as Isabel now used her bound legs to push herself out of the car and kept still as he dragged her along the drive and into the cottage.

Once inside he used a small French Opinel lock knife to cut the binding around her legs. He admired the simplicity of the knife's locking device, the way the mechanism smoothly twisted shut even after years of use.

He told her to go upstairs and followed her as she gained some feeling into her ankles and feet as she climbed the stairs and he manoeuvred her into the bathroom. He went through her pockets, nothing found. She had a bag in the car and he would get that later. She still had her hands and mouth bound with black gaffer tape. She had on a white shirt, black jacket and matching trousers, a kind of business suit for women who want to impress. 'I'm going to unbutton your trousers, pull them down along with your pants so you can use the loo. Turn round.'

She did as he instructed. Emile reached around her waist, struggled slightly with the top button on her waistband as it was a woman's trouser button and unbuttoned to the left not the right. He got it open and pulled down her trousers to her knees.

'Turn round.' She did as she was told and she now had

her back to the loo. He pulled down her pants, slowly exposing her manicured pubic hair. She winced and started to cry again as her pants reached her knees and rested on her trousers. She kept her legs tightly pressed together until he'd walked out of the room. She sat on the toilet and he listened from outside the door. When she'd done, he came back in the bathroom.

'Do not move from there. If you move I will tape your legs together and do not forget what I said in the car.' As he walked off he added, 'Won't be long,' in a cheery tone, as if he was popping to the car to bring her a bunch of flowers or a surprise bottle of fizz to get their break off to a good start. He left Isabel Hart, very late for her job interview, sat on the toilet, exposed and petrified of displeasing her captor.

Hue had arranged to meet Sol at his house. This was risky but he hoped to put him at ease and not have to resort to too intense a strategy. He wished to solicit the information from him in a genial manner. He parked the hire car around the corner and walked confidently into the small, neat front garden and noticed the front door was ajar. Warning sirens exploded in his head. No doors are left open in the cities and suburbs of decent English neighbourhoods. When he conducted his dealings in the poor council estates of London he noticed some doors were left wide open as children and dogs ran freely through the maisonettes, council flats and streets but not in Didsbury, a well to do area of Manchester.

Emile came back from the car, leaving his bag of tricks on the landing and was pleased to see she hadn't moved from the toilet seat. He had his phone out and stood at the toilet door checking the Internet signal was available, as advertised on the cottage website. He was happy with the signal and checked into his account. He went back to his bag and opened it up. He unfolded it out. It was well-worn leather, medium brown, soft and pliable after years of use. Each of the torture implements was spotlessly clean and sharpened to an infinitesimal degree of precision. The reasoning for this was the sharper the blade the less pain inflicted on the victim. He could go for hours, days sometimes if he needed to, extracting visceral feelings from near painless cuts. The thought in the mind of the victim was the most effective and efficient torment of all.

Hue didn't go straight in but nipped round the back of the house to find all the back windows curtains were shut and the blinds pulled down in the upstairs rooms. He was on full alert now, this was not right. He wondered what Charles would have done. Retreat would be considered weak, not an option. Going in would be foolhardy, arrogant and expected. He looked around the back garden. It was not as tidy and organised as the front. There was a shed which was locked with a padlock; overgrown trees provided a degree of privacy. There was always something to aid his need and right enough Hue spotted it. There was a corner rockery, a birdbath made of stone and after a moment's deliberation, working out the weight of the projectile needed, he decided on the birdbath.

Hue was aware that someone may be watching from inside of the house and as he walked across the lawn to the corner of the garden, he turned sharply and scanned the house up and down but detected no movements from the windows, curtains or blinds.

He lifted the birdbath easily enough; some worms fell to the floor and wriggled around, woodlice scrambled for cover. He ran with it towards the backdoor and launched it through the kitchen window. He immediately ran round the front again and stopped to listen before gently opening the door just enough and entered the house. No sound, only silence after the smash through the back window. He pushed open the door to its limit and walked as if standing on light bulbs through the hall, which led straight through the house into the kitchen. He tried to visualise what he was meant to do.

He concluded he was meant to walk into the light, towards the kitchen. The front door started to make a slight creaking sound as if it was shutting on itself. He passed by the closed door to his left which led to the lounge. In the split second he heard movement from above and realised there was someone jumping towards him from the staircase to his right. The door he'd just passed opened, and the front door crashed as it slammed into the porch wall.

Sol had moved first, he'd been hiding upstairs. His gang contact Rennell, who he'd known since childhood had been in the lounge and followed Sol's attack. The third man was another friend of Sol's who used to work in the force but left and now did security work. He'd been waiting in a car and had watched the man in the blazer and slacks walk into Sol's garden. He'd kept a distance as the man went round the back, kept his nerve after the smash and crash and had not moved in. He'd gone into the front garden after the guy had entered the house through the open door and listened, not moving until he heard Sol jump down the stairs.

It was over in less than three minutes. As Sol approached the stairs, Hue looked behind, swivelled his body right from the hip as he lifted his right leg and put his weight onto his straight left leg which was anchored to the ground. He tightened his perineum muscle and expelled all his energy out through the reverse kick, landing it high into Sol's solar plexus. The attacker's forward momentum was met with a greater force and it floored him. In one, as his right leg grounded and Rennell came through the lounge door, he swung his elbow up and connected a back elbow strike to the bottom of his nose. This lifted Rennell's head upwards and Hue used a short rabbit punch to his throat.

The security guard was taken aback as Sol's big frame lay in front of him on the hall floor. All Hue needed was this momentary diversion and he was on top of him in two lightning steps. He was in complete control of his movements as he kicked low into his knee, grabbing the man's neck as he leaned forward to stop himself from going down. Hue now had the head where he wanted it and made the split second decision to end it quickly. A twist and a jerk and the man was dead. A memory, wringing the necks of the chickens when he was a lad during his first paid job at a local farm, flashed across his consciousness.

The black man from the lounge was next. He was struggling to breathe from the punch to the throat. Even though the punch came with no back lift from the shoulder, he used a technique that went through the impact and visualised his fist coming out of the other side of the opponent's body, an old kung fu trick. The man lay on his back, both hands cradling his throat, making choking sounds as his oesophagus had partially collapsed, clogging his windpipe. Hue stood over him and lifted his right knee high. He stamped the heel of his brown leather brogue right into the middle of Rennell's clasped hands and smashed his neck into the floor, possibly breaking it. If he wasn't dead, he wasn't moving anywhere for a while.

Sol was up and grabbed Hue from behind. His stance was unsteady as he stood over his friend's dead body. His grip was feeble, as he was still winded and pained from the kick. Hue jumped slightly off the ground as he spun around and his momentum easily thwarted Sol's attempt to hold him. He grabbed Sol's arm, wrenched it up, put his weight onto the back of his elbow, grabbed two of his fingers, the first and middle and put a three pronged arm, elbow and finger lock into action. He led Sol into the front room. He'd been in the house for two minutes. He held onto Sol's wrist, keeping the finger lock in place but releasing his arm per se. He did this to give himself enough room to angle a kick to the side of Sol's knee. It snapped his leg with a 'crack' sound and he went down to the carpet.

Hue was confident that he was done and unable to fight back in any meaningful way. He patted him down, found no weapons and went to shut the front door, quietly.

On his return he was worried Sol was on his way out of consciousness, so popped to the kitchen, turned the tap on, let it run for a few seconds while he opened the cupboards, found the one for glasses and poured a large pint glass full of cold water. He took a sip then used the rest to wake Sol up, throwing it into his face, as he needed him wide awake and fully conscious. As Sol came round he phoned Sarafian and made sure he was ready.

'I'll make this as quick as possible,' Hue said as he showed Sol the image of Isabel on the toilet, pants round her ankles, gaffer tape round her mouth, crying snot bubbles through her nose. 'What is the name of the gangster who met with Charles Bates, the day he died?'

'Fuck you.'

'Very stupid, Mr Cleaver. Cut her.'

Emile took a scalpel from his brown bag and drew a line across Isabel's forehead. Blood dripped down quickly onto her face, creating a gruesome scene from a slasher horror flick.

'Why are you being like this? What's his name and where can I find him?'

Sol shrugged.

'Rape her … with the knife,' Hue ordered over the phone.

'OK. OK, his name's Dean Shelby, he runs with a Manchester gang, EMD or MMD something like that. Word is he's gone, shipped out, to India.'

'Bull.'

'It's true. Why would I lie?'

'Bull, bull, bull, bull, BULL!' Hue kicked him in the same knee as before.

Sol screamed out in agony.

Hue let out a mock scream, mimicking Sol, humiliating him.

'What shall we do?' Hue spoke into the phone. There was a pause before Sarafian answered.

'Kill both, but first, tell him we will take his family apart and pour hot tar down their throats for his lies,' came Sarafian's voice over the phone.

'Did you hear that?' Hue started laughing, chuckling. He was tickled by Sarafian's reply. 'We'll pour hot tar down your family's throats if you're telling untruths, Mr Solomon Cleaver. Last chance saloon, you're dead already so you may as well save those blissful coons in St. Kitts.'

'It's all true. Dean Shelby. India. True as death.' Sol looked up at him.

Hue leaned in close to Sol's face, almost spitting the words into his eyes. 'I'm not scared of death, I know it's coming.'

Hue went into the kitchen, the room that contains the most lethal weapons in any house. He ripped off a couple of sheets of kitchen roll. He selected an ordinary kitchen knife and held it with the tissue. He kept it hidden from Sol's view as he approached the policeman who sat helpless and resigned to his own demise.

Suddenly they became aware of car doors opening outside. The sound was just perceptible in the quiet suburban surroundings. As Hue glanced out of the window, he heard the front gate clang against the garden wall and then there were several figures running into the front garden.

Split second decision of fight or flight brought his situation clearly to light. He kept the knife and ran into the kitchen, taking a running jump, diving through the smashed window. He landed with a roll on the grass, took two huge jumping leaps and vaulted over the back fence into the garden opposite. He ran across the lawn and hurdled over a low fence, into another garden to his right. He was out of sight and made the decision to get onto the street through a side passage of the house. He stopped running and hid the knife up his left sleeve. The side passage led to a front gate and once he was through, he was onto the lane round the corner from Sol's.

He was inconspicuous in this leafy Manchester suburb, just another professional out and about. He turned right and was on a main road. *Nearly there, keep calm, inhalation one two, exhalation one two.* He got in the driver's door and drove off in the hire car, aware he had left a mess behind but still at liberty, content he had the right information and was already planning his next move.

Emile called Hue on his mobile. He was informed of the situation in Manchester. He made a decision to take the woman back home. He could kill her but disposing of the body would take time and Hue was keen to get moving.

'Stand,' Emile commanded. Isabel stood up, shaking and crying. As he reached down to lift up her knickers he couldn't help breathing in the smell of her and for a second it passed his mind to carry out his earlier threat. This would be unprofessional and even worse, un-gentlemanly. He contented his desire with another breath and he dressed her, informed her she would only be released unharmed if she complied and walked her down to the car. He put her in the boot this time. He cleaned up the place and locked the key in the coded box.

He drove back to Manchester and found a suitable side street, away from CCTV and any passing strangers. He used a knife to slit the binding on her wrist and then on the back of her head to release her mouth. The tape was still stuck to her hair. He turned her towards a wall and he told her to take her time removing it before going anywhere.

Before she realised it, he was gone. She removed the

tape, slowly from her hair, quickly from her skin. She was cold and in shock. She walked past Asian warehouses stocked with clothing, a shoe wholesaler and a jewellery warehouse. They were all shut up for the night and she found herself in a maze of streets, wandering around without a direction and wondering what had just happened to her. She eventually came to realise where she was. She looked up at the huge bleak walls of Manchester prison, Strangeways. The high walls were foreboding with their curls of razor wire on the top. She started to sob. She collapsed in a heap against the towering wall, curled herself up tightly in a ball, hugging herself through the cold and the drizzle.

The tension was taking hold. On the outside Hue was a vista of calm, a lake whose surface was untouched by wind or rain, no ripples or waves upset the tranquil picture. Underneath the water, the currents traversed an unholy broth of chaos and anger. The currents waded into each other, spinning off at tangents, creating turmoil that belied the serene waters on the surface. The undertow was pulling him further and further into the murky underworld that was made up from his past deeds and addiction to inflicting pain and death. This was in the vain attempt to give his own mind some relief from the pressures he was under. This was exclusively created from a lack of empathy; however it was a small part of his disassociation from humanity. His continuing belief that there was no right or wrong had been his subconscious defence, his shield and the veil to hide behind and deflect his thoughts from truth and reality.

The reality that laid bare to his controlled madness was the undeniable truth that his actions consistently ended in ruined lives, creating countless victims and embroiling those victims in years of suffering and emotional pain. Their families left bereaved, bereft of their loved ones. Did any of his victims deserve his justice? Who could judge a man who had no belief in morals? Any rationality of mind had gone years before when his mercenary actions caused the deaths, disfigurements and a lifetime of misery to thousands of unknown military targets, dupes, marks. These were the innocent people the military termed collateral damage. In this truly unholy realm, death was remotely controlled, the loss of limbs dictated by the push of a button.

He had been an expert in mimicking the IEDs used by the hill tribes in Afghanistan. He'd planted roadside devices to take out several British armoured people carriers. It served his employers to do this and he never once asked why. Hue Brooks did not differentiate between the deaths of people born on one piece of land or another. His lack of ability to construe a moral standpoint had consequently left him with an ability to see the world as one, without borders, nationalities, racial stereotypes, prejudices or any significant differences between sentient beings. He would take the life of a fly as easily as the life of a dog or a man or child. He didn't see the world in the typical way; it was almost supernatural the way he viewed things, without fear, guilt or remorse. In his meditative over-mind state, he would often picture the earth from space, witnessing the planet as one, serene and enigmatic, and then transforming this beautiful, rich, diverse globe into one wholly bruised and rotting apple, fallen from its tree, spinning in space, being eaten by maggots to the molten core which oozed igneous rock turds and yellow puss.

11

There wasn't much packing to do, or at least not for Dean. He bundled his laundry and his clean clothes together in his backpack along with a few toiletries and his torch.

Beki spent the last hour packing and unpacking her bag. She seemed to need it packed just so. If everything didn't fit into its anointed space it all had to come out again and go in just right. Dean spent six minutes packing and watched Beki spend sixty.

'Come on, Beki, we're gonna be late.'

'Nearly done,' she said as she tightened the straps up on the front of her bag. She had a quick scan of the room to make sure they'd not left anything behind and she closed the door.

Gaz, Bob and Abdul were still chugging chillum on the roof. The two travellers popped their heads in to say goodbye and everybody was completely underwhelmed in their responses.

'Yep, bye,' from Gaz with a wave.

'Say hello to Hampta for me,' from Kiwi Bob.

'Safe travels,' from Abdul.

The other guy who had never spoken a word, didn't even look up from making his mix.

That's the way it is when travelling, once you're gone that's it, soon forgotten. You may come up in an errant topic of conversation days, months, years from now and if your paths crossed and you ended up meeting each other again by chance, it would be like you were separated at birth and cause for joy and celebration. For now, though, all thoughts from those left behind were about the next mix and who would light the ensuing tube.

They trundled down to the front desk and settled the bill. Again there was no interest from anyone, just a business transaction. They fought through the crowds down Main Bazaar with a steely verve. They were no longer Paharganj rookies. They'd fought these streets several times now and weaved through the crowds without adieu. Begging children were dutifully ignored, grannies on their way to market were given no quarter, other westerners were stared down to move out of their way as they were on the road, in transit, travellers. They weren't just messing about looking in tat shops and smelling incense. They were heading into the unknown and this dictated a wholly different headspace. This was what it was all about.

At the end of the road they were captured by two cycle rickshaw wallahs.

'You want ride in my chariot, faster than lightning? Where you want to go? Train station? Connaught Place? Moon?'

'Connaught Place, Manali bus. It's OK. we'll take a tuk-tuk.'

'We very cheap, very quick. Race? You want race? Lightning and Thunder, see who quickest?'

The traveller's dilemma: cycle or motor rickshaw?

That morning Dean had been up early and had seen these guys who slept awkwardly in or on the ground next to their cycle rickshaws. What did they do if it rained? These guys were poorer than poor and the thought of someone cycling Beki brought up all sorts of connotations of imperialist supremacy of the third world. 'Impoverished Indian man transports beautiful westerner', but then everyone had to eat and this was his job. This was how he made his living and sure as cow dung made fire, he would be getting a better price from foreigners than Indians.

Dean had no dilemmas. This was doing the guy a favour and if they could have a race, all the better. So instead of squeezing both of them and their backpacks onto one cycle rickshaw they got one each. Beki's was Thunder and Dean's Lightning. Both rickshaw wallahs were happy because both Dipti and his friend/rival Kosal were getting a fare. They had worked since six this morning ferrying Indians around Old Delhi, making enough to pay off their loans but not enough to eat. Now with the foreigner fare they would eat that night, maybe have enough for a drink of hooch as well.

They both pedalled as hard as they could, pride was always at stake in a cycle rickshaw race, but both knew that the real race would be won by route, not speed.

Lightning forged a lead but was undone by an errant

cow sauntering across the main road and stopping in the middle. As Thunder had more time he swerved the bovine obstacle and took the lead.

As Beki went past she blew a kiss at Dean, who was at a standstill while Dipti manoeuvred his wheels around the once white, now grey beast.

Now the race was really on as Dipti was going full pelt trying to make up lost ground.

Kosal was cruising and Beki was getting genuinely worried about his pace. As if he read her thoughts he turned his head and reassured her. 'No problem, madam, cow problem,' and he flicked his head backwards, as if those five words and a head gesticulation explained everything.

Indeed he was right, as there was a clear winner in the end. As they stopped at the Manali bus stop area there were jokey words exchanged in Hindi between the two men. Plenty of arm and hand gesticulation and the word 'cow problem' thrown into the middle of a sentence.

Both men were more than happy with the fare and tip and were on their way as soon as the money had been handed over. Not only would they eat tonight they would have enough left over to share a small bottle of illicit liquor. They would both sleep soundly through the hot night.

The travellers' bus was fine, not as grand as a western bus but comfortable seats with recliner facility. It was packed with Indian tourists, mostly couples and families. The driver set off on time and although it seemed to take forever to get out of Delhi, eventually they hit the highway and started to cruise as the sun went down. As the night descended the chatter from the bus dwindled as the kids went off to sleep and the adults ran out of all but essential conversation.

'Want one of these?' Dean held out two Temazepam in the palm of his hand. 'They'll help you sleep.'

'Go on then, I could do with a little help, next stop Manali.' Beki necked one with a swig of tepid water and was off in half an hour with her head resting on Dean's left shoulder as the bus sped along as fast as its engine would traffic it.

The driver, high on speed tablets, kept his foot to the floor and used his horn to warn any lorries he was zooming past them. Anything else on the road didn't merit a warning, as only another coach was as big as him and they were unable to match his speed. He knew all the other coaches on the road, every single one. All other carriers and vehicles would be smaller and duly ignored. Even foreigners soon learn that the rules of the Indian road only merit the horn warning to anyone bigger than you. Anyone smaller needs to get out of the way. It's a simple rule and mostly works well. It may come unstuck if oncoming vehicles fail to adhere to it when they are overtaking round a corner but if both drivers swerve at the last second, even these mishaps can have a happy ending, a nervous smile from the passengers and a nonchalant look to his buddy from the driver.

All Indian coach drivers have at least one buddy, sometimes two, three or four. The buddies are there, primarily at least, to keep the driver awake. Secondly to keep his spirits up by telling him what a superb driver he is, truly a wonder amongst men and how all other drivers are idiots and fools. He is the king of the road and they are privileged to ride with him, the best driver they've ever witnessed. They help unload the bags and pay for the driver's food at the dhaba stop, chai at the chai stop and bidis are continually offered through the night. In exchange they get a reduced fare to and from Manali where they work as waiters, cleaners, kitchen staff and bellboys through the season.

As the sun climbed slowly over the foothills of the Himalaya, Beki slowly opened her eyes and realised she'd slept the whole way. She remembered waking up when the bus stopped at the roadside diner but was off again in no time. Dean was still asleep and the bus was steadily going uphill on a road that was definitely not a highway. This was a road with a view. There were sheer drops from the other side of the bus's window, down to a river valley. The road was all twists and turns and then suddenly you were looking straight down into the abyss. It was as spectacular as it was terrifying and what Beki didn't realise was, she had only just begun to step foot into the majestic splendour of the mountains.

The higher they climbed the more the cloud formed above and around them. The views ceased and the pressure built. It was as if the intensity of the sky came down to visit and was watching their every move.

Eventually Dean woke up. 'Mornang,' he said, mimicking the Kashmiri salesman from Delhi.

'Hoe are yooou?' Beki replied in even grosser, hyper

exaggerated tones.

They both giggled at their little 'in' joke and the excitement was palpable between them.

'I think we're nearly there. It was sunny a bit ago but then the cloud came in. It's hard to tell where we are now.'

'It's that drizzly Manchester rain. I feel right at home. Me nana used to tell me that was "rain that wets ya".'

'Do you miss her?'

'Yer, I do. She brought me up when mum died.'

'I know. You told me in our sessions. That was one of the first times I saw a different side to you.'

'What ya talkin' about? Different side.'

'Well you were just dead cocky at first, then you started to tell me about your mum and dad dying, being brought up by your nana and poppa. I thought the way you spoke about them showed a softer side.' Beki thought for a second and added, 'Almost vulnerable.'

'Vulnerable? Me? I'm not vulnerable.' Dean was feigning shock and horror.

'Almost ... almost vulnerable.' Beki started giggling and tickled him in his ribs.

He had nowhere to go as he was trapped in a coach seat. There were disapproving looks coming from the other passengers as he blurted out 'Stop it, stop it I need a piss ... I'm gonna piss myself,' as she carried on, rendering him helpless, both of them in hysterics, not caring what anyone else thought of them, feeling free and unfettered, living on the boulevard of daydreams, both of them unaware they were still under the spell of the benzo's they'd necked the night before.

12

When the roads became wider and the gradients less steep, they knew they were nearly there. Houses, shops, restaurants, hotels started to line the sides of the road. The cloud covered everything in the drizzly mist and it was impossible to see much higher up than the treetops on the sides of the nearest hill.

They arrived to the usual sounds of horns and engines and they got their bags from the bus and headed off to the nearby taxi rank. When they arrived at the Ashgrove it was as good as Mrs Gulwati the travel agent had promised. They were shown to their room and it had everything you could want, including being spotlessly clean. As Dean looked out of the balcony window he looked over manicured gardens with log huts positioned in small woodlands of what he presumed were Ash trees.

He picked up the phone and dialled reception. 'Hello, Mr Shelby here, we need to change rooms to one of the log cabins in the garden.'

Beki was only just getting over how fab the room was and she was hearing him tell reception they wanted to change rooms, without even consulting her. After initially getting herself worked up about it she decided that, actually, she kind of liked it. He knew how to take charge. So why wasn't he taking charge in the bedroom?

Beki's insecurities started to take hold again. She wondered why he'd not tried it on. Maybe he just didn't fancy her. Maybe he just wants a friend?

She felt deflated on the small trek through the hotel's corridors, past reception, through the garden's gravel path and to the log cabin. The rain had stopped but the cloud was still as low. The bellboy opened up the room, clicked on the dimmer switch and showed them into the most tacky honeymoon suite imaginable. The decor was red, pink and white. Cherubs played flutes and frolicked provocatively with each other on windowsills. The main feature was the giant heart shaped bed with red heart shaped quilted pillows and a pink and pastel green flowered quilt cover.

The bellboy went over to the bed and pressed a switch on a side panel. The bed started to vibrate. He pressed another and it slowly started to rotate clockwise. Beki noticed the mirrors surrounding the bed and started to giggle. Dean was dumbstruck by the candelabra on the dining table for two and the crystal chandelier controlled by the dimmer switch.

'Bathroom.' The bellboy beckoned them through to the only door.

He switched on the light to reveal a round, whirlpool

bath, gold colour taps, more cherubs and a strip of love heart tiles. There was a bidet next to the toilet and they both seemed to realise at the same moment, they were bursting for the loo.

The bellboy was hovering at the front door and Dean realised he was after a tip. He gave him RS20 and he seemed happy enough.

Beki had shut the bathroom door and he was bursting, hopping about from side to side, envisioning she would be in there forever, as all women seemed to do.

'Come on, Beki, I'm dying for the loo.'

'You'll have to wait. Punishment for bringing me to tack city hell.'

'I didn't know it was like this. I thought it would be better for havin' a spliff. Better than a hotel room. I didn't know it was the bridal suite, honest.'

It was the added 'honest' that gave him away. She picked up on it as she was constantly dealing with liars at work and alarm bells rang whenever an extra 'honest' or the other classic 'believe me' were added for no reason at the end of a speech.

'Honest?'

'Honest.'

'Bullshit, you're lying.'

How did she know? 'What?'

'You're lying, there's no way you could have booked this room without the reception mentioning it was the honeymoon suite.'

She'd sussed him. They had told him it was the bridal

suite but he never thought for one second it would be as totally over the top as this. It was all they had left for the log cabins. He thought it might be quite romantic and hoped it would set the scene for him trying it on if the opportunity arose. He had a choice, carry on the lie or come clean.

'Well, yeah, thinking about it they did say something about that, but it was all they had left, log cabin wise.'

Silence from inside the bathroom. She was buzzing. He'd booked the honeymoon suite, how lovely was that? Although it could have been just because it was all they had available. But he could have said no, it's OK, we'll stay in the room.

'Come on, I'm gonna piss me pants, have you finished in there?'

She flushed the chain, even though she'd finished a while ago, opened the door and he dashed in. Relief at last.

When he walked back into the room she was searching for the stash. The papers and cigs already out on the bed.

'So, what do you think, then?'

'I think I need a spliff.'

'No, about the room.'

'It's, erm, different.'

'Yep.' Dean seemed deflated.

'Look, Dean, it's got a rotating heart shaped bed and pornographic cherubs, what do you want me to think?'

'I know.' Head down now, staring at the floor.

'But you are right, it's better for having a smoke, and I do like the whirlpool bath.' All she wanted was for him to ask if she fancied sharing one, but he didn't, another moment gone. How many more could she afford to give him? She was feeling strangely low, not quite there. She sparked up the joint and instantly felt better. After they'd smoked it in silence, she told him she was going to have a shower and then go out and explore Manali.

As she stepped into the bath and pulled the shower curtain round in an arc, she felt really turned on and needed some relief. She washed herself and then used the showerhead to excite her and then used her right index finger to reach orgasm. Her body jerked and twitched as the water fell hot onto her breasts and the steam filled her stoned senses. So at least for the few minutes she was masturbating, she felt cushioned physically and emotionally from the world around her, lost in the fantasy that Dean was the one.

Steve Smart was at home in his detached, four bedroomed family house in Berkshire. Here he was, dad to his two children and husband to his wife.

Here he was Martin Renshaw, city head hunter, provider, all round good guy. He gave regularly to charity and took part in the children's sports days when he wasn't at work. His family had no idea of his real name, job or the danger they were in because of his other life. He stayed in London most weekdays and his wife liked the fact they were not in each other's pockets. She understood the situation. He had to work until late most nights and by the time he had made the commute she would be so tired from looking after the children she would just want to sleep. So the arrangement they had was the better option. Normally when he was at home he could switch off from the job, but today he couldn't seem to get Hue Brooks from his thoughts.

He sent a text to Emile Sarafian.

Call me when free. SS.

Within two minutes Sarafian had called.

'Emile, are you alone?'

'Of course, what can I do for you?'

'How's Hue? Is he holding up? He looked a little downbeat at the funeral, put on a show of course but I'm concerned.'

'He's got a bee in his bonnet about this, taking it all a tad personally.'

'Where are you up to with it? I can't afford to lose you both for much longer, Emile. What you may not realise is that with Charles gone I'm one down in the field anyway. You two running all over the place causing mayhem can't go on much longer. I need you to report in, daily.'

'Looks like we're off to India.'

'India?' Steve was incredulous. 'To chase down some half pint gangster?'

'Yes, seems he's fled. Gorn to India, we're following. He's on the case, using Speedseek to search through flights and online hotel bookings. As soon as we get a hit we're off, apparently.'

'OK, OK. Let me know the details and for heaven's sake make this quick.'

Steve pressed End Call and stared into space. He wondered how long he had before he would be obliged to inform the employers of the situation. He had no doubts they already knew the gist of things, maybe not the details. He would give Hue one week and then it was crunch time. He either came in or a directive from the employers would be needed.

His little girl ran towards him clutching an iPad. 'Daddy, Daddy. Look what I made.' She held up the screen and he watched her wardrobe doors magically open and shut, several times, in a stop motion animation.

'Very good, sweetheart, very good. One day you'll be a great film maker.'

'Daddy, it's just for fun, I'm going to be a vet.'

'Well, maybe you can film the animals when you make them well.'

'Good idea, Daddy, you are the best daddy in the world.'

Steve doubted that, very much.

13

Hue was on 'chat' with Jo90 from Speedseek. He'd last 'spoken' to Jo90 after giving the details of Dean Shelby, about three hours ago. Jo90 had directly outsourced this to their Bangalore office. There they had a small army of operatives who used the black market in information sharing, as well as sheer volume of search hours, to get whatever was needed in a fraction of the time any European outfit could hope to achieve.

The information that came back from Jo90 was that Dean Shelby had boarded an Emirates, Man-Del flight, but had no Delhi hotel reservations. However there was one in Manali, Himachal Pradesh. This was at the Manali Ashgrove, booked through a third party Delhi based travel agent, where he was currently accommodated. He had a double room and was probably travelling with a Rebecca Aston, as they had booked the Emirates flights together and had adjoining seats. CCTV from the airports showed them walking along side each other. Jo90 added that if he wanted, they could provide further detailed information on both parties for a fee.

Hue was delighted. *So you got yourself a bitch.* She was his weak spot, Rebecca Aston, the frailty in the armour. He could taste revenge; a bittersweet flavour covered his palate.

He asked Jo90 for full details of Rebecca Aston and then booked two British Airways flights to Delhi, along with two connecting Air India flights to the nearest airstrip to Manali at Bhuntar, Kullu.

Hue was so thrilled he was now directly on the trail, but the tension was still there. So after a slight deliberation, already aware of the outcome, as it was the unequivocal solution, he decided to go for one of his walks.

'Let's go for a walk, then,' said Beki, feeling calmed and clean from her power shower.

'OK.'

'Cheer up, let's go and eat, I'm starving.'

'Do you always just think food, food, food? Where do you put it?'

'I know, but we skipped breakfast, most important meal of the day. Breakfast like a king, lunch like a prince, supper like a pauper,' Beki said as she walked through the manicured garden of the Ashgrove.

'You'd breakfast, lunch and dinner like royalty,' Dean said, and then wondered when he started saying lunch and dinner instead of dinner and tea.

They walked up the path and through the hotel lobby. It was a walk or a rickshaw ride into either Manali or up the hill to Old Manali.

'Where do you want to go?' Beki asked as they stood outside the hotel, clouds still low around the treetops.

'Old Manali,' said Dean and off they went in a tuk-tuk, up the nice smooth road for about fifteen minutes and then the road went to pot, with holes and stones and gravel patches. They started to hear the rush of the river and then went over one of the tributaries of the Beas that flows through the valley from the mountains up high.

They passed apple orchards and the hotels became guest houses. Travellers on noisy Enfield motorbikes kicked up dust as they overtook them. Some of the bikes were done out with leather tassels hanging from the sides of the handles. Some bikes were half chopped with Easy Rider style handlebars or low-rider frames, fat back tyres, strips of chrome. Dean noticed these were mostly ridden by unshaven little guys with black curly hair, idiotic grins and hippie style clothes. They looked like losers to Dean.

Beki was wondering who all these good looking Mediterranean types were on the bikes. Some of them were very good looking. Some had girls on the back of the bikes and they looked good, too.

As the tuk-tuk reached the edge of town the driver stopped and they got out. He turned a tight U-turn and they started to wander up through the cheap looking restaurants with menus in English, Hebrew and Russian.

There was an Internet café and then a load of tacky

looking choppers, parked outside the Moonlight Restaurant which apparently served Mexican food. All the people in there looked the same. It was obvious they were all trying to look different from their past and future, saying to the world 'look I'm free, I can dress like a cool hippie traveller'. The trouble was with any fashion, the more people clamoured to look a certain way, the more they inevitably became the same.

Dean and Beki looked at each other knowingly, as if to say 'twats' and walked past. Eventually the tackiness gave way to more traditional style cafés and restaurants and then the more fitting village. They started to smell wood smoke and the earthy smell from farm animals, tethered cows and goats in small family herds. Children peeped out from the balconies of the wooden houses and the women were dressed in hardy grey or brown woollen blankets. They were wrapped round them like a dress and fastened at the shoulders with an oversized safety pin. The bland coloured blankets were decorated with thick bands of zigzag woven patterns in red, yellow, black and green. These dyed decorations moved ceaselessly. The women worked industriously, they were matriarchal and proud. They tended the animals, washed the clothes, checked the children, cooked the food, swept the floors and carried the wood and water. The wood was carried in baskets strapped to their backs like a rucksack. The water in buckets, balanced on their heads.

The men seemed to chat to each other in the street quite a lot, passing the time of day.

The travellers came across a café perched on the side of the single file path. The path carried on after they'd walked through the village, heading to nowhere and so it seemed the right place to stop. This was because, sat upstairs on the top deck of the place, there were westerners smoking chillums and drinking chai.

'This looks a good place,' said Dean with a knowing nod to the top deck.

'It certainly does,' Beki replied and they went into the place they would soon call 'home'.

The Mana Café was run by a no-nonsense local man called the Brigadier. He was a retired army officer and ran the best café in Old Manali, possibly in the Kullu valley itself. He was well in with the local police chief and so his place never suffered any police raids and his fried momo with soy sauce was to die for. He kept the menu small so everything he did, he did well.

After taking a seat upstairs they ordered chana masala, four roti, fried momo, two chai, one, no sugar.

The boy waiter took the order and Dean started to skin up a joint.

'This is mint,' he said and Beki just smiled a huge grin.

They were surrounded by huge pine trees and green forest. As they looked out over the other side of the path, there was a huge cherry tree. Birds darted about, cows stomped up and down the path, men chatted to each other and children played, making use of whatever was around them to make believe, spin or wheel along.

When they finished the joint the food came and it was

amazing. The momo were crisp dumplings filled with shredded vegetables like cabbage and carrots. The chana masala was simple and tasty, creamy with a hint of spice. The chai was a different class of spiced tea. Clove, cardamom and cinnamon melded into one refreshing brew.

After they had finished the Brigadier came to collect the dishes.

'Was everything to your good satisfaction?' he asked Dean.

'Yes it was, is this your café?'

'Indeed, now in its ninth year. Did you like the momo?'

'Yes we did,' answered Beki. 'Do you know of any rooms near here, for rent.'

'We have, madam.' The Brigadier called over one of the boys and spoke to him in the local dialect, obviously giving instructions. 'He will show you, madam,' he said and the Brigadier was gone, dishes in hand, contentment on his handlebar moustachioed face.

The boy showed them the rooms which were very basic but tidy. They were basically a square with white walls and a double bed. There was a 'bathroom' attached which was a squat toilet on one side and a cold water tap and bucket on the other. There was a sign on the bathroom door that said HOT WATER BUCKET RS25 and the price per room was a very reasonable RS250 per night.

They had another chai and another spliff and decided to move out of the Ashgrove tomorrow and stay up in the rooms behind the Mana Café. They watched the other foreigners and listened in on their conversation.

The chillum circle was made up of three English, two Dutch, two Swiss and an honorary Israeli, the type who only hung out with Europeans. They were all talking the usual stuff about charas, where to find the best quality and who was making the best chillums that season. Everyone seemed to have their own fancy pants chillum. These chillums weren't like the one Gaz bought in Delhi. Some of these were hexagonal, soft brown colours, patterned, glazed and they were of various lengths and widths. They heard about foreigners charging three hundred dollars for a chillum. Apparently, an Israeli just paid that for a 'William' and a Russian paid so much for a William he wouldn't even tell people the price.

Although the travellers were a bit pretentious Dean and Beki both liked it and when they left they promised to return the next day with their bags.

'It felt like home,' Dean said.

'Yeah, only one night of cherub hell to go,' said Beki and they walked down the path to find a rickshaw waiting by the roadside.

'Manali, please,' Dean said and off they went, heading back into Manali town, down the bumpy road then onto the smooth tarmac and full pelt, downhill all the way.

They went straight past the Ashgrove and headed into the town. It seemed so busy compared to the Mana Café in Old Manali but there were shops and so Beki said if they were going to stay in the middle of nowhere she needed some supplies.

They pottered about and she bought some bits and

pieces. She bought her own jug for the loo, soap, washing powder and some pegs.

Dean bought nothing. He did see a cool looking bar called the Ranch House and asked Beki if she fancied a drink.

The bar was done out saloon style, all logs and tables cut from trees. Dean ordered an Indian Honeydew brandy.

'Best taken with a 7up,' instructed the barman. 'Ice?'

Dean shrugged. 'Yeah, two of those?' He looked questioningly towards Beki.

'Why not,' she replied, happy to go along with things.

The measures were huge and with the sweet fizzy mixer, went down in no time.

They thought they may as well try the local cider as they'd seen the apple orchards dotted about the roadside on the way up to Old Manali.

They were served ice-cold cider with accompanying peanuts coated in a spicy dry roast powder. The cider was refreshing and went down really easily, too. They were big bottles and actually one would have been enough to share but in no time they had downed one each. A barman came with salty crisps and they ordered two more bottles as they started to feel relaxed.

'Wish I had some ching,' Dean said. 'It'd go well with this stuff.'

'Ching? Coke?'

'Yeah, beer and coke, nothin' better in the afternoon.'

'I can think of something.'

'What?'

'Something better to do in the afternoon.'

'Yeah, what?'

'What?'

'What?' Dean was leaning in towards her now, he knew what she meant. He smiled and looked straight into her eyes. 'D'you mean … eat?'

She burst into giggles and the barman brought over two more ice-cold bottles of cider.

'Yes, well, maybe?' She paused until the barman had gone. 'Depends on what you're eating.' She looked at him with her head tipped slightly down.

'I might be hungry later,' he said.

'Me, too.' Beki looked at Dean then added, quietly, intensely, meaningfully, 'Some people would say, get a room, but we already got one.'

'Well, let's down these and get back there then,' Dean said excitedly.

'OK, we will,' she said.

They both poured out full glasses of ice-cold Kullu cider and drank them down in big gulps with Beki struggling to stop it from spilling down her chin and Dean watching her with disinhibited eyes, picturing something else dripping down her chin.

As if she could read his thoughts she giggled. 'Oh, look, I can't help stuff dribbling down my chin,' she said theatrically wiping it away. 'I'm such a messy girl.'

'You're a very messy, dirty girl.' Dean picked up on the game.

'Very dirty, I can't keep stuff off my chin, stuff spills everywhere.'

With this he finished off his drink and she did the same. He held her hand.

'Come on, let's go,' Dean said as he stood up and tried to pull her up, out of her wooden chair. They were both wobbly, losing balance, losing inhibitions.

They took a taxi back to the hotel and got back in the tacky room, made for love.

Beki needed the loo and so Dean thought he'd roll a monster spliff. He was definitely in Beki's knickers, he just had to keep it together and have a laugh, take the piss a bit. He'd had his best nights with girls when he'd laughed them into bed. He knew he had gone too far in the past but that side of him would not be showing, he was too blissed up.

He made the spliff and top loaded it, his excitement plainly growing, waiting for Beki to come out of the loo.

She was washing herself, sprucing herself up. She wanted to be at least clean down there, if not in her potty mind. She knew this was going to be an afternoon she'd never forget.

When Beki did emerge, Dean was rested on the bed, with the joint held out for her to light.

She lay next to him and he held out a lit match for her to spark it up.

As she took the first couple of tokes, he leaned over to the side panel and pressed the two buttons simultaneously. The bed started to revolve and vibrate at the same time, causing mass hysterics to break out. Both of them were laughing riotously at the cheesiness of their rotating, vibrating bed in their cherub nymph love shack. He stood up like he was chasing a wave on a surfboard and Beki joined him. She held the spliff in one hand and held onto Dean's hand with the other to steady herself. They started to bounce up and down, jumping on the bed like kids.

Before he realised it, Beki had smoked half the joint. It hadn't hit her yet, that was for sure. He'd put enough in the top half to down an elephant and had just presumed they would have shared it, but through the giggling and laughter she'd smoked the lot.

There was a creaky sound, then a crack as the bed juddered and stopped rotating. They fell in a heap and stopped the laughter as they looked at each other with surprise and mock concern.

'Flip, we've broken the bed,' Beki said.

There were more giggles as Dean got off and looked underneath, surveying the damage.

All of a sudden Beki looked a funny colour, pale as a ghost. The Kullu cider they had been drinking was 9.5% and the litre bottle she'd thrown down, along with the top loaded spliff she'd just smoked hit her all at once. Beki was in the midst of pulling a 'whitey'.

She looked down at Dean with sadness in her eyes as the overwhelming need to vomit struck her. The room was moving vertically in a rhythmic hop from floor to ceiling. Her eyes couldn't focus on anything that stayed still, as if her brain wasn't able to steady her world anymore. There was a surge of nausea that started in the lowest part of her stomach and rose efficiently upwards to her brain. She jumped from the bed, stumbled once, narrowly avoiding going over on her ankle, seeming to glide and hover across the room, as only the highly intoxicated can, and made it into the bathroom.

All Dean could do was listen at the locked door to the sound of wave after wave of spewing and coughing, interspersed with the sound of snot being blown from her nose and then her sadness turning to wails of tears as she cried and cried and cried.

She was feeling sad to her soul, grieving for Tom, realising for the first time what she had actually done and what a mess she was in. She was absolutely correct, she said to herself in a moment of clarity, as she looked in the bathroom mirror. She surveyed the scene. Hair streaked down her face, wet with tears and phlegm, vomit pieces of half-digested momo around her mouth and down her chin. *I am a very messy girl.*

Hue turned right outside the Bright and then right again. His unconscious knew where it was heading. He turned right at the next main road and found he was walking up a street that catered for the hip Manchester crowd; young people, how he loathed them. There were vinyl record peddlers, X amount of alternative clothes shops, bookshops that only sold design and art publications, cafés selling overpriced but decent coffee and trendy bars fronting backroom music venues. The more he moved towards Piccadilly, the more the standard of the coffee shops and cafés decreased. Instead of imaginative teashops they became viable commodities, franchises without a hint of originality. The propensity of arcades and betting shops increased, promising £500 slots and satellite controlled roulette.

He walked across the grass and concrete 'gardens' of Piccadilly Manchester. Who could have thought this up? Great slabs of dirty arched cement scathed around patchy grass squares with a desolate fountain to one side of the walkway which ran through the centre of all this conformity. Bleak was the word that summed this up, as if this city needed a bigger dose of that. More coffee shops and chain eateries surrounded the grass squares. Drug dealers, so immersed to look invisible, hawked passing trade and groups of immigrants huddled on oblong concrete seats who leaned towards each other in conversation. To top it all there were rows of Hue's pet hate, the idle buses. Stock still with engines running, they spewed out toxic fumes all around you. He felt like running but restrained his urge.

He walked past Chinatown and thought about eating there. He would, as soon as he finished his walk. He crossed over the main road past a huge run down hotel and took his first left. He was now entering the gay village. This was an area of Manchester devoted to bars and clubs catering for homosexual, transgender, bisexual and any other sexual 'ism' or combination of 'isms' going.

Years before, when Manchester actually had a garden at Piccadilly, the area was known for its more than fair share of gay bars. Hue knew of regular gay orgies that took place on the top floor of the multi storey car park every hot summer weekend, or the floor below if it was raining. This was all pre-AIDS, when he'd first visited the city as a young man and dabbled in the gay culture that thrived there. He'd never actually had any meaningful sexual encounters, but he used to like the atmosphere in some of the bars where no one judged him. Now it was all homogenised, so blatant. Subsequently its personality had disappeared into the era of hen nights and pub crawls, commercial and mainstream, nothing much of the hidden left, except the underground world of the rent boy. So naturally, instinctually, that was where he headed, walking through the Manchester murk.

They were sometimes in small packs, smoking on corners, making a show of themselves and sometimes alone. Their ages? Anything from about eleven or twelve upwards. He sniffed one out, immediately he knew. Even he didn't quite know how he distinguished the victims so definitely, so assuredly. How deadly were his instincts honed?

He approached the lone worker. He seemed forlorn, head down, hands in pockets, greasy hair dripping droplets of water from the long fringe. His left trainer had ripped open at the toe and he had no coat in the chill, damp air. As Hue approached down a back street, still littered with last night's takeaway pizza boxes and beer bottles smuggled from bars, the boy pulled out a packet of ten cigarettes and sparked one up with a disposable red lighter. The sky let go a delicate drizzle, the light dimmed and the deal was made. It seemed cheap, twenty quid for head. It was the most costly agreement the boy would ever make.

The boy walked Hue round the corner to a canal bridge,

away from the village, away from any help. They dipped below its arch onto the towpath. He smoked his cig as he started to work, taking the odd drag when he could, the wafts of cheap tobacco burning Hue's nostrils. As he realised this was not a five second wonder he just let the cig burn out between his fifteen-year-old nicotine stained fingers. The thrust became unremitting as Hue rammed his tiny penis into the boy's skull.

Hue noticed the water level of the canal was high and he got even more excited, thoughts raced through his mind. Hue held the boy's head still, looked down now, into his watery eyes. He noticed the acne around the corners of his mouth, the brown strips of tartar that lined the edges of his teeth as he pulled the skin back from his cheekbones, the self-harming scars of a thousand mutilating stripes that lined the bare forearms that gripped Hue's hips, the facial tattoo of a teardrop dripping from the corner of his eye.

'What's your name?' Hue asked.

'John,' said the boy.

I'm the 'John', thought Hue and smiled to himself.

'Turn around, John. I want to do it from behind.'

'I don't do that, Mister, I only blow.'

'Here's an extra fifty.' Hue produced the money and tried to give it to John.

'I don't want it, I don't do that. What's your fuckin' problem?' John started getting upset, instantly angry, his raised voice echoing under the bridge. John saw the flash of worry streak into Hue's eyes.

'ARE YOU FUCKIN' DEAF?' John shouted up into

Hue's face. 'I ONLY GIVE HEAD!'

Hue thought about offering more money but knew it wasn't going to work. The situation was getting out of hand. Not thinking straight, he started to squeeze the boy's head between his hands. John tried to pull his head away from Hue's grip. Hue knew one twist and he could end things there and then but he hadn't finished and he needed to finish, because he must get his release from the whirling in his head.

John was scared, this punter wasn't right. He'd had a few scares, who hadn't on the game, but this was different. He was so strong it was chilling John to the bone. There was nothing left in the eyes, no feeling, no pity and definitely no guilt. John just saw planning and it was deliberated planning at that. John went for his knife. It was a small penknife he kept hidden down the crack of his arse. Getting it was easy and he managed this without Hue noticing. He needed two hands to open it out.

Hue caught a glimpse of his hands moving covertly and in a suspiciously coordinated fashion. Hue used a technique similar to a side impact car crash to stun the boy. He released his right hand from his head and smashed his palm into the skull, the left brain area, repeating this from the other side, then right then once more and lastly from the left. When the brain gets shaken in the skull like this it shunts the brain function for a while until the organ can assess the potential for damage. It's a kind of natural self-preservation.

John was a complete cabbage for a few moments while

his shaken brain aligned functionality again. In the meantime, Hue had turned him around and easily retrieved the penknife from his hand with a twist of the boy's limp wrist.

John was now facing down on the light gravel towpath, head towards the water, his feet against the wall. Hue did two things at once. He opened the penknife and kicked John in the right temple. He crouched over him, put his left knee into the small of his back and thrust the knife into his anus. He ripped open his jeans and underwear once a hole had been opened up by the stab. He used the blood as lubricant and as he entered John's wounded anal cavity, he shoved his body towards the syrupy dark water. John slumped over the side of the canal and Hue pushed his semi-conscious head into the icy liquescence, then fetched it up again. This brought John round and he screamed in fear. Again his face was dunked into the water. How Hue loved this, all the more it was a boy this time. Even though he'd cut him, he was still tight. Perhaps he was actually telling the truth and he didn't take anal. Hue rammed the boy until he was nearly there; each time the boy made a sound he shoved his face into the liquid. He soon learnt to keep quiet.

As Hue reached his climax he put John's head as deep as he could into the drink. He thrashed about as his death throes increased Hue's pleasures and then it was over, he was now still and it was deathly quiet. Even the birds had stopped singing, sensing there was something unearthly happening.

As he came round from the intensity of his orgasm, he heard voices, getting louder, moving towards his playpen. Hue got up and put his bloody member away. His habit of wearing light pastel colour chinos had not served him well today. There was blood around his crotch area and dirt on his knees. He shoved John's body gently into the canal, hardly causing a stir as the liquid night engulfed his slight, teenage frame. Hue brushed himself down as he strode off. He was moving swiftly; bolt upright, away from those 'FACKING VOICES'.

Part Two
The Poulis

14

At the top of the ocean food chain, swim the sharks. They are acutely aware of everything around them. They use their super senses to feel changes so minute in their liquid world, they would be passed off as insignificant by other predators.

Sharks smell blood from miles away. Amazing to us, they can smell the blood's route, as we would hear the direction of sound. A shark can locate a drop of blood in an Olympic size swimming pool in a second. They listen intensely to the ocean and hone in on any distress sounds made by their prey. They can detect a movement in the constantly changing current from their lateral lines, the sensor filled tubes, running the length of their bodies. Sharks 'see' electromagnetically. This is realised through the ampullae of lorenzini receptors. These mysterious glands, located under the skin in their heads, perceive the edges of their prey as a seer observes an aura.

The Poulis family have always hunted sharks. They have prized themselves on taking the lives of the top ocean predators and have scars in their lineage to prove it.

Sycamore Poulis got bitten and rejected by a nervous bull shark, only to turn the tables on the seven foot monster and harpoon her in the head as she turned to swim away. That was more than fifty years ago and he still dined out on the story. Such was the prowess of overcoming and therefore becoming, transforming oneself into, the ocean's top predator.

As is everything with the Poulis family, nothing is ever written down, no records are kept, no ancient scroll depicts the tradition of the shark hunt but it carries on to this day, if not the next, well, who knows.

In the ancient times the oceans, rivers and lakes were sacred and revered as the mother. How apt that the family fought and risked their lives to top the ocean's finest. In the thinking that came later, with knowledge, the family realised that although the oceans make up 71% of the earth's surface, they only account for 0.02% of the total mass. With this realisation the family decided on a ritual earth hunt, too. Who are the top predators on solid ground? There is only one answer that came to the summit, human beings. The realised spirits.

Sycamore's two daughters Reyanne and Anastasia were keen to see their father keep the family tradition alive. They were overjoyed when he took his two grandsons Marimous aged eighteen and Kathar aged nineteen on their first shark hunt. The two mothers waited patiently yet anxiously for their teenage sons to return.

They were stationed at the Lodge, high above the San Juan River which connects Lake Nicaragua and the Caribbean. The two sipped weak Pimms cocktails with cucumber, lime, strawberries and raspberries floating in the tea coloured drink. They were both having foot massages from two naked Swedish hunks and could watch the hunt through telescopic field glasses at their leisure. It was like a scene from the Roman era, transported through time to the modern age.

'Mari's got one, he's got one,' screamed Reyanne in delight. They both watched the party harpoon the distant shark incessantly.

The boys were with their grandfather and several others, the specially chosen employees. It was an honour to be asked on a shark hunt by the employers, as it symbolised so much for the family. It also meant they trusted you with their own son's lives.

The bull sharks travel like demented giant salmon up and down the shallows of the river at certain times of year. Whenever a Poulis reaches age, he will join his older cousin or brother in the sacred ritual. They all work in pairs until death parts them.

Sycamore's brother Tobias had died the year before and he was now the only head of the family, acting alone for the first time in sixty-five years.

Of course the odds are stacked with the human hunters these days. There no getting in the lake like in Sycamore's time. His father had expected to lose at least one of a pair in the hunt, but luckily for Sycamore it wasn't his time. The shark took a bite but as he wasn't the familiar taste of prey, she spat him out.

He remembered launching the famous blow to her head and his brother hit another harpoon through the gills. Their father then launched one from the wooden boat and that was that. Sycamore was rushed to the Lodge where a medical team stitched him up and he survived. Later that year his cousin Randolph was killed when a shark took a bite and pulled him under. He got torn apart and when he came to the surface he had a shredded artery in his neck. The loss of blood was fierce and attracted several other hunters, so it became impossible to save him. This meant his other pair, Oscar, had always been just one.

Oscar now controlled the East and Sycamore the West. The family felt vulnerable as the world was governed by one of a pair, a single man on each side. The pairs had always meant balance and kept the family strong, forever out of the eyes of the world. Two never stood out as one man did. There had already been a near miss with an employee and his secret tapes. Mobiles or any other recording devices were banned of course but now they had tiny cameras, so all employees had to be electronically swept for devices. If it wasn't necessary to be clothed, new employees would be kept naked in the presence of the family. How anyone who was paid as much as they were could ever think about exposing the family's secrets, it was a mystery to all, but it happened once, so may happen again.

Sycamore had a great interest in British politics because of The Crown and the Bank of England, the original bank that still controlled the world's financial direction. Due to this essential factor he liked to keep governments in office for wholly extended periods. This was until they became so obviously corrupt and self-serving, even he could not help them stay in power anymore. Through the Blue rule of the eighties he'd helped promote the new culture of greed. This had been his baby, to stimulate hidden need in the masses. This was how he began to really take things personally, when he actually got involved. It had been his idea to flood the northern cities of Liverpool and Manchester with cheap heroin to keep them quiet after the riots. They needed a stable period to keep the markets content. This enabled the south to bloom, to prosper without relent.

In the next two decades he'd helped the Reds face their demons, to capitulate to his demands and launch an illegal war for profit. It had been so successful they were still embroiled in it today. The knock on effect had been outstanding. As the family controlled the British and American arms trade, they had completed record sales throughout those decades. They had made trillions of dollars from the wars in Iraq, Afghanistan, Libya and now Syria. Who did the world think sold the capability for chemical weapons to the Syrian regime? They never let things get too out of hand in Egypt as that was their spiritual home and they understood there was much more to life than money. The dollar, the pound, the yen? It just helped along the way. Not one member of the family had ever envisaged anything but health, wealth and luxury. So it is and forever will be.

Egypt was the last in the line of cultures that still inspired the families today. Its structures were still visible to all. They were there to be admired by all and truly understood by a very few. The keys to power commenced from the cultures that spawned the Egyptians. The Egyptian culture appeared in history fully formed from the outset due to the inherited knowledge from the Babylonians and the Sumerians before them. The secret lineage went even further, but only the heads of the family were privy to this knowledge. When one of the family's summit pair became unwell, too frail or just felt it was time, he would pass the knowledge down the bloodline, passing on the real source of power. From this initial egg of knowledge the family had survived the millennia and it would forever be.

Sycamore knew that soon Oscar and he would be passing down their knowledge. The appointed time was nearing. Only when the right planets aligned with their sacred place on earth and the human representatives came to them, could the power be passed on. He was confident that his pair, Marimous and Kathar, would be ready as soon as they completed their next task. He hoped Oscar was nearing completion with his two. He had a summit with Oscar very soon and he would know more then.

They were all to visit the sacred volcano and the day after they would summit. He had all the successes of the last strategy event laid out in formation in his memory banks. The cattle were being kept full and fattened. They were being intoxicated day and night. They were slow and dumb. Their vision was blurred by the Arena, the highest rating prime time television show. He now had a controlling stake in Path Productions, the television company responsible for churning out the relentless dross the cattle craved on a Saturday night. The culture was slowly being eradicated and the once powerful church was being replaced with the ecclesiastical belief in sport and celebrity, both of which the family controlled. They had been dealt a blow with the abdication; this new church leader was actually a rare breed, an honest man. Luckily Sycamore knew he had some secrets, he was only a man after all, no god.

Sycamore was anxious to pass on his role to the boys. Mari had done well in the hunt today and his pair Kat had backed him up with skill and precision. If they could take these talents and use them in the world, they would be a formidable pair.

There had been several calls from Steve Smart regarding the situation with Charles Bates' depressions and recent death. Now they were about Hue Brooks.

Intelligence from sources in the British police confirmed that Hue was either renegade or as close to it as it didn't matter anymore. He would have to be dealt with as he posed a risk. Sarafian was not party to the recent bloodbath but had reported in his role. His assessment to Smart was that Hue was letting his psychopathy rule his thinking and was becoming more extreme in his cogent pursuit of Bates' killer.

Sarafian reported they were on the trail of a Dean Shelby, a Manchester hoodlum, who had travelled to India with a woman, Rebecca Aston. Smart had done some digging. He said Aston's partner was missing. She had taken a sabbatical from her work as a probation officer and she had first met Shelby when she'd supervised him.

The boys arrived from the showers, triumphant and euphoric.

'Well done, boys, you have made me proud,' Sycamore announced as he walked towards them, arms wide. Both boys were hugged warmly. As he held them he whispered into their ears, 'Come, let us pray to the goddess and then you shall have your rewards.'

They joined the two mothers and Sycamore commanded all employees to leave the room. Once they were alone, they formed a circle around the ancient symbol on the floor. It was the flower of life, the interconnected geometric symbol that is an allegory for creation.

Sycamore began the enchantment. 'Mother, you have witnessed the coming into age of these two land beings that have made their first assent to conquer the ocean's brave hunters. They achieved this without loss of limb or life, with no remorse and just a little fear.' Knowing looks and polite laughs were exchanged. 'This first task is in honour of you Goddess of All, and they will have their just rewards.' Sycamore stepped out of the circle and took the hands of

Mari, looked deep into his eyes and lifted his arms high in a triumphant gesture. 'Behold the master hunter of the sea!'

The others cheered Mari, clapped their hands above their heads.

Sycamore let him go and took the hands of Kat. 'Behold, the slayer of the beast!' he proclaimed, again holding his arms aloft and looking deeply into his eyes as the others cheered and clapped.

The atmosphere was mounting, gaining momentum, becoming exhilarating.

'Now for your rewards.' He held Kat's hand and joined it to Mari's mother, Reyanne. He joined the hands of Mari and Kat's mother, Anastasia.

Both the couples stared lovingly into the eyes of their partners. 'See the maiden in her. See the woman. See the crone. Now go! Find comfort in each other.' With this he left the room. He was overjoyed at the events of the day.

The decision had been made to send Mari and Kat on their final hunt.

Hue Brooks would be a formidable foe, worthy and dangerous.

15

Reyanne took her partner Kat to the table her feet had been resting on. The one used for her massage. She was an incredible woman in many aspects, not least physically. She was tall and tangibly strong, she had lengthy limbs with a healthy bone structure beneath. Essentially she was a colossal woman, but in physical shape and she wore her size well. Her skin tone was dark brown. She had on shimmering body butter, adding a glow to her body, especially combined with the massage oil on her feet. She wore long black hair that fell in spiral curls. Her oval face was punctuated with high cheekbones, a small but naturally full lipped mouth and dark pools for eyes. Their brown depth radiated warmth and a touch of vulnerability that she used to her credit. She was unaware that this hint of defencelessness made men scurry to protect her and she found this both heart-warming and tiresome at different times, usually depending on the man.

In her world there was no need for monogamy, in fact it

was actively discouraged. Although the patriarchs like Sycamore kept the family in line, the women were the ones who bore fruit of future bloodlines. Naturally they were respected and valued accordingly.

'Sit, be still and comfortable as you are going to enjoy this hour more than any before in your life.' She said this with a shining seductive radiance as she looked into the young man's eyes. 'I will be your every desire, your every wish come true. You can do whatever you want to me. It can be over very quickly and although you will enjoy that, I, will not. However, if you follow my instruction, I will teach you the important skills in pleasing a woman. I will show you the secrets of my body.' Reyanne paused for half a minute, and then asked Kat, 'What is it to be?'

Anastasia was equally as beautiful as Reyanne but in a much more classical way. She was slightly lighter skinned, petite and stunningly pretty. None of the Poulis women ever looked anywhere near their actual age but Anastasia appeared especially young. Mari had been overjoyed when Sycamore announced his partner was Aunty Anna. He had lusted for her since puberty when he'd watched her swimming on a beach in Talum, Mexico. She came out of the water and he could see her nipples through her white costume grow erect as she lay in the sun drying off. He peered at her pubic bone and wondered from that day on what it would be like to make her. He barely heard her talking when she proposed teaching him the arts of making a woman happy and as soon as she disrobed he was on her like a dog driven crazy with desire from a bitch on heat. He was hard and pumped full of teenage lust. He was straight down on her, tasting her, lashing his tongue in and out, in and out.

After a couple of minutes of bad head she resigned herself to the fact she wasn't going to get anywhere with Mari today and switched off, blanked her mind from what was happening and thought about the planned trip to see the volcano tomorrow. It made her smile, as Mari would be erupting pretty soon.

He entered her and pounded away thoughtlessly for the two hundred and thirty one strokes that she counted. He turned her around and stared down at the opening to her bottom and that was that, he came within the minute. She felt him come inside her and was practical in her approach to his mood. She let him rest upon her naked body, his head against her breast. They sat like this for ten minutes while she stroked his hair and held him close. Then he said, 'I have an idea.'

Reyanne began by kissing him, licking him, touching him, caressing him and then instructed he do the same to her. Then she got the massage oil and she let the thick liquid drip from her shoulders, down over her full breasts, down onto her stomach and then towards her pubic bone onto her thighs, which were well developed and strong. He watched and waited patiently, relishing her enjoyment, the look of fun in her eyes, the smile on her face.

'Now, gently, start to move the oil around my body. Do

it smoothly and slowly. Begin at the top and don't touch my nipples, they're too sensitive right now.'

Kat used his fingertips at first and then once he got going the palms of his hands to glide over her skin. It sent tingling sensations all through her.

'Wow. Kat, you have an exquisite touch.'

He said nothing and let her know with his contented smile he was happy to be pleasing her.

After he'd massaged her full body, he slightly increased the pressure and she responded by letting her feet and knees relax, opening her legs a little and exposing her innermost self to him. He took the hint and let his hands glide over her pubis area, then around her body and back to the place they both wanted his hands to go. She steadied his fingers and placed her hand over his. She opened her legs fully now and pressed his hands into the right spot, making precise circles until he had it under control regarding the right place and exact pressure. He tried to stay as distant as he could. To learn from her the right way to love, the right way to pleasure another, but his balls were starting to ache and so he asked in a whisper to her ear, 'Is it time yet? Can I make you now?'

She opened her eyes and brought herself back from her fantasy where she was being seduced by a prince, she being a lowly servant and replied, 'Yes, you may do anything you want to me, anything at all.'

'We have a request from your son,' announced Anastasia to Reyanne and Kat. They had been so in their own scene they had forgotten about the other coupling going on across the other side of the room. They both stopped and looked at Anna.

'He wants to watch us,' Anna said, nodding her head towards Reyanne, 'you and I … together.'

Reyanne looked at Mari, then at Kat. 'What do you want, Kat? It is your time as well as his.'

Kat thought through the request. To see the two women together could teach him something new, to see how they pleasured each other, this detail maybe of use. Then again he was bursting and aching inside to make someone. He came up with the solution.

'Only if Mari lets me make him while we watch. I've got to let this out!' He pointed at his erection, they all laughed at his solution. It was just like Kat to come up with the unexpected yet perfect resolution to one of Mari's games.

'You got me there, bro,' said Mari, 'but next time.' He pointed his fingers gun-like at his own temple and made a 'pshew' sound like a cowboy's six-shooter going off in an old western.

Anna and Mari walked off, hand in hand and left Reyanne and Kat to it.

'Would you have done it?' he asked.

'Yes, of course, you both survived the ocean hunt, you deserve anything you desire. But would you?'

'I knew it was never going to happen, he's such a boy, very machismo.'

'You can do that to me … if you want.'

'I want every part of you, I always have.'

'Then as this is your one and only chance, do as you will. I can enjoy it or not. Sometimes men like it when a woman enjoys his advances, and other times they enjoy it much more when it is forced upon a woman. There is nothing wrong with this, as long as it is consensual. Games can be played out with a partner. Tie me, blindfold me, smack, pinch me … whip me but do it all in the spirit of the game, in play, never become obsessed with this and never let it become real.'

'Wow, I can tie you up?'

'Yes, of course.'

'Whip you?'

'Gently, at first, anyway, we'd have a code word.'

Kat laughed. 'You'd do all this for me? You are indeed a goddess. You look like one and act like one. No, I don't want to do any of those things but I do want you now, right now, I can't hold on much longer.'

'Then give me your water.'

She opened her thighs and he slid inside her. They stayed like this for a while, staring into each other's eyes and slowly started to move. Kat rotated his hips and then made slow, long circular movements inside her. She massaged herself and was totally lost in her own world, so when he came she reacted by coming, too. They stayed locked together until they slept.

Both were unaware of the burning glare covering them from the eyes of her son, Marimous.

16

Sunlight streamed through the cracks in the curtains. Its illuminating shards of light picked up specks of dust that were floating microscopically through air.

Beki opened her eyes and was immediately wide awake. Her whole being felt poisoned. She stared at the moving dust particles and watched their hypnotic dance.

She moved her head and felt the nausea and discomfort return and so stayed stock still for a while. She realised that the bed was still broken, still tilting and that she hadn't totally lost her sense of balance. She needed to get up and use the loo. She managed this slowly and carefully. She returned and found three bottles of water by the side of her bed. Dean must have got them for her last night. She downed about half a litre. She was feeling wretched.

Dean woke up and turned to her and smiled. 'How are you?' he asked gently.

'Bad.' She was sat on the side of the bed, plastic water bottle in hand, taking small sips, one after the other.

He sat up and rubbed her back with the flat of his hand, in small clockwise circles.

'Got a lickle hangover den?' Dean used a mock baby tone.

'Little?' She groaned. 'Whatever I did to my body last night, can it please forgive me?'

'You'll be fine. Breakfast in bed?'

'Oh yeh.' She seemed cheered up by this.

He got up. His hard on had gone down and went to the loo. He came back and grabbed the menu. 'How about scrambled eggs on butter toast?'

'Yes please.'

'Coffee, filtered. Orange juice freshly squeezed.'

'Yep.'

'Or you can have fresh apple juice.'

'Don't take the piss, Dean. I'm dying here.'

'OK, orange, then.'

'Do they have ketchup?'

'Don't know, I'll ask.'

He picked up the phone on the desk and dialled room service, made the order and then went over to draw the curtains. He looked out at their first clear day. The sun was shining over the trees in the grounds and then he looked up.

He went to the door and opened it, took a step out into the chilly morning air and stared in awe and wonder at his first sight of the Himalayan foothills that adorned the town of Manali.

'Beki, you've got to see this. It's …'

'What, Dean, what?'

'It's amazing, Beki.'

She slowly managed to get to the door and narrowed her eyes to the brightness outside. She stood next to Dean and they both stared in silence at the magnificent snow covered valley vista. The sides of the mountain were not fully snowbound and so there were lines of grey rock separating the ice and snow areas. This created a web of pattern on the lower crags that seemed to speak to you. The higher up your vision went the more the white took control and the peaks were completely covered.

The hotel had been positioned so guests could see right down the vale, affording the best views. The hills that immediately surrounded them had lines and patches of snow and were covered with pine forest lower down.

They went back in when breakfast arrived and Beki was very impressed that the ketchup was Heinz. The waiter got a good RS50 tip and she started to feel better. The view of the mountains, the sunshine from the cloudless sky and the tasty carbs and protein brought her round.

They packed their bags, Beki just stuffed hers in today and were out before checkout at 10.30am.

Dean had managed to get the bed back on its base and thought it would be fine until some other drunken potheads decided to act like kids and jump up and down on it. Beki told him she didn't remember a thing about jumping on the bed and he wondered how much she remembered about the way they were acting with each other before she started throwing up.

He paid the bill and got in the first of the taxis lined up outside the hotel.

'I'll take your bags, sir,' the young man said as he got out of his cab and opened the boot of his Ambassador taxi. All the other cabs were modern cars or Maruti mini vans.

'Nice cab,' said Dean.

'Thank you, sir, this was my father's taxi and I'm carrying on the family tradition.' He opened the doors for them and they all got in.

'Where to, sir?'

'Old Manali, please, as far as the road takes you.'

'Where you staying?'

'The Mana Café, in the rooms at the back.'

'Very nice, sir, full nature place. Smoking?'

'Pardon?' Beki asked.

'Are you smoking, madam?'

She looked at Dean as if to say 'what the flip is going on here?' He nodded and so she replied ,'Yes, we like a smoke. Why do you ask?'

'Everybody smokes here, madam. I personally start every morning with chillum and chai before getting into my cab. I pray to Shiv every sunrise and he protects me from all the ills. Ganesha, too. And Laxmi three.'

They both smiled at his turn of phrase.

'My name is Anu, please to meet you.'

He had a certain charm about him. His English was good, he was handsome and friendly. He was the type of individual that gained trust from his naturalness. He was nonthreatening and eager to please.

'So, do you know where we can get a bit of hash then?' Beki asked.

He was confused for a second. In his world there was only charas. Hash was made in other areas of India, but not his. He scanned his memory banks to think of anyone he knew who may hold some hash. He knew they made it in the North East region, Almora in Uttarakhand, but nobody around here would bother with it because it was not charas.

'Sorry, there is no hash around here. You can get it, but nearest place is Uttaranchal, Almora area. Some foreigners brought some here one time. Very hard, pale in colour. Not like charas, madam, inferior quality.'

'Oh, my mistake. Can you get us any charas, then?'

'Oh, very yes, madam. We can make a stop along the way to my friend house.'

They stopped after turning off the main road and drove out of their way for another five minutes through wood-lined roads that filtered the sun's rays in spectacular, strobe like fashion.

They waited for about ten minutes in the cab outside a path leading off from the road. Beki had too bad a hangover to get worried about being in the middle of nowhere in a cab, waiting for the driver to score some drugs, but Dean was getting a little impatient.

'You stay here. I'm going for a walk.'

Beki snuggled into the seat, ignoring Dean by keeping her eyes shut.

He got out of the Ambassador and followed the path for a short walk until he saw a fenced wooden house with a concrete extension on the side. Dogs started to bark as he moved closer. Then he saw Anu and another local sat in the sun, drinking chai. They watched as he approached, spoke a few words and then Anu beckoned him towards them with a wave.

Dean looked for the dogs before he opened the gate to enter the property. They were both tethered with chains and the owner of the house was doing the best he could to verbally calm them down. They only stopped barking once Anu had introduced his friend as Vihar and they all sat down.

'Chai?' Vihar asked.

'Yes, thanks,' Dean replied. He knew this was not what Anu had in mind but he needed to get a feel of how business was done. He understood that Anu would be putting his cut on top of the price Vihar charged for the charas and did his best to explain that he was fine with this and it was what he would do in the same circumstances.

Anu protested that it was a fair price and he wasn't a cheater. Dean reassured him he knew that but Anu was not going to be around the next time he did a deal, so he needed to know the price and how to spot the best quality.

Vihar came back with a small tray of three glass cups, full to the brim with hot, sweet chai.

'So, Vihar, Anu tells me you have good quality.'

'Best quality,' Anu said, not wanting to insult Vihar who was well known to become fierce if he became vexed.

'Sorry. Best quality, sorry, mate. How do I spot the best quality charas?'

Vihar looked up from sipping his chai. He was middle-aged but looked older. His skin was full of deep lines and his beard was grey. He had a thinker's eyes, though they contained a hint of menace, a quick mind and a worker's body. He was dressed in a green wool jumper and had a brown hat that was embroidered with the same colourful patterns that the women had on their dresses. He wore a jacket over the jumper and blue jeans with work boots on his feet. The old boots were covered in dried mud. He looked like a farmer to Dean, a man of the land. Wood smoke made the air smell sweet and pungent. As Dean looked around he understood his life back home was over. This was where he lived now and this was where he was meant to be.

'Always saying sorry, you English. Sorry for this, sorry for that. Always sorry for everything.' Vihar looked very serious all of a sudden.

Dean sat up straight on his wooden stool, there was a taint to Vihar's speech, certainly a smear in his choice of words. He gained his composure and realised this was just another deal. When you deal with gangsters and people who don't give a toss about the law you come up against this all the time. Who you are and how you react says everything about you to the people you're dealing with.

'You're right. It's because the English are always warring with someone. We always have something to say sorry for.'

The two Indian men exchanged a glance.

Dean carried on. 'Let's hope none of us ever has to say sorry to each other again.'

'How is the chai?' Anu asked, hoping to defuse the mounting tension.

'Sweet,' Dean said with an edge to his own tone, using the word to covey two meanings. 'Everything's sweet.'

'Good, good. How much did you want to buy?' Anu asked.

'Depends on the quality,' Dean replied, keeping his eyes busy, flitting between the two men.

'There is only one real way to tell quality.' Vihar produced a piece and showed it to Dean. 'You can split it open, look inside, smell like this.' He took a noseful. 'And all, but until you smoke it, you don't really know quality.'

'We make a chillum and you can see quality for yourself.'

'No need, mate. You've told me everything I need to know. Anu, buy me fifty grams of his best quality. I'll be in the car.' Dean downed the dregs of his chai and little pieces of spice were left in the bottom of the glass. It was good tea and on another day it would have been good company but he wasn't leaving Beki sat in the cab while they all smoked chillums.

When he arrived back at the cab, she was asleep, tucked into the corner of the back seat. She looked much better than she did first thing this morning, when for the first time ever, he'd thought she looked her age. She was a few years older than him but he didn't care about that. It was natural she'd looked a bit rough because she had been puking her guts up all night.

All sorts of sexual thoughts started running through his head. Her jeans were tight to her bottom as she had her knees tucked into her body. He had to have her soon or it would become harder and harder to make the move as time went on.

Anu came down the path and they got in the cab, waking up Beki.

'He likes you,' Anu said. 'He gave you good price.'

Dean took the sticks of charas and paid Anu the rupees, about twenty-five English pounds worth.

They drove up the hill to Old Manali and Anu gave Dean his business card with his mobile on it.

They lugged their bags along the path to the café and the boy showed them to their room. They ordered water and coffee. By the time the boy brought the drinks, Dean had made a spliff from the new stuff. It looked and smelt different from the charas he brought with him from Delhi. This was fresher, dark on the outside and pale brown when you opened it up. It was less sinewy than the first type. There were fewer bits of material in it. It smelt of soil, earth and flower. It almost seeped oil when you rubbed it between your fingers.

Dean sparked it up and passed it to Beki. She had a couple of tokes and passed it back with a puzzled look.

'What's up, what's the face for?'

'Probably me, but it doesn't taste right.' She shrugged.

Dean puffed on the joint, smacking his lips together to get a good taste of the flavour. It tasted of some kind of synthetic oil. Then he noticed he didn't feel anything from it. He grabbed another piece and opened it up. It was the same and then another. Out of the five pieces, there was one that was genuine charas, the piece he'd been shown, and the rest were snide.

He'd been royally ripped off. Dean felt the pit of his stomach empty and he laughed to himself as he went through the whole con. They didn't rob you with a knife here; they did it with a smile, right to your face. He could go back to the place, to Vihar and have it out with him but he knew better than that. He knew he had to swallow this one. He knew it was more trouble than it was worth. India, what a country. Lesson learnt. They told him to his face the only way to tell real smoke was to actually smoke it. Try it, then buy it. He was never going to fall for that one again.

'This is flippin' rubbish smoke, Dean. You've been ripped off.'

He looked at her as if to say 'shut up' but she was feeling better now and wasn't letting it go.

'Headline: The big Manchester gangster gets shafted on his first Indian drug deal.' She was laughing as she spoke and in the end he had to join in.

'Oh my days, do not start on me. Next time you can do the business. See if you can do any better.'

'Couldn't do much worse. Still, one out of five isn't bad going. Shall we try that one, it might actually work.'

Dean made a joint from the stick that looked different from the others, the one that looked more like the stuff from Delhi.

They smoked that and were pleasantly surprised. It was a decent high, fairly mellow but it seemed to make colours stand out. They had another one then went for a walk to see where the path led, out of the village.

17

Emile Sarafian was very good at torture. He was accomplished in the art of death as was his friend. It supplied his income and he was able to provide for his family. In a few months he'd retire. He wanted to live simply, to be nothing more than a man on a porch, looking out over the coast, watching the weather. He would move to an area near to his son and value their time together. He would live through the seasons, year by year, with only his thoughts for friends. After he'd accidently murdered his wife, he knew there could be no more companions to share his life with. He would never even live with his son again, just in case. He needed solitude and bore the responsibility of no bonds.

It was hard for him to figure out why he hadn't been asked to kill Hue. He knew Steve Smart was closely linked in to the chain of command and he'd given Steve all the apposite prompts that would allow him to give the word with no ill feeling but no word came. Now he was worried he wouldn't be able to live out his years on the coast of some forgotten town in a modest maisonette, surrounded by the nature.

He knew a little about the employers, as Charles and Hue referred them as the 'money men'. He knew they were a family that was somehow able to stay behind a wall of silence. An invisible stone so high it was impossible to penetrate it. He knew they controlled things behind the scenes for several governments and he knew they were totally ruthless.

Rumour had it they lived in a pre-Christian world, where the norms and values attached to current society didn't exist. What fun, thought Emile.

Hue was sitting next to him as they flew over the plains of northern India that stretched barrenly below them. The ground then started to become more deciduous in its flora. There were a few hills now, a river here and there. Then the trees turned evergreen, firs lined the gorges. They started their descent without much of a word between them on their flight to the Kullu valley.

The touchdown was bumpy and raised a few gasps from the middle class tourists on the aeroplane. Once through the airport, for what it was worth, they took a taxi to the Ashgrove Hotel.

They had been travelling for twenty hours solid. Hue was as tuned in as ever.

He turned on the charm at reception. 'Hello, Harjeet, how are you, darling?' Hue said to the male receptionist as if he was a long lost friend, leaving Emile in a state of wonder, observing this consummate act.

The receptionist eyes lit up. 'Hello, shur, have you a reservation?'

'No, darling, well maybe. We are meeting our English friend here, Dean. He's travelling with a girl but she's just a pal, you know.'

Hue was camping it up. Emile wondered how he immediately knew the receptionist was gay.

'Oh, I know what you mean, shur. Let me check for you.' Without hesitation the receptionist felt obliged to help out this foreigner. 'Let's see … oh, shorry, he left this morning.'

Hue's face showed a flicker of anger, and then changed back to flirty camp. 'You wouldn't know where to find him would you? It's very important. Mr Ghandi wants to know, too.' Hue slipped him a RS1000 note straight into his hand as quick as a blink.

'I can do my best to find out for you, shur. Wait until my shift ends at sheven this evening and I will talk to the taxi and rickshaw drivers for you.'

'GOOD, let's book a room then. A single for my friend and I'll take a double. Come and see me when you've got something for me. There's more where that came from for the proper information.' Hue winked and nodded.

The receptionist pocketed the tip and thought about the best person to get to do the legwork. He needed to know who took the foreigners called Dean Shelby and Rebecca Aston from the hotel at checkout earlier today. He called Mangla who was on reception earlier and she said she thought they'd got a cab. She said it might have been an Ambassador. Harjeet knew this narrowed it down some. He'd get to it as soon as he could leave the desk.

'Well, thanks for the single, Hue,' said Emile. 'Good of you that.'

'Merely paving the way for the receptionist chappy to come to my room, not yours.'

'How did you know?'

Hue knew exactly what Emile meant but pleaded ignorance.

'Know what?'

'He was a poofter.'

'Lucky guess, I suppose. Just his mannerisms. They gave him away from twenty paces.' Hue paused then carried on just before they got to Emile's room. 'Queers are the same the world over. Should be drowned at birth if you ask me. See you later for dinner, old boy, get some sleep if you can. Might be a busy night.'

Both men were happy with the standard of the rooms and Emile managed to nod off straight away. Hue was unable to sleep. He decided to work out in the hotel gym. He then showered and went to the restaurant and ordered two egg white omelettes, a full roast chicken and steamed vegetables. The food was overcooked but edible. The restaurant was modern, adequately staffed and reasonably hygienic. He had to wipe the cutlery with his napkin before it actually shone.

He thought about a walk but just wasn't in the right

frame of mind. He felt quite vague, almost calm. He turned on the television and watched the BBC news until his eyes eventually closed and he watched the little patterns form in the darkness behind his eyes. If it wasn't exactly sleep it was at least rest.

At the end of his shift Harjeet went out to the taxi rank and started asking around. Eventually he found out it was probably Anu, the son of Anil, who had picked up the two foreigners earlier today. Anil was well respected by other cab drivers but it was well known that his son was of suspect character. Anu had a bad reputation in the area. Harjeet would have to wait until tomorrow to track the boy down. Once questions are asked there is no stopping the gossip spreading. By the law of averages, some cab drivers who are friendly with Anu or wanted to curry some favour from him, might blow the whistle and let him know what was going on. These drivers were less than reputable themselves and would take delight in passing on the information that questions were being asked by the hotel staff.

There was always an uneasy relationship between the cab drivers and hotel staff.

By the time Anu came to work the next day, his story of the foreign couple would be well planned out. He was already worried they may have made a complaint about the drug deal to the hotel manager, as he knew Vihar had sold them a clever mixture of henna, boot polish and flower scent oil. A drug pedalling taxi driver wasn't exactly uncommon in Manali. Selling via the rank outside a four star was pushing it though.

That evening Dean and Beki sat in the open air café. They indulged in two more wonderful portions of fried momo and then got chatting to the other foreigners who seemed to live in or around the same area.

Sometimes after an especially strong chillum … there was a few minutes silence. Generally though there was pleasant chat between the small assembly of travellers. There were the usual charas tales and then talk of how most people made their money. Smuggling drugs. There were tales of friends getting away with it for years on end, living the life, travelling without having to work as such. Only most were now languishing in some jail in Delhi or Mumbai because they became sloppy, over confident or were just plain unlucky.

The group came and went during the early part of the evening but by nine there seemed to be a settled collection of smokers who were going nowhere.

Millie was the only other girl. She was tall, with dark straight hair. She had brown eyes and took no nonsense from the boys. She wasn't especially pretty but wasn't bad looking in her own way.

Dean liked her but didn't fancy her, which suited Beki who'd pick up the nuance of Dean's body language towards the girl, so she was able to talk to Millie without being catty or defensive.

The group seemed to assume they were an item and Millie asked how they'd met.

'At work,' Beki replied. 'Then we became friends.'

'Friends' was all Dean heard. He didn't want to be her friend he wanted to be her … her boyfriend. There he'd said it to himself. Dean Shelby wanted to be her boyfriend. He was falling in love. He had it bad, little chemical rushes of adrenaline were making him twitchy and nervous. His frontal cortex had slowed down, suspending his capacity to make any real judgements.

He was in love, for the first time ever and he was prepared to go for it.

He was lost in his mind for a while and realised Beki had now struck up a conversation with the best looking lad there, Tim. He was a posh boy, a southerner from the Home Counties, wherever that was. He had a carefree air about him. Tim possessed the attitude of the rich and privileged. He carried it naturally. It had been nurtured into him from an early age and it was practically the opposite of the messages Dean had been given as a child. Tim believed that anything was possible and it was his right to have it, no question.

Dean believed he was due nothing and had to work hard for everything. If he hadn't been hitting on Beki, he would have let it go. Instead he honed in on the conversation.

'Ya, I've been to Manchester. My father's company had a box at United v Chelsea.'

'Was it any good? I live near the new City stadium.'

'It was fine, free booze all day. Never been to the City ground, you'll have to invite me when we're back in Blighty.'

'What does your father do? To get a box at United?' Beki asked.

'He owns a chemical company. It's a tax thing I think, the box. He owns a place in India that processes some kind of toxic waste and a plant in Norwich, in the middle of nowhere, that produces it. The locals hate him. I don't like him much, either.'

'Does he like you?' Dean butted in.

'Not much, anymore.' Tim leaned over Millie and put out his hand. 'Hi, I'm Tim, pleased to meet you.'

Dean had no choice. He shook Tim's hand and just said, 'Dean.' Somehow he almost felt sorry for the lad. It was the look on his face when he spoke about his dad.

'We're going on a day trip tomorrow, now the weather's broken. Do you two fancy joining us?' Tim asked them both, genuinely.

'Where to?' Beki asked.

'Out from the village, along the path to see where it leads to,' Millie said.

'Yes, come along, we're up for an early start, meeting here at nine for our special breakfast,' Tim said.

'Why not,' said Beki. 'Sounds like fun.'

'Why not?' Dean said but with an ambiguous,

questioning tone directed at Beki.

'Dean, don't be a prick. We'd love to come along.'

That was him told, he liked the 'we' bit, though.

'Great,' said Millie.

'One last chillum?' Tim asked. He was putting his mix in the tube. He gave it to Dean to light.

He's really trying hard, thought Dean, and his charas is very, very nice.

When they said good night and went to their room, Beki was obviously pissed off with his attitude. In her mind Tim seemed a decent guy, a bit lost but that went with the territory around here. There was no need for Dean to get shirty with him. She got into bed, wrapped in a jumper and leggings. She was really starting to think about who she was sharing a room with, sharing a bed with. Why did he get all defensive with Tim? He was totally harmless, bit of a rich boy geek. Millie was lovely, really nice, thoughtful and friendly.

'Are you alright?' Dean asked.

'I'm fine. You need to chill out with people, Dean. He can't help that his dad's rich. She's really nice. Just relax. I'm going tomorrow, you do whatever you want. I'm going to sleep.' Beki tugged the covers over her side.

Dean didn't really know what he'd done wrong. He wasn't used to these kinds of people. He was used to being around people who were all scrambling around for the scrapings off the floor, the bits and pieces they were thrown, the scraps and the leftovers. These people had it served on a plate and they, well he, Tim, didn't seem content at all.

Well, he'd go tomorrow, give it a chance. That Tim lad did have amazing weed.

Anu was back on the hotel rank at seven sharp. Business was generally slow at that time. However if you got lucky there was a chance a rich tourist would hire you for a sightseeing half, even a full day. No such luck that morning, though, and an hour later, Harjeet the receptionist was walking towards his cab.

The reception and other hotel staff didn't really associate with the cab drivers. This was because of their status. They were considered less of a social class than the hotel staff, on par with domestic cleaners and dishwashers. However, if there was another RS1000 note in it, Harjeet would lower his standards.

The conversation was trite and quick. Anu had said they went to Vashist, the village on the other side of the valley. He'd dropped them at the hot springs and they didn't tell him where they were staying. That's all he knew.

Harjeet relayed the information to Hue when he came down to reception, before breakfast. He was given another RS1000 for his trouble.

'You should have come to my room and told me as soon as you knew, Harjeet.'

'Shorry, Shur, I cannot leave the desk while on duty, I could lose my position.' The truth was Harjeet had met a few sexual predators while working in Mumbai hotels.

Some were there for prostitutes and some were there for anything, paedophiles mostly. They were usually rich men coming to India to prey on the poorest, most vulnerable children. Harjeet could see their intentions in the coldness that lay behind their eyes. There was no way he was going to Hue's room. That would be straying into the cobra's lair.

They arrived at the café to find Millie and Tim waiting, smoking a spliff and having chai.

They greeted each other and exchanged ritual morning pleasantries. Dean had been warned to be on his best behaviour.

Beki grabbed a menu. 'Oh, breakfast. Have you eaten?' Beki asked.

Millie answered, 'Well, we don't want to eat anything before our special breakfast, chai's alright, though.'

'Can you eat before a special breakfast?' Tim asked. Then he handed them both a half centimetre square of white blotting paper. It had faint, hand drawn pencil lines and had been cut with scissors. 'Does my stomach in a bit if I eat first.'

'Acid?' Dean asked in his half question, half statement tone.

'Not just any acid,' said Tim. 'I made this myself. Having a dad that owns a chemical plant has benefits, don't cha know.'

Suddenly, Tim didn't seem too much of a geek to Dean.

He was getting to like him, becoming familiar with his quirky ways.

They took the paper all together with their chai and set off down the path out of the village.

Tim chatted to Dean about the whole process involved in making the acid. Dean had to admit, he knew far more than anyone else he'd met, even Spence, about the science of drugs and how to make them. Dean opened up a bit about his operation back home and before long they were chatting away, interrelating stories of drug misadventure as they walked along the path. Before they knew it, they'd all come up and the morning had virtually gone.

Mari and Kat stared down into the dormant shaft they'd come to see. The shaft went down into a cavern, where for centuries ceremonies had been played out. Now it was their turn, now they'd completed the ocean hunt.

The Tin Zaouatene volcano was dormant and relaxed. Situated on the Mali-Algerian border, they had returned here every year under the strictest militarised protocols. All the close family available were there.

Sycamore Poulis was dressed in his desert cloak. It was so black it shone a hint of blue from the blinding sun.

He stood at the top of the shaft and started the first descent by rope ladder, down the tilting walls to the sacred space. After a few minutes all the family were lined up to take their turn. It was a tricky manoeuvre over the shaft face to get on the ladder but once you were climbing down, a mixture of excitement of what was to come and the thrill of the descent allayed any fear.

After the family was settled around the outcrop of rock where the ceremony was to take place, Sycamore went to each one there to explain the significance of the ceremony. He made certain they understood the choice to remain was voluntary and once the ladder was raised, they were there for the duration.

Each person listened to the instruction and each agreed to their presence in the circle being wholly their own choice. They declared their intention was to stay for the full ritual.

Sycamore led Reyanne and Anastasia to a wooden door in the rock face. He opened it and ushered them in before returning to the circle.

In the centre of the circle was a slab of stone. Sycamore stood on it, aloft, and smiled at the family present until all the idle chatter had ceased. Now everyone's attention was upon him.

The circle was made from immediate family from the Poulis and their pairs, if they had them, from other families of the ruling elite. There was a Coriolis and a Beneviste who had married into the Poulis clan. The only one of the four families who didn't have a representative was the Constantine. There were plans for Mari, Kat or possibly both to breed with them, so Sycamore was confident that there would be a representation from all the four families at their next ritual. He needed the word to be told directly from kin to kin that the Poulis' were keeping the old ways alive. It was all about reputation. He didn't want to have another family doubt his power and the best way of showing power was the ultimate ritual sacrifice.

It was the cleanest, freshest acid and wasn't for sale, as Tim had made it to give away. This added another wonderful dimension to the whole experience. The only criteria were that when he gave it away, the recipient had to drop it there and then and promise him they'd have a great time.

The dose was roughly 100ug or micrograms per tab. Party acid.

This wasn't the end of the road stuff from the '70s when people couldn't move from the couch and just watched the walls melt. This stuff was really mild, just enough to brighten the day.

'Everything seems made of crystals,' Beki said.

'I get it, the world's a brighter place,' Dean said.

'It's like being in a fairy tale, walking through these woods, look at the river,' said Millie, 'it's alive.'

The river's silver sheen did look as if it was moving as one, like an entity. After washing itself over the boulders the river was smooth and rounded, and moved along during the monsoon and then positioned until it was time to encourage them a little further downstream.

The trees had a similar way with them. They swayed in the breeze in a definite pattern. The wind moved through the branches and settled again. This was creating a ripple effect that the trippers could watch flowing along their leaves. This unique experience seemed to grip them all simultaneously. It left them thinking about the view of reality they'd traditionally held as fact.

'Is everything alive then?' Dean questioned the posse.

Tim answered, 'Some people think everything is. It's called the Dance of Shiva, Natraj, the Cosmic Dancer.'

Millie added, 'If you think about it at the cosmic level, everything is moving, it's all movement. Atoms are constantly in a state of flux. They aren't really made of anything apart from energy swirling around, dancing around an infinitesimal particle of solid matter. They say if you took all the solid material in the world and packed it together, it would fit in a thimble.'

'I bet one day they'll realise that even that's not absolutely solid matter, whoever they are,' Beki said. She'd wanted to talk for a while but was finding the whole thing slightly overwhelming. She'd never had any full on psychedelics before and although it was pleasant enough now, when she was coming up it was a bit full on. She'd settled into the whole experience soon enough. Having really good quality drugs was an advantage. Another thing that helped was being in the nature and walking with really nice people. Tim and Millie were friendly, clever and just a bit messed up. Well, Tim was. Millie seemed more grounded. Dean was behaving himself which put her at ease. In fact she'd never seen him so relaxed and happy. After they'd swallowed the paper and started the walk, Dean told her how much he loved taking trips. He first had mushrooms when he was about twelve. They grew on his school field. When they were in season, everyone had a few before going into class.

Dean was having a great time. He needed this. He needed something to take him out of himself, to stop him getting all loved up over Beki.

He realised the path was starting to narrow and the river valley steepened. The edge of the path now looked down on the river which had gathered speed and intensity. It was now just white water, as it rushed through a constricted area full of rapids.

They hadn't seen another soul all day. As they rounded a bend, the river flattened and calmed again and there were local people over the far side. There were three men tending to their crop of ganja. Dean thought they looked like dwarfs and elves.

'Ah, look,' said Millie, 'they look like little gnome people.'

Dean wondered if he was telepathic. He thought something and someone else had said it. 'Oh, my days, I was just thinking that.' Dean chuckled. 'It's like being in Lord of the Rings round 'ere.' His accent sounded really northern to Tim and Millie, even Beki noticed it was stronger now he was high.

They all laughed as they all got exactly what he meant. The path started to rise now, moving away from the river and into the forest. Tim was starting to think they'd better turn back but Dean spoke first. 'Maybe it's time to turn round, better get back.'

'Wow, telepathy's flying about,' Tim said. 'I was just thinking that.'

'Yeah, a good connection. I love it here but come on, let's go back then.' Millie confirmed the decision.

The day trippers took a last look at the forest and headed down the path, back towards the rushing sound of the white water coming from below them. They took up a pace as they were going downhill and in no time they had made it back to more familiar ground. The river was close by, the path wide and they all felt the day coming to an end.

'Let's have a chillum break,' suggested Tim. 'Over here, come on, by these rocks.'

They all sat down on a flat rock and watched the river drift by. They heard the breeze rustle the trees and the birds twittering and singing their song as they darted around.

Tim made a tube and gave it to Beki to light. He thought she needed a buzz as she'd been the quiet one out of the four. She was obviously a bit cooked by the paper.

'Bom, bom … BOOM.' Tim let out a mad wild sound as she puffed on the tube and she passed it round the friends.

This was enough to kick start the back end of the trip into gear again and they all went on their way, rejuvenated and buzzing once more.

They walked along the same path but in the reverse direction. This made it seem like a whole new walk, as the views were different and the sound from the river came from the opposing angle.

'Did you actually make this stuff then?' Dean asked Tim.

'Oh, well. Make might not be the word. The only people who actually make LSD, in its pure crystal form, are the Family.'

'The Family? Who's that?'

'Wouldn't you like to know?'

'Yer, man, what's the big secret?'

'Most of the illicit drug world is controlled by the powers that be, my friend. The hidden powers, those behind the governments. They control the cocaine and heroin trades and have done for years. Rumour has it they're involved in skunk production in Holland and the UK. The one drug trade they have never controlled are psychedelics.' Tim paused while Dean thought through what he'd told him.

'So you sayin' that the Family keep it to themselves?'

'Correct.'

'And you know this "Family"?'

'God no, I'm just really into expanding people's minds. I truly believe that LSD is a great way to understand that the world is not as it seems.'

'So how do you make acid?'

'From the crystal, it's a simple technique, basically melting down the solid into a soluble alternative. Quite easy in the lab. So, it's diluting the crystal and dipping the blotting paper so the dose is spread evenly and doesn't clog in one area.'

'So everyone gets the same hit?'

'Exactly.'

They walked a bit further and enjoyed the views as they

went round a bend in the path and the valley was exposed. They looked over the tree line of the lower ground. The leaves were still moving as one but the effect was less palpable now.

'So what's this crystal acid then?'

'That's the drug in the purest form. You have to be initiated to make it.'

'By this Family?'

'Of course. The Family keep the knowledge hidden, as they're very aware in the wrong hands the sacred aspect of the psychedelic drug would be … debased.'

'So how did you come across this crystal then, if it's all so secret.'

'Ha. It finds you. You don't find it.' Tim chuckled to himself. He looked at Dean with a knowing smile. His eyes were still glazed and Dean thought he suddenly looked very wise, older than he'd appeared when they first met. He had a long goatee beard and looked a little like a wizard.

'Do you buy it?'

'No money was involved with me but if you know the right people, I'm sure you can. I was given the chance to meet someone in California and took it. They put me up for a few days and got to know me, got to understand me and eventually they accepted me into their world, just enough to let me try out some of their stuff.'

'You tripped with them?' Dean was really intrigued; he wouldn't mind getting some of this stuff. It was nothing like the other trips he'd had.

This stuff was hardly there, almost subtle if there was

such a thing as subtle acid, but you were well off your box at the same time. There was nothing uncomfortable about it. No hairballs stuck in your throat. No body aches or anything weird going on with your breathing. There was a purity of sound, vision and mind, a transparency of reality. It may as well have been a different drug to the tabs he'd had in England.

'In order to use their product, you have to taste it first. They're all really into what they do and try it with you,' Tim carried on.

'What. Try it how? Take a tab?'

'It's called a thumbprint. You lick your thumb and touch the crystal.'

'What's it like then? The thumbprint experience.'

Tim thought a minute and then realised they were quite far ahead of the girls who were lagging behind. He stopped and looked at Dean.

'Have you ever tried DMT?'

'No, mate.'

'DMT is intense, mate, full power, a fifteen, twenty minute psychedelic rush. You go into another world, a new dimension. Tasting the crystal was like that … only it lasted for eight, mind melting, hours.' Tim smiled as he recalled the trip of his life.

'That must have been mad.'

'It was wonderful, magical, surreal and the ultimate education.'

They waited until the girls caught up and carried on walking.

'Anyway, if you fancy some DMT, let me know. I've got some with me, well, back at the house. We have a smoke of it now and then, for special occasions.'

'OK, mate, will do.' Dean wondered what he meant by house. Did he mean guest house or did he actually have his own gaff.

They neared the end of the road and the edge of the village came into view.

'We off to the baths, Tim?' Millie asked as they approached the café.

'Ooo yes, we'll be just in time.'

'What's the baths?' Beki asked.

'The hot springs, sulphur water in Vashist. They have private baths for the tourist but we use the Temple baths with the locals,' Millie replied.

'Actually, at this time of day the Temple's going to be filthy,' Tim added.

'Good point, wise old, Timo.'

'Timo? Your name's Timo? Not Timothy?' Dean sounded surprised as he'd just presumed it was Timothy.

'It's a shortened derivative of Timothy, but I was actually christened Timo. It means God's Honour or something like that.'

'I know someone back home called Timo,' Dean said.

'Really, how strange. The only other one I've ever heard of was the racing driver, Timo Glock,' Tim replied.

Dean's thoughts started to race. His past flew through his head in pictorial form. He thought about his world back home. The gangsters like Timo, the gun's like Glocks and the difference from the honourable world of psychedelic drugs to the way he dealt. How could he have thought it was all right to put crack in his weed? He'd been really proud of his Chronic, sold before it hit the street. Maximum kick for minimum buck. Well, he'd turn it all around, he'd make amends. From now on he was only going to sell really good, clean drugs. Today had been a wonderful day. He looked at Beki and felt pure love for her. He loved her more than anything. He would do whatever it took to be with her, to protect and cherish her. *Dean*, he said to himself, *you have changed.*

18

Sycamore Poulis had spent the week following the last ritual with a fixer in Nigeria. He had sourced a woman who was keen to escape her life of poverty and who had a belief in witchcraft and magic. She was paid for her services and the fixer carried the deal through.

The tension was mounting in the circle as Sycamore started to name the lineage of Poulis from memory. Nothing was written down. He was back in time now, sighting the Egyptian names of his ancestors. None of the names were of the pharaoh dynasties because, as it had always been, the lineage was never famous. They had always stayed out of view. They always stayed in the shadows. They let the politicians, religious leaders and the royalty take the stage. More recently with his ideas about television shows like the Arena, Sycamore had infiltrated the daily lives of the cattle. He kept them fat and content. They were subliminally bombarded by a message of subordination and fear. Fear of terrorism, drugs, crime, war, immigrants, poverty, job loss but the most effective was the fear of standing up for their rights, lest they be identified as a trouble causer, an outsider.

It was the poor, the sick, the disabled and the weakest in society that Sycamore had been targeting recently. He'd hatched a plan to label them as scroungers and painted a picture through the media of them as the scum of society. He'd created 'the other' within the social order.

This deliberate attempt to victimise the weakest and neediest had been a success. There had been little protest, as they weren't able to mobilise anything across the board. The thing he realised was that they all had separate conditions and viewpoints. Each disability charity or action group was its own body, with its own agenda and they never thought to become a conglomerate, to rise up as one.

The estates of poverty were so fixated with skunk and alcohol that they kept themselves low. There was no need to use heroin anymore to keep the estates quiet, skunk did the trick, especially as they started smoking it so young. There would be no political will from the cattle, as they could hardly function without their hit of medication, their painkillers. They were kept far too busy scrambling around to get the money for the next ten pound bag or bottle of cheap vodka. Ripping each other off, robbing and stealing from the others on the estate, the ones they deemed weaker than they. It was just the same gross human nature being played out again and again.

It had been a stroke of genius to genetically modify the innocuous cannabis plant. There was no hippie ideal left in skunk. This turbo charged Frankenstein plant had taken over. He would have to get Smart to kick start the operation again, once Brooks was dead and buried.

As he neared the end of the open lineage, he started to raise his voice and added a bit of pomp and ceremony to the ritual. He produced the sickle in a swift movement from beneath his cloak. He raised it high above his head and started the chant, quietly at first, slowly gathering pace and volume, the circle around him joining in and after a short time they created the intensity of atmosphere that Sycamore had anticipated. Everyone thrives on ritual. There is something in the human psyche it touches. How did the churches maintain longevity? They repeated a winning formula.

Inside the wooded door there was a cavern illuminated with large black and crimson candles. There were five passages going out from the room, faint moaning sounds seemed to emanate from them. Every now and again there would be the echo of a muffled shout or scream from the Mislaid.

The light held a certain quality, a flickering mystery. There were four people in the chamber and they could hear the chanting of the names of lineage outside becoming louder and more flamboyant. Incense smoke filled the air and the woman Sycamore had found last year was sitting on a wooden chair with her newborn baby, suckling at her breast. The two Poulis mothers, Anastasia and Reyanne looked fondly at the scene.

'Do you recall doing the same for yours when they were

in arms?' asked Reyanne.

'Yes I do. It is one of the gifts of life. The warm sucking of a babe,' Anastasia replied.

The women exchanged a look and then both nodded in agreement, smiled and said in unison, 'The time has come, the deal is done. Our gods await your infant's fate.'

They paused a few seconds and repeated the chant. 'The time has come, the deal is done. Our gods await your infant's fate.' And as they moved towards the mother and child they repeated the poetic chant again, almost singing it, using their voices to calm the woman and her child, now full of her mother's milk, sleepy and satisfied. 'The time has come, the deal is done. Our gods await your infant's fate.'

As they each linked the woman by an arm, they carried on the chant and led her out into the awaiting circle of the invocating family.

The circle opened and as the woman and child entered, the chanting died off. The repetition of the lineage stopped. They had gone back as far as Sumerian pre-history. The hidden lineage was only known to the heads of East and West. Soon Sycamore would be passing on the hidden gen to Mari and Kat and they would become the keepers of the ultimate understanding, the power source that kept the family in authority and supremacy.

Sycamore gave the woman his most grandfatherly smile. 'Have you come here today of your own free will?' Sycamore's speech was now completely natural, as if he'd just asked her what the babe's name was or how was she enjoying her stay.

'Yus, ma own free will.' Her English had a proud African tone but she was fluent. She understood what was being asked of her.

'Then we shall proceed,' Sycamore said with a theatrical swish of his gown.

Anastasia moved in and gently took the baby from the woman, keeping the tiny swaddled body warm against her own.

Nyo, was the name the woman. Uchechi, she had christened her daughter. It meant 'God's Will'. She was a beautiful baby girl. Her mother's belief in witchcraft had been confirmed when she'd been selected to provide a baby for the rich foreigners. Only weeks earlier she had paid Kimata Obesayo, her witch doctor and purveyor of potent magic, a tidy sum of money to put a petition to the spirits to provide her with opportunity and prosperity. She had no doubt in her mind that what she was now doing was the culmination of that ritual, the spell Kimata Obesayo had cast. He had sacrificed a chicken for her and she would now sacrifice her child for the same spirits, because it was obvious to all that is what the spirit demanded.

It was paining her, naturally, but the higher power must be appeased. That is what she knew for sure and if she would become a rich woman in the process, then that was proof enough that the sacrifice had worked.

She would consult Kimata Obesayo on every life decision from now on. He must be the best witch doctor in Nigeria. How lucky that he was from her town and had agreed to father Uchechi, as this guaranteed the success of the sacrifice.

Reyanne led Nyo towards the raised stone alter and as she'd been instructed to do she stood aloft, taking Sycamore's place. He joined the circle and then they moved into a choreographed line. He stood at the back with Anastasia. She was still holding little Uchechi and stood in front of him. One by one the members of the clan took turns thanking Nyo for her ultimate sacrifice. They told her of the riches she would receive, the wonderful life she will have, the gratitude they felt. When it came to Anastasia she stood aside and let Sycamore, still looking full of fatherly devotion speak. He told Nyo not to worry, that there were no babies sacrificed by his family. Her child would be safe and live a full life of luxury and that she would die one day, but most likely from old age. He told her that they would never take the life of an innocent, and that he did not worship the owl.

'We would certainly not forfeit one who couldn't tell us that they came here today of their own free will. One without a full grasp of the intention. So behold your daughter, Uchechi, she will not be sacrificed to the goddess of the mountain.' He paused, smiled and as if he'd flipped a coin with his personality, instantaneously changed from caring to contemptuous. 'But we do need to let our friends and family know that we are not cowards and we do not stray from the path of the old ways. Did you come willingly to this place, knowing the intention of the day, which is to perform human ritual sacrifice?'

With nascent understanding, Nyo, trembling, sweating now, looked down on the surrounding horde and replied,

'Yes, but I made a mistake.'

She sounded as English as she could, subconsciously trying to assimilate her voice with theirs. A tactic people use when faced with the realisation that they are in implicit danger.

'Yes, you did, you made a grave mistake. Do you take us for barbarians? That we would take the life of an innocent child? Those days have ended, Nyo. And so have yours.'

They all moved as one organism. They grabbed her and pushed her off her feet. They raised her struggling, screaming body high above their heads. She pleaded for her life in English and in her native tongue, Yoruba.

She lost control of her bodily functions and urinated as the procession moved towards the edge of the great shaft. A waft of heat rose up from the bowels of the earth, way below them.

Mari tasted her fluids as he tried to wipe it away from his face with one hand while keeping a grip of her with the other.

They stopped at the edge of the pit and Sycamore raised his voice above Nyo's screams. The family could just about hear him, he spoke quickly.

This is what they heard. 'We give you, Nyo! Beseech her now, to the ancient tribe, to the no god. She is a gift to you, red fox. Take her as your own Lord of the left club foot.'

They all reached frenzy point. The complicity of the woman's murder ran through them as wind through the braches of a tree. They hauled her right to the edge and then threw her as one into the shaft of the volcano. Her final scream became silent. She had joined the rest of the human sacrifices, the bodies that lay at the bottom of the pit. They all lay still, a new friend adding to their number. There were rotting corpses, skeletons, some now turned to ash from the heat at the motionless depths. All supposedly dead to appease a god that over the centuries had become an amalgamation of something Sycamore Poulis knew had never existed.

19

Hue decided he stood out too much. He needed a camera; he could pass as a rich British tourist, so needed to look like one. He went to a camera shop in Manali town called Camera Magic. He bought a Canon PowerShot G X 1 compact digital. It was light enough around his neck and looked the part. He might even take a snap or two of the mountains. It was spectacular scenery, the forests and Himalayan foothills.

Emile was the type to blend in effortlessly wherever he set foot in the world. He had the knack of being in the background, moving unnoticed through shopping malls or highland peaks. If you asked somebody about the man they just passed they wouldn't recall much, if any, detail.

Emile wore a plain grey baseball cap and a dark grey Patagonia Los Lobos fleece. He wore Oakley Half Jacket sunglasses and Hanwag Tatra Top GTX walking boots with Keb trekking trousers by Fjallraven in the same, nondescript dark grey and black colours. He looked like a trekker, a

European used to the outdoors. His boots and clothes were worn but not scuffed, as Emile understood the dress code for trekking in India. Not many who trekked the arduous Himalaya did it twice. One trek was usually enough for the average hill walker from Europe who fancied a challenge. His clothes were meant to portray someone who had bought the outfit, done a little walking round the Lake District or Snowdonia to prepare and was now going to stomp around the Himalayan foothills before his Nepalese Annapurna Sanctuary adventure.

Hue on the other hand seemed to have lost track regarding his attire. He still wore the same clothes he had in England, beige chinos, shirt, blazer and brogues. The camera he'd purchased was a good move as it did make him look slightly more touristic and he could have gotten away with this look in Manali town, but not in the hippie hangout, Vashisht.

Even he had realised once they had their first, unsuccessful look around the hot spring baths and then the village of Vashisht that he stuck out like a bulbous red pustule on the face of Keira Knightly. His look just didn't fit. He had been stared at by every face he'd met, the villagers included and they had seen a few sights by the look of the place. Hue felt the stares and that's when he'd decided to buy the camera.

'What do you think, Emile? Do I blend in a bit more?' Hue asked, as he fiddled with the camera lens.

'Well, Hue, if you want honesty, no, you don't really blend in at all. You look like you just had lunch at the

British Embassy and we're in the middle of hippie heaven, searching for a travelling gangster who probably now looks more like all the youngsters do when they land for more than five minutes in this wretched country. Like him.' Emile pointed to a stereotypical traveller. He wore a pale green Indian style shirt, the type with the rounded collar, a sleeveless Nehru jacket made from rough looking wool dyed burgundy and striped trousers in various shades of blue. He wore big open army boots and had a kind of man bag made from wool and intricately embroidered in a mesh of clashing colour. He stopped on the other side of the road and mounted his Enfield 500. Thankfully it wasn't chopped to look like some rejected heavy metal from the set of Easy Rider and still had the original British classic design in place.

'We need to do two things,' said Emile.

'And what are they?' replied Hue, sternly.

'First, get you looking like you belong here and you've not just stepped out of a meeting in Whitehall and second, we need to hire two bikes. I suggest Enfield 350s.'

Hue didn't reply, he just walked off in the direction of the Rhotang Motor Cycle Hire sign. They both chose a Royal Enfield Bullet 350, as Emile had suggested. There were a few minor changes to the original British design but apart from that it was still a fully-fledged piece of classic Empire.

'Now, some clothes. Come on.' Emile led the way.

They walked up and down the main street but could not find anything that both of them agreed on. Hue was in no mood to be kitted out like some trekking hippie and Emile failed to persuade him that blending in would get him what he wanted. So in Emile's eyes it still looked as if he was so wrapped up in himself he was failing to recognise the bigger picture. This insular attitude was a problem. A new order had just come in. This latest instruction from Smart was to keep Hue safe at all cost. He surmised from this that Hue was still viewed as an asset and so he considered his own position to be safer than it was yesterday.

Finding two young travellers in this maze of winding village streets which seemed to accommodate endless streams of similar looking young travellers, was not only a chore but a costly waste of Emile's valuable time. He was willing to think outside the box for Hue who was walking at an exaggerated speed. It was almost as if he thought moving faster would get the job done quicker.

'Hue, slow down will you, please, we need to talk, plan this out. Shall we take some tea? A bite to eat perhaps?' Emile was aware he was dealing with a man obsessed. He hadn't seen Hue eat or drink anything all day. He suspected he wasn't sleeping well either as dark circles lay around his eyes, causing him to look even more intense than usual.

'Yes, tea. What a splendid idea. Is it three o'clock?'

Emile didn't really understand what he was on about so chose to ignore him.

They went into the first decent looking hotel they came across. It was called the Himachal Sanctuary. Hue ordered a pot of tea and fresh fruit salad. Emile ordered a beer and a palak paneer curry with two roti.

They sat in silence for a while until the drinks arrived. They exchanged a few pleasantries about the standard of hotels in the region. After the food was served Emile took his chance.

'How about we put up some posters saying something like, DEAN SHELBY, in capitals. Then underneath, contact me, urgent, and a phone number.'

'Smoke him out?'

'So to speak.'

'Good idea.' Hue thought for no more than five seconds. 'Problem. It gives him the heads up. He might go underground.'

'Spook him, er, yes, you're right, it might do. Well what about the girl? We could put a poster up with her name on it.'

'Better. Much better.' Hue started to eat his food instead of picking at it. 'This fruit is quite good. How's the curry?'

'Nice, tasty. There's spice but it's fairly mild, a little creamy, quite rich in fact. Here.' Emile offered him some bread as he'd finished his fruit and said, 'Try some.'

He scooped up a piece of paneer expertly with the bread, using his right hand. Years of living in tribal areas, making the most of whatever diet was available meant he was adept at eating with his hands, chopsticks or just eating things raw either plant, meat or fish. It was a common rule to eat a mostly vegetarian diet in places like India, at least until you became accustomed to the spice and microbes.

Hue ended up finishing the plate, covetously. The best way to stimulate an appetite from the starvation mode the body enters into when faced with a limited amount of food is to eat something that's easily digested. Then you find you can't stop. He then ordered another curry of sabji, a dish of mildly spiced mixed vegetables and a classic, tarka dhal. He added on five tandoori roti and onion salad that came with a wedge of lemon. They both ordered mango lassi and Hue seemed to be the most relaxed Emile had seen him since they'd left the UK.

After Hue had polished off the meal he ordered coffee and two Martel VSOP brandies.

'Those bikes.' Hue paused to sip his liquor. 'They remind me of a story.'

'Pray tell,' encouraged Emile, just happy he was communicating.

'Charles and I were in the middle of an adventure, a paid mission. It was to do with someone high up in British politics that had an agenda. Something to do with an arms deal gone sour. We were initially in the company of others, who shall remain nameless, but essentially they'd bailed, gone west, or was it east. Anyway, they left us to do the dirty work, as usual. We were using some local boys, paramilitaries. They were a rough lot, all high on something or other. Some as young as ten. Brutal way to live. Forced to fight. Kill and rape. Maiming and mutilation were routine occurrences. Those boys, the facking guns were as tall as them. Anyway, the job was to take out some top brass in Kinkala.

'Ultimately we were after a coup d'état, but we had to start somewhere. We paid these blighters ten thousand US dollars, and they took our money and tipped off the government troops to what was going on as well as our location. We were pinned down in this god forsaken village, moving from one dusty road to the next with them hot on our tail. Dogs barking, children screaming. Every corner we turned seem to set off a cock crowing or we'd wake up a sleeping pig and it would make off scurrying and squealing, giving up our position.

'Anyway, Charles saw two bikes parked outside a shop, well, kiosk really. It was still open and he bought those bikes for a thousand US each. Cheap when you think that's what saved our lives. We sped down the main street, guns blazing, bullets flying everywhere but neither of us took a single hit. We sped into the jungle and made it to the airstrip just in time. They were close enough to get a few rounds off at the helicopter. He missed all that, Charles. The things that man knew.'

'Like what?' Emile felt he was getting somewhere. 'What did Charles Bates really know?' Information sharing is a rare commodity in his line of work so when someone's guard was down take full advantage. Emile ordered two more generous measures of Martel.

'He was party to the man at the top.'

'Above Steve?'

'Well above Steve Smart.'

'How so?'

The waiter carried the drinks on a stainless steel tray. He then placed them on a round paper doily mat by the side of each guest. He put Hue's glass down on the white doily but slightly off centre. Hue immediately moved it to the midpoint of the mat and stared at the waiter's back as he walked away.

'Charles Bates worked for the family, off and on, for thirty years. He met Sy Poulis, more than once. He went to meetings at the highest level with Sy and helped set up the original '80s blueprint for the operation to keep the masses quiet.'

'The opium overflow?'

'Indeed.'

'What did he say about Sy Poulis?' Emile asked, he was now intrigued.

'Charles told me he operates from a different sphere of consciousness. His words, not mine.'

'Meaning?'

'He doesn't think like you or I.'

Emile was slightly worried, and slightly flattered that Hue put him in the same realm of understanding as himself. 'So … how then, does Sy Poulis think?'

'He only ever sees the bigger picture.' Hue shrugged. 'Apparently.'

'The New World Order?' Emile asked and Hue ignored his somewhat clichéd question.

'He sees the world on a grander scale. Charles gave the example that when he talks about a country or a people he uses the terms brothers or sisters. He sees the world as one. It's all an interconnected existence to him. Charles said it was refreshing just hearing him speak. He really sold Charles the idea of a one nation world.'

'With him at the head, of course.'

'Well, yes, I suppose, who else. He had the imagination to actually do that kind of thing, munificently creating a one nation state.'

'For the benefit of us all.'

'Exactly. For all.'

Emile had heard enough. Charles had done a number on Hue and this Sy Poulis had done a number on Charles. There had been some master manipulation at play. None of these men were easily seduced, but the stench of power is as intoxicating a smell as the garrigue on the mistral breeze and as deadly as the almond scented cyanide.

20

The daytrip was coming to an end. They all popped into their rooms and got towels and swimming costumes for the baths. They met up outside the café and went into the village, jumped in a Maruti taxi and drove through Manali town. They climbed the winding road up the other side of the valley to the tourist baths. The entrance was a fairly nondescript government run building with blue painted doors and window frames surrounding frosted glass.

Tim and Dean went to the counter and paid for an hour each. Tim advised they get two baths with a glint in his eye towards Dean.

Beki and Dean went into a big room with a sunken bath area taking up most of the space. It had an oversize tap at the end. It was a good size for two people, with space to get changed and enough of a ledge around the side of the bath to sit. There was a high window which was again frosted. There was a bare light bulb that was permanently switched on over the door.

Dean took off his shoes and socks then walked into the bath and put the monster plug in the hole. He turned the huge tap clockwise with two hands. It made a classic screeching sound and then the red-hot spring water started to gush out. He was surprised how warm it was and there was no cold tap. The sulphuric aroma was penetrating their trippy senses but after a few giggles about the smell coming from Lucifer's farts, Beki realised she was quite enjoying the rather dark thoughts and imaginings this place was conjuring up.

Today had been a day of change for her, as well as Dean. She had become insular at first as her whole understanding of reality had been challenged. Was the world pure illusion? Could things ever be as beautiful now she was coming down? She was still a little high but nothing like she'd been when they were walking. Everything she felt and saw was amazing to her that day. She'd had a lot of trouble putting anything into words and this freaked her a bit at first but then she remembered thinking 'I can talk, I just can't right now and that's fine' and the fear retreated. Then a real sense of wonder took over. She was consumed by her constantly evolving amazement at the immense beauty of the nature they were walking 'in' not 'through' as she would have said in the past. She was astounded at the completeness of it all and the complexity of simplicity. She had a wonderful day and was intent on having a wonderful evening.

Dean knew it. From the look she'd just given him, this was their time. He didn't say a word as they both discerned what to do. He walked to her, paused a second as he looked into her wide eyes once more to be sure and then as he kissed her she seemed to melt in his arms.

The steam from the bath filled the room as he fiddled with her jeans, trying hard to unbutton them from in front of her, a reversed angle. She understood his struggle and turned around, so he was pressing hard against her bottom. From this angle he managed to undo her jeans and peeled them to the floor. Then he took off her top and vest, lifting them slowly over upstretched arms. Thank God he was now perfectly placed to undo her bra. It gave him just a hint of trouble, catching on itself just the once. As she stood with her back to him she stepped off her jeans by keeping one foot on each hem and he took off all his clothes. Modestly, she kept on her pants. They were proper girly, white with tiny pink hearts in a random pattern.

She turned round and he held her close. They kissed again and he took her hand and led her into the hot bath. She saw him fully naked for the first time and thought she was in heaven. Everything she'd imagined had been given life. He had the body of a model, his broad shoulders created a full chest and as she looked down he actually had a defined six-pack. The end of his cock was level with his navel. It stood bolt upright.

The bath was full and he let her go to walk gingerly to the end and turn off the giant tap. Sounding overly loud in the relative silence, the classic ancient tap screech seemed to echo off the walls. She was a bit chicken and stood in the shallow end near the door. He liked her modesty, keeping her pants on but he'd like her naked even more so moved towards her and knelt down in the bath.

The water made his skin tingle. He stared up at her and smiled before slowly kissing her on the belly and upper thighs. He put his hands around her bottom, stroking her and then gently pressed her from behind, not enough to unbalance her but to allow her hips to move towards his kisses.

Once she had opened her legs a little he knew the time was right and he kissed her through her white and pink pants. That seemed to work so he eventually put his fingers into the top of her pants. He began to slowly pull them down.

Practical as ever, she moved her legs up, one by one, so the pants didn't get too wet. When they were off she threw them on the side. Now they were both naked, in a steamy hot bath, having kissed and made the initial moves towards each other. They walked hand in hand into the water. She noticed the water felt thick and it had flecks of grey running through it. She presumed that was the sulphur.

Dean didn't notice anything apart from enjoying the most wonderful hour of his life so far.

Kat and Mari were flying towards Kullu on one of the jets. It was an immaculate, brand new, twenty three million dollar Cessna Citation X, a luxury midsize jet. It was powered by two Rolls-Royce turbofan engines providing a long range capacity and superb in flight stability. The jet had been made to the specifications given to the UK factory. No more than two family members ever travelled in the same jet. It had two bedrooms and a seated area. Everything was paired up identically. The thinking behind the design was to promote a sense of bonding between the occupants. This plane had been specially commissioned for this flight. The landing at Kullu was on time to the minute and light as the pilot could make it on the neglected short runway.

Sycamore wanted to make this hunt the culmination of his plan to move the boys into their rightful position of power in the family. If it all went well he was confident things would be in place for the ceremony of the passing of power.

He needed to back down; he needed new blood in charge. He would always take an interest in their progression and would be there for them to consult but his mind was not as sharp as it used to be. He'd noted the memory banks were not as potent as they were only a year or two ago. He'd noticed new aches and pains coming through his bones in the mornings.

His sex life needed a boost, too. He needed extra help to get through a session of lovemaking with his partners and used a Viagra tablet, which always did the trick. He was sure this would be the move he needed to get things back on track. He was sure the problems in the bedroom were connected to the stress involved in his high ranking position.

Once he had passed on the true origins of the family bloodline to his grandsons then he would be free to do as he pleased. His life had been devoted to keeping the status quo, the order that was required. Soon he would find peace and contentment when the boys took control.

Kat, Mari and their small entourage walked through the airport without even a look from the bribed officials. Their plane took off again as soon as they were through the other side of the building. They walked straight to the awaiting Tata jeep with blacked out windows. Steve Smart was waiting aside the open passenger door.

'Kathar, Marimous. Get in and we'll talk while were travelling. It's a way up the hill and I need to give you some details before we part company.'

'How are you, Steve?' asked Kat as he got into the jeep. He was as cordial as ever.

Steve gave him a nod and the faintest of smiles. Mari said nothing and slumped down next to Kat.

'Here are your new passports and identity documents. I'm sure you read the back stories on the flight.'

Both boys answered that they had.

'Here's some images we took yesterday of Sarafian and Brooks.' Steve handed over the latest photos. 'Emile Sarafian is the best assassin we have ever employed.'

'We?' questioned Mari.

'Sorry, Marimous, *you*, have ever employed.' Steve sat up in his chair, uncomfortable about being pulled up by the supercilious boy.

The jeep went over a pothole and they all got shuffled about.

'He will be briefed in the next hour as to what is going to happen and will be told not to intrude. I can pull him out if you want me to.'

'If he's just there as a backup, then we don't need him,' Mari said.

'OK, as you wish. How are you two feeling?'

'Good thanks,' said Kat.

'Bad, Steve, I'm feeling really bad.' Mari gave Steve a frozen stare.

Steve thought he looked like a boy trying desperately to become a man.

Kat looked comfortable in his own skin. He kept an eye on the world outside. The boys had stayed in Africa, Central and South America and so they knew what scarcity was but each continent has its own take on poverty and India's was particularly ironic.

The fact that you were born into a caste resonated with the Poulis'. They fully understood this concept. The fact that it kept millions of people in abject poverty, with little or no chance of ever moving up the social strata, was just the consequence of fate to them. They justified their philosophy by desensitising themselves from the masses. They used terminology like 'cattle' to refer to the Western population. They spoke of the people of the east as 'ants'.

'So, you're both fully briefed about who you're up against?'

Both boys nodded and said yes.

'Tell me about him.'

'What?' Mari was exasperated.

'Tell me what you know about Hue Brooks, whatever was in the brief. Then, I'll give you the real Hue Brooks, the one they didn't tell you about.'

Dean held her in the palm of his hand. He was stood up in the bath as she floated next to him. She was being kept afloat by the flat of his hand in the small of her back. She had her eyes closed and a contented smile seemed set on her pretty face. He looked at her perfect breasts, lay flat being pulled down by gravity. They moved as if possessed by their own force in the small waves he was creating by moving her body slightly up and down, side to side. He stared at her body. She was pure woman. When he first touched her between her legs he had never felt anyone as soft. She was innocent in a way.

This was in massive contrast to the women Dean was used to. She just seemed to fade into his arms and he was the one who took control. She had no problem reaching orgasm; in fact she had three separate climaxes before he came. Now she was resting, happy and spent. He was ready to go again but the water was getting colder and their time was up.

He moved her towards the edge of the bath and she opened her eyes.

'Finally.'

'Finally what?' asked Dean.

'I've wanted to fuck your brains out since I very first set eyes on you.'

'I know,' he said, rather sheepishly. He was aware of what might be coming next.

'Then why the hell has it taken you so long?' She had some bitterness in her voice.

'Steady, you've started swearing again then. That's two swears in the last ten seconds.'

'Dean.' She put on her most officious tone. 'Promise me you'll never make me wait again … promise.' She went for his ribs with her right hand then when he was helpless grabbed his limp cock with her left. 'Or I'll pull this motherfucker off.'

'That is really bad language now,' he said, laughing.

Bang, bang, bang, on the door. The light flashed on and off.

'Time's up, better get dressed.' Dean climbed out of the bath.

They towelled dry and hastily pulled on their clothes against their damp bodies.

Tim and Millie were waiting outside for them, smoking a joint and watching the sunset over the mountain. They told Dean and Beki they were going to get some food in Vashisht and asked if they'd like to join them.

'No thanks,' Dean said, 'we'd better get back. We'll just chill out at home. But thanks for a perfect day.'

They went their separate ways after arranging to meet up at the café for dinner the following night. Tim said he had a plan and would talk to them about it tomorrow.

The taxi ride back to Old Manali couldn't happen soon enough for Dean. He wanted her again and again.

As they rode through town they passed two awkward looking tourists walking down Manali high street, slightly tipsy on brandy, who in turn were being stalked by three undistinguishable surveillance operatives working for Steve Smart. They were good but not so good they could fox Emile Sarafian, who had felt the net close in around him day-by-day, now hour by hour.

21

'Hue Brooks,' said Steve Smart, 'is a high end psychopath.'

The boys both looked up, he'd gained their attention.

'How do you know that?' asked Kat.

'It doesn't say that in the manual,' Mari added, with a slight concern in his voice.

'It doesn't say it, Mari, because they'd never admit it, even if they knew. Right, when they talk about his military career on paper, it looks fairly impressive. His work as a "Security Operative in several conflicts, notably the Middle East and Africa" sounds good, doesn't it?' Steve didn't wait for or expect a reply. 'So, let me fill you in about who you're dealing with here, let me explain a few things.'

This was the first time he had ever been 'alone' with the boys. He'd known them since they were kids, youngsters, seven or eight years old and he'd watched them closely. He knew they were his future and as much as it repelled him to do so, he knew keeping at least Kat alive was his best chance of keeping his six figure salary and maintaining his own survival. Kat was spoiled, but he had a compassionate side to him. Mari was just like the rest of them, maybe worse. He was totally self-centred, a classic precocious brat and a teenager to boot. He was egotistical and wilful.

The problem Steve could foresee was that Mari was the most likely to come out of the encounter with Brooks alive.

'He has less feeling or remorse than those sharks you hunt. I believe he's currently at his most dangerous as his only friend in the world is recently deceased. He will take this completely personally, as if the whole scenario was all about him being left alone in the world. I think he will stop at nothing to avenge his friend's death and this is your chance to get to him, that's his weakness. He'll be so preoccupied, so engrossed in finding this lad, Dean Shelby, he'll let his guard down.' Steve looked at the boys' faces and was pleased he still had their attention. 'Brooks has been involved in killing for many years. He's been responsible for some of the most dreadful atrocities, killing many innocent women and children, along with a countless number of genuine soldiers, paramilitaries, mercenaries and paid security forces.'

'He's killed a few cattle, so what?' Mari interjected and gave a flippant laugh.

'He's also a serial killer. He preys on young men and boys.' Steve looked straight at Mari as he spoke, hoping to quieten him down. It seemed to do the trick.

'Steve, how do you know this? It's not in the literature,' Kat asked.

'OK, well, that's true. I'm in the process of pinpointing

his movements and tying them in with several homicides at present. It seems that every time we place Mr Brooks somewhere there is a similar case of sadistic killings of young men. The latest was in Manchester only a few days ago. He messed this one up and the police have DNA evidence so as all our, sorry your, employees are DNA checked I'm awaiting confirmation from my sources that it's definitely him.'

'You seem sure,' said Kat.

'Oh, yes, I'm sure.'

'So in your eyes we'd be doing the world a favour, taking out this nasty cattle killer.' Mari smiled. 'Who I'm beginning to get a liking for. He sounds like an apt foe.'

'So he's a homo, then?' Kat asked.

'As far as we know he's never engaged in any kind of relationship or consensual sexual behaviour.'

'I was thinking, we could use Mari as a honey trap.'

Both the boys found this hilarious. Steve Smart really did wonder if he came from the same planet as they did. They seemed to have no fear, no regard for their own lives and certainly none for others.

'So, let me just reiterate the pertinent points from the manual and from my personal knowledge. He's expert in hand-to-hand combat and uses a mixture of martial techniques. He's very powerful and keeps in good physical shape for his age. He has a killer instinct and will hone in on weakness and will not hesitate to use deadly force. He seems to have no fear of consequences. He's completely self-centric and my personal belief is he's a sadistic, psychopathic serial killer... Any questions?'

'Apart from delectation with beautiful young men like Mari...' The boys pushed each other and jostled for a second. 'Does Mr Brooks have any other weakness?' Kat asked.

'Only that at present he's obsessed with finding this Dean Shelby. I'll let you figure out the rest. I'm pulling Sarafian out altogether. He's done his bit for now and I've a job in Syria for him.'

'What job?' asked Mari.

'Well, it's a mess over there. Your grandfather wants it to carry on a while longer and so we need to dispose of a few of the Syrian top brass, the ones who changed their minds, who wouldn't defect to the rebels when they saw the balance of power shift back to the government. And it's nearly a hundred years since the end of the Ottoman caliphate; it's a great time to have a new one. It's all a game, like chess. Your grandfather wants the players to compete a little longer for the prize, that's all. We do the best we can for him.'

The jeep slowed to a stop, the security detail in the front got out.

'He wants it to play out so he can sell more weapons.' Mari said this as a matter of fact.

'He needs an eternal enemy,' Kat added.

'Come on, let's go, I'm starving.' Mari brought the conversation to an end.

They both got up and without a thought to thank or say goodbye to Smart they went with the security guard up the stairs and into the foyer of the new building at the side of the road.

They went straight into the kitchen of the apartment they were to use as a base. They munched out on the food that had been cooked and delivered before they'd arrived. Mari particularly enjoyed the wild smoked salmon with lemon and dill aioli sauce and organic quinoa salad. They then took their food supplements of organic spirulina, high strength multi-vitamins and minerals.

They did some research into the local area, customs, terrain, weather patterns and then read the associated files on Hue's target, Dean Shelby. They also read up on his partner, Rebecca Aston. Everything came with precise detail.

If the Poulis family wanted to know what colour knickers she had on, they would find out.

When Hue brooks woke up he had a fuzzy head from the alcohol. It was late in the day, he'd aberrantly slept in. He was instantly annoyed.

He got up, brushed his teeth and showered. He ordered a room service brunch and while he was waiting tried doing some half-hearted press-ups and stretches.

After the greasy bacon, scrambled eggs, fried potatoes with onion and peppers, butter toast and filtered coffee on a stainless steel tray, he called Sarafian's room but got no answer. He tried Sarafian's mobile and he picked up first ring.

'Where are you?'

'On the road, called out this morning. I'm off, on a job. They assured me you have as much time as you need but I'm required elsewhere.'

'Who called you? Smart was it?' Hue asked gruffly.

'Yes, why? Who else?' Emile sounded earnest.

'Have a good trip… I have to tell you, after Charles you were always the one I … well, er, erm, enjoyed working with the most.'

'Thanks, Hue, that means a lot. Goodbye.'

Hue clicked off the phone. He knew they'd be monitoring the calls. He knew he was being watched. He wondered how much time he did actually have. Pulling Emile out was a bad sign. Why hadn't they got Emile to delete him? Surely a sip of one of his potions was all they needed to do. Perhaps Emile refused. Can you refuse them? Hue didn't know anyone who had.

He slumped down on the big bed and had a nap, something he would never normally do, but even he had to admit as a man who clung on desperately to order, these were not ordinary times.

Beki had never made love so often, so hard, so gently, so intimately, so flippin' wonderfully as this. She'd never had such varied sex as she'd had today. He was like some kind of machine.

For Dean it was as if the last twelve months frustrations of wanting her but never having her had been offloaded that night and all of the morning, too. They had sex, smoked a joint, more sex and then slept a while. Beki woke up with him going down on her and it started all over again. He'd got up, slipped out and brought back supplies. After eating they showered with a hot bucket, cleaning each other, pouring the water over each other and then once he was clean it was she who got carried away this time. She felt irresistible. Growing in confidence, she started it off again by going down on him.

As the day went on they talked about how tough it had been for him, when he used to see her at the probation office and about their dual fantasy, the one where they were having sex with each other over the office table. How crazy it was that they were both thinking the same things and that eventually their dreams had come true. She insisted he did her from behind while she bent over the desk in their room.

She pointed out that while he was on probation she was probably smoking some of his weed through Aidy. She admitted that occasionally, she used to unbutton her top before she interviewed him and he used to stare at her with complete lust in his eye.

'Are you surprised? Have you actually seen yourself?'

They eventually got up at five in the afternoon. They had another hot shower and then met up with Tim and Millie in the café for dinner. They ordered lemon soda, coffee and momos. While they waited for the food they smoked some of Tim's excellent charas.

'Where did you buy this stuff?' asked Beki.

Tim smiled.

'That's what we wanted to talk to you two about,' Millie replied for him.

'We're going on a charas hunt and wondered if you two wanted to join us?'

'Hell, yes,' said Beki.

Dean was a little grumpy as he'd envisioned the next few days were going to be mainly spent in bed, not trekking up the Himalayas scoring dope.

'Where to?' Dean asked.

'Thela valley, there's a man I know who helps me out.'

'Is his name Manu?'

'Wow, how do you know Manu?'

'Well, I don't but we met a guy in Delhi, Kiwi Bob. He said find this guy and tell him hello. Said he's got good stuff.'

'Kiwi Bob, Kiwi Bob.' Tim searched his memory banks. 'Na, don't know him. Might know the face. Well, it's fate then. We set off first thing.'

'And he means first, thing,' Millie added.

'Up at five and away by six. It's a fair journey. Taxi to the start of the valley and then hopefully we'll make it to the village by dark.'

'What do you think?' Dean asked Beki, somewhat hopefully, now she knew it involved a pre-dawn alarm and a trek.

'Fab, can't wait. Come on, dinner, we're going to need you, fill up for the trekking tomorrow.'

When the plate of momos arrived they ordered rajma, a mountain speciality of kidney beans and tomato curry, a mixed dhal, an aloo palak, potato and spinach and a mutter paneer, peas and cheese. Accompaniments were one plain, one veg fried rice and eight tandoori roti. They had cherry pie for pudding and Horlicks with the last couple of chillums before settling their bills for the rooms and the food with the Brigadier.

The Brigadier said he would order them a taxi for six in the morning and told them it was good they were going to bed early as he doubted they could make it to Thela village in a day without an early start.

Dean and Beki spent half an hour packing and had a final spliff in bed. They made love again, slowly this time, before cuddling up and falling to sleep in each other's arms.

22

After a night sat at the hotel bar, sipping his way through a bottle of imported Johnnie Walker Red, Hue was very drunk. He gave the barman a wave goodnight and he plodded back to his room, bumping into the walls down the corridor more than once.

He slept in his clothes. As he hadn't shut the curtains and his sleep pattern had been disturbed lately anyway, he was woken shortly after dawn by the light coming from the sun. Then there was the need to both evacuate and imbibe water.

He lay on the bed and his head started to spin. Once the water hit his stomach he started to feel giddy again. He got up and looked out of the window, over the gardens and further to the forest and hilltops.

What was he going to do? He could run but he knew they'd find him. He could do nothing and wait until they called to finish him here. Sit like a rabbit in a cage waiting for the fox to appear. That wouldn't do at all.

Fack it, just carry on. Just do what you came here to do, Hue Brooks. Stop this boozing, drowning your sorrows and get to the job in hand. Finish this job and then start another, or don't.

He brushed his teeth and gagged as the toothpaste hit the back of his throat. What was he going to do with two Royal Enfield bikes? Something will come up, it had to. He seemed more hopeful this morning. He had a good feeling about the day. He liked being alone, having Emile around was fine but he worked well by himself. Nobody telling him what to wear or what to do. Now things would be done the Hue Brooks' way or no way at all.

The breakfast was good. No grease on the bacon, crispy, as he preferred it. Maybe because he'd gone to the restaurant. The eggs were fresher, too, they lacked the slight skin they possessed the day before at brunch and were as soft on the outside as in the middle. Even the toast was served warm. He asked for a strong filter coffee and it came just as he needed it, with an extra caffeine kick. He felt great, almost as if the hangover was spurring him on. The fact he was still a little drunk from the night before never entered his mind.

After the hearty breakfast he walked outside the hotel into the crisp mountain air and perused the taxi rank. He went back inside and walked over to the desk. The old Hue was back, picking up on the minutiae, the inescapable signals that gave people away and gave him the information he needed.

With the young Indian woman behind the desk, it was

the way she froze when she saw him.

'Mangla, I believe you know me?' Hue paused, gripping her eyes with his glare. 'Hue. Hue Brooks. I'm a friend of Harjeet.'

'Oh, yes, sir, Harjeet.'

'I've seen him talking to you, Mangla, our mutual friend.'

'Yes, sir.' She gave a nervous giggle. She forced a smile. 'Talking, why not?'

'What did he tell you? Anything … about who I was looking for?'

Mangla looked about furtively, breaking his trance but the morning was a quiet time in the hotel lobby, nobody had checked out yet and nobody had arrived early. There were no allies around to turn to.

'Nothing, sir, we do not discuss the client's business.'

'Now, Mangla. Let us get this straight. I know you're lying, you know you're lying so just tell me what you do know and I'll leave it be.'

She couldn't comprehend just how she felt threatened. It was if a wild animal was stood over the other side of the reception desk. A very well mannered, polite wild animal but she got the impression if she didn't tell him the truth she would suddenly have her throat ripped out. She felt he was just like the leopards that came down from the mountain at night, to take the chained up dogs near her home village. They went straight for the throat, excellent hunters. They clawed your belly out for an instant kill.

'He asked about the English couple who left that

morning and I told him they went with an Ambassador cab.'

'Who drives that cab, Mangla?'

She didn't hesitate. 'Anu. He's outside, waiting for a fare.'

Hue moved with the alertness of a hunting tiger. It reminded Mangla of pictures she'd seen on television of predators in the jungle, speed and stealth in one fluid movement. He was out of the door before she'd realised she was safe.

He walked straight up to the old fashioned car, even though it was fifth in the row. This attracted the attention of the other drivers. He opened the door and got straight into the passenger seat.

Anu was still sat reading the paper at the wheel when he registered there was some white man next to him. He looked up, startled, suddenly feeling the world fall out of his stomach but just stared straight ahead. The other drivers kept an eye on things after they saw the foreigner get in his cab, either directly or by adjusting their mirrors. Even the ones who thought Anu a scoundrel would rally round if needed. They had all come across the odd foreigner who thought they could throw their weight around. This was still the Kullu Valley, though, and as everyone with any amount of sense knows, you don't mess with mountain folk. Hue was instantly aware of the eyes upon him.

'Anu. Do you want to be a rich man today?' Hue knew how to push the right buttons.

'I want to be a rich man tomorrow, too.'

'Good. We both want the same thing, then.' They looked at each other for the first time. 'The story, the one you gave Harjeet.' He paused, building a little gravitas. 'It doesn't … add … up.'

'Oh, that story, about the English couple.'

One of Anu's friends came to the driver's window and asked in the local Pahari dialect if he needed any help. Anu said he was fine but to keep an eye on the guy, because he stank of booze.

Hue gave the man a polite smile and he went on his way.

'So, Anu. I'm right in guessing you didn't drop them at the hot springs in Vashisht after they'd checked out of this hotel, with all their baggage on their backs, am I.'

'Well. How much are we talking here, boss?'

'How much do you earn a day? On a good day?' Hue asked, aware it wouldn't be much.

'Good day, RS500, after expenses.'

'So, if I was to say five thousand for the correct information, how would that seem?'

'Good, very good. Come on, let's go.' Anu started the car and pulled out of the queue without a look or a word to anyone. The prospect of one month's salary was too much to miss. He didn't want anyone else knowing his business either. He'd take a drive to see Vihar. He got the impression this guy was after these two for reasons he didn't want to get involved with. Way too much for him, but Vihar was a different story. Rumour had it he'd killed a high ranking police officer and never got charged with it. He would be good to have around if this guy proved trouble and if he was throwing money around like this, then maybe they could fleece him, too.

'Where are we going?' Hue asked after a couple of minutes.

'To a friend house, for chai. Five minutes. No problem. Just not good doing business there, too many eyes around. This is very bad area for blah, blah. Always talking, talking, talking. Blah, blah.'

'Yes, I get the picture,' interrupted Hue. He'd wait this one out, see what came. After all, he'd changed his luck today. Hue understood that there was no such thing as luck. He knew that people created the luck around them by their own actions.

They drove to Vihar's house and left the car outside the path. The sweet smoke from the burning pine wood wafted about in the airy breeze. The dogs barked their traditional welcome. Vihar appeared in the doorway, he had an axe in his right hand. He was dressed in the same clothes as always, apart from a new hat. Anu thought he must have bought it with the money from the last deal they'd done, the one with the Englishman.

'Vihar,' Anu said as they approached. He then spoke in Pahari. He told him not to speak in Hindi as this guy was not who he seemed and may understand some words, even if he wasn't fluent. He spoke about the money he was banding around using slang words and the information he wanted on the English couple.

Hue got the gist of the conversation. He didn't

concentrate on what they said as much as how they'd said it. Non-verbal language changes slightly from culture to culture but a skilled interpreter can gleam any major meanings.

Hue saw that Anu was this man's subordinate. That he was trying to explain and possibly get advice on the situation. The older man said little and kept his composure. He held everything in. Hue liked that about him. He also liked the way he kept his hand on the woodcutter.

'This man will help you. He is willing to work for the same amount you pay me, RS5000.'

'How will he help me? Why can't you help?'

'I'm known around here. I have my good family name and want to keep it so. This man has no family and he is willing to help you find these foreigners. Just take the help on offer please, boss.'

The two Indian men spoke again and Vihar disappeared inside his house, leaving his woodcutter resting against the outside wall.

'Sit.' Anu offered him a seat.

Hue sat down and thought about things. He'd come this far, just carry on, get the job done. He liked this Vihar. He looked to Hue like a proper man. He disliked Anu. His brashness. He would like to take a walk with him though, when this was all over.

Vihar appeared with three glasses of very sweet and pungent chai. He sat down then so did Anu who passed round a packet of unfiltered Wills cigarettes. Both men took one and they all lit up. Hue didn't smoke, unless it seemed the right thing to do of course. He'd sat with tribal leaders, stood with dignitaries and smoked cigarettes and cigars when the occasion called for it. Bonding, especially male bonding, often took place alongside pursuits that were either immediately life threatening, parachuting for instance, or when there was a tokenistic nod to death over the long term. These were things like smoking, drinking or a bar fight. The social crutch that was the cigarette broke down barriers of mistrust and promoted a shared experience.

'Why?' was all Vihar said to Hue.

'Revenge.'

'For what, revenge.'

'For a friend. A brother. A man.'

'Good. Five tousand PER day.' Vihar emphasised his speech with a raised finger. 'Noting less.'

'OK, five thousand per day it is.'

'Give him five tousand now.' Vihar nodded towards Anu.

Hue pulled out a wad of rolled cash and peeled off ten five hundred rupee notes. He handed them over to Anu.

'OK, Anu?'

'Yes boss, very fine.'

'Now, where did you take them and if I don't get the truth this time, I'll take his axe over there and gut you like a strung up goat.'

Anu gulped, Vihar laughed.

'The Mana café, Old Manali, boss.'

'So why all the mystery?'

Anu looked at Vihar who shrugged and told him, in Hindi now, that he may as well tell Hue the full story.

'He wanted some smoke so I took him here, to Vihar house. He was supposed to wait in the cab but after only five minutes he arrived here, uninvited so to speak. Vihar a proud man, good man. He doesn't want one uninvited guest. Sold him makka wakka, fake charas. I was worried about my job, if word got to the hotel about some dealings or other.'

'So you made up a false trail?'

'Yes, boss. Sorry, boss.'

Vihar had a right go at Anu in Pahari, telling him he had nothing at all to be sorry about. Vihar scooped up the empty chai glasses and put them in a blue plastic washing up bowl that lay on the floor, outside in his garden. Half the glass peeked out of some grey water in the bottom of the bowl.

Hue knew Vihar was still listening even though he was pretending to rinse out the chai glasses.

'I may well have done the same. Don't apologise. Let us all move on. It's history, past, gone. Can you go with me to this Mana place?'

'No, but he can.'

'Vihar?'

'Yes.' Anu was sat slumped now, head down.

Hue turned in his seat and spoke to Vihar's back.

'I've hired two 350 Bullets. Fancy a ride to Old Manali?'

'You pay, I go.' Vihar turned to Hue and shrugged. 'Business.'

'Is business,' added Hue.

They all drove back towards the hotel in Anu's taxi and he let them out a quarter mile from their destination, down the hill road. He did a three point turn amidst the beeping traffic and headed off to his favourite brothel in Manali town to relieve some stress with his five thousand rupees.

Vihar and Hue walked slowly uphill. It was Hue who opened the limited conversation.

'What's so good about the smoking up here?'

'Best quality in whole country.' Vihar made a wide circular movement with his arms, and then held out a hand. 'Now, look.' Vihar held out his palm to reveal a black ball of charas and a smaller red ball next to it.

They stopped at the side of the road with cars, motorcycles and rickshaws passing them by with a beep of their horns, just to let them know they were there and had passed.

'This is charas, best quality and this is—'

'Opium,' said Hue, before Vihar could get to the end of his sentence.

'You know opium?'

'Oh yes, my man.'

Vihar wasn't sure he liked that phrase but let it go, this once.

'This piece, three fifty.' Vihar looked him in the eye for the first time. 'Take.' He gave Hue the piece; both men knew it was a gift, for free. Hue wasn't the only operator in this fledgling relationship.

As they walked along Vihar and Hue compelled the passing drivers and some of their passengers to rubberneck.

They looked an odd pair but both had an air of danger about them, a fact not lost on Steve Smart's security detail.

They arrived at the hotel on foot and departed riding two 350 Royal Enfield Bullet motorcycles. No helmets, the chilly wind streaming through their hair, a symbol of freedom and a look of the outlaw about them. They sped uphill, overtaking the slower moving vehicles that were being forced into a slog by the steadily increasing gradient. Hue followed Vihar's lead and beeped his horn as he passed a driver or fellow rider.

They slowed down as they entered the village and gained a mixture of stares from the Israeli bikers. Some were curious as to the nature of the relationship between a white European and a local. The others just admired the way they rode into town and soaked in the air of menace that extended around them, hoping to clasp some of it for themselves. It was always a good prop to have on the road, looking tough. It meant car drivers kept their distance.

This view came from the men and women who had a world view moulded from their service in the army. The special forces operatives, the night patrollers, the intelligence gatherers and the interrogators. Hue noticed these lost, soulless men and women, mostly in their early twenties, the ones who were constantly hanging out. The ones smoking too much, riding their bikes without any style to call their own, acting dismissively and aggressively to anyone they meet on the way. They had all been actively serving in the military weeks or months before. Hue felt their pain, he knew it well.

The older crowd who settled for the hippie dream India gave them were usually the most affected. They were the fighter and helicopter pilots, black ops intelligence and espionage operatives. They had been through the system and had been spat out with a lump sum of shekels. They were determined not to be suckered back in, at least for now. They'd had too much time to think. One of the best reasons for smoking good dope is it gives the user one pointed concentration. This is an excellent state of mind to deeply explore a train of thought.

When Shiva's neon blue light appears in your thoughts, in the mind's eye, the internal switch is turned to on and when the necessary conclusions are determined, the one generally deemed by all, is the necessity of love for your fellow man, planet and every living entity. So after a single or a series of revelations that cannot be ignored, the charas smoker follows their path of knowledge gained from their own insight and stays in the mountains, beaches and jungles of the east. Here they can spend their days recuperating from their pain, curing their diseased minds from the abuse they'd suffered. They can heal their inner child or at least temporarily forget. This could be anything from religious proselytization from birth to state sponsored indoctrination. Whatever the reason, for many young people, getting very stoned in India is a better option than being in the army in Israel.

There were no Israeli customers in the Mana café that morning, though. They mostly kept to themselves, separate, in a kind of safety in numbers mentality. The foreigners in the café were European, mainly English and instantly recognisable as such to both motorcycle riders as they let their bikes glide to a stop, engines cut. They came to a halt over the other side of the path from the café, with its open plan tables.

'You vait. I know him. The Brigadier, owner.' Vihar gave a chin forward, jutting, upright nod with each short phrase.

Hue thought it best to leave it local to local and although he got off his bike and put it on the side stand, he just sat back on the seat, a leaning side saddle, as relaxed as he could be, waiting and watching, scanning and sensing.

23

After another briefing from Steve, with the latest information about Hue's whereabouts and the fact he was now travelling on a motorbike, the boys received the best news of the day. They too were getting bikes. Steve had already gained permission from Sycamore and he had ordered two BMW 1200 RTs in black. They were a go-anywhere bike, powerful for a cruise but also good for off road and scrambling.

The boys were given directions and they both had a weapon. Mari had a knuckle knife. It had a six inch blade and a spiked knuckle guard. Kat was given a nunchaku. They were made of steel and had a concealed, spring loaded knife hidden at the base of each handle. If he needed the knife he just had to twist the base clockwise.

The boys had spent years training for this day. Hours in the gym, combat exercise with the best teachers. They had studied and trained more or less every day, for the last ten years. They didn't start their education until they were nine.

The girls started theirs at eight as they matured earlier. Before then the children of the ruling elite were free to daydream and play, to develop their imagination, to wonder through their childhood. By the time they'd reached nine the boys were both interested and capable of learning. They could properly hold a pen, they could concentrate for more than a minute and they were comfortable sitting still for more than thirty seconds.

Since then they had been educated in a unique manner. They were asked their opinion on things all the way through their learning. They were asked to think things through for themselves and come to their own opinions about a subject or problem. Being right or wrong was not the issue; there were never any tests, never any stress. Once the basics had been taught it was a cooperative learning experience. This gave the children a way of thinking for themselves, a sense that any problem could be solved by a creative approach and a will to achieve.

This was in stark contrast to the education system Dean had been through. His was more akin to containment, to a legal prison for children. The learning was through reparation and there was little or no scope for actually working things out and empowerment. All the power in Dean's school had been with the authority. The children were barely classed as people, more like drones. The whole education system was a game. The aim was to turn out workers to keep the system churning. It was to rotate the lives of the masses on a permanent hamster wheel. To make sure they worked their arses off to get nowhere. To give them just enough to survive in relative comfort, but never too much. If they all had too much then there would be no incentive, no 'need' to work hard, to step up the ladder. The problem with their ladders was that they never even got half way up because then the wheel would turn again and something would keep them permanently at the bottom.

Dean always heard his nana and poppa talk about their contemporaries in terms of 'he or she was a hard worker'. This being the ultimate compliment they could bestow. It never occurred to them that all their hard work got them nowhere. They all struggled through their late years. Just eating hot food and heating their house in winter took most of poppa's pension.

The biggest surprise to the people who ruled the world was that the masses kept on falling for it. They were constantly astonished that the millions of ants and cattle believed the propaganda from their televisions and newspapers. Who did they think owned the televisions and newspapers? Who did they think fed them this constant drivel of fear and hoopla?

Sy's best idea this decade had been a new television show The Arena. What a lark. It had been sold to almost every country in the world. It was a mixture of all the worst prime time fodder. Contestants had to outdo each other in a variety of fields. These were combatant, where contestants had to literally fight it out with each other. This was in a boxing ring with slightly oversized, padded gloves and then on an assault course. The assault course was outdoors and full of mud and freezing cold water between the obstacles.

The contestants were encouraged to spend as much time pulling back or fighting their opponents as they were scaling the ramps and crawling under the barbed wire. Clothes were ripped off and the television screens were often full of blurred patches to cover the genitals, bottoms and breasts on show as they battled it out on the course. This puritanical view of nudity persisted to this day. This was another amazing fact the elite could never really understand.

They believed it came from the church and its influence on the common mind set. It was still taught that nakedness was shameful and it was taught through myth at a tender age, before learning should really be exposed to the delicate mind of a child. So the myth was perpetrated from generation to generation, down the line. Innocent Adam was corrupted through the pernicious Eve and he realised he was naked and shamed by his penis. Pre-Christianity the penis was worshipped, and still is in certain cultures. Even they who honour the Shiva lingam in India are tainted by the Victorian values of the recent European rulers. If one needed to be reminded of the old ways, take a good look at Khajuharo temple in India, the pyramid temple of Candi Sukuh in Java, Indonesia or the Cerne Abbas giant in Dorset, England. This was more suited to the Poulis view of sex and nudity.

The hidden use of pornography through the mainstream web was proof if any were needed that the vast majority desired an outlet for their fantasies but they all kept their public faces clean. They were happy to watch hardcore, S&M, bestiality, coprophilia, child abuse and rape online but would then go and pick up the kids from school and ask what they had learnt about maths or religion that day, nod politely to their neighbours, chat with their friends and pass the time of day with their child's teacher.

At least in the world of the ruling elite all these tastes could be catered for in an honest and open way. The truth was that this rarely needed to happen. The elite were generally very earthy in their sexuality. There was never any good or bad desire. They were brought up to be sexual beings in whatever fashion they naturally developed and so most just developed into people who had sex with other age appropriate people. They didn't crave youngsters. They didn't want to watch others defecate on glass tables. They didn't want to rape or corrupt as they felt empowered in themselves for being whoever they turned out to be.

Kat was definitely into women but sometimes he fancied the odd guy. It was nothing more than playing about with his own erotic fantasies and he'd never actually had sex with a man, but the thoughts and feelings had been there. Kat liked the idea of it but when he actually pondered the reality of sex with a man, the bits and pieces, it started to turn him off.

Mari was so heterosexual, it was strange for the others around him. He was thought to be hiding something by those who didn't fully understand his ways. Those closest to him knew he was just an out and out boy, nothing more or less. He loved competition and physical activity. Half the idea from the Arena came from watching Mari compete and play with Kat.

He was at every girl he laid eyes on. He tried his luck and wasn't bothered if he failed, he'd just move on to the next challenge. Sooner or later he'd find one who was impressed by his arrogance and money. The boys weren't encouraged to make it with the cattle but it was impossible to stop them.

As they rode their BMWs they both felt as free as birds. As they were used to having either security or other employees around them constantly, it was a great feeling, knowing they were alone in the world. No more communications from Steve, no more intelligence from his watchers. It was their hour: the hunt was on.

'This is it … this is what it's all about,' Kat shouted to Mari before accelerating away, his front tyre lifting up from the road with a mini wheelie.

Mari took the bait and burned out his back tyre in a wheelspin trying to keep up. The smoke from the scorched rubber tasted acrid in the air.

They weaved in and out of the traffic on the Manali highway and shot down the hill, soon coming to the road off left, heading towards Thela valley. They slowed down the pace as the traffic was lighter now and the road narrower, winding like a moving snake. This meant most of the time they could ride along next to each other. Now and again one would fall back if a fancily decorated, burnt orange painted lorry came towards them, but most of the time this riding position allowed a shouted conversation to take place.

'Bet I take him, knife through the neck.'

'Nah, I'll knock him out and then slice open his throat.'

'You take him down and I'll stab through his ribs, jolt it up into his heart.'

There was a loud beep, beep, from a white Tata 4X4, headlights flashing, who wanted to overtake them. Kat dropped back and let the impatient tourist go ahead. He caught back up to Mari. 'Shall I pull out my nunckucks and rattle his window?'

'Do it. Do it,' Mari chanted.

Kat pulled out the steel bars connected with a chain. They were an excellent weapon. Originally used for cropping wheat in China, they became popular after martial weapons were outlawed. A fighting system was devised using regular agricultural tools like sickles and rakes. Nunchaku or nunchucks were made famous by Bruce Lee when he wielded two sets at a time, a highly impressive stylised display. The reality of using nunchucks is very different from these katas or set moves. The authentic martial artist does not spend five minutes swirling sticks of metal around their own head and elbows as they know too well this is going to lead to them seriously hurting themselves and not the opponent.

As a show of force it could be a deterrent but a real expert in nunchucks will strike from a hidden place, usually holding the two bars together behind an arm or if facing an opponent head on, hiding them round the back of the body, the end of a bar in each hand with the arms straight down the sides or slightly bent at the elbows for a hip length attack. The recoil from the first strike is the most important part of the blow. This generally determines the way things are going to pan out. A few generalisations may occur. Either the opponent will run or they will stay and fight. If they run and you think they can be caught, a wide, sweeping strike to their ankles may take them down. A last resort to a running man is to throw the nunchucks and hope they hit or tangle in the legs of the runner, slowing or taking them down. Once the opponent is on the floor it should be a simple task to finish them off, but you must be aware, if you have thrown your weapon, they may pick it up and use it against you.

If they do that then get in close, because only a skilled martial artist would have the knowledge and ability to successfully use the nunchucks as a club or even the third method taught, the pinch. If you can get the chain around a limb, for instance a wrist, then wrap the bars around it, the pain created from the pinch is incredibly debilitating. The user can gain complete control over the opponent and then use a kick to the knee or back of the legs to drop them.

If the opponent stands and fights then you have generally not given them a good enough first blow. Anything to the temple or head, elbow, knee, shin would send a person running if they were still capable. A body blow or one that didn't connect to bone would not be sufficient to cause a flight reaction in all but the lamest of foe. On top of this, if the user receives unpredictable recoil, then the opponent could take the advantage and move in close. The unpredictability of the recoil is where a skilled martial artist, one who has spent hundreds or thousands of hours in drill, perfecting their response to jump back, has the advantage over a novice. Gaining mastery over the strike means dealing with many forces at once and reacting to all the possibilities with speed and precision. The faster the arm and wrist move the branch through the air determines the amount of torque created. A reasonable strike can generate a 300km/h blow, with 350 joules of kinetic energy. This is the equivalent of the average bullet fired from a pistol. The difference between a bullet and a nunchuck hitting the body is all about size and shape. The bullet penetrates the body easily due to its pointed tip and spinning velocity. A nunchuck will cause the most damage when the edges hit, that is why Kathar was using a Japanese style, hexagonal design rather than the round Chinese sticks.

Kat decided to teach this guy a lesson. Mari watched as he accelerated away, slipping his clutch this time to create a sustained wheelie. He kept the bike at 7000 revs and the throttle steady. He was pulling a cruising wheelie now, nunchucks held tight under his right arm, front wheel at head height, not leaning forwards or back but keeping his weight centralised.

Kat flicked his throttle and the bike came down to the normal riding position with both wheels on the ground. He dropped a gear and accelerated until he was level with the 4x4.

Mari was lagging behind. He was less comfortable on a bike than Kat but refused to be outdone. He thought he'd wheelie, too. He thought he knew the technique. He was so concentrated on copying Kat he didn't notice the 4x4 had slammed on his brakes when Kat whacked the top of the car with a branch of his nunchucks.

The car driver, a tourist from Delhi staying in Manali, chauffeuring his wife and two children, thought a tree had hit them at first. Once he realised it was the crazy biker who'd smashed something onto the roof of the car and sped off, instinctively he hit the brake.

Mari realised he was going into the back of the car and leaned forwards to get the bike down from the attempted wheelie. He also used his brakes and leaned over to his right to try and lay the bike down. The adrenalin rushed through him, slowing down his perception of time and giving him the extra few tenths of a second he needed to make this judgement. Luckily he was going slowly enough and by the time he hit the car was far enough down so that the bike took the brunt of the collision. As the car had not come to a complete stop, the crash and then the slide along the tarmac was not as traumatic as it could have been if he'd smashed into a stationary lump of metal.

The car driver wasn't hanging around, though. He did a three point turn and went back the way he'd come. He wasn't waiting for the other guy to come looking for his friend and start smashing up his pride and joy again.

Mari lay with his bike. He didn't move apart from switching off the engine. The handle bars and canopy at the front, along with the side panel storage boxes at the back saved his legs. As he'd lay the bike down in a reasonably controlled manner and not crashed into the back of a completely static object, there were no broken bones. Coming out of the attempted wheelie and braking saved his body and pride.

Kat was oblivious to the accident as he was away and round about five bends before he realised he should slow down and wait for Mari. He was disappointed the 4x4 hadn't given chase but he was just happy to be on a bike again. He'd loved riding since he was a child. He loved scooters, cycles, skateboards but most of all motorbikes. He loved scrambling best. Second stunts and third just plain cruising on a long stretch of straight, empty road. He'd not done much of this though, none on a real open highway, not really. He'd just imagined it when he was riding bikes up and down on the private airfield the family owned. He'd pretend it was this day, this very moment, when he was truly free for the first time. He had waited patiently for this, for today. He had hoped beyond hope they would have bikes but there had been so many variables as to where and when the hunt would take place it was sheer luck that they'd been riding today.

He turned round and slowly rode back down the winding bends until he saw Mari, slumped against a tree with the bike still on its side.

Kat laughed inside but then it hit him, it juddered up from his belly and the laugh came out loud. He had a big advantage now, he was the best placed to make the kill if Mari was injured. There was a lot at stake; it meant everything to some. They would all ask who had made the kill.

He pulled up, revved the engine for a touch of theatrics and killed it when it settled on a purr. 'What happened?' Kat asked, innocently.

'I was speeding up behind and he broke. His brake lights came on and I had to lay the bike down.'

'You alright?'

'No broken bones, bit shaken up.'

Kat moved close and offered his hand to help Mari up. 'Come on then, get up. Best thing you can do is get back on, straight away.'

Mari was in shock and wasn't aware of the severe bruising he'd sustained to his side. He wasn't aware of the pain he'd be in or that the adrenalin was still active in his brain. He got up with the help of Kat's arm. They held each other forearm to forearm as Kat pulled and Mari lifted himself up, putting most of the weight on his left leg.

'You're going to be sore in the morning.'

'I know. Come on help me lift it up.'

The boys pulled the 230kg bike up from its sorry position. Kat took it and clicked open the stand.

Mari checked his gravel rash and rubbed his shoulder and hip.

'Come on, Mari, get on. We'll stop at the next town and get you something sweet.'

Hesitantly Mari got on. He clicked the ignition and pulled up the stand. Then he realised he should have pulled up the stand first.

Kat just gave him that knowing look, the one he'd given him all his life when he'd taken things too far, when he'd overdone it and when he royally messed things up.

Mari gingerly rode off in first and then upped the gears until he was taking the bends like nothing had happened.

24

The four travellers arrived at Manu's house well before dark. They were in plenty of time. Manu wasn't in but his son, Tara, a lanky teenager who spoke good English said if they could wait he'd fetch him. They all sat around outside the ramshackle home. There were goats with their kids dotted about, eating practically anything they could find. There were chickens pecking the ground and crows, too many crows. Their caw wasn't pleasant, their mean gait intimidating to other, smaller birds. They were survivors though, adaptable, never ones to back away from trouble. As the evening was coming in the crows started to circle. All four were watching as they smoked a chillum but Dean couldn't take his eyes off them. He was trying to work out what was going on as they flew in a controlled frenzy above them. They flew straight at each other and waited until the last second before collision for one to change flight.

Then things grew darker, both in the evening sky and with the birds. They stopped the games of chicken and all started to attack one young crow.

'It's called a murder of crows,' said Millie.

'They are dark creatures. Look, they're all going after the baby one,' Beki added.

'Survival of the fittest, nature's way,' said Timo.

'They're taking out the weak link, the one who lets the others down. It's got to be done.' Dean spoke grimly, with full understanding of what was taking place.

They never got to know if the young crow survived as the birds flew off chasing the young one down.

Manu arrived with his son Tara and welcomed Tim and introduced himself to the others. He said hello first to the two girls, then Dean, while Tara went into the house.

Dean spoke after Manu said hello. 'I'm Dean, a friend of Kiwi Bob.'

Manu looked completely blank. 'He said hello?' Manu didn't know who Kiwi Bob was, not by name at least. He asked them to sit and Tara came back with a bundle wrapped in cotton cloth. He gave it to Manu and he opened it out on the ground.

Dean noticed his fingers wore rings. There were two on each hand. They looked like gold with different coloured stones in them. One blue, one green, one red and the last was small, sparkling and looked yellow.

'Two quality. Thish bagicha, RS400, thish jungli, very nice shmoke, RS850.'

'850?' asked Tim.

'Yes, set price, no likey no buyey. Thish Asda price.' He broke off a piece from the jungli. 'Here, take, tryey before you buyey, nooo problem.'

He seemed a bit camp to Beki. He was certainly a character. He gesticulated wildly as he spoke, almost telling his story with his arms and hands.

Tim made a chillum and while he was mixing it, made small talk with Manu. They talked about the police cutting down some fields and about the dams the government had built locally. He said they had better roads now but that meant it was easier for the cops to get up high. He joked they were all too fat years ago, living off the baksheesh, the bribes, the farmers paid them. Now there was more state pressure to be seen to be doing something, so everyone had lost the odd field. However they were in the process of working out a deal with the cops. They would plant some low lying fields each year so the cops could cut them down and not have to walk too high up.

'A kind of sacrificial field?' laughed Tim.'

'Exactly brother, so the copsh stay fat. They can take some shnaps and show the even fattier copsh in Shimla, that they're tackling the drugs menashes.'

Nobody realised that after smoking Manu's stuff they were all sat in a circle talking and joking about the cops and corruption, telling stories and laughing with the proper giggles.

'I'm starving,' realised Beki, out loud.

It seemed to hit a chord and everyone agreed they should go and find a café and a place to stay in the village. They all said that this was the best weed they'd had in years. Everyone bought a few tolas and off they went.

Beki's stomach was rumbling. They'd walked from the end of the road up to Manu's house and it had taken a good few hours. The village of Arna was about a half hour walk from Manu's and was a welcomed sight. It was pitch black and cold by the time they'd arrived. They'd had to use their torches for the walk and on the way they all had wittered on about the pros and cons of the traditional handheld Maglite, versus the newer style head torches. Then about the new types of bulb, halogen, krypton, LED and what gave the best light out at night if you needed the loo or if you were out walking in the dark, as they were. It was agreed that the bright halogens were better for walking but a softer LED better for the bedroom. They were all completely engrossed in talking about torches and bulbs. They were very stoned.

They booked into the first place they'd come to, View Guesthouse and ate dinner there. It was basic, lightly spiced dry cabbage curry, dhal and rice. It was home cooked and did the trick. Beki was full of food, very stoned and very tired. She had a happy contented smile on her face after dinner that Dean loved to see.

After a last spliff and a cup of mint tea they all went to bed. Beki was asleep within five minutes and Dean nodded off soon after, dreaming of the crows circling overhead and his old friend JT.

Vihar looked at Hue as he slept. He wondered about this odd fellow. He was a full Englishman, full of manners, full of money and full of hate. Vihar studied people. He never appeared to, they would never have known but he did. Most people he met were fools. This one was different. They had arrived at Arna village after the Brigadier told him they had gone to Thela valley, as it was the obvious place to stay for at least the night, but there had been no sign of this Dean. There were about five guest houses in the village and a few rooms you could rent straight from the families. They hadn't time to check these out as it was now dark so Hue had said they should sleep and make an early start. They were staying at the Rainbow Guesthouse in a double with twin beds. It was a basic room with attached shower and toilet. The only light was from a candle Vihar had lit when Hue fell asleep. He got a cigarette from his packet of ten Wills. He leaned over and lit the end from the candle on the windowsill and smoked it slowly, with purpose, thinking about this Englishman and what he was capable of if they found this foreigner, Dean.

Kat and Mari found a room in the worst kind of Indian hotel, a motel. It wasn't cheap by Indian standards as the owner knew anyone who stayed there had no other choice and would never be a returning guest. It was stay there or chance the mountain roads at night. Signs for the end of the road started a mile back. If you're near the end of the road, can't face going back down it and can't trek up into the valley at night, it was a better option than the car or roadside. The boys didn't know there was a much better place round the corner, right at the end of the road that was clean and well run. They just stopped at the first place they'd come to.

Their room was truly disgusting. They were the only guests in the place. There was a smell from the drains like an open sewer in the room. The beds had a worn thin Indian-made quilted mattress that cost a few hundred rupees in the market. They had sheets that had been washed but were still stained with blotches of yellow and brown. Urine and blood sprang to Kat's mind. Their quilts smelt damp and musty, made in a similar way to the mattresses, cheaply.

The attached toilet had turds floating in it. That explained the smell. Kat threw a bucket of water down to try and flush them away.

The bowl itself was stained brown and black from years of use. It looked as if the cleaners gave up on it years ago.

Mari lay on his bed and thought he was hallucinating as he watched the whitewashed walls start to move. There were tiny grey dots, in lines, moving along in almost military fashion. He showed Kat.

'Bed bugs,' Kat said. 'They're coming for you …' and he walked off to his own side of the flea-pit room.

There weren't many mosquitoes left in the mountains at this time of year but the few that had survived the cold all seemed to be living in the Motel Krishna. The constant attack from the smallest insects and creatures that descend on the human food source during the dark is the speciality of the house. Fleas, bed bugs, mozzies and all, joined the attack through the night but a special was saved for morning.

As the sun shone through the impossible to close curtain windows, Mari sat up from his interrupted sleep and was puzzled to see several earthworms in a wriggling mass on the floor of the bedroom.

Their trails were still visible and upon closer inspection of the bare tiled floor many of their previous, now dried up trajectories could be made out. He watched them for a minute. He was quite curious to see them wriggle around in a tangled, moving blob on his motel room floor.

By this time he was immune to any further surprises the Krishna could throw up at him he got up and went about his business, scratching at the night time bites and sidestepping the worms. He was slowly coming down from the adrenalin hit from his crash. It had left him feeling wired. He was sore from hitting the hard top and felt stupid and lame. He tried a stretch but it was too much. He undressed and although it was freezing water, he dabbed it on his gravel rash straight from the tap in the filthy bathroom. It stung like crazy. The skin was red and starting to show signs of puss around the edges of the cuts. It hurt to move. His brain felt like it was swimming around in his head. He felt numb on the outside and shaky inside. He had a weird, clouded headspace and couldn't seem to think straight or care about anything. If he was really honest he felt tearful, too.

Kat woke up, shoved past and took a long time on the squat toilet.

Mari thought he would never have shoved past him yesterday.

They both knew Kat had the advantage, now he was lame. Kat's unsubtle change of temperament towards Mari showed it, shouted it, to the world.

'How you feeling?' asked Kat, in a matter-of-fact way.

'Good and you?' Mari showed no pain in his voice.

'Fine. Hungry, though. Fancy a curry breakfast? Or some road kill? Tarmac on toast, extra gravel? Human pizza?' Kat looked closely at the red cuts and winced inside.

For once Mari maintained his demeanour. He ignored Kat's childish jibes and carefully dabbed a damp bed sheet onto his cuts. He tried to pick out the remaining bits of dirt and road from his legs. He needed new trousers as his had ripped. Logically he should have gone back to Manali but there was no way he was letting Kat go on alone, no chance. He was pretty sure if he suggested they go back this morning Kat would have an immediate riposte, something like, 'yeh, you go back and I'll try and stay upright on my bike and go and finish the hunt alone'. Mari wasn't going anywhere but up the mountain.

They didn't bother with the motel breakfast as neither wanted food poisoning. They stopped further down the road at the clean looking dhaba café with rooms, the place they should have stayed last night. They ate chana masala with puri. The puffed up bread was delicious and went well with the lemon sour, chickpea curry. They had salted lassi and sweet weak coffee.

The boys had rarely had to use money and didn't know

much about tipping and so as the whole meal came to RS243 Kat just left a RS500 note and they were gone. They boy who collected the dishes showed it to the owner, Mr Singh and he immediately ran out to the boys to rectify their mistake.

'Sirs!' Mr Singh caught up with them as they stood next to their bikes, pondering their next move. 'You mistake.'

It seemed like the entire kitchen staff were watching from outside the back of the dhaba, following the unfolding morning drama.

Mr Singh tried to hand back the note but Kat, wondering what all the fuss was about, told him to give the boy the change. Then he had a better idea.

'This is the actual end of the road, then?' Kat said it as half question, half statement.

'Yes, rasta, uppur, Arna village. Yes, good.'

'So this is the way to Arna village. Good.' Kat turned to Mari. 'Where are their bikes?'

Mari asked Mr Singh if he'd seen two men on Bullets, one white and one Indian yesterday.

Mr Singh thought. He'd seen them but he wasn't a man to part with this kind of information to two foreigners who threw money around like dry rice at a wedding. Especially not to a kitchen boy. The tip was more than his weekly wage. He'd made Mr Singh look cheap. Throwing money around like that would only lead to trouble.

Mr Singh gave them the Indian, side to side, head wobble as their answer. This was the non-descript gesture that means yes, no and anything in-between, all at the same time.

Kat and Mari both looked at each other. They'd been briefed on a few things about India and its cultural norms. The first was nothing happens quickly. The second there were no rules that couldn't be at least bent if not broken. The third was everyone takes a bribe, it's completely normalised, and there is no better way of getting what you want.

Kat pulled out another RS500 note. He did it discretely enough so the viewing public didn't see. He had noticed there were an ever increasing number of young men watching them from a distance now. He presumed correctly that it was genuine curiosity as not much went on at the end of the road, especially in the mornings. It seemed really quiet; they were the only customers in the dhaba.

Mr Singh took the note and held his head in his left hand, pretending to think and search his memory. 'Two man, one Indian, one foreigner. Look.' Mr Singh pointed with his finger and the boys spotted two 350 Bullets parked up, just off the road, partially hidden behind some bushes.

'Arna?' Kat pointed to the two Bullets and then the path.

'Arna, rasta,' said Mr Singh and decided he'd had enough, turned around with a, 'you go, uppur, Arna, good.' Mr Singh waved his hand in a dismissive gesture as he told them to go up the mountain on the Arna path, rasta in Hindi. He then walked off, back towards his dhaba, short and plump, wobbling as he went.

'Hey, can we leave our bikes here?' Kat said in a loud enough voice so Mr Singh could hear but Mr Singh had cloth ears, the type young boys and men in their own little kingdoms develop. These ears only let you hear what suits you and Mr Singh was getting hungry after all this drama. He heard very little when he was hungry.

The boys were not used to being ignored but they had to swallow this one. They left their bikes anyway and pretended to walk away, towards the path to Arna village.

When they were sure the watching eyes had got back to work Kat scuttled back and using the blade from the bottom of one of his nunchuck sticks he slit the tyres of each Bullet, just enough to give a slow puncture.

The going up the hill was tough for Mari. He didn't feel good and he knew he was slowing Kat down. He had to stop and rest about every mile and he was drinking more than his share of water. Even in the fresh climate he was sweating profusely. His head was aching and his side was being irritated by the constant rubbing of his clothes against his sore skin as he walked up the mountain.

Kat noticed it all. He was happy that Mari was there because nobody could then say it was a one man hunt. He was constantly planning strategies, scenarios and running through possibilities. They had the biggest advantage possible, surprise. What an enemy didn't know was coming was impossible to plan for.

What Kat had not figured out was that Hue was fully prepared for an attack. Hue had it all worked out that Steve Smart's men would be coming for him. What Hue couldn't understand as he strolled down Arna's one and only street that bright Himalayan morning, was where they had got to.

Hue never took his eyes from the passing travellers dressed in Nepalese and Indian garb. He stared down alleys and into guest house gardens and cafés , scrutinising any occupants, sexing them from a distance as some of the lads had long hair, some of the girls short and as for the ones with dreadlocks, they could be any sex at all, scruffy buggers. He walked past the View Guesthouse and took a good look at Tim and Millie but they didn't match Dean and Beki's description. The Brigadier hadn't been asked by Vihar what they had looked like, so he hadn't divulged any picture.

Inside their room, Beki had woken up first and decided to give Dean a treat. She felt his hard on and had started to go down on him while he was still asleep. She would never have done this before she'd gone travelling. She'd also found new freedom and she liked it.

He woke up as she caressed his balls and licked him. It usually took him a while to finish but not today. After no more than five minutes of her best attention he was done. His body tensed, his hands clasped into fists and he let out a little cry of relief as he came in her mouth. She swallowed and then looked at him with a beaming smile and said, 'Mornang,' before she got up and cleaned her teeth for the second time that day.

When she went back in the room he pretended to be asleep and watched her out of narrowed eyes as she pottered about. He grabbed her from behind as she started to get changed and he pulled her onto the bed as she screamed a little helplessly, a fun squeal.

'Your turn,' he said and gave her the slowest, most intense half hour of her life, teasing her and then going in for the kill in the last five minutes as he licked and sucked her into orgasm. How he loved this feeling of her flowing into him as she came. He had never experienced true intimacy before. He had always got off on the opposite of affection and tenderness. He was head over heels in love with this girl. Everything they had been through together just seemed to make them stronger. He loved her more than life itself, completely, utterly, totally. As she lay with her back to him on the bed he reached into the bottom of his bag. He found the oblong case and placed it next to her head on his side of the bed.

'There's something for you, Beki. I love you and I want you to have it.'

She froze. Suddenly stiff as a board. Did he just say that? Was she still hallucinating? She rolled onto her back and saw he was sat on the end of the bed with that same staring schoolboy look he'd had when she'd first met him. She leaned up and then sat upright against the wall. She took a good look at the black case before opening it. Inside she found herself looking at the most ridiculously ostentatious, bad taste bracelet she had ever seen. Its yellow gold looked practically orange in the morning light and how anyone could think she would wear a rope gold bracelet like some blinged up chav or gangster rapper was beyond her comprehension.

She realised just how far apart their worlds really were. They were from other sides of the coin. She knew there and then, as if it had been placed on a billboard in Times Square and blown up to the size of Manhattan that Dean Shelby and Rebecca Aston had absolutely no long term future together. Though she also knew she was going to have as much fun as she could while it lasted.

'Oww, you sweetie.' She put out her arm and he clasped it on her wrist. It looked totally gross to her. Then she realised just the gold alone was probably worth a couple of grand.

'It must have cost you a fortune …' she said unconsciously emphasising the last word.

'Nice, though, in' it?'

'Oww, thank you. How can I show my appreciation?' she asked with a seductive, almost sly look on her face and then she moved on top of him again. As she straddled him, she thought how divine it was to have a younger man. They just kept giving and giving.

25

Mari and Kat were able to spend time resting when Mari needed to. They had little choice. Kat had to suppress the little voice in his head that suggested he go on alone and leave Mari to catch up. Neither of them had ever been seriously hurt or even properly ill. They'd picked up viruses when they were young, coughs and colds but that was it. They just didn't understand that Mari needed to rest and clean up his wounds. If they left it to get infected, out here in the middle of the mountains, he could be in serious trouble but they just didn't know that was the case.

Being constantly sheltered had its downside. They wanted for nothing but failed to learn how to interact with the world at large.

This ritual, this rite of passage they were going through, was the first time they had experienced being amongst the cattle and ants they had been conditioned to loath.

The other times they had been amongst them were carefully configured. They had been to parties and nightclubs, met with royalty and celebrity but never had they been allowed to interact with just anyone.

Mari didn't get it. He was fine with his world and just wanted to get back there. He wasn't that bothered who made the kill now.

If it was Kat, so be it. He had won the ocean hunt. Kat had joined him but he'd made the first strike into the shark.

Nobody could understand how terrifying it was to be waist deep in a flowing river with a massive shark heading your way, armed with only a harpoon to kill it. He had felt brave and indestructible then. Now he just wanted one of his own beds. He wanted his mother Reyanne to hold him close as she had when he was young. He wanted to feel the heat from her and smell her familiar perfume of honeysuckle rose and jasmine.

Kat was completely opposite. He loved being outside the family's grasp. He loved the open space around him, the feeling of making his own decisions, mistakes, choices and future. He liked that during this hunt, nothing was planned out for him. It was spontaneous, dangerous and fun. He'd never just been allowed to have fun, not on his own terms at least. Sure, he'd had anything money could buy. He'd had love from his mother throughout his life. He'd had some wild times on his yacht with his friends but they were all 'chosen' people. All of his peers, the sons and daughters of the super-rich, who through no fault of their own were as shielded from the world as he was.

The easy option would be to carry it all on, to limit his experience of the world to this one adventure, this one challenge but he had other plans.

He wanted to know more of the world than Patek Philippe watches and Bugatti Veyron cars.

As they walked along the path they saw a lone figure of a local woman. She was probably about forty but looked fifty. She carried a big wicker basket full of tree branches on her back.

Kat watched her slow pace up the steep path. He followed her, not just with his eyes but with his mind. He realised for the first time in his life that he was no better than her, that she was not better than him, that he was no worse than her or she him. He stood still and watched this woman, a person. He would never know her but she had taught him so much.

'Come on Mari.' He gained his senses back. 'Once we get to the village I'll get you somewhere to rest up and see if there's some medicine or something.' He almost felt compassion for Mari now. He'd watched him struggle on the relatively flat part of the path. Now it was all steep, truly steep in parts. It felt like straight up to him, so it must have been really tough for Mari.

To make things worse the sunshine had stealthily been replaced with cloud. This wasn't the white fluffy stuff either; it was matt grey, dark and foreboding. The wind had picked up and it contained a real chill when there was a rushing gust. The trees saved them from the worst of it as the wind's strength was broken down.

It all changed when they hit a small clearing at the top of the straight stretch he'd watched the local women climb.

The wind bit through their skin.

Kat was both enthralled by the mauve light coming through the rainclouds and the view from the valley. The space around him seemed overpowering in its scale and grandeur. He worried how Mari was going to cope with the approaching downpour, now visibly moving towards them from the far side of the valley.

When the rain came they were about half a mile from the village. If Mari had been fit they would have made it in plenty of time but during that last half mile they got soaked to the skin. It stopped being a crisp mountain fresh morning and had turned into a close, muggy afternoon. Even though they had Berghaus Ulvetanna Gore-Tex jackets, chosen by Sy Poulis himself, the rain was so torrential, the humidity so encompassing that the moisture seeped into their whole being.

As they dragged themselves into the village there were no tourists on the street. A few locals hurriedly went about their business, jackets pulled up around their necks or over their heads for tame relief from the torrent.

It did seem to be easing off now they were … somewhere, not out in the wild.

Kat looked down the main street. The shops were just one-man booths. There was no chemist but there was a store that seemed to sell more than cigarettes and soap bars. It had an actual door, not just a front you had to stand outside.

They went in and a strange mixture of spice and fragrance hit them.

Soap powder and chilli battled for prominence

depending on where you stood.

Kat bought Dettol soap and bandages. At the counter he asked for a doctor. The young woman serving him told him in good English there was no doctor or chemist but asked what the problem was. She was used to being asked such questions by foreigners.

Mari showed her his knee and arm. She went off into the back room of the shop and came back with a tin of antibiotic powder, a glass bottle of iodine and some antiseptic cream. She looked sternly at them.

'Firstly use the soap and clean thoroughly. Use some clean bandage to dab on some iodine. Let it dry naturally. Then apply powder. Do this twice a day, morning and night. After some days it will heal, then use the cream. Keep it covered in day and open at night or when sleeping. Two hundred and sixty five rupees only, doctoring is free.' She said the last bit with a slight giggle and her look softened.

'Where's the best hotel?' asked Mari, happy now they had something to put on his wounds.

'All are best. My aunty has rooms. You want me to show you?'

'Yes, you OK with that Kat?'

'Yes, Michael, I'm fine with it.'

Mari had forgotten to call him Matt. They both had false names and passports.

The girl called into the back of the shop and an old man came out. It was her father but he looked like her granddad. They spoke briefly and she led the boys out with a 'come on', and a wave of her hand.

They doubled back and took an alley left. The narrow paths were muddy and had mini streaming floods flowing down them. The girl seemed to know just where to land her feet, using stones and drier parts of the path to navigate her way.

The smell was lush now. The rain had eased to a stop. Steam materialised from the valley. The wooden houses with their verandas and balconies became more prevalent.

They came to a house and the girl shouted, 'Aunty,' into the front doorway.

A kind looking woman appeared with two little tykes at her feet, one crawling, the other a toddler. The two women talked and negotiated a price for the room. The girl would take a finder's fee of twenty five rupees. The room was RS250 per night she told the boys, fully expecting them to say it was too expensive and to bargain her down to the two hundred mark, which was the going rate for a family room. There were no guest house facilities here, no toilet, no bed, just a mattress on the floor. Some foreigners preferred it like this, though she never knew why.

The girl went on her way knowing she would collect the money from the next member of the Lal family who visited the shop. Everyone looked after each other in Arna village. It was like that because no outsiders were going to look out for them. All the promises from the politicians were broken. They had no medical centre and no school. It was only because her family had the shop that she had been educated in Shimla. If they hadn't had the money for school fees and a relative willing to look after her, she would have been just like the other families here, uneducated and conditioned to the rural life of the village.

Personally she didn't mind the tourists, they were a colourful distraction. She had been brought up around charas and didn't understand the fuss the police made about it. It grew everywhere. If they had to do a hard day's labour collecting wood or tending to the animals on the hilly terrain, are they saying they couldn't take a few aches and pains away with a bit of charas? It was considered medicine to her people. Only the men would smoke it, the women chewed a lump. It was said to work better if you ate it, so that made sense to her as the women in her village did most of the back-breaking work.

One day she would have some. One day she would sit around all day doing nothing. She worked six and a half days a week in the shop. She had one afternoon off per week for her English lesson and to visit her friends. Even so she had it much better than most. They had to work seven days a week, sometimes until dark from before sunrise, depending on what had to be done.

She arrived back at the shop and her father left her to it and retired to the back room where he was sorting out some new stock for the winter. She knew the weather would be changing in roughly two weeks from now. More storms would come. Then after about a month, they would turn from rain to snowstorms. The mountains would be white all the time. The tourists would have gone and the village would be cut off for at least ten weeks. She liked this time of year, though, because there was less work to do in the shop and she could concentrate more on her studies.

'Pritti,' her father called from the back room. 'Come here. Help me with these chillies.'

26

Mari used the fresh water tap that Aunty had shown them to wash his wounds and he cleaned himself up. It was at the front of the courtyard and from there he looked down the forested valley to the plains below.

In Switzerland he had viewed something similar but when he realised that here was much grander than the Alps, he wondered why he'd never been to the Himalaya before.

Kat was keen to get out and about. He checked Mari was fine with him taking a stroll, as if he had much choice. He needed to rest, even he knew that. He made him promise he would not take the target out without him at least being there. He reminded him that they were a pair and he'd been fine with Kat launching his harpoon in the shark after his initial hit, sharing the kill.

Kat promised he wouldn't do a thing if he saw Hue Brooks other than watch and learn his movements, routines or anything that would give them an advantage. Smart reckoned he was a worthy foe and so he had to be given respect.

Once Mari was cleaned up and lay on his bed on the floor, Kat was off. He practically glided down to the village. The water had disappeared from the path, the rain was a distant memory and the sky was mostly blue, punctuated with the massive whiter than white clouds he loved.

Kat stopped at the junction of the alley path and the street. He looked right and left and settled on a place called the Chrystal Moon. He took a deep breath and walked in the open plan café, took a seat upstairs on the balcony and waited to see what happened next. He just wasn't used to walking in places by himself. In his life everything was preordained. Things like who he sat with for dinner, who he spoke to after dinner and, if they had their way, who he made it with, too. He understood the principle was that Sycamore had the power over them but he wasn't around much and so essentially it had been the most trusted employees who had governed his life. None of the Poulis' would ever admit this, but that had been the reality of his teens. There was constant pressure to conform to the old ways. It was fair to say he had his doubts about some of what went on but felt powerless to challenge the order of things. As they were constantly being reminded, it had worked for thousands of years that way, why should he question it.

He listened in on a conversation between the two women who sat at a table close by with one ear and with the other listened to Dreamy Days by Roots Manuva from the café's decent speakers, via the owner's iPod.

Soon the music won and when one of the women offered him a go on her joint, he was in total harmony with this London rap and this whole India experience.

'Hey there, you're not supposed to smoke the lot. It's a sharing thing.'

He handed her back not much more than the roach.

'Sorry, I'm so very sorry. I got carried away by that music.'

'It's alright, I'll make another.'

'I'm Matt. How do you get a drink in here?' He was genuinely confused. Why wasn't someone taking his order? He'd never smoked much pot before. He had some at a party once but that was to come down from some cocaine. He liked this feeling, though. It was as if the world had taken on an extra glow. He felt relaxed and happy. Nothing was an issue for him right now, his stresses and strains were on hold.

'Someone will come in a bit. It's India time. I'm Emma, this is Jules. Where are you from?' Emma liked placing travellers from their accents. She couldn't pinpoint this guy's, though, if she had to guess he would be South African.

'Good question, bits from here and there. As far as I know Egypt, well the general area.'

'You don't look Egyptian,' Jules said. She was leaning forwards to get a better look.

'Well, that's where I was born. I've been raised all over the place.'

Emma started making another joint.

Jules liked the look of this guy. He was dishy and didn't have the usual traveller thing going on. He was different and she liked different. She moved chairs so her back was to the view and she was now able to talk directly to him.

'Anywhere interesting, where you've been brought up?'

He had been warned about this. He'd been advised not to engage in conversation about his life or who he was because it was all a cover story and he might get caught out. He couldn't be bothered with all that. He was going to spill stuff to the girl. She seemed really pretty and interested in him. Not because of what he had, where he came from but because she was friendly and genuine.

'Different parts of Africa, South and Central America. Europe and the US, obviously. The best place depends on what you like. There's Switzerland in Europe. Belize is nice but my favourite place is the ranch near Cape Town. That's where I could ride my bike.'

It was a bit of a conversation stopper. Jules looked at him and decided he was telling the truth. She knew there and then that the universe had conspired to bring him to her. She'd felt the Union at work, even after Rupert had left she'd been telling herself the last thing she needed was another man.

'What bike?' Emma asked.

'Ducati Monster, 696. Custom fitted.'

'Have you a bike here?'

'Yer, a BM. It's down at the road.'

'Emma loves bikes,' Jules said as she became more intrigued than ever.

'Who doesn't love bikes, Jules?' Emma asked, setting her friend up with the question.

'Rupert Farringdon-Jones, he didn't love bikes,' Jules retorted with a bit of grace and humour. Both girls laughed at the fact that Rupes wouldn't ride a motorcycle. He thought they were too dangerous and he always bleated on about being too stoned. He'd happily take a lift off others who were equally as stoned, though. He'd never take responsibility for anything and that was the real reason they'd split. He just never pulled his weight in the relationship. Jules did everything for him; it was like travelling with a kid.

A waiter came and stood by the table. Emma took the initiative. 'Two chai, shakkar nakkar, no sugar. Do you want something, hot, cold? A drink?'

'Something cold, nothing sweet, though.'

'Lemon soda, no sugar?' asked the waiter. This was what they usually had if they didn't take soft drinks.

'Fine,' said Kat, 'lemon soda.' As the waiter skipped down the stairs Emma gave Jules the joint to light and they all smoked in silence, unless the looks flying between the girls counted for words.

'We need a plan. Mohammed won't come to the mountain, so we must bring the mountain to Mohammed.' Hue spoke rhetorically to Vihar who just sat and smoked his cigarette. 'How about you go round the guest houses and tell the owners you have a message for Dean Shelby. Say it's from the Brigadier and he needs to get in touch. Say it's his grandparents. They're gravely ill, dying. We need to flush him out. Then I'll finish him.'

Vihar thought for a second. So he was to do the dirty work. Get his name tainted with this village as the one who was asking around for the foreigner who then disappeared. He didn't like Hue's plan.

'I go now.' Vihar stood up, stubbed out his cigarette. 'I tell whole village I look for Dean, no problem. Grandfather sick. Death coming.'

'Yes, yes. Exactly.'

'You have my money?'

Vihar was out. He was promised a good fee for his company but he'd had enough. He wasn't getting embroiled in murder. Not for a few thousand rupees.

Hue weighed up the possibilities. He raced through his options as he slowly looked in his bag for the cash. He decided to ask, be upfront. He liked this stoic Indian. He was as guarded as they came. He handed him the money he was promised and respected his decision to leave, if as he suspected, Vihar was going.

'You're leaving, then?'

'Yes, leaving.' Vihar wasn't in the least surprised Hue had worked this out.

'Will you ask at the hotels?'

'No. Nothing personal, no offence.'

'None taken.' Hue sat down on his bed. 'Thank you for coming this far, showing me the way here and for the company.'

'I go now.' Vihar kept an eye on Hue as he opened the

door. 'I drop bike at hotel?'

'Yes, thanks. I can't ride two bikes back. Leave the keys behind reception.'

Vihar left and all the way down the hill he kept stopping and hiding, waiting to see if Hue was following. Once he got down the mountain trail to the road he saw the tyres had been tampered with and thought about going back up to warn Hue. His better judgement told him to hitch a ride back to Manali, buy a bottle of his favourite Indian whisky Highland Laddie, go home and drink himself into oblivion.

Hue was left in a state. He was getting nowhere fast. He could walk through the main street again if he wanted. He could do the guest house run himself but he needed a new angle.

He reached into his pocket and pulled out the opium Vihar had given him. On close inspection it was a reddish brown, sticky and clean. He rolled a ball from the big piece and holding it in his closed hand, pulled down his trousers and underpants. He bent forwards and pushed the opium ball up his bottom with his first finger. An opium suppository should get him thinking.

Half an hour later he did another one. He lay on his bed, dreaming while awake.

He thought through his life. He thought about Mr Kinsey his teacher, the one who'd tried to break him, the one who'd made him cry. He thought about what he had done to Kinsey, years later, when he'd tracked him down. It had been the way Kinsey looked upon him when he was little that he'd hated most. That look that told Hue he was powerful. That he had had power over him. The one that made him cry. He recalled how Kinsey had smelt after he'd soiled himself in terror. He had kidnapped, bound and tortured Kinsey for a few hours before finishing him. Hue started to masturbate as he went through his most sadistic pleasures. He'd gouged out Kinsey's eyes, held his head in a vice like grip and fucked him in the bloody sockets, his penis fitted well he recalled.

He was imagining doing those things to Charles Bates' murderer. He was going to take this handsome, fit young man and make mincemeat out of him. He was going to rape him and slit his throat while he came and … and then he was done. His climax was very intense. He lay on the bed and wiped up. He slept, he woke, he dreamed and eventually found himself sitting up.

He walked to the door and opened it. The air was nice on his face. He was still a little giddy from the drug but was in a carefree state of mind and walked out into the afternoon.

It was obvious to Emma that she was the gooseberry between Jules and this Matt. After another round of chai she made her excuses and she left. It was hard being around Jules as she was so pretty. That was all most boys were interested in. Once they got to know Jules and all about her Union beliefs they would realise she was a nutjob, but some would stay around just to have her as a trophy girlfriend. Emma went back to her room at the View. She'd go and read her new book, a bit of chick lit to while away the afternoon.

'What shall we do?' asked Jules.

Kat was very stoned and really was quite happy sitting there but this girl was very nice, he would like to please her.

'Is there anything to do around here?'

'There's the river, the forest, the temple.'

'Temple?'

'Yes, the Kali temple. There's a cave, too. Fancy it?'

'Let's go. Have you got any more of that smoke?'

'Yes, back at my room. We can get some.'

'I'll pay the bill then.'

The two new friends talked about the charas on the way to Jules' room at the View and she explained how it was made and how much better it was than the skunk they had in England.

'It's a natural product, just rubbed by hand. The stuff in England's full of chemicals.'

When they arrived at the View Kat had a sudden and intense feeling he had to get Mari. He didn't know why but he just knew he had to. He'd stopped to think for a few seconds at the bottom of the stairs which led up to the first floor rooms and balcony. He followed Jules' bottom with his eyes as she climbed the stairs to her room and heard her 'OMG' and some more chatter as he started to follow her upstairs physically.

Jules had her arms wrapped round the most beautifully natural woman Kat had ever seen. Still high from the first time he'd been properly stoned, he stood at the top of the balcony and just took in the scene. He would have made them both but the blonde woman was definitely number one. She looked like a Scandinavian goddess; she looked to him like the essence of beauty itself, perfection, love. She was Inanna, Isis, Ishtar, she was the one. She was his Venus.

The Poulis' had over the years slowly altered the iconography of their goddess for mass consumption. She was now a pallid representation of the original. As time had passed their own clan had become slightly lighter skinned, as they spent more time in other, colder parts of the world. Kat's hair was more brown than black now. It wasn't unusual for iconography to depict the goddess in a more local form. Did the pictures of Mary the Virgin depict a Jewish matriarch? She would have been naturally dark skinned with black hair but today she was almost universally whiter than white, sometimes with blue eyes and light brown or even blonde hair.

The Poulis' knew it was important to depict their icons in a form with which the viewer could identify. They realised that the power in the world had shifted from the Roman times. This was when the Egyptian dynasties faded and a European, not African aspect made it easier to go undetected behind the ruling faces.

Some lines like Reyanne's and Mari's were still pure. Mari had black hair and brown eyes. His skin wasn't as dark as his mother's but was darker than Kat's.

'So amazing to see you again!' Jules was gushing.

'You, too,' said Beki, slightly underwhelmed.

She was sat alone on the balcony having a joint and a mint tea. She was smiling politely and hoping desperately she wasn't outwardly appearing as patronising as she felt inside towards Jules. Then as she had her third hug she looked over to see the most handsome, well groomed guy she'd settled eyes on in her life. He leaned against the wooden post at the top of the balcony and gave her the sexiest look she'd ever received. Her entire world stood still. Her heart jumped a beat. She felt a degree of anticipation in her whole body; her complete being was suddenly alert. She had excited butterflies flitting around her belly. She was in … well if not in love at first sight, certainly in lust with this guy.

'Have a seat.' Beki pulled a chair out for Jules.

'Oh, we're off to the Kali temple. This is Matt, say hello, Matt.' Now Jules sounded patronising, maybe it was catching.

'Hi, Matt, I'm Beki.' She gave him her best cat like smile. 'Have a seat.'

'I've got to check on my cousin. He's had a slight accident. He fell off his bike. Nothing serious. I'll bring him along. Jules, can you wait half an hour while I get him?'

'Fine.' She looked at Beki. 'We can catch up.'

Beki wondered what they had to catch up about but her Englishness meant she agreed out of politeness. 'Dean's just gone to the shop, he'll be back soon. We can all go.'

Then it hit Kat. Beki was Rebecca Aston. She was

waiting for Dean Shelby. He had to get Mari. Nothing would stop him coming to the temple with them now.

'Twenty minutes, promise.' He spun round the post and jumped down the wooden stairs. He practically flew down the main street and then the alley. He was back at the door of their room in record time.

'Mari, I've found Dean Shelby.'

Mari had been dozing off and on since Kat left but now he was wide awake.

'Where, how?'

'He's, well, I got talking to a girl and then we were going to a temple then we went to get some pot.'

'Pot?'

'Yeh, I know, but it's different here. Really good stuff, I've been smoking all afternoon.'

'Is there such a thing as good pot?' Mari looked perplexed. 'Everyone says it slows you down.'

'This stuff makes you feel great … everything's clearer, sharper, more vivid.'

'Take your word for it. I'm not smoking pot. No way.' Mari slowly got up from the floor and pulled up his trousers to examine his scrapes. As the cuts were on the classic knee and elbow, moving around tended to make the skin break again but now there was no sign of infection. He sprinkled more antibiotic powder on from the packet and covered it up again, this time with a bandage under his clothes. His elbow was less troublesome. It was stiff and sore but showed no signs of the initial infection.

Once Mari was up and about with his boots on, he

realised he didn't have a swimming head anymore. In fact he felt really wired. He was a bit jittery still, but no headache or serious pain anymore.

They walked along the path and once Mari found his pace, he felt quite good. His confidence was coming back, his chest filled with air and he started to take bigger strides, rather than the tentative steps he'd taken on the way to the room.

Once they'd got to the main street the pair caught their first glimpse of Dean Shelby. He was leaning over the balcony, looking down at them, staring, sussing out who was approaching. He was smoking a cigarette and flicked it nonchalantly onto the main street before turning away.

Hue Brooks could have sustained his step and picked up the burning butt end if he'd have bent down. Instead he carried on walking past the two boys coming the other way. He smiled as they both looked at him, recognised him? No, they were far too young to be Smart's, anyway one had been limping. He'd never be using a novice to take him out. Nice looking boys, though.

So that was where the blighter had been hiding. He'd a room on the top floor with his bitch. Hue walked into the shop across the road from the View.

'Ten Gold, please,' he said.

Pritti, the girl behind the counter had seen this one walking up and down the main street. She had wondered if he was German.

'Anything else?'

'Do you sell knives?'

'Yes, for kitchen?'

'Hunting. Do you sell hunting knives?'

She gave him a 'wait there' stare. She went into the back room and came out with a standard nine inch blade khukuri. It had a black scabbard and two smaller knives next to the black buffalo horn handle. It was second hand but when he inspected it and felt its balanced weight, he knew that didn't make much difference. The edge seemed to be as sharp as he needed it to be. The curvature in the blade had a slightly thicker top edge than the base or end. This gave the knife a real advantage over the standard straight blades. It was the traditional Budhuna design. That is the heaviest of all the three styles of blade, which suited Hue fine. He envisaged chopping it straight into Shelby's skull, jerking it sideways once it was embedded and exposing his brain to the air.

'Perfect. How much?' The foreigner had shown his hand and the price had just doubled. Her father had told her he wanted fifty US dollars for the piece. She doubled it to a hundred.

Hue knew he was paying way over the odds. He knew she was trying it on but he liked her, she was to the point and had brought him a very decent weapon. He was short on time and given his clumsy opening he kept his bartering skills closed for a rainy day. He just asked for the cigarettes be thrown in for free so he didn't have to bother with loose change.

27

Sycamore and Oscar, his counterpart in the East, were sat drinking fresh Darjeeling tea. The leaf was evident at the bottom of the fine bone china. They were gold leaf rimmed, St. James Eau de Nil teacups. The brew created a slight lift in the senses once consumed. Oscar considered it the best tea from his estates.

The two were coming to the end of the summit. They had discussed the oncoming shifts in leadership and thankfully both agreed it was time for change. Oscar had a few points of direction he hoped the future pairs would pursue.

'Sy, we may need something really big again in the next ten years, so why don't we start that process before we relinquish our roles. The boys won't be able to think as big as we do.'

'Well, Mari might but I understand you. Anything in mind?'

'Come on, Sy, work with me. Guy Fawkes was the last

decent attempt on British parliament. It can't be America again. Too many catastrophes there last time.'

'You mean by the administration?' Sy asked, almost innocently.

Oscar raised his eyebrows and smiled. 'You gave them too much scope, we both know that. Tower seven … a really foolish move.'

'They're idiots all right but are the Brits any better? Tower seven had to be pulled because all the planning was done there. The documents were all stored in the Secret Service department in seven. It had to go.'

'This lot, these new Blues seem ruthless,' Oscar said. He was still digesting the reason why Tower seven was pulled.

'True enough. So what were you planning? You've got this figured out already, I know you.'

'An attack on parliament itself. Last time it was just a bunch of low grade cattle in the US. Next time we need to hit the politicians. Who could say anything about that? They all think those stuck up fools run the place. Who could say anything about it if we blew them up? In ten years we'll be old men but it'll give the boys something to aim for. We could start a new phase of restrictions. We'd get ID cards through parliament for sure if they'd think they're on a kill list. Not just the breeders next time, we go for the prime rib steak, I say.'

Sy thought for a moment. He joined his hands and put them up against the bridge of his nose. He put his hands down before taking a final sip of tea. 'It's a fine idea. Fine, but if you want to go really big we could aim for China.'

Sy knew Oscar would hate this idea. He was so dismissive of his part of the world but whether they liked it or not, the Chinese were now big players in the world and they had never properly been infiltrated by the families.

'Not China, Sy. They'll never sustain anything without our help. Who would care less about an attack on the communist party? They'd just shift a few clones around and act like nothing had happened.'

'No, you miss my point. What if we staged it so a few Chinese bits of wire or bomb case were found.'

'Like when they found a hijackers passport next to the trade centre, the one that fluttered down from the firebomb when the plane disappeared into the tower? Something subtle like that?' Oscar shook his head, he knew he'd won. He had never forgiven Sy for the fiasco of 9/11. What was supposed to be a dramatic false flag attack had turned into an embarrassment for all concerned. Next time they had to do it big, but hidden. More like London when most of the action happened underground.

9/11 had been handed over to the CIA as they were responsible for overseas escapades and not generally associated with homeland security. They had succumbed to the American state of mind that says everything should be bigger and better than the original. The initial plan they handed over was for one plane to smash into one of the towers. This would have been enough to justify their cause. It would have been dramatic enough and with the one and only camera crew around to capture the footage, rather like a Sun God, their message would have lived on forever. But no. That just wasn't brash enough for the American psyche. Why have one plane crash when there are two towers. They obviously needed two. Oh, and while they were at it they could take down their New York office as a party trick, Tower seven. They just stashed all their fuck ups from the previous decade in the New York office and Hey Presto! They were gone when the skyscraper that wasn't even hit by the planes collapsed vertically, in seconds. This happened a few hours after some debris hit it and set a few fires off. It is the one and only skyscraper to fall like this from some fire. The sprinkler system wasn't powerful enough to kill those initial flames and most of the firemen were either dead or too traumatised to tackle it said the official report. Now it seemed the plans for the whole job had been obliterated there, too. Shrewd move doing all the planning in the building next door.

The upshot was still that they went completely over the top. Anyone, even the dumbest, Arena watching, burger chewing, low-grade heifer could see it was fake.

Next time Oscar was sure the Brits would be more subtle. They couldn't be any less. Now that was impossible. However they would balk at the idea of taking out their own paymasters, so maybe getting a foreign power to take the hit of blame could work. They'd finalise the detail, they had time.

'What about hiking up the gas prices again this winter in Europe? Have you got that under control?'

'Already done.' Sy knew he'd ask. It was fine for him as most of the East was warm anyway. It was his pet hate, the fact that most of the ants were so poor they died before sixty. The cattle had to be helped along and they had found hiking the gas price at the end of summer worked surprisingly well.

'And how's the fast food revolution in the East?' Sy smirked. 'Going well?'

'Really well, thanks. You'll never let me forget that was your idea, will you.'

Sy had initiated the plan to flood the East with cheap, fattening, unhealthy fast food two decades ago. They put pressure on the Indian government to open up their doors to the usual fast food and sugar drink corporations. People had forgotten that it wasn't until 1993 that the government capitulated and allowed the multi-nationals to move in. Now they were expanding inexorably, both in profits and in waistlines. They pre-empted this by taking control of the leading manufacturers of diabetes drugs and so it was a perfect storm for the Poulis'. They created the problem, let it fester and were now solving it. Similar strategies were being used in various theatres of war, currently in Syria. They'd created the dictator, armed the rebels and once it was calm again would go in and rebuild the country. If they could keep a presence there like in Afghanistan and Iraq, all the better. Iran was next on the list.

'So, we are all done apart from the Last Detail.' Oscar gave Sy a pen and paper. This was the only thing they ever wrote down. It would be put inside a sealed box and kept for posterity. They were both to write their most outlandish idea, swap papers, read it back to the composer, hopefully laugh about it and then maybe one day even use it. They'd done that before. The idea for cloning had come from a Last Detail fifty-five years ago. They still bankrolled these science projects because yes, they did want to live forever.

Sy was done in a few seconds and so was Oscar. They did this every year and so had it all pre-planned. They swapped papers and Oscar went first.

'So, your Last Detail is to "IMPLANT AN EYE CAMERA THAT TAKES A PHOTO WHEN YOU BLINK". It's a spy in the eye.' They both laughed at the ridiculous idea and silly joke.

'So, yours is "TO MAKE A FALSE FLAG ALIEN INVASION".' They both loved this one.

'That's so stupid the sheep might actually buy it,' Sycamore said when he'd stopped his giggles. 'Orson Welles, for real.'

28

By the time Kat and Mari arrived at the View there was a whole posse waiting for them. Tim and Millie had joined Emma, Jules, Dean and Beki.

Jules had persuaded Emma to come by telling her Matt was bringing his cousin.

On the way down the boys had decided to do away with their false names. They'd say Matt was his real name but he was nicknamed Kat. They would just leave Mari as it was. They could say he was called Marian, like John Wayne if anyone asked.

The fact that Hue Brooks had just walked past them meant the hunt had officially started. They had a quick conversation before climbing the View stairs.

Introductions were made and they all agreed an evening stroll to the Kali temple was a fab idea. They let Mari take the lead and Emma soon found her way to the front.

There was general chatter between the group, with Tim taking the lead in conversation about Kali. He told them about the goddess and about her followers the Thuggee, who befriended travellers then strangled their victims to appease Kali. He told them she was the Goddess of Time and as all things came to an end, she was the ultimate being who consumes us all.

Kat and Mari didn't like to hear this as they'd been brought up to revere the stories of ancient Sumerian, Babylonian and Egyptian goddesses. They knew better than to get bogged down about a concept, though.

The Kali temple was only a ten minute stroll from the village but was out on its own, with no village houses around. They had walked through an area of pine trees to get there. The trees had long, bare trunks and were very tall. The younger ones had smoother bark than the older ones, whose outer layer was more ridged. The canopy was high above them and the forest floor filled with millions of green or brown fallen needles and thousands of small pine cones, which were mostly still closed. They all took their time, mindful of Mari's stiff leg. They enjoyed the conversation, the forest and the beautifully fresh pine scent carried on the breeze. Their footsteps made crunching sounds and their chatting competed with the birdsong to break the silence.

'Here we are,' said Tim. He sped up ahead of Mari and Emma. He stopped outside the temple which was made of wood and stone. He said a little silent prayer and rang the bell on a rope at the front. They all stood around the open entrance and Tim asked them all to take off their shoes and boots. Kat had a good look round and then took his boots off. Mari wasn't happy about it either as he felt vulnerable enough but he was confident Hue Brooks wouldn't go after Dean with so many people around.

The temple looked to be ancient. The inside was made of stone, the kind that's been weathered smooth. The canopy around the stone interior was made from beams of wood and looked much newer. There was a space inside that they all entered comfortably. In the middle of the floor there was a square fire pit or dhuni. In each of the top two corners of the temple there stood a wooden chest. They were identically carved in spiral patterns apart from the lids. One had a carving of a basic sun, the other a crescent moon.

Millie had brought several small candles with her. She placed them one by one around the inside of the temple by heating up the base, then pressed them into the stone or wooden shelves dotted around. She waited a few seconds for it to go cold. She then made sure it was set, by applying a touch of pressure to the side of the upright candle. If it fell over she did it again until it stayed erect, and only then she got to light the wick. She just loved lighting candles and admired the way they gave a warm glow to the sacred space inside the temple.

The actual alter was quite baffling to the uninitiated. It was a circular pyramid of stone, painted black, dressed in a blouse of shiny red material which was edged with fancy white embroidery, rather like an elongated doily. At the top of the pyramid there was a painted eye. It had a red oval circumference with the actual eye being white and the pupil black. The one eyed mound had an obdurate stare. It was a stare that penetrated through you, beyond you and onwards into infinity.

Around the temple in the flickering candlelight were iconographic pictures of Kali. They differed slightly but all had similar characteristics.

She wore a band of human skulls around her neck. Her skin was either dark blue or black. Her blood red tongue stuck out in a defiant gesture. She wore a golden crown and had four arms. She carried the severed head of a demon in her top left hand. In Her upper right hand she possessed a straight shafted sword with a curved sickle shape at the end of it, perfect for beheading. The severed head dripped blood and the lower left hand held a bowl made from human skull, called a kapala, to collect the blood from the seeping neck. The sword was raised high, giving the impression she had just beheaded the demon. Her lower right hand held a trishul, an Indian trident. Her long black hair flowed abundantly behind her back and over her breast to her waist. She stood on top of her consort Shiva's corpse. She was magnificent, angry, hellish, fierce, uncompromising. Yet she was also strikingly beautiful, powerful and strong.

Kat and Mari both immediately loved her. They were both forming their own ideas around her. When they compared her to their goddesses they struggled to marry the two. Often a goddess has similar traits, so alike as to be interchangeable. Looking around this atmospheric place, there was little they could relate to Ishtar or Isis. Maybe some similarities to Inanna, the earliest goddess with her sexualised nakedness and her treatment of men. That struck a chord.

Tim was stood nearest the altar and turned to face the group. He looked at the entrance and noted the Maha-Kali yantra above the door.

This mandala held a green background with three diminishing inverted red triangles inside a lotus petal circle. A square with four gateways surrounded the circle and in the centre was a white dot, the seed or bindu.

The whole mandala is created around this bindu, as it initially represents the un-manifested universe as well as the creative spark of existence.

The inverted triangles symbolised the yoni, the female sexual organ, the vagina. Everything must be born from a mother.

'Let's sit in a circle. I've brought a treat for you all,' Tim announced.

They all sat down cross legged, letting their eyes adjust to the light and their flickering shadows on the walls.

Millie took six small pipes from her shoulder bag, the type you might use for smoking hash in. She then reached down into her knickers and pulled out an elaborate stash bag attached by string to the inside of her jeans. As she opened the drawstring at the top of the multi-coloured bag from Rajasthan, Tim spoke.

'I don't want anyone to feel under any pressure to do this but Millie and I have brought along some DMT. I made it for you to try, only if you want to.'

Millie pulled out a large snap bag of white crystallised powder. She closed her eyes, held it up and seemed to say a little something under her breath. Then she opened her eyes, smiled broadly, waved the bag around and said, 'This could change your life …'

Tim carried on. 'The whole trip lasts about ten to fifteen minutes and I guarantee it's perfectly safe. DMT is a naturally occurring …'

Dong went the bell outside the entrance. They all looked round in unison.

Sy Poulis spoke to Steve Smart on his mobile as he waited for his private jet to taxi down the runway. 'I'm coming over there. I take it there's no news.'

'Nothing yet. They're supposed to be in a village chasing him down. He's no idea what's going on but he was aware he was being shadowed in the main town, Manali. This village is a few hours walk from the road. If anything happens while you're travelling I'll let you know.'

'Alright, then. Call me first. Under no account speak to the mothers without consulting with me. Is this understood?'

'Understood.'

Sycamore clicked off the phone. He wasn't pleased with the news. The Airbus ACJ800 now stood waiting for him. His entourage of employees paved the way, opening doors, fussing around him. The cabin crew greeted him with bowed heads.

He climbed the boarding steps and walked straight into the cockpit.

'I'm taking her today, captain, I need to think.'

Sycamore was an accomplished pilot and although he mostly left his travels in the hands of others these days, when he needed to meditate on an idea or problem, he loved to do it while looking out over the earth below and the sky above.

'Check that, sir,' said the captain and he got up from his leather, sheepskin coated seat.

The ACJ800 was the epitome of luxury flight. Even the cockpit was fitted with super comfortable seats, walnut panels and light gold coloured metal surrounding the LED dials and gauges. These included tachometers, accelerometers, altimeters and airspeed indicators. Hydraulic and manifold pressure gauges, directional gyros, vertical speed indicators. The list went on.

He liked nothing more than being in control of this super jet. It didn't publicly exist. There had only ever been one officially commissioned by an oil rich prince from the gulf. Sy and the other families owned one each. He'd bought his first and the others followed his lead as they knew he understood aircraft.

From the outside it just looked like an ordinary ACJ380, the difference was the interior. It was kitted out to his personal specification. He had a gold theme running through the plane. Everything was the best quality. The meeting room had a polished burr oak table surrounded by thirteen oak chairs with sheepskin linings covering the hardwood. Thirteen was considered a lucky number by the Poulis'. He had a four piece bathroom suite with a whirlpool bath, gold taps of course. There was a dining room for thirteen and twelve individual bedrooms with his master suite making up the numbers.

The kitchen could accommodate a banquet for the guests and the relaxation area was suitable for an orgy, harem or family occasions.

He got comfortable and breathed a sigh of relief. The summit was over but he had to think a few ideas through.

'The checklist's been done, sir,' said his number two, co-pilot Lance Kessel.

'Parking brake off. Easing on the power now, ten, twenty, thirty per cent.'

The huge plane crawled into motion.

'Clock on, sir,' said Lance as he started the stopwatch.

'Prepare for thrust, rudders steady … check.'

Lance had respect for anyone who could fly this bird but extra respect for someone to just could walk on and take her up like this.

'Hundred knots, twelve and a half degree attitude, visuals lost.'

The aircraft was ready to lift from the ground and then she was up.

'She's talking to me. Increasing the power.' Sy was now working off the digital displays around him as the ground was a memory and the only thing he could see out of the windows was blue. He dipped the nose and put the power into thrust climb.

'Auto thrust set.' Sy moved his hand to the flap lever.

'Flap now at one.' He paused a few seconds, moved it

down a notch. 'Flap zero.'

Now the speed was really increasing and they were almost at the initial flight altitude of 7000ft.

'Levelling off at seven.' Sy flicked a switch. 'Autopilot engaged.'

He sat back in the chair. 'Once you get over the size of her, she really just needs a gentle hand.' Sy paused while he thought about how simple she was to pilot. 'Keep an eye on things number two, I need to relax.'

Sy kept a watch on the main display until he was happy there were to be no last minute adjustments and then he started to mull over some of the talks he'd had with Oscar at the summit.

Oscar had told him how well he was doing in bringing the Japanese machine down. He said the xenophobic ant colony was in serious free fall. They were steeped in national debt, had zero growth and most of the population were deflated pensioners. The youth were obsessed with gadgets and unable to communicate normally. They would rather sit next to each other and text than talk face to face. The girls were seen as sexualised children and the boys couldn't face responsibility. They were ready to be plundered.

Traditionally the family had found it really challenging to gain ground in Japan. They were so stuck in their ways that unless you were Japanese, spoke the language, considered their customs as the law, they were a closed shop.

Over the last ten years Oscar had been working hard to demoralise the nation, devalue their economy and increase their national debt to unsustainable levels. Now they would have to seek outside assistance. They would never look to China because the historical scars ran too deep. Their traditional allies South Korea and Taiwan would be where they would turn. That was the issue he needed to think through. How could he get them to ask for help from the UK and US? The Bank of England and the Federal Reserve were both in his pocket. If he could do a deal to secretly bail out Japan via these routes, the money he could siphon off would be astronomical.

Oscar was up for it. He was already thinking of ways to drive a wedge in between the three allied nations. It wouldn't be difficult to do. They were so rigid about stuff like honour and keeping face he'd just blow up a few money laundering scandals or commercial espionage stories and they would all stop doing business with each other until the wind settled.

His job was to key up the British economy again and he had no doubt how to do that now he was flying, it came to him as he watched a line of lightning flash from one cloud base to another issued from a storm in the distance. As if his prayers had been answered, 'Ching!' it went in his mind.

Cocaine.

29

The group remained seated and quiet as a figure entered the womb of the temple, through the yoni, the entrance. Everything here was symbolic to the man who was informed. Everything had meaning and most meanings were of either an earthy or spiritual nature.

The fact that there were several foreigners sat in a circle on the floor was taken with neither surprise nor significance. That was just the way it was today in this sacred place.

RamaBaba sported his dreadlocked hair in a tight top knot on the crown of his head. He wore the red robes of the tantric and over the top of his gown, the furry skin of a black bear. His beard was long and had mostly turned to grey. There was a sparkle in his eyes that seemed to go on forever, through time. It was mischievous, awake, beguiling and marvellous. His gaze was completely free of judgement or duplicity. His only view of the world was as one. He didn't make any separation between different types of matter, as he created all of this in his conscious mind. His consciousness was separate from his physical form and was eternal, as is creation or destruction. He worshipped Kali-Ma as the ultimate being of compassion because she takes us all when our time comes. She eats us up and then spits us out until we have learnt life's lessons and when we have no further need of this earthly education. She was everything to him. She was the divine spark of creation that first came into being and would never cease or diminish. She was the energy that kept Shiva's cosmic dance alive. She was the moving atomic particle that could never be seen, because as soon as you found her she had gone, moved, changed form, been affected by your view of her. This was because you did not realise she was you, you were her and all is all. Everything in existence is one and there are not two of you.

There lies the secret of time. It is not a horizontal level that you travel across. It is a vertical. All that has ever existed or will ever exist is now. Your perception of the now can never actually be measured as there is no definitive of the present. All that we know is only the experience of it. Kali-Ma is the goddess who shows you this, if you truly let her. However she is fierce, she is powerful, she is omnipresent and if you are fortunate enough to be blessed by her, after that there is no going back.

The initiate of Kali-Ma cannot live in the world of ignorance or surround themselves with the unfortunate ones. The initiate is much better secluded or living with the forest, ocean or mountain dwellers. The initiate is better to live with the trees and flowers, the animals and the weather.

His friends are bears, monkeys, apes, dolphins, whales, tigers, buffalo and birds. They have more to say to him than a hundred thousand humans who abide in ignorance.

RamaBaba walked through the circle and Tim moved quickly aside, rather than be trodden on. He approached the effigy of Kali-Ma and applied red powder to the bottom of the black mound. He joined his hands in the traditional prayer gesture and raised them to his forehead.

The guttural noise that filled the chamber touched all those present in a universal way.

'Auuummmm … Shiva, Shakti, Kali, Laxmi. Auuummmm.' RamaBaba turned round with a huge cheeky smile and in perfect English told them all what was going down. 'It's the last day of full moon. She has her period, menstruating.'

All the women in the room got it immediately but the boys were left behind. Only Tim really understood.

'Is she real? To you,' Tim asked.

'As real as anything else. She is real because she allows me to see through her veil, her transparency, her Maya, so into the real.'

Tim was straight into this sadhu. He'd met plenty along the way but mostly the ones who stayed around tourists. The ones who blagged your charas. It was very rare to meet a genuine sadhu, a wandering holy man, who completely authentic.

'What is the real?'

'The real is whatever you make it,' RamaBaba answered as he always did, cryptically. He was not there to answer these questions. He was not there to be some kind of guru or teacher. He knew they were all at different levels of understanding and they all had to follow their own, individual path. He would respond to their request for knowledge with riposte, not solution.

'You mean the Union!' said Jules, not as a question but a statement.

'If you like.' RamaBaba decided he should sit. Tim and Millie made space for him and he effortlessly contorted into the lotus position. He had a routine that he'd worked out for himself. He rose at sun up and spent some time in meditation. He then spent some time doing hatha yoga. He then drank some nettle tea by making a fire and heating water and using the top sprigs of the nettle plant as flavouring. He boiled up some porridge with the remaining water that he took from a spring in the rock face. He then went for a walk if the weather allowed it. He then came to visit the temple to clean it and make sure all was well.

He would visit other sadhus or spend time in the forest with the animals. He would visit the temple again, around this time, early evening and then go back to his cave to be asleep as it went dark. He always did exactly as he felt he should. If he wanted to stay somewhere all day his routine would be put on hold until the next day. He found having this unstructured structure in his life the best way to be. He answered to no one, owed no one anything and was never a burden to others.

RamaBaba was fearless and courageous. He was neither arrogant nor meek. He just felt the need to sit, so sit he did.

'Why have you come here, to the temple?' he asked.

Tim thought too long before answering.

'To smoke some drugs,' Dean swaggered in the conversation.

Beki, who was all over the place emotionally after meeting Kat, the real man of her dreams, couldn't believe what Dean had just said and elbowed him sharply in the ribs. She was looking for any excuse to get at him.

'Charas?' RamaBaba asked.

'Well, no. Actually. Show him, Mills.'

Millie raised up the stash of white crystal.

'DMT,' said Tim who was looking quite perplexed. He was out of his comfort zone. He'd been all ready to be the pied piper of the group's Dimethyltryptamine session, leading them through the trip of their lifetime. Now this sadhu had usurped his role.

'What's it like? DMT.'

'It takes you to another dimension,' said Dean.

'Where did you learn such good English?' asked Emma, bluntly.

'Boarding school, do you think I was born into this poverty and enlightened state?' replied the sadhu. 'Anyway, is this other dimension worth being taken to?'

Dean couldn't believe it, even the holy man was from the upper classes. 'Dunno, not been there meself, yet.'

Flip, thought Beki, *he's gone all Manc again, that means trouble.*

'I'm Millie. This is Timo, Emma, Jules, Beki, Dean, Mari and is it Matt or Kat?' Millie said, trying to be polite.

'Kat, pleased to meet you.' Kat directed his greeting towards the sadhu.

'So, it's considered polite and natural for me to tell you my name now, isn't it.' RamaBaba thought his name out loud in his head. He imagined it echoing around the chamber and the vibration resonating in their eardrums. If any of them were awake, they would hear him first before he spoke. 'RamaBaba, my name's Rama.' He gave them all a big toothy grin showing off his widely spaced teeth. 'Baba.'

He reminded Dean of some of the old school Rasta from the Moss.

'Wow, how the heck did I know that?' said Jules.

'No way, Jules.' Dean was only half looking at her because he was laughing as well. 'It's easy saying you know his name after he's just said it.'

'Sorry,' Jules apologised for no reason. 'I know I get carried away sometimes.'

'Let's smoke those drugs,' said Tim. 'Baba, would you like some?'

'Sure. Is it natural, potent and very bad for you?'

'Absolutely,' replied Tim, smiling.

He nodded to Millie and she handed over the stash bag. While he was putting the powder in the first pipe Jules broke the silence.

'I know you're wearing one, but do you eat animals?' she asked the sadhu earnestly.

'Oh, no, I don't really. Animals are nice, they're my friends. Why would I want to eat them? This one died of old age. I don't want them rotting away inside me, eating the dead is not to be taken lightly.'

'But, you're a tantric, aren't you? I can tell.'

'I wear red cloth? Is this how you know, Jules?'

'No, actually you did something before. I don't know how you did it but you did.'

The sadhu put up his hands as if to say 'enough' and he changed the direction of the conversation. He wasn't prepared to talk about his party tricks. He wasn't prepared to tell them he'd eaten a morsel of human flesh once in Varanasi.

'Do you know what DMT is?' RamaBaba asked the question but didn't wait for a reply. 'We'd better find out.' He reached under his red robe and produced his iPad mini.

Dean smiled in total admiration. 'Can ya get a signal?' Dean asked, well impressed.

'Oh, yes, the tower's just up from here, very good signal. Better than Manali.'

He typed away and announced triumphantly, 'Ayahuasca!'

'Well, it's ayahuasca's baby brother,' Tim advised.

'There's no inhibiter, so as it's a naturally occurring drug in your body, the brain assimilates it really quickly after it's broken down by a liver enzyme. The whole trip is all over in ten or fifteen minutes,' Millie informed anyone who'd listen.

'Right then. Who'd like first go? Tim asked.

Hue Brooks waited patiently in the bushes along the side of the path with the entrance to the temple in his line of vision. It had been easy following the chattering crowd unnoticed. There was an outcrop of rocks he could hide behind so when they came out he could see where they'd go next. If they split up he could take Dean down. The girl would be no problem.

Facking holy man, why hadn't he thrown them all out of his temple? Hue was getting cold as the sun was low in the sky and teetered on top of the mountain, ready to sink behind the wall of stone when a chill would holiday on the breeze.

'If the boys take out Brooks and he doesn't get to this Dean Shelby, I want him brought in.' Sy Poulis spoke to Steve Smart at the apartments the boys had used for their briefings in the Kullu Valley. He'd landed the 800 in Delhi and taken a Cessna Citation X the rest of the way. He sipped scalding hot, freshly ground Monsoon Malabar coffee from Kerala, South India.

Smart knew better than to ask why he wanted to meet Shelby. 'How's the supply chain coping without the Brooks and Bates partnership?'

'It's not coping. I'm directing Emile Sarafian down there

as soon as he's finished his current assignment. He's a safe pair of hands. He will sort it.'

Sy sipped the coffee. It tasted of the colour black. It was dry and dark and awesome, like tasting the night. 'Do you know how they make this coffee, Steve?'

'No sir.'

'They let the roasted beans wallow for the monsoon in the warehouse, deliberately exposing them to the winds and the constant moisture. The beans swell up, they gorge on the weather, just like they had done when the British Raj sailed them home, when it took six months by sea.'

'They copy the conditions at sea?'

'Exactly. They swell the beans up by any means they can. It creates the perfect pH equilibrium.' Sy put down the cup and looked straight into Steve's eyes. 'That's what we are going to do to the British economy.'

'Swell it up?'

'Who do we have in South America? Columbia or Peru?'

'Several key allies, sir. It depends on what you want.'

'I want the UK flooded with cocaine, Steve. I want to forget the dampening process and I want the streets painted white with snow.'

'That should be no problem, sir.'

'It doesn't matter about the quality, as we both know, you Brits will sniff anything. It's quantity I need. Get that economy working again.'

'Yes, sir. I'll direct Sarafian onto it.'

'Good man. Now, about these boys. Is the clean-up team ready to go?'

'Helicopters and motorbikes on standby. I've got some trekkers already in the area.'

'Good work, Steve. Let's hope it turns out well.'

30

'Why don't we all do it together?' Emma asked.

'Yey, there might be some telepathy flying around,' said Jules.

Millie looked at Tim. 'Why not. Has everyone got fire?' asked Tim, using the European traveller's term for a light.

They all took out matches or lighters. Millie passed round the pipes. She'd bought them in a roadside stall in Old Manali. She gave one to the baba, Dean, Beki said she wasn't having any today, Kat, Mari, Jules and Emma.

'You not having any, Beki?' Dean looked at her accusingly.

'No, there aren't enough pipes anyway,' she said lamely.

'I've got one,' said Emma, who carried a small hash pipe for smoking small boulders of charas when she didn't want tobacco. She flushed it out from a hidden pocket in her coat and passed it round to Beki. 'There you go, lovely, wouldn't want you missing out.'

'Hell, no. Once in a lifetime, smoking the most

powerful hallucinogen on the planet in a creepy Kali temple. What's not to like?' Jules said in her jolly way as she passed the hash pipe on.

'Oh, thanks.' Reluctantly Beki took the pipe. She noticed it was slightly smaller than the others. She heard her mum's voice in her head. 'Be thankful for small graces, Rebecca' and she watched as Millie filled the bowl with the white crystal powder.

'A little guidance for you all. You are about to experience your true self. Don't be afraid. Relax and enjoy it. You will know when it's time to come back and when you do I suggest you stay still, lie down and think about where you've just been.' Tim was back, anchored in his role now.

'Alright, Tim and I will be here to make sure you're all fine and nothing will happen to you while you're out.' Millie paused. 'One more thing, please take all the smoke in, don't waste it. Timo here worked very hard to make this batch. It's completely pure and we've both done it a bunch of times ourselves.'

'It's really good stuff,' Tim added.

'Shall we light up?' said Dean.

They all lit their pipes up together.

Nothing's happening thought Beki as she put the pipe down after inhaling the blue grey smoke. Then as she lay down she thought the sadhu was starting his auming again. She realised that the sound was getting louder and louder and she felt as though her very being was the sound and that she was rushing with that sound and wasn't stopping. That all-encompassing hum, the very noise of creation was taking her quickly into infinity. Her real self, her essence was that sound and all abruptly the colossal rush stopped. She looked at a scene of the most intricate quantum geometrical patterns that were moving into and out of each other with the most ultra-vivid colours of neon blue, red, green, violet and yellow. There was a turquoise hue in the background shimmering with moving flecks of silver and instantly she was there looking back at the scene from the other side. She was surrounded by these flecks of silver that shimmered in the air and she realised they were entities, they were real. The entities moved all around her and they had wings that caused their shapes to fluctuate. They were upright beings but moved like rays do in the water, gently swaying their wings to move their bodies. Bodies, these beings did not have bodies as such, they were translucent and then she realised they had no bodies because they were just made from souls. *My, God, they were angels!*

Mari had a milder auditory hallucination but more of a visual one to start his trip. He heard the hum but he felt a flash of energy go right through his body. It was cold and bright. It was white light without heat. He felt the cold go right to his core and then the ball of white light evaporated around him and left him looking at the earth from space. He was out in space. There was the earth below and he could see the moon, too. It was the most beautiful thing he had ever witnessed. He was surrounded by the universe and he realised he was part of everything; he was really part of it all. He wasn't separate from anything, he was just it. He felt as though he wanted to be part of it, too, that being part of it was the most natural thing in the world. This was the first time he'd ever felt like he truly belonged.

Within a blink of his eye he was somewhere else and he was looking at earth from a distant planet. He was standing next to a telescope. When he looked into the telescope he could see the earth. He started to feel very far from home and then in a language he had never heard but completely understood a voice next to him said he could go home now to his own people. He took his eye out of the scope and there was a little green cartoon pixie man next to him who reached up and took the eyepiece side of the scope away from his head and then the scope telescopically shot out and he was sucked into the eyepiece. He went through the scope in a kind of vortex and landed back down on earth.

Emma was in the streets of a megacity made from green glass. There were no shops or offices but she felt perfectly at home there. She then realised she didn't have to walk as she could fly around and so she just took a leap of faith and she was soaring above the glass city. In the distance she could see a blue glass city, then as she turned a red one and then a yellow glass city. It started to rain and the rain was made of rainbows, little dashes of rainbow and all of a sudden she saw a huge tree between the cities and she flew towards the tree as she realised that the tree was at the centre of all the cities. When she got close to the tree it was colossal and its branches and roots were the lifeblood for all the coloured glass cities. The cities would not be able to exist without the beautiful multi-coloured tree whose leaves she could see were like paisley or more like fractals. When she looked into the leaves they went on deeper and further and she was in a spiral and she was flying into the essence of the tree of life and it went on and on forever. Each new shape or form had a new colour of pink or lilac, black or cobalt blue until she realised she was in the infinite spiral of life that spores us all.

POP! BANG! An instant, a hit, Kat was there. He felt like he'd been broken into a million tiny shards of light and put back together in a few milliseconds. Where he'd been put back was a beautifully complex multidimensional universe of colour and light. He was it; he was a part of the light. His body was made up from this wonderful glowing substance and his mind was fully involved in creating this stuff, too. He was in it and he was next to it at the same time. Logic ceased to exist. In some way he was part of it all and separate at the same time. He was no better or worse than it and it did not judge him. He then felt surrounded by a luminous glowing light that was not part of this realm but was feeding it into being.

He was suddenly in a craft that was flying through the universe and he was watching all these dimensions come together as one. They all had different civilisations and all had different beings living in them but they all had one true underlying connection and this was the luminous light being that held them all in place.

Hue had been waiting patiently but was getting frustrated. What were they doing in there? He thought through the option of just walking in the place. After all they just looked like a bunch of young hippie types. They wouldn't know what hit them.

He drew the knife from its sheath and felt its perfectly balanced weight in his hand. To pass the time he recalled how the Gurkhas used to play around with them at drill. There was a myth that if a Gurkha soldier drew his weapon, he had to spill blood. It had certainly kept a mob at bay when he was stationed in Afghanistan one time. The Gurkhas were given the task of guarding the small base that had been set up in a village in a remote district in Helmand province. Hue had been staying there doing some reconnaissance on a suspected tribal leader who was trying to work both sides. He was taking money from the West and protecting freedom fighters from the local area. Hue had been there for three days, in the heat and dust. He had another night before he reported in. He was either going to give the order to take this brute out or leave him be.

There had been an incident with some local goons and a trigger-happy infantry grunt from the Royal Anglican. He had let off some steam and fired a couple of warning rounds at a jeep that looked like it wasn't stopping at a checkpoint. It did stop and the locals inside were in a rush as one of the women in the back seat was pregnant and in labour.

This minor incident had the whole village on the street after Friday prayers and they were all coming down the main drag protesting.

Hue had gone up to a vantage point to see what was going on. The ramshackle crowd were just farmers and shop owners as there was no other work in the area. You either grew things or sold things. As they approached the guards on duty, two incredibly brave Gurkha soldiers walked out of the gate and stood in the road, facing the crowd. Hue watched in amazement as the mob approached. The two soldiers simultaneously raised their right hands so all could clearly see their intention and then pulled the kukri's half way out of the scabbards, showing enough steel to vow intent.

The crowd knew that if the Gurkhas fully withdrew their blade then blood would be spilt, or so the legend goes. The noisy mob ground to a halt as the ones at the front soon realised they'd be first to get it.

They stayed at a safe distance, made their protest and dispersed after a half hour standoff with these two fully committed, if slightly crazy, Gurkhas and their kukri blades.

Hue let the weight of the curve take the momentum of the knife and made a few moves he'd watched these boys practice in the base. There were the classic slashes and thrusts but it could also be used as a guard for the forearm by letting the handle spin in the palm of the hand to a reverse position, so the blade ran vertically down the arm while still being held in hand but with the bottom of the handle facing upwards.

There were other guard moves, like protecting the head from a high strike by holding the knife horizontally and using the free hand to back up the large blunt side of the knife where it bends. This meant any stick, knife or fist coming towards you could be blocked.

When the Gurkhas made a strike they let the knife do the work. They didn't hold it rigidly but let the heavy part of the blade slash through whatever they were attacking. In the drills, Hue had witnessed these were wooden posts and the sharpness of the blades was evident. However if the Gurkha wanted their man alive they just turned their weapon around and used the heavy blunt side as a club to knock them out.

Hue practiced some more moves, using the weighted area to balance the knife and flicks of the wrist to manoeuvre it into and out from the classic fighting position. He thought about the headlines if he went in there and killed them all: *Massacre at Indian Temple. Blood Sacrifice at Indian Temple. Human Sacrifice at Indian Temple* … maybe he could get away with it. When he thought it through he'd be covered in claret by the time he'd finished. Anyway, ideally he wanted to torture Shelby first, spin it out a bit and have some fun.

Jules was the most experienced of those taking part, with psychedelics. She was able to relax as she took the smoke in but nothing she had taken before could remotely be compared to this.

Snap! She was being sped through millennia of time to the source, the creation, the initial birth, the beginning. Then she was in a beautiful field of psychedelic tall grass that swayed and parted as she walked through it. She turned round and there was a line of cheerful, playful, childlike pixie people who were jumping around in pure joy. Two held her hand and they all started running through the tall grass that parted for them as they approached each strand that came up from the ground. She looked down to the terracotta coloured earth and realised that was also alive and organic. They came to a river of flowing mercury like water. It was dense and silver coloured. The pixies gave a hoot of joy as they hurried her towards it.

'Come on, come on!' they seemed to say but they weren't talking, they were communicating with thought. They all ran now, hand in hand towards the silver river and they jumped off the red earth. She thought she would sink in the river but they could run over the top of the flowing torrent. It was slippery underfoot and they skidded from side to side but they made it across, still holding hands.

On the other side of the river there was a fairy castle and the pixies ran faster and faster and told her telepathically she was 'going home'.

The castle was made of crystal and the quartz gave off a wonderful energy all of its own.

'Go on, go on!' The pixies let go of her hand and the drawbridge lowered as she approached. She turned to see the pixie people were all in play again, jumping around, doing cartwheels and forward rolls and were being very silly and free and loving every second of their existence.

She ran into the fairy castle which seemed much bigger as she walked in and she was picked up by two fairies that were just as loving towards her as the pixies had been but who seemed to know her every thought and deed. In a strange way she thought they were part of her. They asked her why she had come to visit them and she replied she wanted to see her true home and they loved her without judgement or agenda. She knew she was home and then they told her it was time to leave them but she was always welcome. She vowed to return one day soon. They said she could stay longer next time and she could come straight there to visit but she really had to go now … and then she was back in the temple, the candles were flickering their subtle, dainty light and she felt a little lost but warm inside.

RamaBaba had been to some strange and mystical realms in his mind before and so when the drug hit him he also felt relaxed and secure. His visions were astounding, though, even for him. He met the Buddha Avalokiteshvara whose multi-dimensional form blended into his own and seemed to emanate from him. His vision was of himself as a Buddha or more precisely a Bodhisattva, which seemed a perfectly natural state to reside in. There were several heads and arms which he seemed to own although they were more the Buddha's than his. They went up from his head and out from his shoulders respectively. The Bodhisattva body was not real as such but was made from the pure essence of reality. He knew he was alive but may as well have passed over to another realm. He meditated in this form and sensed an overwhelming force of love and compassion coming from and to him contemporaneously.

Dean was hit hard by the initial blast from the smoke. Millie had put a bit more than the others in Dean's pipe. Subconsciously she thought he was being a tad brash and she didn't like it. She saw to it that he got a good dose.

Dean was the only one to stay sat upright after smoking the DMT, everyone else lay down. His eyes stayed open, staring, unblinking. His eyes looked black as if the pupils had taken over. He looked ominous and departed. He moaned a bit as his head filled with the loudest rushing noise, an encircling sound. Round and round, this sound, the vibration of matter went. It was like standing in the middle of a Jah Shaka sound system on full volume with a mega low bass tone on loop. His whole self was the vibration. He then emerged from the initial sound with a BOOM and he was then just energy. He was the energy of the world. There was no up or down, no in or out. He understood time had no relevance to him as he knew it could not possibly exist. He was part of these beautiful patterns he could see and suddenly these patterns took form. They formed into mobius symbols, more and more, coming in and out of existence, spiralling into the infinite. They looked like they were the very principle of reality, which made an impeccable, sagacious, distinct, faultless, flawless truth. The fact that they never needed to stop, the fact that they were all able to continue forever without any outside interference or help made it all seem so simple and yet so profound. The key to life was there in front of him, was part of him. There were no rules, no regulation, nothing to conform to, no boundaries. Anything was possible, everything was allowed, there were no more limits. There was nothing he would ever put on himself again. He knew he would continue in one form or another forever. In the distance there was a shining light heading towards him at an impossible speed and as soon as he registered what was happening, it hit him with a supersonic high pitched, immortal tone, light as sound and sound as light. It was too much, his limited brain couldn't cope, then bang, bang, bang, bang, bang, like a midnight firecracker going off in his head he was back, staring through watery eyes at his lost infinity.

Dean blinked away the tears. He was the last to recover. There was silence as he looked round at his fellow travellers.

'Everyone home again?' asked Tim to the trippers.

'How long was that?' asked Emma.

'Dean was the longest, just past fifteen minutes.'

'Oh, my God! It felt like hours in there,' Dean said.

They all started to laugh and chat to each other about their experiences as if they had known each other their whole lives. They all agreed it was the wildest quarter of an hour any of them had ever experienced.

31

'Bab.'

'Yes, Jules.'

'Can you teach us any tantric tricks?'

'No, Jules, we have no tricks. We only work with rituals.'

'Rituals, then, can we do a ritual? Please RamaBaba Ji.'

RamaBaba was in a playful mood. 'The compassion I feel for you all is very great. You have been educated in Western ignorance.'

Mari and Kat gave each other a sly glance. Kat noted Mari's eyes were still heavily dilated.

'So … Baba, can you help us overcome our ignorance, then?' Jules was persistent.

'Do you all wish to learn the tantric ritual of Shiva-Shakti?' asked the sadhu. He was already aware the answer would be yes.

They all agreed that they would like to take part in a ritual.

RamaBaba stood and walked over to the Sun chest. He placed his hands on either side of the lid and pressed the secret panels and released the inner catch.

He lifted up the lid and placed it open, against the wall. He removed a drum, a Tibetan singing bowl along with its wooden stick or mallet and a wooden flute. As he placed them next to Tim and Millie he asked the boys to go around the back of the temple and fetch several logs from a wood store covered with a plastic sheet.

While they were gone he spoke to the women. 'You are the Shakti. Without you, Shiva lies as a Shava, a mere corpse. During this ritual you will be the ones to give the Shava life. You are the empowered ones. You have the power over the man and this ritual will allow you to believe this to be true.'

'So we're in control?' asked Beki.

'Yes, indeed. You are the eternal flame of desire and passion but some of you may not fully be aware of this. You are in command here, this is the Temple of the Goddess.'

The boys came back and the sadhu arranged the logs in a certain formation. He used kindling from some splinters off the logs and started a fire in the dhuni. He spoke some ritual words that nobody understood over the flames and then told the awaiting acolytes what was going to happen.

'Millie and Tim are going to play the singing bowl and flute.'

'I can't play the flute,' said Tim.

'Then just make it up, it's really not important,' Baba said. He turned his head back to the group who now sat in a circle around the flames. 'Each of you will have a natural partner that you feel is right for *you*. Stand in front of one another and join hands.'

Dean and Beki, Mari and Emma, Jules and Kat all stood up and faced each other. They all held hands, interlocking their fingers, palms facing inwards towards one another. They were spaced out around the dhuni and there were a few giggles coming from Emma and Mari who seemed the most relaxed couple.

Baba nodded to the two musicians. Millie had used a singing bowl before. This was larger than the average bowls she'd seen in Tibetan shops and stalls. The wooden stick was placed on the outside of the rim and slowly moved around in a steady circle. The vibration caused the bowl to 'sing'. The sound created from each bowl was slightly different and this one was a deep 'om' sound.

Tim was a capable guitarist and so he just trusted his instincts and went with the flute as the sadhu had told him to. Soon a tune emerged, a random set of notes that seemed to want to repeat themselves.

RamaBaba started to play the drum. It was a typical Indian style piece, double sided and he tapped out a gentle rhythm onto the stretched goatskin with the tips of his fingers. His left hand played the larger side, setting the constant loop of the beat and his right fingers tapped a complicated tune that seemed to accompany Tim's notes on the flute. As Tim had just been playing a kind of improvised jingle he had no idea how this was happening, but it did seem to work.

Once the play was established RamaBaba spoke to the couples.

'You are all free souls. You have no restrictions anymore in this sacred space.' Bom, ba, ba, bom, ba, ba bom went the drum as the constant resonance from the singing bowl filtered through the gaps and Tim's ditty on the flute flew over the top of it all. 'Here you are free from all your shackles. You are free to express your true selves. Look deeply into the eyes of the other. Understand that they are part of the everlasting cycle of birth and death. Know that your time here is both limited and unlimited. Know that you can be free if you understand this. Breathe as one, see as one, melt into each other.'

The fire was now well caught. The flickering light it created was both hypnotic and warm. The couples were starting to enter into a kind of trance. They were pliable enough from the DMT to let their minds go with the music and the gently persuasive voice of the tantric master.

RamaBaba was well beyond what the general population consider to be normal. He had spent the last twenty eight years of his life on a quest for realisation of the human condition. He knew we were all sexual beings and that repressing this caused untold harm. His philosophy of doing exactly what he felt like doing was being played out in a rare opportunity. He was slightly increasing the tempo of the rhythm as the show went on. He was subtle and manipulative. He was in complete control.

'Now you're engaged in the timeless merging of the Shiva and Shakti. Only once they are together can the world exist.'

All three couples were completely past their initial discomfort and were intimately moving with the sound of the ensemble. Beki and Dean were smiling into each other's eyes and gently swaying, moving their hips and touching each other occasionally.

Mari and Emma were much more serious. There was an intense gaze between them that seemed to reach down into their very being. This was coming more from Mari than Emma. The knocks from the accident and the hallucinogens were having a definite effect on his psyche. Emma was amazed at his intensity and was happy to go with it even though she knew she should be taking the lead.

Kat and Jules were now hugging and caressing each other. They were moving with the beat from the drum, in and out, round and round.

'Now, to represent the world as it truly is we must change partners. The only certain in life is that it is in a constant state of flux. Gently move away from each other and turn to the next partner along. Do it now.'

The drum changed its rhythm. The story took a left turn. They did as they were inculcated to do. Mari was now with Beki, Dean with Jules and Kat with Emma. They started where they'd left off. The intensity in the room was palpable now. It was hot from the fire and a little surreal, dreamlike.

The music seemed to be of a more exciting nature. The group response was to move with it, sway with it. Tim and Millie were completely enthralled in creating the scene. They were both wide eyed and Tim was fully engrossed in his new found skill as a flautist. He felt like the ancient god Pan was showing him how to play. He spontaneously stood up and moved around the circle, playing his flute to each couple like a violin player in an eccentric Italian restaurant.

Once the sadhu was there himself he commanded another move round and now it all went with his imagination. Only Millie who was a pure soul stayed still and peaceful, lost in her own world, going round and round the singing bowl, immune to his thoughts, his will.

As Jules moved across to Mari she unbuttoned her shirt and then took it off. All she could think of was becoming naked like Kali. All she could do was to give in to the heat and atmosphere in the temple. She started to dance and then like a virus, her intuitive movement spread round the room.

Beki was with Kat and she just didn't care anymore. She took hold of him and kissed him. He was the most beautiful boy she had ever seen. They started to remove each other's clothes as if they had been together for lifetimes.

Dean was aware of what was going on but something deep down told him it was OK and he should be happy for her. He was with Emma who had a deep sexuality who took control of him, completely.

The orgy of sexual expression went on until the fire's flames were spent and a cold chill once again filled the air. Only Millie watched as the others all entwined with one another now slept or rested. She decided she had seen enough and wanted to go back. It was dark outside and so she woke Tim. As they weren't a couple she had no hold over what he did but there was a sense of loss about him in her mind. He pretended to be asleep and although she knew better she left him. The others who had smoked the DMT would be tired, she understood that from her own trips but Tim was just playacting. It wasn't even ten o'clock at night. He never crashed until after midnight.

As she gathered her things and headed for the door RamaBaba spoke.

'Millie.'

She stopped but didn't turn around. She kept looking at the door. Mari stirred as he hadn't actually been sleeping.

'When I arrived there was a foreigner hiding in the bushes watching the temple. He may still be there.'

Mari sat up. 'How old was he?'

'Middle aged, forty, fifty.'

'Kat, wake up.' Mari nudged Kat who had drifted into a post orgasm glow. He and Beki were still cuddled up. She was warm and wonderful but when he heard the news from Mari that Brooks was hiding outside, he was instantly awake.

32

Both the boys had brought shoulder bags that housed their weapons and they both searched for their bags and checked the contents. They huddled in a corner of the temple under the watchful eye of the sadhu.

RamaBaba was quick to work out there was a serious issue with these two. Mari knew who the waiting man was and now they were planning something.

Kat felt like he was coming round again from his altered state and was trying to figure out what the hell had gone on with the orgy. Had he been hypnotised? He'd certainly felt in some kind of trance and not entirely subject to his own free will. He'd just made Dean's girl, how was Dean going to react to that?

Kat looked down at her. He had never connected with anyone before. All the women he'd been with had shallow imprinted into their DNA. She was different because she was pure inside. He was convinced she was the one he'd been looking for. It was time to hunt and if he survived he was going to take her for his own. She would be his prize; she was what he would fight for tonight.

Mari was working from an unknown place. He was still slightly spaced and wired from the accident. Not only that, he'd then smoked some powerful drugs. It had been a very strange night so far. He had felt obliged to go along with the sex ritual. It troubled him to think he wasn't in control. That was his conclusion when he thought through it all. The whole hour had been very bizarre. Now he was supposed to hunt down and kill a human being. He'd never even considered this act to be anything other than his duty. From being a small boy he'd heard tales from the older family members of hunts and the bravery shown by the Poulis'. This was how you became a man in his culture. After this night he would be taken into the breast of the clan. He would be ready to head the family.

'Dean, Dean, wake up.' Kat shook him and he opened his eyes. Mari watched as the boys had agreed, ready to intervene if Dean caused a problem.

'Wow.' He woke up to the scene. He felt like it was a movie. 'What happened?' He seemed as confused as the boys. He was asking Kat what had gone on.

'Strange days, my friend,' Kat replied and they both looked at RamaBaba who was sitting upright against the wall, watching, listening with an unmitigated expression of innocence.

'Did you do her?' Dean asked him, as straight as bullet from a gun.

Kat looked away, half in shame and half not wanting to give away his delight. He nodded yes.

'Good, isn't she?'

'The best,' offered Kat. 'You're a lucky man.'

Dean got up. The voices made the girls stir although Beki kept pretending to sleep. She even tried to blow her breath out to replicate a sleeper's breathing sounds. Nobody was fooled, though.

Dean chuckled to himself.

'Did she mention she offed her last boyfriend? Sliced his cock off with a kitchen knife.'

Beki tensed instinctively. Dean caught the momentary lapse in her breathing.

'Didn't you tell 'em that?' He was talking to her back as she lay on the floor. She didn't move as she spoke.

'What, Dean?'

'Didn't you tell 'em you killed Tom Fisher?'

'Must have forgotten to mention that, you prick.'

'Oh, she forgot to mention it.' Dean walked towards the door where his shoes lay. Taking off shoes and lining them up reminded him of the growing rooms back home.

He sat on the floor and started to put his on.

The boys approached him.

'There's some bloke watching the temple. Baba said he's hiding in the bushes.'

This got Dean's attention. Especially as he'd just been reminded of what had gone down in England before they'd left. Could it be Tom's family had found out he was dead? Word might have got out. People talk, even gang members tell stories.

'What we gonna do about that then, lads?' Dean tied his laces nice and tight. 'Cos I'm in no mood to be messed about with.' He looked back at Beki.

'Us neither,' Kat said.

Dean stood up and the boys laced their boots. He thought through the angles and came to the only obvious conclusion. The man watching the temple was there for Beki and him. To hell with it then. How he wished he had his night vision goggles. He knew he would have to close his eyes before going out into the night but did the lads? Now he looked down on them as they sat on the floor.

'Right, wake up, ladies, get your stuff together.' It was like he was back home giving the orders out again. It felt good and natural. 'This is what we do.'

Hue was freezing now. He'd used two more opium suppositories to kill the cold. He'd stood as long as he could but now had to walk up and down behind the rocks to keep a bit of body temperature and circulation. He'd thought about approaching the temple and listening in a few times but he didn't want to lose the element of surprise when he hit them.

As he stepped back to check the temple door from the little soft trail he'd made from going back and forth for the last hour, the temple door opened. Hue froze to the spot, aware the world around him was still and silent. He watched two young men go around the back of the building as had happened earlier.

No,no,no,no,no! Hue was livid. They came around with more firewood. *They must be staying in there all facking night!* Once he got over the rant in his head he realised they had left the door ajar.

Now he was sorely tempted to just steam in there and grab Dean Shelby, drag him out and butcher him in front of his friends. He had to hold himself back with the thought that he wouldn't get to torture him first, that it would be too swift, too noble a kill.

He could see the flickering light from the doorway. It made him think warm thoughts and with the painkilling effect from the goof balls, he suddenly felt better than he had in the last two hours.

'So are you two lads up for this or what?' Dean asked Kat and Mari.

'Sounds good.'

'Right you. I know how hard it is for ya to keep ya clothes on, so swap coats wiv him, pants too if they fit.'

Beki didn't protest. She was scared, too, nervous of who was waiting for her outside and alarmed by her behaviour with Kat. What had she been thinking? But that had been the whole point, as if she hadn't been able to manage herself, as if she had been a device, beguiled into operation beyond free will. Now she was paying the price for living completely in the moment, for doing exactly as she pleased without any thought of consequence.

She took off her trousers and although he couldn't fasten the waist button, Kat kept them on by the belt. Her coat was a tight fit but with the hood up, in the dark he would pass for a girl.

Kat took his bag and went into a corner. Only the sadhu saw him take the chained sticks from his bag and push them up his left arm sleeve, chain end first.

'Ready?' Dean asked the room but aimed it to Kat in particular.

They walked out together and Dean then put his arm round Kat, as if to keep his partner warm. They left the door slightly more open than before and walked down the path as if they were heading home. Dean had initially had his hood down so there would be no mistake it was him.

'Cold innit?' Dean said rhetorically and pulled up his hood.

Hue was feeling sick with excitement. *Come to Daddy, come to Daddy,* he kept saying to himself as they walked towards him down the path. The moon shed some light but was hampered by the clouds. The cloud cover would keep the heat reflected from the earth but he would have preferred the moonlight now.

He would take out the girl with the back of the knife. A single blow to the head with the blunt edge should suffice. In the confusion of the attack he would take out Shelby's legs and drag him behind the rocks, arm round his mouth to snuffle any noise. Stab him in the arse if he protests too much.

As they approached he wondered how unbelievable it was that they came out alone, as if delivered to him by the gods and then the first spark of caution erupted into paranoia. *Was this too easy?* Self-doubt did not sit well with Hue Brooks. It was an unknown entity that bounced around his mind like a tiny warm squash ball rebounding off the insides of his skull.

Mari couldn't help it as he looked through the crack in the door where the hinges met the wall. He had his hand wrapped round the handle of his knife buried inside his shoulder bag. Tim and the girls were all sat along the back wall and the sadhu had been instructed to lead them to safety when Mari left the temple.

Mari's heart was pounding in his chest and his hand felt lined with sweat around the handle of the knife. His mind was playing tricks on him. He could taste a metallic tang in his mouth. His thoughts raced about what had gone on in the last day, his accident, the drugs, the sex. Now he was ready to kill or be killed. It really didn't get any higher octane than this.

He felt like he was behind the cut out steering wheel of a yellow Lamborghini at the start of a race, revving the engine, waiting to wheelspin into oblivion.

33

It was a strange sensation that Hue Brooks had just felt. For the first time since childhood he had doubts about his actions. Was he being set up? This was impossible. He was the most effective killing machine the forces had ever seen. He was the go to man for the richest, most influential family on the planet. He was mentored by the top spook of his generation, the late Charles Bates. All this training, Black Ops, spying, field combat and psychopathy had taught him well. You could never trust good luck. Luck did not exist, only probability and what were the odds that of the two people who made a timely exit from the temple, one was the very person he was here to see. Hue calculated the odds were very lucky, nearly one in ten. An unusual note of caution would be needed.

In Hue's past he had worked on instinct and an unmitigated self-belief. He never hesitated and just went with situations, took what came his way and made it his own. Hue was acutely aware this was his last mission. He would be executed, squashed like a fly by the machine that towered above him, the Poulis family. He had worked out the only reason he was still alive was because taking out Dean Shelby was tying up a loose end for them. They liked to use and manipulate their employees and if Hue had any respect for anyone, it was for those who explicitly attained their goals at any cost.

The opium was dampening down some of the more extreme symptoms of Hue's increasingly problematic mental state. He was not a fool; he knew he had been depressed by Charles' demise, the nagging thoughts, eating away like maggots through his brain. It was the unbearable image of Charles jumping voluntarily from the hotel balcony. He had to have been shoved over. He had to have been pushed, and this runt, this council estate scum walking towards him was responsible for his death.

'What shall we do Timo?' Millie asked, breaking the silence.

There was an atmosphere of dread taking hold of the room.

RamaBaba was sat in meditation. Tim was feeling guilty about joining in with the orgy as he'd taken full advantage of Jules who had been completely out of it while he went with her. He'd watched the group go under as RamaBaba had worked his magic. Tim had never seen anything like it before. This wasn't stage magic, this was real. Unless he'd been influenced too and not realised it? Yes, that was it. He had been under the spell and not comprehended it. He'd been tricked, too. He'd had no choice but to join in.

Then the image of Jules beneath him, moaning incoherently, eyes flickering open and closed, rolling back to their whites as he came inside her bore into his consciousness. He'd always fancied her, who wouldn't have. She was the pretty one out of the two. Emma was the more grounded, plainer looking. Jules was out there all right, a real space cadet. He wondered if she even knew he'd been with her.

'Wait here, I guess. Let's just wait and see, Millie. The guy might have gone ages ago. We could all be back at the guest house in half an hour, smoking a chillum and laughing about it all.'

She gave him a look that said this was no laughing matter and then stood up and walked over to Mari. 'Anything going on?' she whispered and felt the tension in his body as she touched him. She looked through the crack in the door out into the dark night. She could see Dean and Kat walking down the path with a single torch beam illuminating their way. They were approaching the rocks and bushes—that must have been the place where the guy was hiding. The path then opened out for a short clearing before you entered the pine forest.

Hue hid behind the rock and heard their footsteps increase in volume as they approached his hiding place. If they were aware of his presence, by the time they cleared the cluster of bushes and stones they would let their guard down. They would think he had left. He held his breath as they walked directly past him and when the shuffle of feet reached the crunch of the pine cones and needles, he made his first move.

Hue threw a medium sized stone into the forest and it hit a tree with a flat crack before hitting the floor with a soft thud.

The two walkers immediately stopped and held their ground, listening for anything, senses on full alert.

A sleeping bird instinctively flew from its perch and a shrill warning call filled the sound waves, becoming more distant with every passing second.

Adrenalin thumped the two boys hearts into speedy motion, their flight instinct was difficult to subdue. Both wanted to run while Hue brooks suffered no such feeling. His only thought now was to fight and so the other, bigger rock he'd secured in his long and cold lookout had just been discarded towards the heads of the two frozen sentinels.

On hearing the crack of the stone in the forest Mari shoved past Millie and swung open the temple door. He ran down the path and she just caught the image of the lethal knife emerging from his shoulder bag as he went.

Mari was at full speed and was at the rocks in seconds. He jumped into the bushes, slashing at the foliage as he went through it.

The rock hit Dean on the shoulder and then carried on to smack into his ear. The shock was enough to take him down, though. He was still conscious but felt the blow. The adrenalin brought him through and with a hand from Kat he was on his feet again.

Hue's plan had been to follow the rock up with a running dive, taking the two of them down but when he heard the bushes behind him being stomped through, he'd stopped in his tracks. Hue held the big blade across his chest and kept his back to the rocks. As the moon peeked from the last of the cloud he met Mari's silhouette, still slashing through the dark with the fierce frenzy of a frightened teen in his first real fight.

None of the training, coaching, teaching, killing of animals or even a shark can prepare you for close quarter combat. Even Hue had rarely been in this situation. His close kills had usually been with easy, vulnerable prey. This type of situation was best avoided due to the amount of variables involved in hand to hand fighting. One such variable was rapidly approaching him, wildly thrashing a deadly blade through the air.

Hue took a chance and crouched down, hoping he was enough in the shadow that he wouldn't be caught out.

Mari was moving too quickly, he wasn't thinking of his teachers who had schooled him to slow down, to take in his environment and use it to his advantage. He was panicking, lost in an emotional rage. He had started his advance towards the goal from a position of disadvantage. He now realised this was a big mistake. He was mad at Kat and fuming he'd let Kat persuade him to keep back. There was no way he was going to get the kill now. Tears began to well in the bottom of his eyes and his vision became so blurry he did not see the squatted figure of Hue Brooks until the knife had been stabbed, straight and deep, into his stomach.

It was a fast, hard thrust that pierced square into Mari's intestines and carried on. The momentum of his forward movement took the point of the blade into his left kidney. Hue had trouble then. Due to the boomerang shaped blade and the way Mari fell forwards onto him, he didn't get it out in time. He held on as long as he could to the black bone handle, trying to rip it out, but it went from his grasp. He may have broken his wrist if he'd held on too long.

Then the other two, torchlight in hand were coming at him from the forest side.

Hue was on his feet and the torch beam flashed off the blade in Mari's right hand. Hue stamped down hard on his right elbow. The reflex caused his palm to open and Hue then stamped on the back of his wrist, pinning it to the ground causing it to bend backwards in a ghastly manner.

Mari struggled desperately to keep his fingers round the handle of his weapon but failed. Hue wrenched the knife from his useless hand and quickly stabbed it into his lower back, no twist or turns, a quick in and out through his right kidney and into his liver.

Kat realised Mari was face down on the ground as they approached he felt like he was going to soil his pants. His whole stomach and bowels felt as though they were going to fall out. His heart thumped rapidly and sweat now ran down his forehead, even though the outside temperature was low. He brushed back the hood and let the nunchucks slip out of his sleeve, into his hand, whipping them around his back to cover them from sight. He stopped in front of Hue, still short of slashing or thrusting distance, he was not going down like Mari. As soon as Dean caught up and Hue's face acknowledged Dean's presence with a lustful grin, Kat swung the leading stick straight out from behind his back. No fancy show, no elaborate kata, not any warning or quarter given.

The bottom edge of the lead branch hit him straight in the mouth. It went into that snarling grin like a hammer hits a nail and his teeth shattered, flying into the back of his mouth. He struggled to gain composure as the splintered enamel was causing him to gasp as he choked on the bits of himself that were scattered around his throat and across his tongue.

Hue spat out and coughed up his teeth as Kat delivered a swinging backhand blow to the side of his head. Hue knew what was coming and managed to duck away to his left, so even though there was a connection it was more a glance than a full on strike.

Hue reached with his left hand into the back of his throat and scrambled around with his fingers, trying to retrieve his lost bits of enamel, dentin, cementum and pulp, all mixed together from his smashed in teeth.

He stood up, erect and projectile vomited up the contents of his stomach with a combination of his fingers down the back of his throat and the effects of the opium that stop the digestive process and rather promote evacuation of this sort.

Once the boys had been sprayed with Hue's vomit and bits of his teeth they felt like throwing up themselves but Hue was over it instantly and was seizing the advantage. He slashed the knife towards the boys and they both stepped a pace backwards. Once they had that narrow distance again and had gathered their minds back from being splattered with puke, Dean realised he'd been duped.

Where had the nunchucks and fancy knives with spiked handles come from? Why were Kat and Mari so intent of taking this guy down? Nothing made sense here. Whose fight was this? Because when he left the temple he was sure it had been his.

Hue was at them again and this time he didn't stop coming. Kat had taken him by surprise with the first strike, the second had been useless, just a partial blow. Hue was back into his empty mind fighting mode now. He had cleared the majority of his teeth from his throat. He was sure they had lost the advantage by being so repulsed by a bit of stomach lining. They had missed their chance and the pendulum of the fight had swung back his way.

He advanced in short darting movements, sometimes changing directing from left to right, at times retreating when a branch of the weapon parted the air at head height.

It was after one lower swing that he moved in and slashed at Kat's arm as his body turned slightly from the missed strike. Hue cut through the skin with the slash and immediately went for a stab to the neck but Dean read what was coming and just in time pushed Kat from the back onto the floor.

Hue's eyes followed Kat as he sprawled and fell. Dean used a front kick to Hue's torso and although it failed to inflict any damage it pushed Hue back towards the area Dean needed him to be in.

Hue staggered backwards, headed for the rocks and it was Dean's turn to advance towards him. He kicked out again, connected well with his body and then Hue was off balance and unable to stay on his feet. He fell backwards and landed with enough momentum to roll away from Dean, even further towards the outcrop.

Kat got up, he was vividly aware he'd been cut on his arm. It smarted and throbbed but he had enough left in him to hold the bottom of the nunchucks and turn the top of the branch with his good hand. The end came off to expose the concealed blade which he pulled out to its full length. Kat was going to finish the hunt with a stab to the enemy's heart.

Kat tried to ignore the pain but he knew his arm was useless. He held his weapon with his right hand and ran towards the melee.

Hue got up and it was then as he raised his eyes from the body on the ground that Kat saw the silhouette of a figure standing atop the rocks.

34

'Come this way,' said RamaBaba ushering the group from the temple and away from the direction of the fighting. They silently filed out and then he hurried to the front of the queue as they waited in the dark. The lack of light was made more acute as they had just left a relatively illuminated place and their senses were on full alert.

Jules felt it most. She was the sensitive one after all. Normality was back with a vengeance as soon as she left the temple. Inside there had been something going on, but she could only guess at what it was. The best way she could describe her time in the temple was that there was magic in the air, not completely white magic, either. Now she felt as if something had been lost.

'Come, this way,' said RamaBaba. He led them along a path that would have been invisible to a foreigner, one made by goats and sadhus alone.

The path stretched right round the outskirts of a hill and if it had been light, they would have really enjoyed the trek.

By torchlight it was quite arduous as the trail was narrow and with most seldom used paths, well camouflaged and overgrown.

Once they had circumnavigated the hill, the path climbed. Luckily the vegetation ceased and they were now on a rocky and well defined route.

'Follow the rasta, wait at the top,' Ramababa said to Emma who was behind him and he stepped to the side until they had all passed. He stood stock still and listened intently for any kind of noise coming from below.

If anyone had followed them he would have heard them on the rocky path but there was quiet serenity, compared to what they had left behind.

Sy Poulis was pacing up and down the apartment, taking sips of coffee from a white mug and constantly felt he wanted to smash the blessed thing against the white walls around him.

'We have a live feed,' said Smart. He moved away from the monitor set up on a table in the main room to let Sy see.

It was being transmitted by their operatives in the area. They had helmet mounted cameras with night vision facilities. The green hue on the screen was pixelated and blurred but they got the gist of the situation.

The operative had climbed up the trunk of a pine tree on the edge of the forest while the fight had been in the early stages. He had centred in on the noise, got down and then crawled in the direction of the grunts and commotion.

With the moonlight behind him, camouflaged fatigues and his blacked out skin he became imperceptible to the naked eye as he lay motionless and observed the show.

At first they all presumed it was Mari and Kat who were going at Brooks but the first doubts sprang into Sy's mind when they were next to each other and Dean's frame, his wide shoulders, didn't seem to fit with Marimous' body shape.

Smart spotted it, too, but kept quiet. He wasn't going to be the one to speculate as to where Mari was if he wasn't one of the pair fighting. Anyway the picture wasn't great and as they had moved back to the rocks the operative from the snatch squad had to move around to get them in view again.

The camera settled in time to see the outline of a woman. She was standing on top of an outcrop of rocks. They watched her lift an object of considerable size in the air, directly over her head. They were transfixed as she waited and waited. Then she launched it down into the area below.

As Beki hurled the log from the timber stock downwards towards Hue's skull, she nearly went over the edge, too. It was the way she threw it, with such force. She wasn't going to let her boys go down. Neither of them.

The noise when it hit the top of his head was a sickening

combination of crack and splat as it smashed into his skull and reached the grey matter.

Was this the actual blow that killed him? Undoubtedly it was.

He staggered about for a few seconds, his life events ran through his mind now. There was no fight left in him, he was gone in less than a minute from the time the heavy log had left her hands.

The boys just stood in amazement, watching him die. He twitched and shuddered.

They say when you die DMT gets released into the brain to help you on your way. Dean shone his torch into the split cranium of Hue Brooks' head and stared at his brain and bits of splintered skull. His brain was intricately veined and a thin membrane reflected the beam and glistened, gossamer like, around it.

Kat went to Mari who was still breathing but in really bad shape. He dared not move him as he was bleeding out from the two stab wounds. He tried to apply pressure to the one he could see but it was a useless effort.

The snatch squad were on it. They were ordered in by Sy as soon as it was apparent that Brooks was dead.

Sycamore sat down and wept. These were no tears of joy or triumph. These were tears of woe and disappointment. How could they be so stupid as to let a random girl make the kill? In all the centuries of the hunt, this was a timeless ritual going back further than current records began. An oral tradition passed down from the very beginning of their bloodline. The shame he felt at that moment. How could they do it to him, how?

Now that coffee cup flew at the wall, the black liquid creating a splatter pattern in contrast to the plain white beneath. It started to drip downwards, as gravity ruined the initial bland aesthetic.

It had been that same force that helped kill Brooks. The weight of a log thrown vertically at someone would have little effect but thrown down towards the mass of the earth with force, the same log was lethal.

He watched the coffee splatter drip dejectedly down the wall and although he felt like raging, he started to laugh. So what? He may as well laugh because every other ruling family would be laughing at the Poulis' when this came out. Their boys couldn't even make their own kill. It was the shame of it he found hardest to handle. He would have to think carefully about how to proceed. He must use this outcome and turn it to a positive.

The beams of light surrounded them and were moving in at speed. Beki had climbed down and was wondering what the flip was happening. Where were all these torch beams coming from? It had to be the police. She panicked as she ran up to the boys, still standing next to the two bodies.

'Dean, say he fell. Say they had a fight and he stabbed

Mari and then he fell. Dean, he fell.' Beki panicked.

'Whatever.' Dean turned to Kat. 'This is seriously messed up, mate. We should do one.'

'It's the cops, I'm not waiting around here to explain this one to Indian police, lads, I'm off,' Beki said.

'Stay here. Wait. I know them,' said Kat. 'They'll help clean this mess up. Mari's hardly breathing, just shallow gasps.' He reached out and took Beki's arm. 'Don't worry. It will all be taken care of. You two killed him, really, he's your kill.'

Beki looked at Dean as every part of her wanted to run, but where to? The beams were almost on them now. Then she heard the beating whirr of helicopter blades moving in.

35

'Hello, it's Dean, isn't it.' Sy Poulis gave Dean his most grandfatherly smile as he walked into the conference room of the Hotel Kailash.

'Yes, you must be Sy,' Dean said as he sat at the big circular meeting room table. He didn't get up. In fact he kicked back, pushed his chair away from the rosewood Corniche, the Arios-Maler designed slab of manicured dark wood and leaned it back on two legs.

Sy sat down and poured a glass of iced water with lemon wedges, from a cut glass jug, into a tumbler. He took a sip, just enough to wet his lips. The water pouring gave him the time to evaluate Dean's body language. He picked up that he had no respect for age or authority. He was at ease and would be open to suggestions that he thought had some benefit to him.

'This hotel.' Sy paused to make sure he had his full attention. 'Is the finest hotel in the region. They cater for the rich and powerful. Politicians, rock stars, film stars,

Russian oligarchs. They have the best restaurant in the area and a suite costs per night more than the average Indian earns in their lifetime.' He took another sip of the lemon infused water. This time offered Dean some. Dean accepted and Sy's aim of getting him off the two legs of his chair worked, as he had to lean forward to take the glass. Dean then kept his weight at the front of the chair, arms on the table and Sy was no longer irritated by his arrogant stance.

'But who owns it?'

'Dunno. You?' Dean asked, hopefully.

'No, I'm not in the service sector. The truth is that it's impossible to find out who actually owns this place. The owners are lost in a web of several different companies and lawyers who have off shore interest and shield the actual proprietors from any direct accountability. This is what it's like in India. There are no rules that cannot be bent if one has enough money to bend them. Luckily for you, I have enough money.'

Sy could see Dean slowly understood his pitch. He could see that it was registering that he was being given an opportunity and was not just being told what to do.

'What is it someone like you needs from me? 'Cos from what I've seen, yous don't need my help.'

'Oh, yes, but I do, Mr Shelby. You are the very person I need. You know the way things work. You understand the people I don't want to deal with. My operatives come through Eton or Harrow. They are completely removed from the 'street' as it were. They can bully or bribe their way through but they don't know how to make a play with gangsters and hoodlums. You do.' Sy stood up and walked over to Dean. He stood near to him and looked right into his eyes. 'You will have my full support and backing if you agree to work for me. I will take a personal interest in you and see to it that the risk to you and your family is kept as low as possible.'

'What risk?' Dean thought a second. 'Risk to my family?'

'Your family were at risk from your previous activities and I will minimise any future negative outcomes on your behalf.'

'My family weren't at any risk until my meeting with Charles Bates. He made the threat against my family.'

'And you dealt with it … bravo. There will be no more of that as you will be in charge of the operation.'

Dean thought for a moment. He liked this man, for all his airs and graces he wasn't like Charles Bates. He was more down to earth, more approachable. You didn't see many people like him in such a powerful position.

'So what is it you have in mind, Mr Poulis?'

Sy smiled and went back to his seat. 'It's a simple plan. I find they are the best. You are going to smuggle some kilos of Indian charas to England. Once you've sold it, you are going to buy some pure cocaine and from there you are going to expand your cocaine business extemporaneously. Thus you will be creating a multi-million pound cocaine empire, almost overnight. I want the UK saturated. I want the streets paved with snow.'

Sy stood up and asked Dean if he had any questions.

'Why? Why do you want the UK flooded with cocaine?'

'Well, I could tell you the official version. It's all to do with geo-political economics and the balance of power between the East and West, but really, Dean, are you sure you really want to know?'

'Yer, go on then, spill, big man.' Dean leaned back on two legs again.

'It's to keep the vibrational frequency of the masses low and chaotic. So they will all be obsessed with food, booze, sport and celebrity. So they will be kept ignorant, fat and greedy. So they won't notice that half their brothers and sisters are hungry, and if they do notice, they won't care because they're all right. They have a game to watch or a crate of beer to drink. However most of all, Dean, it's to do with keeping the masses so removed from the vibrational frequency of "love" as possible. Love, you see, is very, very bad for business.' As he walked towards the door he asked again, 'Are there any more questions?'

To which Dean replied no and found his chair was back on all four legs again. He needed the grounded feeling of stability. 'Oh yer, actually. There is one more question.'

Sy stopped just short of the hotel suite's door and stifling his irritation, he turned around with his winning smile etched on his face.

'If that's bad for business, then what's good?'

'Easy, Dean. Fear. Fear is very good for business. Keeping them so in fear of their future they dare not question anything. Imagine a world with no protest, no uprising or insurgency. No more riots. Things have reached the point again.' He could see the puzzled look on Dean's face. 'Dean, you have been lied to your whole life. Human civilization is not a few thousand years old, it is a few million years old. There used to be a collective spirit that maintained balance and equilibrium. The plants and animals lived in the garden and they had balance. They had no need for anything because they were never aware there was anything to need. They lived in harmony with their surroundings and adapted to the natural changes around them. They were able to map out a line of energy related hotspots around the planet. They knew where to place their sacred sites by intuition and by their deep understanding of the natural sequence.

'Look it up for yourself on a globe. Easter Island, Machu Picchu, Nazca, Ollantaytambo, Cuzco, Paratoari pyramids, the ones in South America that they say are a natural phenomenon. Pah! So then we go through to our homeland in Mali. Go onwards to the Tassili N'Ajjer in Algeria, Siwa, Petra and Persepolis in Iran. Mohenjo Daro in Pakistan, Khajuraho in India, Pyay, Sukhothai, Angkor Wat, Preah Vihear, Burma, Thailand, Cambodia and back to Easter Island. You may wonder why I missed out the Great Pyramid, Giza herself. Do the maths. Use the Golden Ratio, nature's sequence. Find the links for yourself. See how she fits in.'

Before Sy left the room he said that Steve Smart would fill him in some details and that it was a pleasure to meet him after his escapades last night in the forest.

Dean was left with his mouth open, staring at a closed hotel door.

Steve Smart walked in with a blue file in his hand and sat down on the other side of the table.

'You alright?' Smart asked.

'What the hell was that all about?'

'Blew your mind did he? Tell you about the speed of light being hidden in the circumference of the pyramid? That's a good one to get you interested. Wasn't that one was it?' Smart searched through Sy's tall tales of disinformation. Truth and fiction all sold as fact.

'Was it that the observer is the intrinsic element of creation, you construct your own universe?' Smart drew more blank looks. 'The Tablet of Shamash showing the frozen resolution of high pitched sound?'

'What?'

'Well I think he's got that one wrong. It looks like the sun to me.'

'Who the hell is he?'

He's the stuff of myth and legend. There's no record of him anywhere. There's nothing written about him or any proof he actually exists. Look him up. You'll find nothing. He pulls the strings. He's a magician, a business man, a seducer, a pilot and one of the best people who have ever lived to have on your side.' Smart paused and straightened the file he had just opened on the desk. 'The counterpoint to that of course is if you fail him or try to get one over on him, the cost to you will be as immense as his generosity. In brief young man, he's someone you say yes to.'

'He said he wants me to buy a load of charas, smuggle it to England, sell it on and buy a load of ching.'

'That's the start. It's all about building a seemingly legitimate drug empire to boost the UK economy.' Smart searched through the file as he spoke. 'You can keep ten per cent of the money. The rest gets ploughed back into the economy. Buy and sell more drugs, basically.'

'Yer, I can do that.'

'Oh, we know you can, Dean. That's why you're now an employee. There are certain conditions, outlined here.' Smart twisted the file and pushed it across the desk so that when Dean stopped it he could read the three conditions.

1~I will be silent, truthful, unfailing and trust my employer.

2~I understand that my employer will terminate this contract if I fail.

3~I understand that I will burn in the fires of hell if I fail this contract.

'Burn in the fires of hell. Are you serious?'

'What do I know?' Smart flicked his wrist and a gold fountain pen shot across the desk. 'If you don't believe in hell, then there's nothing to worry about. All I know is, it's worked for the Catholics for centuries.'

Dean scribbled his signature across the bottom line and closed the file.

'Where's Beki?' he asked.

'She's being taken care of, counselled. She's just killed a man.'

'Self-defence.'

'Yes, from the top of a rock, by plunging a rather large log into someone's skull.'

'That man would have done us all. He'd just killed Mari and striped Kat on the arm. That was self-defence, yo.'

'Anyway.' Smart stood up. 'You must be tired. You have a suite waiting and there's a nice surprise for you before bed.'

The door opened and a butler walked in. 'This way, sir, to your suite.'

He had a posh Southern English voice and was decked out like something from a bye gone age.

Smart walked out and so Dean just followed the butler. They walked along a grand corridor with white half columns with gold leaf edging breaking up the vertical striped wallpaper of green and red. The carpet was dark green and the ceiling of white was speckled with gold.

They arrived at Room 432. The butler opened the door and they went in. It was huge. In contrast to the rather elaborate room they had been in, this one was current. There were swirling patterns of pastel green and blue on a coffee brown background. The windows looked out onto pine forests and had a view of some snow peaks in the distance. There was a scented essence of citrus in the air. The separated bedroom contained a super king sized bed with a sixty five inch TV set on the opposite wall.

'I have arranged a wardrobe for you, sir,' the butler said as he opened up the bedroom fitted doors. Dean looked at seven different outfits, all colour matched from day wear to a dinner suit and everything in between.

'I expect you're tired, sir, but I have arranged a masseur to visit you in a half hour if you would care to shower first.'

Dean wondered if this was a polite way of saying he had a brass coming.

'I'd like two. At least one Asian or black. Can you get me some weed, boss, I's proper need a spliff, yo.'

'Anything else, sir?'

'Yer, man, keep that bitch Beki Aston away from me. Feed her to the lions or somat.'

The butler nodded and left the room.

Dean grabbed the remote from beside the bed, switched the beast on and flicked through the menu of channels on the TV. There were news, sport, music, film, documentary, history, drama, religious and sales channels. He stopped at channel 369. Free hardcore porn. He settled on watching a lesbian scene, although back home the lesbians he knew were all big and butch. They didn't look remotely like the ones on the telly.

36

Beki was having a pamper session after her spa treatment with Kat. The Rasul is a tiled room with subtle blue and red lighting. In the centre are two tiled heated loungers, fixed to the floor.

The occupants began the treatment with a warm shower, big enough for two and continued by rubbing exfoliate onto each other. The tiny grains embedded in the refreshing mint and eucalyptus gel exfoliate the dead skin, the epidermis, leaving a tingling sensation on the body. Slightly raised patches of red appeared on Beki's pure white skin where he had rubbed the gel in a little too vigorously.

The cut from Hue's knife had been long, shallow and superficial. It hadn't needed stitches but there was bruising around the area. She was careful not to let any eucalyptus gel get near it.

They then showered with still warm, wet skin, they slapped on handfuls of Rasul healing mud. It had herbs and minerals to promote invigoration and positive energy. It was also great fun to slap and rub mud all over each other. Then they went and lay on the heated tile loungers, as steam filled the room and soft tones of an Arabic flavour came from the hidden speakers.

At first they did as they had been instructed by the treatment advisor and lay motionless on their separate beds. They felt the warmth coming through the heated tiles and the cleansing steam filled their senses. Soon Kat found his eyes wander across the room to Beki's naked form, wet yet opaque from the mud. She looked like an art house nude in the blue and red lights. Staring through the cloudy atmosphere, the sheen of her skin as the mud slowly melted into patches was too much for him. His hard on was impossible to hide as he got off his bed and went over to her.

He massaged the mud around her body, sweeping his hands gently over the surface of her skin. He was careful not to go near her vagina but did touch her breast and nipples which became immediately erect and she flinched slightly as it was too sensitive, too horny.

Beki took a peek. *OMG! Look at him. It looks like it's about to self-combust!*

He went back to his bed and she wondered how long she should make him wait. The treatment advisor had said the whole hour was on a timer and the lights would change when the next programmed event was about to take place. She didn't wait long. She got on top of him and rode to orgasm in less than five minutes. She was completely selfish and when she was done, got off him with a contented smile.

Kat was having none of this. He was not being left feeling used by her. As he watched her get one leg onto her heated bed he caught a glimpse of her from behind and he jumped off his bed, careful not to go flying on the slippery floor. So before she was properly up on the bed again he grabbed her by the waist. He moved her back, feet to the floor and bent her forwards over her hard hot bed. He didn't care anymore. His cock was still moistened from being inside her but as an extra precaution he wet the end with spit, spread her legs and put the tip of his cock to the outside of her butthole.

'Just the tip, OK?' He'd asked a question but made it sound like she had no choice in the matter at the same time.

Before she had time to say one way or another, the tip was in. Beki felt it slide inside and although every feminist principal she knew said she shouldn't like it, in this setting, on this occasion, she did. She felt like being taken further than usual and liked the way he took control. She let herself believe she didn't have a choice. Sex and death go hand in hand with each other and trigger the basest human emotions. The dark, shadow, hidden self comes to the fore.

Neither of them noticed the lighting had changed to green and yellow as the final part of the treatment started. By this time he was all the way in and watched it slide in and out of her bottom in the steam filled half-light.

Suddenly a sound caught their attention from above, hot water power showers erupted from the ceiling, rinsing their muddy bodies from all impurities. It was a kind of baptism, as she moved herself to a second coming and he held her still by the waist and shot inside her.

Just as Dean realised he wasn't getting turned on by the porn there was a knock at the door. He opened it to see a huge blonde guy, a proper muscly type. He had shoulder length wavy hair, a vest top that showed off his ample arms and shoulders and spoke in a foreign accent.

'Hi, I'm Stephan your masseuse.' He carried a large black folded table and a case. Dean opened the door wide and let him in. Without much talk between them, he had by far the most powerful massage of his life.

Stephan used lots of scented oil that he warmed by vigorously rubbing it between his hands. He used his palms and fingers at first then once he'd got Dean relaxed, went at his shoulders with deep tissue kneading. As he moved down his back he used his elbows to really move below the surface.

When Stephan left, Dean was left in quite a sedative state and slept like a baby for the next ten hours. When he woke it was light outside. He got up and showered. He put on some brand new clothes and wondered what to do next. He was hungry so thought he'd find some food.

There was a knock at the door.

He opened it to find the butler with a trolley, complete with silver domed covered tray.

'Breakfast, sir,' he announced. The butler pushed the trolley into Dean's suite.

Dean did justice to the full English complete with fried bread and black pudding. There was freshly squeezed orange juice and strong coffee to sip as he stared out at the forest and snow peak view.

The butler came back after he'd completely finished and told him Mr Smart would like to visit him at eleven.

Dean flicked through the channels until Smart arrived, bang on time.

'How are you, Dean, rested? Ready for some action? Good.'

Dean hadn't said a word. Smart seemed in a hurry.

'I've arranged a jeep to take you to meet a friend of ours. He's going to take you to the best source of dope around here. He'll explain everything. Mr Smyth, the butler, will provide you with all you need for the trip. We won't be meeting again. Certainly not for a good while. I've arranged for our best man, Emile Sarafian to get in touch when you're back in the UK. Treat him with the respect you've shown us, we're all very professional. So is Vik, the man you're meeting now. He's a little unconventional but he can be trusted.'

Smart got up and hurried out without a goodbye. A minute later, Mr Smyth arrived with another set of clothes, outdoor ones and a kind of rucksack in reverse, one that fitted on your front, not your back.

Dean left the hotel and jumped in the awaiting jeep. He had an Indian driver who sped downhill and went as fast as he could uphill. He was constantly on the horn, overtaking at every opportunity. Blind bends were not an issue for this guy, in fact Dean thought he relished taking over a lorry or bus just before a corner, or so it began to seem.

As they left the tourist area the roads became quiet and they started to climb steadily. The drops to the valleys or rivers became vast. One wrong move and they would be away, rolling down the side of the steep mountainside, dead for sure.

They made it in one piece to what could only be described as the middle of nowhere. The driver stopped down a cut off and gave it three horn blasts. He got out and opened Dean's door.

'Come, you come,' he said. He beckoned Dean to exit the jeep.

Dean followed the driver down the grass cut off. They climbed up a slight incline, moving away from the road. They had driven up most of the way and as they reached a clearing Dean was taken in by the sight before him.

The Himalayas stretched out in their magnificence in the distance. Forested slopes with mountain peaks lined the foreground.

Dean could see several Indians milling around and what looked like two … *Oh no,* he thought. Walking towards him was a white guy. He was little with a slight limp and a mischievous grin. He seemed slightly out of sync, as if his right side was a bit higher than his left.

'Hi Dean, I'm Vik, Goa Vik. Ever done a paraglide before?'

Vik had a long nose and tight mouth. He was wiry and spoke with a nasally yet soft, Southern accent, not London, but definitely Southern. He had a familiar way with him, as if he was a long lost friend.

'No, never done this before.'

'Right, then, we'll give you a "crash course" so to speak, huh, huh. Don't worry, it's easy once you're up. Anyway, we've got engines in the ones we're using tomorrow. I'll take you up tandem today and show you how it's done. Fancy a chillum first?'

While they sat round in a chillum circle with the Indian boys, Goa Vik told him the basics of flying. 'Pull left to go left and right to go right. Be easy with everything unless you feel you need to be strong. Go with your instincts, feel the air. Remember, there's nothing to crash into but the ground, so always keep a height you're comfortable with and never, ever, go too low. Saying that, you got to be careful of a thermal taking you around here. The problem with this place is scale. Everything's big, including the wind. We use thermal streams to get us where we want to go but never get caught in a biggy, they can keep taking you higher and higher.'

'So high you die?'

'Yer man, so high you die. Come on, let's take you up.'

There was a kind of controlled chaos as Vik gave the orders to the several Indian guys to lift up the wings, just far enough off the floor to be ready to go when he gave the order, but not high enough so the wind caught below as they waited for the right air.

'Right, man, run when I tell you and as we go off the edge you have to get yourself into your seat when we're in the air. Just push yourself in, it'll all be fine.'

There was an anxious wait as Vik shouted orders around to the lads on each side then suddenly it was a 'Go. Go!' from Vik and they were running as best they could towards the edge of a cliff, the Indian lads either side picking up the wings. Dean's heart was racing as he felt helpless but had to carry on with it and then all of a sudden, 'STOP! Stop!' Vik called and ground his feet into the floor, metres from the edge. The helpers all skidded to a stop and wondered what was wrong. 'The wind's not right. Sorry about that, Dean. Come on, boys, help us back, we'll do it again.'

There was more tension around now, Dean could feel it. He was really starting to wonder if this lot knew what they were doing.

'Second time lucky, huh, huh.' Vik laughed through his nose and they set it all up again.

This time Dean was ready for anything. He decided to give it one more go and if this messed up, he was off. He'd walk across the valley.

'Where are we actually going?' Dean asked.

'Nowhere today, this is just fun. Tomorrow we're off over there.' Vik pointed to a distant hill, across the huge valley. 'Makala valley, that is. It's impossible to cross on foot because of the river, see. Over the other side is the best charas you'll ever find. Come on, wind's up again.'

This time the wind was the right kind and they ran off the edge and immediately they were up. Dean struggled to lift himself into the seat but eventually he managed to get most of his bottom in it.

Vik used the air to sweep round in arcs, giving them great views of the valley, the river and then as they turned, the snow peaks in the far distance.

They stayed up for about half an hour before Vik decided he'd let Dean take control.

With Vik's expert guidance, Dean soon got the hang of it and learned to use the wind like a friend, never to take too much and always be respectful. He could see how easy it would be to get completely carried away up there. Some of the lifts from the invisible currents were beyond powerful and the skill was to judge their strength before your wings become immersed in their influence.

'Landing's fun. Start running while we're still six feet up and you won't end up six feet under, huh, huh.'

They touched down on a grassy piece of flat land. After undoing the harness they sat and stared out at where they'd been flying.

Vik spoke at length on the basics of flight and explained how thermals form and how they dissipate as well. 'Don't get caught flying on empty air, move away if you feel the bottom fall out of it. That's bad air, ultimate fail.'

They stayed the night in a Government Forest Rest House. Vik said it was all that was available this remote. They cooked their own meals with firewood, a basic dhal and rice. They slept in hard beds with layers of blankets to keep warm. There were no electricity cables this high up so they relied on the solar panels for light. They slept well and Dean was woken by Vik just before dawn.

'Come on, let's watch sunrise over the hill.'

It was cold and still as they walked into the morning. There was silence, no bird song, traffic noise or background sound of any kind. The light was coming. The sky started to turn into an unfolding picture before their eyes. Vik sparked up a joint.

As Dean smoked it he noticed the taste. It was sublime. The whole scene became brighter, colours more concentrated. The mauve and burgeoning blue of the sky had a mystical element to it. Light changing dark. And then there was light. He seemed to understand that for the first time. The stars slowly vanished as their cousin the sun gulped them in. The first rays illuminating the backdrop behind the mountains and then there he was, orange and yellow, enveloping all with heat for another day.

'It recharges your batteries,' said Vik.

Dean knew exactly what he meant.

After breakfast Dean did his first solo flight. He landed with a bit of a thump but stayed on his feet. The Indian lads applauded. He couldn't wait to do another. They were at it all day. He loved the feeling of being in control but also being totally at the mercy of the all-powerful air. He found out for himself what good and bad air was and how to manage it to your advantage. Never getting caught up in good air or caught out by bad.

Dean was starving by lunchtime and one of the lads had made more dhal and rice but this was small brown bean dhal and was very filling. Mountain dhal, Vik called it. After they all helped to wash the pots they sat down for tea and a spliff.

'There are a few things you need to know about the Kala

people. They don't really like foreigners. They put up with us because they want the money but we're definitely seen as, well, dirty or something like that. They can't have any direct contact with outsiders and so you have to make the deal and then put the money down on the floor. You can't hand it directly over, oh no, it would be seen as unclean if you're still touching it. The whole deal could be off. There are stories of people being thrown in the river at the side of the village for that kind of thing, so leave most of it to me. Mr Smart sent you this.' Vik pulled an inconspicuous bag from under the kitchen table and opened it up. It was packed with rupees, all crisp and new. Each bundle was kept together with a paper band around the middle of the wedge. 'There's enough for forty kilo.'

'Forty?'

'That's what we're buying. It'll be fine. Come on, let's get the engines, piece a cake.'

Dean was knocked out by the spirit of this little man. It was apparent he had some kind of slight physical disability but he truly didn't give a toss. Dean liked him. He thought about all the moaners and haters back home. He saw in his mind's eye all the people from the estates that constantly brought their world down around them. It was like a disease, a virus that spread by osmosis, one of negativity and depression. It was all about who could be worse than their neighbours, who could moan the loudest, who was poorest, the most skint but they still all ate at Macky D's. Who was more psychotic, who was the most mentally ill, physically ill? Who could rip who off, who was the hardest or the chief psycho, the best burglar? Who would use torture on you if you didn't pay your debts, who had the biggest gold chain, latest gaudy 18k Rose gold Breitling watch, Audi 4X4 or the prettiest drug whore girlfriend driving round in a brand new £40,000 white BMW when she worked part time in your uncle's flower shop?

It was messed up back home. He was going back home to mess it up even more, if he survived Goa Vik's crazy adventure. Just then he heard the first mechanical sound for two days as Vik fired up the spiral blades of the propeller.

37

'That is exactly as things are Beki.' Kat was in bed telling her about the way the world is run. This was the world behind the veil, the transparent cover that the masses fail miserably to see through.

'So I was "bovine" until I met you and ended up here? Is that what you're saying, Kat?'

'No, no. Not at all. You were always destined to be here. Everything is precisely as it should be. As far as I can see you are the goddess incarnate. You are Inanna, Isis, Ishtar. Names for gods are many but broadly they are the same. Everything comes from similar root myths. You were never one of the cattle, Beki, you just didn't realise it until now.'

Beki thought about being classed as a goddess. She liked the idea. It appealed to her vanity. 'So, I've always been a goddess, I've just not known it?'

Kat looked at her deeply. It was as if he was penetrating her with his eyes, searching her consciousness, feeling for her.

'Kat, stop it, that's creeping me out.' She got out of bed and he watched her perfect body walk naked across the room to the dresser. She sat down in front of the oval mirror and started to make a joint with only silence between them. She then lit it and walked back to bed. He stared at her manicured crotch. She'd been waxed clean of hair. He couldn't wait to make her again.

'Here.' She passed him the joint and got under the covers again, keeping her perfect breast exposed. She knew how to keep him interested.

'Thanks.' He took a drag and told her more. 'There are lots of things going on already, but more in the planning stages.'

'Like what? What's being planned?'

'Well an expansion of fluoride in the water. You tell them all "it's good for you, good for your teeth" and like sheep grazing on grass, they bite, chew and then they just swallow it. Sheep and cows don't think about the grass they're given. The bovine out there don't actually think about the water they drink, they just drink it.'

'Why, what does it do? I thought fluoride is good for your teeth.'

'It is in tiny micro levels, it's naturally found in most water, anyway. It's not the teeth they're interested in. You're warned not to swallow toothpaste due to the fluoride content but it's in the water you do swallow, see how dumb they are? Do you know what your pineal gland is?'

'It's in your brain.'

'Correct, but what is it?'

'Go on, then.' He had her attention now. One of the benefits of cannabis smoking is the ability to concentrate fully on something. Another is you develop a diverse outlook. You find a new reality.

'The clue is in the title, as with many things. Pineal, pine. There is a pine cone shaped part of the ancient brain that if controlled can keep the masses just where we want them to be. The symbol is around if you care to look. The biggest pine cone symbol in the world? Do you know where it is?'

She shook her head left and right, pushed her lips together, raised her eyebrows and opened her eyes wide.

'It's in The Vatican. One of the states within states. The City of London and the United Nations being the others. Anyway, our little pine cone is the key to raising consciousness, it's always been known. If they were conscious beings, realised spirits, they would be dangerous. The last thing we need are prisons without drugs, right? If there were no drugs in prisons then there'd be riots every other day. It's the same with cattle. Block up the brains with fluoride and it stops them thinking straight. They have no spirit gland left, it gets all calcified up. Well it does more than that actually.'

'So fluoride in water makes people less spiritual?'

'Absolutely.'

'What's the other thing?'

'You'll love this. It makes girls come into puberty earlier so they breed younger, much earlier actually.'

Beki had reached puberty much earlier than her mum

and several years earlier than her gran; she knew this was fact because they'd talked about it back home. She started to feel slightly sick in her stomach. This stuff was affecting her. 'Go on, anything more. Why do you want girls to "breed" earlier?'

'Better stock of course. It's a world economy now. They buy more over a lifetime, produce healthier kids. I don't know everything yet. Soon I will. Let me tell you about history.'

'Go on.' She leaned towards him thinking he was going to tell her it was all made up, all a lie.

'All my history is there for you to see. You just have to know where to look and more importantly, how to look.'

'What?' Beki slumped back now. He watched her breast jiggle as she hit the headboard of the bed with her shoulders, pillows supporting her lower torso.

'Yep, the whole of our history is there for you to see. Isis is alive and well. She rules today as she has in the past. She is worshipped and admired everyday by those who know and by those who are ignorant of her true nature.'

'Where is she worshipped?'

'New York Harbour for one. Who do you think the Statue of Liberty represents, Beki? Liberty Enlightening the World. She is Isis, you are Isis.'

'I'm Isis?' asked Beki, more confused than ever.

'We are the representations of the gods. We hold sway over the world. What else do gods do? If you join me, Beki, you will become a goddess. I've seen the signs. Anyone who knows anything will know as fact you are her, she is you.

When you went to school you learnt about reading, writing, history, geography, yes?'

'Amongst other things, yes.'

'So did I but I also learnt about many other things. Things that are hidden, concealed from the … profane, shall we say.'

'You mean the herd, the sheep, cattle. Ordinary people.'

'Exactly, ordinary people. I don't want to use the word occult as it has several connotations, as have all things as it goes, but, erm, well occult as in hidden, nothing sinister.'

'Shall I make another spliff?'

'Good move,' said Kat as he watched her get up from the bed and walk across the room to the dresser to ritually roll another one.

He carried on talking with her back to him. She listened to every word intently.

'We have been taught from birth to believe in and use our energy ritualistically. We have in place something that works, Beki. It keeps us hidden and in power. I can tell you more or less anything you want to know. About anything really.'

'Anything?' she asked as she rolled up the joint and turned to face him. She wet both lips and then lay her tongue on her bottom lip. She kept her wet tongue still and slid the layer of gum along before using her deft fingers to roll the paper round into a perfect cone. Kat didn't know why this turned him on so much. Had she left her tongue hanging out a fraction too long?

'Anything that's meaningful, magical, important. I can't

tell you much about the Arena TV show, apart from we own it.'

'Why do you own that?' Beki answered her own question. 'To keep the people watching pure rubbish?'

'Now you're getting it.' He took the spliff off her, then put it in his mouth and she lit it for him.

'Tell me about the Kabbalah, I've always wanted to know about that.'

'Kabb-alah. Think about it. Alah. It has the name of a god in it. The ancient text tells how a soul can transcend the realms from earth to heaven and warn you of the potentials on the way.'

'Potentials?'

'Yes, the great abyss between worlds.'

'OK, what about the Catholics? Why have they been around two thousand years?'

'Easy, because it works. Have you ever sat through a Catholic Mass?'

'No.'

'Then you should. The ritual ticks many boxes, believe me. When the priest rings that bell, changing the wafers and wine to the body and blood, it's pure magic, what else? Ritual, magic, the occult, religion, they all work, Beki. They change the psyche, alter reality for that brief time and we all love a bit of altered reality. What do you think we're doing now with drugs?'

She had to give him that one.

'So how deep do your rituals go?'

'As deep as a dark pit and as high as the tallest mountain.

Our beliefs are firmly about what works. There are certain rituals that when I'm in power, I'm going to either change or stop.'

'Why?'

'Oh, because I have to. They've lost their power. My grandfather says they're not barbaric but I know they are. He's meeting me later to pass on some untold truth, some secret only he knows. They're archaic, out of touch, unnecessary. My family are steeped in a tradition much older than you could possibly imagine. It's time to … modernise. Now without Mari to stop me, I think I can do it, too.'

38

'Here, put this mic on, it wraps round the back, earphones in, that's it.' The din of the engines was blocked out and he then put on his helmet. Vik had it all under control today. The chaos seemed to have been replaced with order and professionalism. Dean realised that this was it.

They strapped in the seats and Vik told him he would be going up first and went through a few safety drills, how to switch off the engine for landing and how to switch it on again if the landing had to be aborted.

At the last minute the rucksack that went on your front came out and Dean put his arms through the straps. The Indian lad clipped it around his back and then Vik was in his ear, telling him exactly what to do. He told him they had good air and before Dean had time to really think about it his wings were being lifted by the Indian lads and Rik shouted 'Go. Go. Go!'

Dean ran, or more like fast walked towards the edge of the cliff and the feeling of jumping off took his stomach away. Then he was up, the air caught his wings and he had to pull the sides in to stop himself going up.

'Switch your bloody engine on,' Vik shouted in his ear.

Dean flicked the switch and the blades kicked in. He'd had to use his right hand to do this and that meant letting go of the wings for a few seconds. That was all the thermal needed. He was climbing quickly.

'Brake. Brake, come down.'

'OK, OK.' Dean could see Vik below him. It was cold, the extra height made a difference. There was definitely a comfort zone and he wasn't in it.

'Look, I'm not coming up there. It's too bloody cold. You need to come down. It should be easy now the blades are helping you.'

Dean was struggling even with the blades. The thing didn't seem to want to go anywhere but up. The crisp air bit into his face now. He used all his strength to try and control the wings so he could stop himself climbing but at best he was treading air. Then he saw her.

He knew she was a female. She was serene. She held the air when she wanted to and when she needed to move she tilted and dipped. She was showing him how to do it. Her brown feathers, sleek body, tucked feet, hooked beak and sharp eyes all worked as one to float, soar or dive. He watched her as long as he could and then he understood.

It wasn't about fighting your way through the air, it was about using the air to your best advantage. You would never win the fight but the air may be your friend, your partner in a dance.

Then he got it, he started to act like the Kite.

Vik watched as he tilted the left wing and circled down in an arc, using his head, using the wind now. Vik realised he would be fine. He'd stopped trying to control the uncontrollable and was reacting to the air.

'It was that bird. She showed me what to do.'

'Good, they're the masters. Best teacher you'll ever have.'

Now they were out of the big air and were able to keep a steady course, arching through any rough patches and with the aid of the blades they quickly made it half way to the other side, this was the deadline.

'So, decision time. We either carry on to the other side of the valley or turn round and go home. What's it to be?' Vik knew the answer. Once you get it there's no going back.

'Let's go on,' Dean said.

They headed on towards the mountains and Vik was impressed the way Dean handled his wings. There was no more panic and he was now flying with the air, not against it.

With about another ten minutes to go Vik decided to take his mind off things.

'So, Emma told me about your goings on,' Vik said, opening things up.

'Emma, you know Emma?'

'Everybody knows everybody here.'

'What did she say?'

'She said you all got strung out by a baba after taking some DMT. Hypnotised she said. Something about an orgy, where you all swapped partners. Ha, ha, ha. Very nice that, getting strung out by a baba.'

Strung out, what did he mean? Dean was worried he'd been duped.

'What do ya mean, bro? Strung out?' Dean asked.

'Played, he played you all like a fiddle. Got you all in a vulnerable time after a massive psychedelic experience and tricked you into performing for him. Emma said she was the only one who he didn't get to. Even Tim got stung.'

'No way. No … way. I knew what I was doing, yo.'

'Did you really? Did you choose to get off with whatsit?'

Dean thought it through. The answer was no. Of course it was no. He would have never willingly got off with Jules and let Beki do it with Kat. The more he thought about it the more he realised that at that time he never questioned any of it. He just went along with whatever came his way. Could he have stopped if he'd wanted to? Yes, but he just didn't even want to, even though he'd lost everything he ever secretly wanted. The world would well pay for that.

'Right we're heading for that flat clearing on the left. It's a bit rocky here and there but mostly grass. The wind's going to drop as we move in so you'll have to be prepared for that. There's always a chance of a blast of air more or less anywhere this high, so keep your wits about you.'

They curved through the dry air left and right. All the time Dean could feel what Vik had said about the quality of the air dropping the closer they got to the landing site.

Suddenly he realised the landing site was approaching fast. Just as he thought he needed to switch off his engine,

Vik gave him the word and he flicked the switch. Now he was dropping and pulling in his wings, slowing down, dropping towards the fast approaching ground and this was it.

He started to run in the air, doing bicycle kicks in preparation for his landing. It was a time in life when you were literally hitting the ground running. They were both down; they had both avoided the rocks and came to a dignified halt, still on their feet.

Once the rush of the landing had stopped Dean realised there was still wind around and he felt it try to get under his wings. He also realised there were people clapping and little boys whooping as they ran towards him.

Vik was out of his harness and as he stepped free the lads got hold of his wings keeping them firmly on the ground.

The lads who ran towards Dean just stood around his paraglider watching him struggle with the harness. Vik jogged over.

'Keep it down, they can't touch it until you're out of the harness.'

Vik helped him unclip his straps and then when he walked free of the frame the lads closed in and held it down. 'Remember, don't offer to shake hands or touch anything they're holding. You'll be run out of the village and they'll have to sacrifice a goat that you'll have to pay for.'

The wings were covered with thick khaki canvas sheets and then rocks placed on top to secure them.

The youngsters were excited but the older guys took it all in their stride. They looked old before their time, weather-worn faces from the harsh mountain climate. They had pale brown skin and some had blue eyes, some green, others hazel. Two spoke to Vik and they left Dean out of the conversation. After a minute or two the talk stopped and Vik came over.

'Things have changed a bit since I was last here. They want us to deal with some foreigners who they tell me handle their business now.'

'Foreigners?'

'I know, they get everywhere. Look, there's no point arguing with these people. You've got to understand it's village law here. We do what they say, no rumpus, got that?'

It was the first time Dean had witnessed another side to Vik. He could turn it on if he needed to. He was ruffled by the news of the foreigners. He'd not known about it and it had put his already broken nose a bit further out of joint.

The two men Vik had talked to led them along and up a path, through some forest and right past the village. Dean noticed some of the houses were less traditional than those further down the valley. Some were made from wood with the traditional balcony structure but some were brick and breeze block. Tin roofs with blue plastic covers seemed popular. They were much more practical but looked much less romantic. The village had some money. It was very obvious.

They passed a small school-come-community centre. There was no medical centre Dean could see but there had been a shop selling hardware and groceries. Goats wandered around in small flocks, bleating on about this and that, goat stuff. Dean looked at their eyes. They looked very strange and at first he just couldn't fathom why. Then he realised their black pupils were horizontal rectangles. Their eyes were square. It just didn't seem right. Then he couldn't stop staring at them. Their pale yellow eyes with rectangular pupils were freaking him out. He had to jog a little to catch up to the others after being mesmerised by the goats' eyes.

Once past the village they walked through more forest and bush. He noticed thick foggy spider webs in the more dense scrubs. There were more birds in the trees here, too. This was remote, it felt different to Manali. The air was thinner, dryer, crisper. The forests were more diverse, random bushes and varied trees filled the route. In Manali it was mainly fir trees with pine needles and cones but here there was a mix of nature. It was stunningly beautiful.

They trekked on and then the subtle smell in the air changed. The forest thinned and he stopped in his tracks as he looked out on the biggest field of ganja he'd ever hoped to see.

'Bagicha,' said Vik.

At first Dean couldn't understand why there was no real smell other than the one you get from a meadow of grass. Then as he approached the plants he realised their magnificence. He was tall but some of these plants towered over him. They were massive, giants, mutants. He was speechless.

'Vik,' Dean said eventually. He was as excited as a child on a birthday morning. 'They're ten feet tall.'

'I know, it's kind of awesome here, isn't it.'

Dean stopped and pulled down one of the stalks to smell the buds. There was nothing immediate about the smell. Back home the plants were stinkers. Here you literally had to bury your nose in the bud. Then he took in a sweet fruity smell, like … mango? The plant he just inhaled smelt like a ripe mango.

He hurried on to catch up to the others but couldn't resist stopping and smelling another giant further down the path. He inhaled deeply and registered a grassy, mossy smell this time. The leaves on this one were broad and turning pale green, almost yellow lower down. The stems were thick and hardy. The buds grew out directly from the branches. He'd never seen anything like it. The further up the increasingly rocky and less defined path they went, the scraggier the plants appeared. There were no fields anymore and there were gaps between the clusters of plants.

'This is more jungli now, wild plants, more mutants. This where you get the best smoke in the world, believe me.' Vik spoke with a knowledgeable grin on his thin face.

The two men stepped aside and let Vik and Dean through.

'Greeks,' one of the locals said as he beckoned them towards some smoke rising awkwardly through the air.

39

Beki was sitting thinking about how she had ended up in this mess. She'd somehow managed to totally misread Dean. She was supposed to fall in love and he was supposed to treat her badly, but it had been the other way round. He'd failed to live up to his bad boy stance. He wilted in her eyes as soon as he'd given her that stupid piece of gold. He was supposed to hump her senseless, leave her wanting him more than ever, convinced she could change him into someone good, someone better, while he made her do unspeakable acts of sexual depravity. Instead he'd been a kind lover, trying his best to meet his perceived view of her sexual needs. How wrong he'd been. She just wanted rough sex, end of. Now it was well and truly over. She knew there was no going back, no reconciliation. She'd probably turned him into a misogynistic nightmare. He'd probably had his illusion of true love shattered into a million pieces.

She didn't feel too bad though because he'd done hippy dippy Jules while she'd ended up with Kat. The more she thought about it the more she realised that … she actually couldn't remember how any of it happened. She knew it had, but as hard as she could she ran through her memory banks, searching for details but couldn't find any. She remembered smoking her DMT. She recalled the trip where she'd been surrounded by angels and those patterns and the colours had been the most vivid, complex 'things' she'd ever witnessed. However she knew they were just made from her mind, her thoughts. Although she could swear they were as 'real' as anything solid, rationally she knew better. The world around her now was real. What a world it was, too. Talk about luxury. Kat had ordered some mixed world nibbles and they came on a silver platter complete with domed silver lid, served by a kind of old school butler. He was very polite but she didn't like the way he looked blankly down on her.

She had caviar on crisp bread, wrinkled olives from Thassos, strips of crispy, streaky, salty bacon. It was all yum. Garlic mayo and fresh lime and chilli salsa, the fingers crisp on one side and soft on the pitta, hummus with tangy olive oil and paprika sprinkled over the top, tandoori chicken kebabs, lamb shami kebabs, onion salad with a citrus dressing, fried aubergine, paneer 65, Kerala paratha, lamb shawarma, tabbouleh and a Persian rice and lentil dish with a tahdeeg finished with a crispy onion topping was offered. The tahdeeg is a crispy, almost burnt bottom of the pan, that's turned over and served as a crust. It was perfect munchie food, all served in tiny portions in silver dishes.

Kat dug straight into the Persian rice dish. 'This crispy bottom is broken up in my mother's recipe. It's called a hkaka.'

Beki gave him a questioning look. 'You know what kaka means in some languages?'

'Nooo! Hkaka, huh, Aitch, whatever, it is delicious and no one makes it like she does.'

Warning bells rang in Beki's head. 'No woman will ever make apple pie like their mum', she'd been advised by a friend once in England.

'Right, time for me to go. Are you good here?'

'Erm, yes, I think so. How long are you going to be?'

'He's usually straight to the point about things. An hour I guess. There's everything you need at the other end of the phone there. Name it and they'll sort it for you.'

Kat left the room and walked the long corridor to his grandfather's suite. He knocked once and Steve Smart opened the door. They exchanged civilities and Smart left the room.

Sycamore Poulis came in through the bedroom door. He was dressed impeccably in a black Prada shirt and black trousers. On his feet were polished ankle boots by Jeffrey West and as he sat down and crossed his legs Kat noted thick dark grey cashmere socks by Burberry, with their distinctive check rim.

He supposed comfort was more and more a priority with his grandfather now. Years ago his socks would still have been Burberry but made from a thinner fabric, one more fitting with the rest of his outfit that day. His still looked amazing and dressed like a man twenty years younger but there was no denying it, he was getting to be an old man now.

'Drink?' he asked.

'Please,' Kat replied.

Sycamore got up and poured two measures of Pimms into tumblers and filled the rest with sparkling Pellegrino, a dash of sugar syrup and ice from a stainless steel ice bucket. He finished it with two slices of cucumber, stirred it with a silver spatula and handed the finished drink to Kat.

'Cheers.' They touched their glasses. 'To Mari,' said Sycamore.

'To Mari,' followed Kat.

'There's nothing formal yet but as you know, I'm stepping down and you, alone now, are taking over. There are a few pieces of the jigsaw puzzle that are still left to fit and before you formally take over, you need to know them.'

Sycamore paced the room very slowly, glass in hand. He reached round with his free hand to scratch the back of his neck. 'Your basic education was supplemented with profound and comprehensive knowledge of the entire ancient catalogue of man's beliefs. Rituals, myths, religions, meta-physical, spiritual, magical and scientific. They enable us to understand the psyche of the world. They keep us informed of how the world thinks. They are all in their little bubbles. The Protestants and Catholics, Jews and Muslims, Sunni and Shiite, Buddhist and Hindu, Black Magician, White Magician, Wiccan or Pagan. Do you know what they all have in common?'

'No, sir.'

'They are all right and their opposing believers are all wrong. They all want their angle on the world to rule and some are prepared to vanquish those who think differently to their view of god. Think about the crusades, the witch hunts, the suicide bombs in the Arab world and the car bombs in Northern Ireland where both parties were peace loving Christians. And what do we think about "Holy" war, Jihad or the American invasion of Iraq with god on their side. How could they have failed so badly?'

'I remember you telling me about "Shock and Awe" and how they would just be slaughtering cities of sheep,' Kat said.

'We lost over one hundred thousand in Iraq alone.' Sycamore went back to the table and sat his glass down. He stood looking at Kat. He put his hand on Kat's shoulder to make sure he had his full attention and to convey the full truth of the world. 'They all have their own creation myths from antiquity, whether it's the Greek Golden Apple of Immortality in the Garden of Hesperides, the Sumerian garden of Heden or the more fashionable Christian and Muslim tale of Adam and Eve. They all have a man and woman, the primordial couple, in the garden, Heden or Eden, the Utopian paradise and along there cometh a serpent. The one who speaks to them. One who talks their native tongue and tells them to eat the forbidden fruit, the apple of knowledge. I've heard it called some things, eh. So of course they eat, or fuck, whatever you need to believe and she gets the blame, not in all accounts but certainly in most.

Then they're banished from paradise and realise they have shame. They cover their cocks and labias. Their god cursed them with knowledge of good and evil so we can all play out this game.

'Then they all have a flood. There are just too many to tell you about but they all centre on a family, told by a god to build a ship, or ark, and take their herds and any other animals they could find along with the birds of course.' He turned away and paced the room as he spoke, picturing the myths in his mind's eye. 'From Central America Coxcoxtil and Xochiquetzal. From the Norse people the myth of Bergelmir, the Chinese Gong and Zurong, Babylonian Unapishtem. In Serbia they had a flood myth where a man called Kranyatz saved the world by hanging on to a grapevine.'

He stopped as if in trance, staring at nothing. 'The Persian myth of Ahura Mazda and Yima. The Native American's Lone Man, born of a virgin. From our homeland in Mali, the Manday people had Faro and Pambe. The Incas from Peru, Virococha. The Great Father and Mother of the Mayan. From Columbia, Bochica and Chia.' He paused and seemed to regain his wandering mind. 'You were always told that these myths were based on fact. That these various legends were all sourced from an original truth. A truth that the Poulis' were central to and the keepers of that truth were the Pairs.

'Do you now see how easy it actually is to indoctrinate a deluded believer? That's how we have survived because I am telling you now that all you know is a lie. I will tell you the truth but not until this has had a chance to sink in. Go to your Isis, your Ishtar. She will be our Venus. Make her every way you can tonight because as of tomorrow at midnight, the time between times, you will be told the secret that endures.'

40

There was a small camp of three wood cabins, set in a circle with the doors all facing towards a camp fire at the centre.

The smoke they'd seen had been rising from the fire and around it sat three men and three women.

As the locals had backed off it was just Dean and Vik who approached the camp. None of them looked up. Two of the men were sitting doing nothing, just staring out over the view. One man sat cleaning the biggest chillum Dean had ever seen. He was using a stick with cloth tightly bound around it and was repeatedly rubbing the inner part of the tube, lifting it up and inspecting it and then rubbing it voraciously again. It was like he was cleaning a gun barrel.

All three women were sat with polished bowls made from half a coconut. They were all making mixes of charas, ganja and tobacco. There was a look between them of the hardcore traveller. These were olive skinned, long haired or dreadlocked dope heads. They were an ugly bunch, too. None were blessed with good looks although one of the girls looked very young. There was an obvious alpha male sat bolt upright with a pile of dreads tied up on top of his head in a twisted top knot. He was the first to bother to look round at the two trespassers. Once he'd moved his head round the others all looked, too.

'Hello,' Vik said in his chirpiest voice as they were right next to the circle now.

It was slightly uncomfortable for a few seconds as they all just sat looking up at them. There was a definite vacancy running through the eyes of the Greeks.

Then the head guy spoke. 'You wanna charas?' he asked. He spoke with the most petulant tone of dismissive disgust Dean had ever heard.

'Oh, yes, please,' piped up Vik, unperturbed by the abrupt tone.

'Sit,' said the Greek and Vik realised there were two spaces conveniently open in the circle. They'd been expected.

They sat down and life went on. Nobody spoke. The women made the mix and the one man cleaned the daunting tube. Dean guessed it was nearly fifty centimetres long. It had a massive head with a design of a cobra on the side. The thick brown clay was turning black from use around the top.

Then the young looking woman spoke in Greek to the head guy. There were a few words exchanged and he seemed to use a similar tone to her. Then the cleaning man gave the head guy the tube and the women all placed their mixing bowls in front of him.

As he inspected the tube's insides he spoke again in Greek and this time they all laughed. He grinned at Dean with yellow nicotine stained teeth. Dean looked into his watery narrow eyes. He noticed ingrained dirt in the wrinkles around them. The guy had a long thick beard that showed flecks of grey. It was impossible to tell how old he was. His hair, beard and wrinkles aged him but beneath that there was a youth like quality to him.

He started to fill the tube with great care and attention to detail. Every time he emptied a mixing bowl in, he would knock in any errant grains of mix that had settled around the top of the tube, then gently tampered the mix with his thumb and inspected his work as an artist would inspect a painting. He turned the tube around and looked down the top from various angles. The last bowl went in and there was a perfect symmetry to the whole tube now with the mix sitting perfectly flat at the top.

The man who had no job suddenly went into action. He burst into life and ripped a strip of cotton safi cloth, wet it from a bottle of water, wrung it out so it was just damp and then he was handed the tube while he expertly bound the bottom of it. He handed it back to the head guy.

Dean's heart was pounding. He hoped beyond hope they didn't give him this monster chillum to light. Three mixes in one tube, what was that about?

As if he could smell the fear through the air like a dog, the head guy handed Dean the tube. It was heavy and hard to actually handle. Dean's chillum skills were limited. He'd had a few in Delhi and a few in the mountains but these were made from one cigarette and charas. He had no choice but to give it a go. The safi guy had another role. He got up and was now stood over Dean with three matches positioned next to their box for lighting.

'Boom Shiva!' Dean was willing the god of chillums and charas to help him out here. He wrapped both hands around the extra-large safi bound bottom of the tube and was conscious that he must keep the weight balanced or risk some of the precious mix, so precisely packed, falling out.

As the matches exploded into action he shut his eyes and started to suck the air as best he could down through the huge mix. The irony of smoking chillums is you have to use lung power to suck the air and then smoke down through the tube and into your lungs. This in turn messes your lungs up. The more chillum you smoke, the less able you are to handle smoking them. As Dean still had good lung capacity he was able to light the cobra chillum, just about. If he'd had a better technique with his hand position it would have been simpler but he left a gap with his hands so some air seeped in through the small space between his palms and this small error failed to make a perfect seal. If there is no air coming through the hands then all the air is sucked from the tube. Even with this he was able to get it going and the head guy was impressed.

Dean handed it to him and witnessed years of professional chillum smoking in action. He puffed and sucked and sucked but he couldn't manage a lungful. His hands wrapped around the tube with grace, his lips pursed around the gap he'd left between his thumbs and all but the smallest amount of smoke went up in the air. He couldn't manage to suck much into his lungs. He took the tube away from his lips and held it out to the next guy. Then after letting it go he put his left hand across his chest and desperately held in what little smoke his lungs could take.

The tube went round the Greeks with similar results. Coughs abound as they all tried their level best to hold in the smoke. Only the young looking woman and the safi man were able to hold in a serious lungful.

Then it was Vik's turn. The tube somehow looked way too big as his wiry hands held it next to his mouth and it towered over his head. He raised it to his forehead while saying a little invocation. He placed it to his mouth and took the best hit of the lot. The mix was about half done and it was passed round again with the accompaniment of splutters and rasping coughs.

Then the high started to creep up on Dean. As he watched the chillum being cleaned by the safi man he realised the whole world had taken on a sparkly quartz glow. He also felt stuck to the floor. This was some serious stuff they were smoking and the women all started making mixes again.

Now he understood why they didn't speak much. It was actually difficult to talk he was so stoned. His thoughts were on hold. Vik looked just as wasted which came as some relief. Dean looked at the mixes being made. Two were the usual black charas, no need to burn the resin here, just pick it off the block and roll it into tiny balls before adding it to the tobacco and ganja in the glossy mixing bowl. The young looking one had a block of resin with a red tinge to it. Her block was smaller than the others and Dean couldn't help staring at her as she went about her job in a meditative state.

'You like my wife?' The head guy's words came out with a piercing tone. It took Dean completely by surprise.

'Erm, yes, of course. Not like that, mate, she has some red charas, different charas.'

He spoke to her in Greek and she quickly answered him with a smile. She broke off a piece and passed it to her friend who leaned over and gave it Dean.

It was smooth and ochre coloured. He smelt it after pulling it apart with his thumbs. It smelled of the earth, of pollen, of flowers.

'This is the best charas. Only smoke here. No sell this one.'

Dean realised the Greek spoke English like an Indian. He offered the piece back but she shook her head and so he pocketed it.

'Shall we talk business?' Vik asked, starting up a new line of conversation.

The Greek nodded.

'We need a monthly supply of forty kilo.'

Monthly, thought Dean, he'd not realised.

'No problem. Only forty?'

'Only forty,' replied Vik.

The Greek had just had to say it, only, as if that was a paltry amount.

'No problem.'

'I come here each month, OK, with the money.'

'Good, no problem.'

Another chillum was ready. Vik's negotiating skills were through. He settled into a mind numbing chillum session, happy to repeat this scenario each month.

Then the Greek seemed to relax. The business had been settled. It would be good money for the village. As the broker he would be seen in good light.

'You like chai?' the young looking woman asked after the chillum was dead.

They both said yes and soaked in another massive hit of the strongest mix they'd ever had.

As they sipped their sweet, milky spiced tea Dean realised he was looking out over the foothills of the Himalaya, in a village that survived on growing and selling weed. He thought about home. He lived in a district of Manchester that survived on growing and selling weed. Same, same but different. This traveller term he'd heard summed it up perfectly. It didn't matter where you were in the world, it was all the same stuff, just a different location. Dean realised for the first time that he was part of this planet and its goings on, not separate to it. He wasn't just a walking individual, a set of detached space. For the first time in his life he felt infinitesimally small, out here in the vastness of this magnitude of nature but at the same time he was aware of his own place in the whole.

'Dean.' Vik brought him back from his thoughts. 'Dean, give him the money.'

He handed over the money filled bag. Then Vik told him it was time to go.

There was little coming back from the Greeks as far as words but they all nodded goodbye.

The flight back was done in a kind of dreamlike state. They both felt invincible and at one with the air. There was no panic or worry in them and they landed with ease. The little group of Indian lads were there to greet them and Dean thanked Vik for everything. He was in the back of a van on his way down the mountain before he started to come round from the Greek's chillums.

He liked India but he knew he was ready to go home. He was going to sell this stuff in England. He was going to buy sniff with the money he made and he was going to become the biggest dealer in the North. Forget Liverpool. Manchester was going to be where it was at from now on.

He looked out of the window and locked eyes on a boy who was standing staring at him from the side of the road. He was wide eyed, dressed in orange robes with long black hair. He held a stick in one hand and a brass handled container in the other. The van was going slow, trapped behind a lorry and as Dean looked into the boy's eyes he thought he was looking into infinity, into the eyes of an old soul even though the boy was just a teenager. India, thought Dean, it got to your soul. He was really going to miss it.

Made in the
Charleston,
16 November 2